GOD OF CLOCKS

ALSO BY ALAN CAMPBELL

Iron Angel
Scar Night

GOD OF CLOCKS

THE DEEPGATE CODEX:
VOLUME III

ALAN CAMPBELL

SPECTRA

BALLANTINE BOOKS

NEW YORK

Copyright © 2009 by Alan Campbell

Published in the United States by Spectra, an imprint of The Random House Publishing Group, a division of Random House, Inc., New York.

SPECTRA and the portrayal of a boxed "s" are trademarks of Random House, Inc.

ISBN 978-0-553-38418-5

Printed in the United States of America

Book design by Lynn Newmark

For my brothers, Neil and Alex

ACKNOWLEDGMENTS

My sincere thanks to Simon Kavanagh, Peter Lavery, Juliet Ulman, and David Pomerico—and to everyone at Bantam and Macmillan. I appreciate all your hard work.

GOD OF CLOCKS

A boy was given a riddle and told that if he worked out the answer he would understand the secret at the heart of the universe and thus know god. The riddle went:

A man and his new wife step down together from the altar of a church, walk hand in hand along the aisle, and reach the door at the same instant. During that short march, which one of them travels the greater distance?

Scribbles from the Severed Hand of Polonius. Deepgate Codex, Ch. 339.

When I was dying on that battlefield, I got set upon by ticks. I had enough life left in me to pull their tiny paddle bodies off, but the heads stayed in and I lived. The wounds healed right over those heads and now they're part of me forever, like canapés for the soul.

"The Tale of Tom Granger." *Deepgate Codex, Ch. 88322*

PROLOGUE

PREPARATIONS FOR A FEAST

In the dark heart of Cospinol's great wooden skyship they boiled a demigod. Her wings and legs had been broken with hammers to fit them inside the iron cooker—a witchsphere now strengthened to resist steam at high pressure. It was clamped in a mighty vise set upon a brazier. A lead pipe fed carbolic water in through a nozzle in its paneled shell. Another pipe channeled the demigod's spirit to a glass condenser, for collection.

For fifty days the slaves had pumped water and stoked the brazier while red shadow-figures loomed over them like some infernal puppet show. Steam issued from valves and moiled the tarry bulkheads, but the workers neither perspired nor complained. They moved with the mute efficacy of men long used to a task. All around them the *Rotsward* shuddered and pitched, her joints sorely tested by her captain's desperate flight westwards.

The slaves observed as sparkling liquid gathered in the condenser flask like a colloid of starlight, then crept up the glass and cascaded back down in furious scintillations. It seemed to whisper to itself in voices edged with madness. They paused to study the vise clamps each time the cooking sphere rattled or boomed. Yesterday they'd brought their hammers and laid them out on the floor where they could be reached in a hurry, poor weapons as they were. And then they added more coke and curried the furnace with blasts of air from bellows. The booming sounds intensified as Carnival continued to kick within her pressurized prison.

A boy with hooks for fingers watched the stewing process from a crawl space above the chamber ceiling, his small red face afloat in the gloom up there. Why didn't the demigod just die? He had never seen Cospinol's workers take so long over a boiling. Only after the light had bubbled clean out of her would they tip out the water from the sphere and let him fill his kettle. The black tin vessel was the only one of his meager possessions that he had not stolen, and he glared at it now accusingly. It remained mournfully empty.

He looked on for a while longer then scratched another line into the ceiling joist, joining up four vertical gouges with a long diagonal. Then he turned and wriggled back down the passage in the direction he had come.

Smoke from the burning city below the skyship had leached freely into her tattered wooden hull. Air currents buffeted her endlessly. She rolled and creaked; she sounded as though she would not survive for much longer. The boy hummed a fragment of a battle march he had once heard, repeating the same notes over and over again just to block out the other frightening sounds. He blinked and rubbed his eyes with his sleeve. His shirt smelled of brimstone. He crawled onwards, deeper into the maze of filthy ducts and passageways.

Urgent voices came from the stern: the god of brine and fog himself, clearly angry, and a woman with a strange soft accent. The hook-fingered boy wormed around another bend and found a place where he could peer down through one of the many chinks in the floor.

"... The assassin saw everything," Cospinol was saying. "Coreollis is leveled, Rys's palace reduced to ashes by some unknown cataclysm. Are my brothers dead or simply scheming?" He paced before a bank of windows at the far side of the room, his crab-shell armour clicking with each step. Lank strands of grey hair fell back from his noble face and rested in the hollow between his wings. Behind him the windows framed nothing but fog, crosshatched by the dim lines of the *Rotsward's* gallows. "All Rys's Northmen are now slain or have fled," he went on. "Pollack's Outcasts, too. The war was over when King Menoa released his arconites."

A female voice responded: "The war is not over, Lord Cospinol. Have some faith in providence."

The hook-fingered boy adjusted his position over the hole to see who had spoken. Directly underneath his hiding place sat a woman in a cowled grey robe, glittering red gloves clutching a tiny scrag of a dog to her chest. But then the boy peered closer and saw that the gloves weren't gloves at all: The woman had glass scales for skin.

A Mesmerist witch?

Cospinol halted his pacing, his pinched expression evidence of this verbal lash against his pride. "Whose providence? My mother Ayen's?" he snapped. "Or were you referring to my missing brothers? Are they truly lost? It matters little. Mirith is a mad coward and knew nothing of warfare. Rys, Hafe, and Sabor possessed some skill on the battlefield, but they were all in Rys's bastion when it fell. Likely their souls are now lost in Hell. And Hasp is useless to us." He looked away from the woman. "No offense intended, Hasp."

From up here the boy could not see the room's third occupant, but the reply sounded gruff and fierce. "I am well aware of my value to you, Cospinol."

The woman glanced back at the hidden speaker before returning her gaze to the old sea god. "Your *own* providence, Lord Cospinol. *You* must seize control of this wayward situation. Many of Rys's Northmen fled the battlefield at Larnaig. Hafe's troops are now leaderless and there are militia abroad. Tens of thousands of men, armed and ready to fight."

Cospinol threw up his arms. "To what end? Menoa's arconites cannot be killed. We learned that in Skirl."

"If you do not recruit them, Menoa certainly will."

He snorted. "Menoa will simply disband them—or murder them."

"He's not that much of a fool. Rys's disappearance has robbed these warriors of their leaders, their purpose, *and* their income. How will they earn wages to feed their families?"

"You really think these soldiers would actually turn traitor and fight for their sworn enemy?"

"They will unless they prefer to starve." She set the dog down on the floor, whereupon it pissed and then sniffed at the pool it had made. "Menoa uses lies and persuasion on people. In Hell he turned the dead to his purposes, and he *will* do the same in this world. Lord Cospinol, if you yourself do not recruit these men, the king's arconites will soon acquire a formidable foot army. We do not need any more foes."

The sea god shook his head. "How can I be expected to maintain an army? They will devour the *Rotsward*'s stores like an infestation of weevils, and then empty my coffers of gold. And when we're out of turnips and coins they'll come looking for soulpearls, mark my words." He gave a short bitter laugh. "Yet you ask me to employ these purposeless men simply to prevent them from being used against me—legions of combatants who are entirely useless against my real enemies."

"They cannot fight Menoa's arconites, but they can still fight."

"Fight *who?*" he exclaimed.

The witch's dog growled, and nudged her leg. She picked it up again. "Since we are defeated, ill-equipped, and presently fleeing for our lives, I propose we pick a fight with a new foe."

Cospinol just stared at her, but a great gruff laugh came from the back of the cabin. The boy heard Hasp's deep voice booming out: "I think I see where this is going. Oh, Mina, you've offered us an end that will shake history!"

The conversation went on, but the boy had lost interest. He was watching a beetle crawl along the dank wooden passageway. He stabbed his steel fingers down around it, trapping it in a cage.

The beetle tested its prison. The boy watched its antennae moving. He scooped it up and ate it, then slouched back a bit and began to scratch a maze into the passageway wall. Bored with that, too, he crawled further down the rotting conduit into deeper gloom, and on through a ragged hole that snagged his sailcloth breeches. He found Monk waiting for him in a narrow gap between an inner bulkhead and the *Rotsward*'s cannonball-chewed outer hull.

Monk claimed to be an astronomer, but he wore an old musketeer's uniform and looked like a grave-digger's apprentice. He squatted there with his filthy knees poking through the holes in his breeches, like partially unearthed skulls. His eyes were as fat and moist as globes of frogspawn, their black pupils trembling as he searched the shadows. He clutched a wooden bowl and spoon. "Who's that?" he said. "Boy? Don't skulk in the dark. Where is my soup?"

The boy shrugged. "They're still boiling her," he said.

"After twenty days?"

"Fifty days. She's still kicking at the inside of the pot."

Monk frowned and set down his bowl and spoon. "You could kill me a gull," he muttered.

"Ain't any gulls here," the boy replied. "The air's too smoky. There's crows, though, down there on the battlefield. You can hear them from the lower gallows."

Monk said, "I wouldn't go to the gallows, not to hear no birds cawking."

The astronomer had been dead for a hundred and fifty years, or so he said. He wouldn't return to the *Rotsward*'s gallows, not ever. Not after all the time he'd spent hanging out there on a gibbet next to that wailing filibuster from Cog. Besides, they were liable to just string him up again if he went outside, weren't they? No, it was best to hide in here, stay quiet, and keep his head down. Work with the boy and share all the beetles and birds' eggs they found between themselves.

But Monk never found any beetles or birds' eggs. He never left his hiding place, never got up except to stagger down to the big hole in the hull where he kept his musket and his battered old sightglass.

Monk followed the boy's gaze. "No stars last night," he said bitterly.

"Maybe there aren't no stars no more," the boy replied. "Maybe they all fell down like Cospinol did. What if Pandemeria is now full of gods, and the skies above are black and empty?"

"I don't think we're in Pandemeria anymore," Monk said. "Last I saw of the world was when they cut me from my gibbet to fight at Skirl." His gaze now focused inwards on his own memories. "Needed us old veterans to stand against the Maze King's first giant," he said. "Guaranteed freedom for those who took up arms against that thing." His tone became animated and mocking. "'No more gins or nooses and that's a promise.'" He spat. "Fat lot of use, anyway. You can't kill a thing that can't be killed. And we couldn't even see to shoot at it in this damn fog."

Monk had been in Pandemeria during the uprising, attached to Shelagh Benedict Cooper's Musketeers. He said he'd read the stars for Shelagh herself, and shot seven Mesmerists, too.

"Never saw the stars neither," he went on. "None of us could leave the fog without just melting away into Hell. We started to fade as soon as they lowered us from the *Rotsward*'s deck, and when our feet touched the ground we were nothing but ghosts on the battlefield, spectres dragging muskets we could hardly lift. We were about as effective against the Skirl arconite as a fart blowing round its heels."

"Because Cospinol ate your eternal souls?"

Monk nodded. "He stole the stars from me."

"I don't want to leave anyway," the boy said. "I like it here."

"You like tormenting the god of brine," Monk observed. "He'll chop your head off if he catches you."

The boy just grinned. "Then I'll make myself a new head, a metal one."

"Shape-shifters." Monk sighed. "You all think you can do what you like. How are you going to make yourself a new head if you don't have a mind to imagine the shape and feel of it, eh? It's not like forging those fancy new fingers of yours." He made a chopping motion with his hand. "One deft *shnick* and that'll be the end of you. Cospinol won't be bothered about losing one soul to the Maze, not when he has so many hanging from his gibbets already."

The boy shrugged. He hadn't thought of that.

"Don't see why you can't change yourself into something useful for once," the astronomer said. "Something to help your old friend Monk pass the time." His eyes narrowed, the pupils like peepholes into some cruel realm of night. "A weapon, maybe...or something softer."

"I'm not a shiftblade!" the boy cried. "I'm not like them."

The old man chewed his lip. "No, you're a good lad who brings his friend Monk kettles of soup. Except there's no soup because that scarred angel just won't die in her cooker. Fifty days? What the hell is wrong with her?" He looked at the boy. "You wouldn't be holding out on me?"

"No."

"You wouldn't be *lying* to your old friend Monk?"

"No."

"So you won't mind if we go take a look together?"

"But..." The boy took a moment to assemble his jumbled thoughts. "You don't go anywhere."

"And *you* were counting on that?" The old man surged forward and grabbed the boy by the nape and dragged him back down through the sloping inner space of the hull, his grey hair as wild as a busted cord of wire.

The boy panicked and began to change his shape, willing his bones to wilt and flow out of the man's grip.

Monk punched him in the face. "None of that," he growled. "You'll keep the bloody body you were born with, for once."

The shock of admonishment emptied the young shape-shifter's mind. He scrabbled against the inner bulkhead, his fingers scraping gouges in the wood. But Monk simply stuffed him back into the narrow conduit and pushed the boy ahead of him like a clot of rags. "Which way now?" he demanded. "Larboard or starboard?"

Not knowing, the boy turned left, and they bumped and shuffled onwards in a noisy brawl of knees and elbows.

Once they reached the crawl space Monk shoved the boy aside and peered down through the spy hole. The brass buttons on his epaulettes shone dully in the light of the brazier below, while the hooked tip of his nose glowed like a torch-heated spigot. He was silent for a long time.

The boy looked at the kettle on its hook above the spy hole, and then he looked at the astronomer's head.

"A witchsphere," Monk whispered. "And they've reinforced it." He frowned. "Witchspheres don't open from the inside and they don't break. They were designed to contain a whole world of torment." His frown deepened. "So why bother to reinforce it?"

From the chamber below came a mighty boom. Steam blasted up through the gap. The astronomer flinched.

"That's why," the boy said.

Monk stared into the shadows for a moment. "She just kicked like a babe in a womb."

"Told you," the boy said.

The old man rubbed condensation from his brow. With a grim expression he went back to studying the cooker below. "The vise plates have been arranged to keep pressure on those core panels," he said. "But those braces set against the top curve haven't been welded properly. Witchsphere metal won't take welds. That's the weakest point. Come here, boy, look where I show you."

The boy did as he was told. He saw the witchsphere clamped in its vise over the brazier, the hot coals, the pipes, the wheel valves, and a whole nest of steaming iron braces. Cospinol's slaves were shoveling coke and pumping in air through leather bellows. White light boiled inside the condenser flask and threw long mechanistic shadows across the floor.

"Those plates are held together by bolts through opposing corners. You can see where they fused the nuts into the flanges. That's just normal steel." The astronomer scratched his chin. "But the braces are only fixed at their outer ends, and those joints have already started to rust in this steam. A good whack with a hammer would break through them quick enough."

"But she'll get out."

Monk looked back down at the witchsphere for a long moment, chewing his lips again. "The sphere will leak enough for us to fill our kettle, before the slaves reinforce it again. That's all." Then he shrugged. "But if she gets out, she gets out." He grinned. "That's what they call someone else's problem."

I

THREE HOURS AGO

Twelve angels had been released into the world from the Ninth Citadel of Hell and would return there only in the wake of all mankind. The earth shuddered and broke apart under their heels of ironclad bone. Engines pounded in their skulls and from behind armoured ribs still steaming from the portal through which they had passed. They crushed Rys's Northmen on the battlefield at Larnaig and then moved on to Coreollis, where they stove in the gates of that gaunt city. Shadow-angels on thin legs trailed them across the rolling acres of darkly stubbled grassland, burnt forest, and corpse-strewn mud. The cames of their wings made stark black silhouettes against the bloody dusk, the low sun blazing through like a leadlight vision of apocalypse.

Those defenders upon the city ramparts who had remained loyal to Lord Rys now lifted their catapults' pawls and swung the wooden machines inwards. Sulphur pots arced up and burst against the giants and then fell in flaming yellow showers over innocent homes. But the battle had been fought and lost at Larnaig, and these doomed buildings were now home only to widows and fatherless children.

And thus bathed in red-gold radiance, dragging chains of brimstone through the streets of Coreollis, the Twelve converged on the palace of a besieged god. Gables broke against their advancing shins, and roof joists shattered. Chimneys toppled; the slates flew spinning or slid in sheets to break upon flagstones under a veil of red dust and lemon-coloured fumes.

Half a league to the east, Rachel Hael stood on the battlement of an abandoned keep set atop a motte. Rys's men had built this timber-and-sod outpost an age ago to watch the Red Road, and the heads of Pandemerian traitors and Mesmerist demons still adorned the spiked palisades around its bailey. She had laid out a simple picnic of bread, butter, and fruit on a bench behind the rampart wall.

Now gripping an apple between her teeth, the former assassin raised her sightglass to follow the eyeless gazes of those grim sentinels arrayed on their spikes. She searched the road where the soil had been churned black under the armoured boots of King Menoa's legions, and then she swept the lens over the metallic pink waters of Lake Larnaig. Stands of white willow dotted the scalloped shoreline like silver pavilions; their ancient trunks crowded underneath in dens of red shadow. To the east the steel curves of the Skirl railway shone brightly beneath the ink-dark heavens. The track bisected a hamlet of burned station buildings and sheds near the northern bank, before terminating at the end of the Larnaig pier. The steamship *Sally Broom* had once carried Menoa's treaty of peace towards that same stone dock. Now the battered vessel lay at the end of a deep gouge in the Larnaig Field, three hundred yards from the point whence she had been thrown.

Beyond the lake, the Moine Massif reared up into the clouds in gaseous blue layers of scarps and saws and cones like simmering temples. A closer and less natural mist blanketed the broadleaf woodland just a league to the northeast, indicating where Cospinol's skyship was creeping away from Coreollis. For a long moment, Rachel watched the *Rotsward*'s sorcerous cloak recede, before turning her sightglass towards the west. Here the Larnaig Field was strewn with many corpses and uncountable parts of corpses, both human and Mesmerist, all burnt and spattered with mud, figures sprawled in attitudes of death across the blasted earth like fossils of men and beasts uncovered by a sudden cataclysm.

Veins of darker mud connected one tableau of violence to the next, so that it seemed the very skin of the world had grown old and thin. Dust sifted through metal wheel-spokes and blades and spears and pikes or hammers, flanged maces and hobnailed bludgeons still gripped in gauntlets or claws. It scoured ridges of bone and dry teeth, the iron limbs of altered men sheared or bent as if windblown, and cages of ribs and scorched flesh as dark as petrified leather. Engine parts lay scattered everywhere: cogs, bolts, chains, brackets, and snarls of wire, all dark with mineral grease that soiled the ground. Scraps of steel plate or mail glimmered dully amidst white-and-blue plumed helmets and filthy rags and entrails.

Most of the battlefield was littered with butchered horses, war hounds, and jackals with pink-and-black tongues, and the partly eaten hulks of armoured siege aurochs, and uncounted heaps of blue-lipped warriors with their clammy faces and eyes seething with flies.

Rachel took a bite from her apple.

Menoa's portal to Hell formed a red crater in the heart of this killing ground, but its perimeter had already begun to crust and shrink inwards like a wound. Soon it would close completely. A hundred thousand warriors had died to open that rift. Twelve arconites had drained all but the last breath of power from it.

Tails of smoke were now rising from Coreollis and drifting through the bones of those terrible giants.

They had finally reached the palace. Now the mightiest of the Twelve stepped over the sixty-foot-high rampart girdling Rys's courtyard and gazed down at the white pinnacles and rose-decked balconies of the besieged god's inner bastion. The others held back, their shins laced by flames, their wings as thin and luminous as sheets of rain. Embers harried them with the persistence of wasps. The lead arconite stooped and picked up something from the courtyard to examine it.

Rachel tried to focus on the object, but the giant had already crushed the thing and let it drop.

It waited. Twelve priests in Hell would be gazing through the Maze-forged eyes of these mindless ambassadors, just as Rachel herself now peered through her lens. She expected Rys to attempt to bargain for his soul. Yet what could the god of flowers and knives offer that King Menoa could not simply take by force? The events to come would certainly not be decided in this world.

The assassin took another bite from her apple, then focused the tube and scanned the bastion windows for signs of life.

Smoke clouded her narrow field of vision. She lowered the sightglass in time to witness a score of projectiles make fuming arches across the rooftops of Coreollis. From the city walls the defenders had renewed their onslaught with the vigour of men who had abandoned all hope of saving their homes. Explosions bloomed. A series of distant concussions sounded, followed by a furious crackling noise and then silence. Fronds of yellow sulphur smoke wilted in the breeze.

Rachel spat out an apple pip.

One of the arconites was burning. It remained motionless, its cavernous eye sockets fixed on Rys's palace. And the others stood rigid beside it, towering over the palace like rawboned citadels themselves.

Down in the bailey beneath the motte, Rachel's mount whickered, pulling at its tether and stamping its hooves like an impatient master demanding attention. She pressed a finger to her lips and then quickly lowered it and shook her head. *Horses.* This animal had belonged to the Heshette raiders, and had been ruined before it was passed to her, all knees and ribs, swaddled in a filthy cloth saddle. Yet, despite its sorry origins, its white eyeballs still rolled with an inbred contempt of Spine, recognizing her as one of Deepgate's temple assassins. At each step on the track to the outpost it had bucked against her clumsy attempts to steer it, almost throwing her twice.

She took a last bite from the apple, then threw down the core to the miserable beast.

A sudden change in the texture of the sunlight brought the Spine assassin's attention back to Rys's palace. Eleven of Menoa's arconites were moving back from it, their wings turning in the twilight like great lucent sails. The first and greatest of them, however, now knelt before the god's bastion as if in supplication. Rachel trained her sightglass on the palace itself.

On its highest balcony stood a white-winged figure in shining steel armour. He wore a cape of battlefield roses as vividly red as the living blossoms that cascaded over the balustrade around him. The glass doors to his quarters had been thrown open behind him, and the myriad panes shone blue.

Rys had come to plead for his life.

Rachel saw the god gesturing angrily, but even with her sightglass fully extended, she could not discern his face with enough clarity to read his lips. Whatever words he spoke to the kneeling giant went unheard. Yet after a moment the arconite's reply resounded across the heavens, as deep as an echo reverberating from the throats of all of the world's tombs.

"King Menoa rejects your proposal outright, Lord Rys, for he suspects that your brothers' souls are not truly yours to bargain with. Furthermore, he demands that they present themselves before these assembled ambassadors as a gesture of goodwill. The Lord of the Maze is magnanimous. He will not punish such worthy adversaries. He simply requires that all sons of Ayen enter Hell before the portal expires. As guests of the Ninth Citadel you will be spared all the horrors of the Maze and denied none of its pleasures." The arconite's maw was an affectation, for it could not speak as men do. The voice issued from a metal simulacrum of a larynx, and yet the thoughts behind those words were born in the depths of a citadel built under a different sky.

It was talking about Rys's brothers: Mirith, Hafe, and Sabor. Rachel was hardly surprised that the god of flowers and knives had attempted to sell his own kin, or that King Menoa now purported to offer them sanctuary. Should the sons of Ayen be killed in this world, their souls would be lost in the endless reaches of Hell. Clearly the king wished them nearer to hand.

Rys must have recognized this offer for the lie it was. He turned his back on the angel and gazed through the balcony doors. And for an instant Rachel thought she spied *another* archon within the building, an armoured figure identical to Rys himself. It must have been a reflection in the glass doors. Rys inclined his head. His cape of roses ruffled and lifted in a hot updraft from the burning city. He stepped suddenly from the balcony, back into his own chambers.

As the sun's lowest edge touched the rim of the world, Rys's palace imploded, evaporating into white powder before that great motionless, kneeling observer. The concussion that followed seemed to crack the air apart and left Rachel's ears ringing. The falling bastion and its sentinel towers became ghosts of themselves that bent leeward in unison, and began to drift away in the breeze.

Rachel spread butter on a hunk of bread. Had she truly observed the last clash of gods in the world of men? Those deities whom the ignorant claimed to be fallen stars had seemed to her to sacrifice their souls too easily. She sensed trickery here. The glimpse she'd caught of Rys's own reflection had looked...odd. Something about it troubled her, but she couldn't say exactly why. Had Cospinol sent her forth from his fogbound skyship to deliberately witness this very display?

The kneeling arconite now stood and joined its eleven fellows. Sulphur fires clung to the shins of two of these automatons, and yet they appeared to be untroubled, perhaps even unaware of the flames. The Twelve moved north towards the walls of Coreollis, over which the haze of Cospinol's fog glowed dimly in the final light.

King Menoa had at last turned his attention to the *Rotsward*.

Rachel stuffed the hunk of bread into her mouth, gathered the remains of her picnic into her satchel, and then descended the log steps from the motte rampart, jogging down a further set of steps to the bailey, where she unhitched her horse's reins.

The animal tried to bite her, but she slipped past its neck and, grabbing its mane and placing a foot in the cloth stirrup, swung up into the saddle. She pressed her heels into the beast's flank, whereupon it snorted and sidestepped.

"Natch."

The horse blew and stamped a hoof.

She whipped the reins. "Natch."

Her mount began to walk backwards.

"Natch. Natches. Forward, you obstinate Heshette..." She dug her heels in sharply. "You *know* the command I'm trying to say. Ha!"

The beast lurched towards the bailey gate.

But time was against her, for the arconites now shared her destination and Cospinol's scouts would have noted as much. To reach the *Rotsward* before her foes she would have to ride quickly. She urged the horse into a gallop and clung on for her life. It bolted down the earthen track, throwing up clods of muddy grass, its worn hide sliding over ribs gripped between Rachel's knees. The path rounded a conical grass mound, the remains of some earlier fortification now overgrown with birch and black brambles, and veered northwards again towards a gloomy tunnel in the misty broadleaves. With long, slow strides, the arconites traversed swaths of ground at a pace Rachel's mount could not hope to match, but she had half a league's start on them—and she had the help of a thaumaturge waiting onboard the *Rotsward*.

Or so she hoped. *Now would be a really good time, Mina.*

From the battlefield to the west arose a new mist. It poured from the mouths of ten thousand slain men and demons like a final cold exhalation. A little blood yet remained in those warriors and, aboard the *Rotsward*, Mina Greene had used this to her advantage. Tendrils of fog intermingled above the corpses to form a thin grey pall that swelled and heaved and then rolled out over the Larnaig Field like a seawater tide. It consumed the slopes and the railway buildings and the lake and plains beyond in sorcerous mist. It billowed against the walls of Coreollis and swamped the forest where it merged with the *Rotsward*'s own shroud of fog.

Rachel rode into the misty gloom of the forest. The sound of the horse's hooves grew duller as it thundered down the arboreal tunnel. A faint nimbus of light defined the gap in the trees through which she had entered the woodland, but the fog ahead hoarded a deep and varicose darkness. She could not see the path clearly, and her flight into those grey and flinty shadows felt like a plunge through the borderlands of delirium. Black branches intertwined with the mist around her, limp with dank brown foliage and lines of gossamer. The boles of oak and elm leaned over the narrow track like leering youth or stood back in the greyness like sullen old men. Twigs stabbed at Rachel's eyes, and the rushing air felt cold and damp against her face. The horse blew and huffed; its unshod hooves bore down upon a carpet of sodden mulch, kicking up leaves that smelled of worms and spiders.

From somewhere behind came the long low drone of horns. Rachel urged the horse on faster and, to her surprise, it responded. Perhaps that hunting call had finally given the beast the wits to share its rider's urgency, for it now thundered along the track like the true Heshette warhorse it once must have been.

They leapt over a collapsed tree clad in plates of white fungi, like the armour of a fallen Icarate. Rachel felt herself begin to slip from the saddle. She clung to the steaming animal's neck. The rich odour of its hide filled her nostrils. Its breathing came in hot quick gusts. But, rather than bucking, the horse eased up a little and allowed the assassin to drag herself back upright in the saddle.

"Thanks," she whispered.

The beast surged forward again, almost throwing her a second time. She gritted her teeth.

The track skirted a huge lichen-spattered boulder and then opened into a glade of beer-coloured ferns, young hazel and grass flourishing amongst granite outcroppings. Rachel heard singing. She reined in.

John Anchor was sitting on a rock in the center of the clearing, muttering a tune while he sharpened a stick with a short sword that, in his big hands, looked to be no larger than a simple knife. In the forest gloom he looked like a huge black bear.

The great hemp rope that tethered him to his master's airship rose skywards from the harness on his back, but otherwise there was no evidence of the *Rotsward's* presence here, nor of the many passengers floating in the fog above him. He was quite alone. He looked up and grinned.

"Rachel Hael."

"I thought you abhorred blades," she said with a glance at his handiwork.

"Only when they are used in battle," he replied. "The Heshette gave me this weapon as a parting gift. It belonged to Ramnir's father and his father's father, and so on. It is very useful, as you see."

"What are you making?"

"I had not thought that far ahead," he replied. "Kindling, perhaps." He stood up and peered into the gloom behind her. "The Twelve are in pursuit of us now, yes?"

She nodded.

He waited a moment, his ear cocked to the heavens. The rope on his back gave a sudden vibration. "Cospinol asks if Lord Rys attempted to sell out his brothers."

"Naturally."

"And what has become of him now?"

Rachel described how the palace had fallen to dust. John Anchor listened carefully, and then waited. After a long moment he inclined his head towards the sky. "Now they are arguing," he said. "This may take some time." He went back to sharpening his stick.

The former assassin shrugged. "Take your time, Cospinol," she muttered. "We only have *twelve* arconites moving this way." She dismounted. The horse huffed and began to graze. She patted it, uncertainly, and then scanned the fog for signs of Dill. Despite his vast size, she saw nothing in that bleak greyness but the merest sketched outlines of trees. Cospinol's mist enveloped him as thoroughly as it would shroud a mountain.

A horn lowed in the west; it sounded close. Rachel dug out another couple of apples from her satchel and handed one to Anchor. "They're moving quickly," she warned, taking a bite. Her gaze lingered on the tethered man's harness, on the bulwarks of muscles covering his broad chest. The rope above him thrummed again. Rachel slung her satchel back over her shoulder, then tossed the apple core to her horse and wiped her hands on her leather breeches. "How fast can you drag that thing?"

"I can run with the *Rotsward* when Cospinol needs me to," Anchor said, chewing. "But now your Deepgate thaumaturge has extended the reach of the fog. The land is completely hidden, yes? All cloaked in mist from earth to sky. There is no need for me to run, and with luck we can reach Coreollis by stealth."

"Coreollis?" She looked at him, and then back over her shoulder. "What do you mean, *Coreollis*? John, that's where they're coming *from*."

John Anchor slid his sword into a gap in his wooden harness, examined the stick he had been sharpening, and then put that away, too. Then he said, "Menoa's arconites do not tire, nor can they be killed. So we must go to Hell and slay the priests who control them, yes?"

Rachel just stared at him.

"It is fortuitous that the portal leads directly to King Menoa's citadel." The big man beamed. "So we do not have to walk far."

"Surely you're not going to take the *Rotsward*, and everyone aboard her, into Hell?"

"Not everyone," Anchor said. "Alice Harper will lead Cospinol and me to the Ninth Citadel, since she knows Hell so intimately, but your thaumaturge stays here with you."

Rachel had met Harper briefly on the Larnaig battlefield, a dead woman who had seemed more at ease amongst the remains of Mesmerist demons than she had amongst the living. Since then Harper had kept herself hidden in one of the *Rotsward*'s cabins, choosing to have little involvement in the ensuing arguments and decisions. "Harper *agreed* to go back to Hell?"

Anchor nodded. "She's dead. She belongs there." His eyes brimmed with mirth. "But Mina Greene has devised another mission for those who choose to remain here. Cospinol agreed—how you say...? 'Whole-headedly'?—with the thaumaturge's idea. We must divide our party. Cospinol has decided to declare war against both Hell and Heaven."

2

DEPARTURE

In the last moments of twilight a heavy gloom settled upon the forest. An owl hooted, and was answered by a distant cry from deep in the fog. Rachel waited beside John Anchor, and yet in this darkness she could discern little of the giant but the whites of his eyes. He remained as still and as darkly imposing as the oaks around him. They had moved a quarter league further north, to rendezvous with Dill. The bone-and-metal angel was somewhere nearby, but Rachel could not have said where exactly. He might have been standing just ten yards away.

She heard the *Rotsward's* elevator creaking before she saw it descend out of the murk, materializing amidst the forest canopy overhead. It was a simple basket suspended from ropes, hauled by slaves on the midships deck. The elevator's two occupants, Mina Greene and Hasp, looked like a strange pair of heavenly ambassadors in their grey cowled robes, their bloody glass-scaled hands clasped before them.

The basket landed with a soft thud. Hasp leapt out, seemingly unconcerned that a single crack in that Maze-forged armour would have spilled his lifeblood and returned his soul to Hell. Rachel realized she was staring. She looked away. Mina lifted out her demonic little dog, Basilis, and set him on the ground before cautiously climbing out after Hasp.

The pup sniffed at Anchor's feet and then bounded off into the shadows.

"Cospinol's slaves have transferred provisions and gold from the *Rotsward*," Mina said. "Our friendly arconite made an impressive packhorse. They've stored tons of wheat and dried fish inside his ribs, and caskets of coins in his jaw." She smiled. "Cospinol wasn't happy to see that gold go. His mood now suits this sorcerous weather."

Rachel glanced at Hasp. The Lord of the First Citadel scowled, lifted his hand inside his cowl, and pressed it firmly against the side of his glass helm as though a sudden headache had gripped him. His red eyes flinched, and he bared his teeth.

"Hasp?" Rachel ventured.

He ignored her.

Hasp had become increasingly irritable and sullen since King Menoa had implanted a parasite inside his skull. A tiny demon of brass and flesh, it compelled the Lord of the First Citadel to obey Mesmerist orders. And poor Hasp, who had once stood alone against Hell's armies, had already been abused by the weakest of Menoa's servants.

His mouth tightened. He muttered soft curses to himself.

Such a cruel punishment. Menoa had stripped Hasp of everything that defined him, denying him even the glorious death in battle Hasp had coveted. She looked up, but she couldn't see or hear anything of the work going on overhead. "What about Menoa's Twelve?" she said to Mina. "Can you sense their presence?"

The thaumaturge inhaled a deep breath of the misty air, and then hesitated. "I can observe them while they remain in this fog," she said. "Four are waiting at the western edge of the forest.

Another two stand in the Larnaig Field south of Coreollis, guarding the portal. But the remaining six are moving north. They're following us."

"Who are they after? Dill or Cospinol?"

"Both, I imagine."

"How long can you maintain this fog?"

She shrugged. "That all depends on Basilis." She picked up the hideous little pup, cuddled it in her arms, and kissed its ear. "Doesn't it, sweetie?"

The dog growled.

Anchor beamed. "I must be on my way to Hell now. The priests who control these golems won't kill themselves, eh? Good luck with Ayen, Mina Greene."

Rachel looked between the two. "Hell is one thing," she said, "but Heaven is an altogether different matter. Even Ayen's own sons didn't consider themselves powerful enough to intrude in their mother's realm. The goddess of light and life will butcher us all."

A myriad of tiny glass scales around Mina's face crinkled. "But she'll kill the enemy, too."

The young thaumaturge planned to use Dill to attack the gates of Heaven, reasoning that if the goddess of light and life perceived a threat from *one* arconite, she might destroy the rest of them, ridding the world of Menoa's unholy Twelve. Yet not even her son Cospinol knew exactly how to find the gates of Heaven, nor how to breach them in order to reach the goddess shuttered within. His kin had never been ones to share their knowledge, it seemed. The thaumaturge's plan was nothing more than a leap into the abyss. Yet it was still the best plan they had.

"We'll search Sabor's palace," Mina explained to Rachel, "and then Mirith's. If anyone knew how to reach the goddess, it was them. They had to know something if they were planning to storm Heaven themselves."

A hunting horn sounded somewhere to the west.

John Anchor stepped forward. "Hasp, Mina, I will not shake those glass hands of yours, but I must go now. Hell awaits."

Mina rushed up and hugged him, while Rachel merely nodded. Hasp fixed his dark eyes on Anchor. "Give my regards to King Menoa," he said.

The tethered man laughed, and strode southwards across the glade and then faded into the misty trees. The great rope trailed after him, cleaving a path through the forest canopy. The sound of snapping branches could be heard long after he vanished from sight. And then he started singing.

That's his idea of stealth? Rachel shook her head. The fog hid him and the skyship above, but it couldn't hide the noise of his passage. *How can he hope to slip past his hunters and drag that vessel into Hell unnoticed?* Rachel didn't really believe he expected to. King Menoa would know the precise moment when the portal was breached but, from what she had seen of Anchor, the big man from the Riot Coast relished confrontation.

And so Rachel found herself standing there in a forest in a strange land with a thaumaturge, a dog, and a debased god in glass armour. The hunting horns called again from somewhere closer. Hasp winced at the noise and clutched his head, but he said nothing.

They encountered Dill several hundred paces to the north. Or rather, they found his shins rearing amongst the oak and elm. The rest of him stood obscured in the misty grey heights. They stood beside his heel and looked up. From the heavens came the distant sound of machinery.

"Dill?" Rachel called.

A bony fist descended, snapping through branches, and formed a cradle on the ground. The three climbed into his upturned palm.

And then they were rising up through the chill damp air. Rachel clung on to Dill's knuckle as they surged through the forest canopy. The trees soon fell away below them, dissolving into the mist. Huge bones wrapped in metal tubing loomed on her left as they soared up past the arconite's pelvis and spine—their pitted yellow surfaces etched with the same complex whorls she had once seen on the hull of Deepgate's Tooth. A citadel of machinery shuddered behind the giant's ribs, composed of dark metal forged in Hell—perhaps from the broken chains of the city she had been born in. The mechanics of it were vast and unknowable. She smelled oil, and another ripe and coppery odour, like that of butchered meat or the killing fields of Larnaig, yet tainted in some chemical way she couldn't identify. Lime? It reminded her of the poisons in Cinderbark Wood. She sensed the pressure of tons of blood and hydraulic fluid within those piston housings and tubes and vats.

Dill's skull finally came into view—huge and naked and hideous, and devoid of anything that suggested a living mind inside. The cavernous eye sockets held naught but echoes and pools of dank water, providing shelter for birds or bats, whose shit spattered the lower ridges of bone. His jaw was partially open, and the yellow teeth stood motionless. Green moss clung to the underside of his jawbone. Rachel could see the barrels Cospinol's slaves had unloaded heaped in the darkness deep within that maw—enough coin to buy an army.

Dill's hand came to a halt beside his mouth and Rachel realized that he meant for them to step inside, beside the gold. Tears pricked at the corners of her eyes but she could not say exactly why. They climbed from the hand and into the giant's mouth.

Mina set her dog down and headed into the gloom at the back of this dim bone-and-metal cave. Her glass-shod feet echoed on metal floor panels. Hasp stood looking up at the golem's palate above his head, his face in shadow. Rachel sniffed the damp air. It stank of the battlefield, of iron and blood.

"Dill?" she whispered.

For a moment she imagined that the floor had trembled, yet there was no answer but the echo of her own voice.

Mina looked up. "I warned him not to speak," she said. "He has a voice like thunder, quite loud enough to betray our position to our enemies."

Rachel stared at her. "I need to talk to him." She hesitated. "I need to know that he understands where we're going."

Mina beckoned her over and then took her hand. The thaumaturge led the Spine assassin over to the very back of the oral cave, where a dark crawl space led up out of the main chamber. "This leads to the topmost vertebrae of the spine," she explained. "From there you can climb up into the skull."

"His *skull?*"

"It's not a *living* creature," Mina said quietly. "The arconite is simply a machine, a golem, a rude simulacrum of an angel. King Menoa chose this form to ease the stresses put upon the soul trapped within. This way Dill's subconscious can still function. He can move his limbs without having to consciously direct any unfamiliar mechanisms. It is a suit of armour for his soul, brash and hideous, yet functional." She stared at the crawl space above her, perhaps unwilling to meet Rachel's eye. "Climb up inside the machine and you'll find your friend's soul. Speak to him there." She looked at the floor. "He won't need his larynx to answer you."

Rachel climbed. Crystals encrusted the walls, less like jewels than chunks of tarnished glass. The passage rose steeply, then opened into a dark atrium a little wider than her shoulders. She reached out in the darkness and felt a tangle of arm-thick pipes running vertically, more crystals, and hexagonal metal pins. She stood there in the dark for a long moment. *It isn't you. It's just a prison . . . like Ulcis's abyss or Cospinol's ship.*

Mina was right. This was armour: a suit created by the Lord of the Maze to allow his servants to walk freely amongst mortals—and to destroy them. When her eyes grew accustomed to the gloom she noticed a dim light shining overhead. The passageway now rose directly above her head. She gripped the pipes and pulled herself up.

A room had been created inside the arconite's head. There

were no windows. The light she had previously seen came from another source entirely.

Rachel put her hand over her mouth and began to sob.

King Menoa allowed the Ninth Citadel to glut itself with power from the Maze, and then he gave the walls and steps within that living stronghold his permission to breed. Aeons had passed since these Mesmerist constructs had been human, but their souls remembered lust and exulted in the freedom granted to them. Flesh born of subconscious thought flowed and melded with uncountable partners in an orgiastic frenzy that pushed thousands of souls over the brink into madness. They produced sentient offspring to strengthen the citadel's own hive mind, but occasionally they also birthed mutants: fragments of dreams or memories that could not think in any useful way and merely mimicked the shapes of the faces around them. And these faces shouted and barked or simply licked their teeth and stared.

Whenever such deviants were discovered by functioning constructs they were murdered and absorbed back into the citadel. Hunters with fists grown into knives flowed through walls and ceilings in pursuit of imperfection. The whole process of unfettered copulation continued until Menoa's fortress had grown by almost thirty levels and the House of Faces set high upon the building's teetering summit had sprouted many new chambers, stairwells, and eyes.

When it was over, the citadel exhaled. Bloodmists hissed from vents in the foundations, and then drifted out over the great wet labyrinth of the Maze.

Menoa stood upon a freshly birthed balcony high on one side of the House of Faces and watched the mists recede. Ribs of new bone and crystal eyes glistened in the platform floor and made the surface uneven, yet he was prepared to allow that for the moment. He would wait and see how it matured before determining its value to him.

Far below him a witchsphere was rolling through the Maze on its way to the citadel. Barges lolled in deeper channels, their decks crammed with cages full of souls for the Processor. The great inverted pyramid continued to whisper and issue gouts of steam, but its forming ovens and arconite pens were empty now.

All of the king's children had now left Hell, yet the instrument of their passage still dominated the skyline. Menoa's portal writhed above the Maze like a vast ribbon of flies. From a fixed base of scorched and blasted stone the portal rose to impossible heights, becoming narrower and narrower until the last thread of it vanished somewhere inside that dark sun that lay at the very heart of the Maze. Both ends remained fixed in place, but the length between them undulated like a whip. It had lost most of its substance since the arconites had passed through, Menoa noted. He could almost see through it in places.

A fly settled on one of the claws of Menoa's black gauntlet. He glanced down and changed the tiny creature from living flesh to glass, then crushed it.

His reverie was broken by an unspoken query from the citadel. The witchsphere had reached the base of the fortress and it wished to speak to him.

Admit it. Allow it to pass through the citadel unmolested.

A short while later the witchsphere rolled onto his balcony. Menoa had no name for this construct, but he recognized it nevertheless. Its scraped and dented metal panels were evidence of the many years it had spent in the living world.

"We bring word from the Prime," it said in the voices of numerous hags. "They have confirmed your expectations. The thaumaturge has conjured a mist to hide the traitorous arconite. It engulfs Cospinol's own fog and reaches far across the lands beyond."

"And the portal, too?"

"Yes."

Menoa sensed his glass mask contort as it mimicked his own

expression of grim contemplation. "I did not expect this fog," he admitted, "but certainly treachery. Cospinol cannot kill my warriors, so his agents must attempt to kill their controllers." Menoa's Prime Icarates were ensconced within the Bastion of Voices deep inside the Processor, their minds watching the living world through the eyes of his arconites, their thoughts steering those vast iron limbs that had crushed Coreollis. He had already taken steps to protect them. The thaumaturge's fog was an unnecessary precaution, amateurish. Did they truly expect that he had not anticipated and planned for an attack on the Maze? "Perhaps his smokescreen has been engineered to allow an assassin to enter the portal?"

"They will send the arconite Dill?"

The king shook his head. "That young angel alone possesses enough strength to resist my own warriors. Cospinol needs him to remain on earth." He turned back to the portal. The vast ribbon writhed and spun, but the twelve angels had all but drained it of power, and it was growing weaker with every passing moment. "Cospinol owns another assassin, the Riot Coast barbarian who drags his skyship. That is who he will send."

The balcony had not yet grown itself a parapet, but the witch-sphere rolled closer to the edge of the precipice. "Without Anchor, Cospinol will be grounded and helpless," it declared.

"He cannot allow himself to be stranded," the king agreed. "And so the god of brine and fog must accompany his slave. After all, he has an entire army of men hanging from the gallows of his ship. No doubt he plans to set them upon us as some form of *distraction*."

"Shall I instruct the Icarates to stoke the furnaces within the flensing machines?"

"Yes," Menoa said. "All of the furnaces."

John Anchor took a deep breath. He relished the smell of this old woodland, the wet leaves, the cool rain-laden air. If he was ever required to walk across the bed of an ocean again, then this was the sort of air he'd prefer to fill his lungs with. It was a fine place in which to take a stroll. The soft brown mulch compressed under his feet and bounced back up in his wake. As he walked he scooped up a handful of soulpearls from the pouch at his hip and tipped them into his mouth. Then he began to hum a tune.

The rope thrummed.

He laughed. "You worry too much, Cospinol. My voice is no louder than the sound of these snapping branches. And we can't silence the woodland, eh?"

His master's voice came through the rope. *The arconites are bigger than you, John.*

"But not stronger."

Now is not the time to test that theory. Save your strength for Menoa's Icarates, I beg you.

"But I am quicker than the golems, Cospinol. Like a rat around their ankles, eh? I jump in the portal and pull you down after me while the giants stumble after us. Easy as swinging a boar." *You are tethered to me, John. Do not forget that.*

Anchor grinned. In truth he hoped to confront at least one of these arconites. He felt strong today: A million souls howled in his blood, their voices like a war cry at the back of his mind . . . so long as he didn't listen too closely. If he concentrated too hard on it, he would recognize their moans and pleas, and that would take the edge off his good humour. He ducked under a low-hanging branch and then heard it catch on the *Rotsward's* rope behind him and snap loudly.

A hunting horn again bellowed in the west.

Anchor altered his direction subtly, moving more in that direction.

I'm warning you, John, Cospinol said. *Mina Greene conjured this fog to disguise our own camouflage. Don't ruin it by trying to confront these things. I want to reach the portal without incident. Turn back to the southwest, away from that horn.*

"You are reading my mind now?"

No, John, I just know what you're like.

The big man sighed and did as Cospinol instructed. Fog shrouded the view ahead, but he could see that the woodland here sloped down towards the south. In places he spied low walls amongst the oaks—the remains of some long-abandoned settlement now soft with moss and wrapped in snarls of black bramble. Fungi clumped in earthen hollows, like bones protruding from graves. He could not recall if he had visited this place before, and he wondered what tragedy had befallen the owners of these dwellings. As if in response, a lone soul cried out in the back of his mind. Anchor frowned and ignored it, not wanting to know. He began to hum again, half singing under his breath.

> *"One summer's day on Heralds Beach,*
> *I met a girl who had no teeth.*
> *I kissed the collar of her pretty frock*
> *and she—"*

The rope shuddered. *Please try not to enjoy this, John. That's all I ask.*

Anchor snatched up a stick and swung it before him like one of the swords he so despised. "Since you deny me the arconites, Cospinol, I can only hope that all Hell awaits, and that Menoa has had the good sense to arm them."

That, Cospinol said, *is something I can promise you. The Lord of the Maze will not have wasted the souls of all those he slaughtered.*

The tethered man left the wood not far from the place where he had first entered it. The rope snagged on the last of the branches and then tore free. Anchor's eyes were long used to this grey gloom, and he saw a series of low humps in the ground and the remains of a palisade wall to the southeast. Earthworks dug by Rys's Northmen. He was near the edge of the Larnaig Field.

He scanned the mists all around, but saw no sign of Menoa's

Twelve. He frowned. "Why would Menoa leave the portal unguarded?" he said. "A smarter man than me might suppose the king wanted us to enter Hell."

There was a pause before Cospinol answered. *I suppose it's possible—perhaps even likely. If I were to die here on earth, my soul would become lost somewhere within the Maze. His spies might search for it for years. But killing me at the door of his Processor would spare him all that trouble. The Ninth Citadel is the seat of his power. It will not be undefended.*

"Good. Then we needn't waste any more time being stealthy."

We were being stealthy?

Anchor began to jog down the slope towards the Larnaig Field.

Soon they came upon the dead. Armoured bodies covered the killing field like some queer steel crop, harvested but then left to rot. The metal took on the dull lustre of the surrounding fog, scattered weapons and shields as grey as stone. Gas had distended the bellies of soldiers and now whistled softly through punctures in their flesh. Ravens cawed and hopped through the stink, pecking at lips and eyes. Here and there the colourful blue and gold plumes of helmets stood out like exotic birds come to feast alongside their ragged black cousins. And there were Mesmerists, too: machines of flesh and iron, jackal-like beasts, dark stains left where Non Morai had dissolved. They had been butchered in their thousands. Anchor stepped amongst them, his good mood rapidly fading.

Rys's warriors had been cruel men, but they had not deserved to die in this way. That he would soon face their souls in battle offered Anchor no consolation.

He had proceeded less than a hundred yards when he spotted Silister Trench. The First Citadel Warrior who had possessed Dill's body lay partially buried under the summit of a huge heap of Mesmerist scrap, his dead eyes staring at Heaven. He had lost most of his teeth. Something blunt had cloven in his skull.

Anchor walked up the pile and then gripped the corpse's shoulders and dragged it out. It was incomplete, for Trench's legs remained inside the crush of broken machine parts. "He fought well," Anchor said. "There are many more Mesmerist corpses here than elsewhere. He was making a hill out of them."

Up ahead, said Cospinol. *The portal.*

And Anchor saw it. It had indeed been left unguarded.

A large chamber occupied the inside of Dill's skull, yet there was so little space amongst the crowded machinery that Rachel could barely move. Banks of gears surrounded her in the semidarkness, the cogs clicking like hundreds of little black teeth. Wheels whirled inside wheels. Piston shafts heaved up and down in a sequence of irregular whooshes and thumps. Crystals hummed and threw out gouts of white light that splayed briefly across the metal surfaces. The whole room smelled vaguely like the air after a thunderstorm.

Rachel sensed all of this at the periphery of her vision, for she was staring at the glass sphere in the center of the chamber. Almost all of the illumination came from this device, or from the phantasms within it.

So many!

She counted at least a dozen of them trapped inside that sphere: human men and women, all naked, a brawling knot of figures crammed into a space hardly large enough for one or two people. All were struggling against their confinement and against each other, yet there was no substance to their gaseous forms. Their fists passed easily through each other's faces and torsos. Their lips mouthed silent cries or curses. They grinned and frowned and spat. Forks of light rippled and flashed between them like manifestations of unheard revilement. She glimpsed Dill's tortured expression before it became lost again in a tangle of elbows and legs. His mouth had been open wide, as if pleading.

But there was no sound in the room bar the persistent tick and thump of machinery, the icy crackle of crystals. The sphere grew momentarily brighter and then diminished. Wreathed in lightning, the ghosts continued their silent brawl.

Rachel had seen soulpearls, the beads John Anchor consumed to give him such great strength, and she knew that ethereal consciousness did not necessarily need body shapes to exist. With the right technology a soul could inhabit almost anything. Alice Harper's Mesmerist devices had once been alive, and still remembered fear. Yet it seemed to Rachel that some deliberate action had been taken to keep these particular figures here in their physical forms.

She wormed through the banks of machines, stepping over cables as she approached the sphere. Reaching it, she pressed her palms against the glass wall of the globe—

killed him . . . move to that place . . . no I can't do . . . my head, stop shouting at me . . . no . . . me . . . and it was so dark in there . . . I hate you, I hate you . . . I don't want to remember that . . . isn't me . . . it's you, stay away . . . no knives . . . liar, I talked to her . . . nothing but the dark . . . the murderer . . . don't speak, don't . . .

—and then jerked away, her head reeling from the cacophony of voices that had assaulted her mind. She took a deep breath. "Dill?"

The whole room gave a sudden jolt to the left. Rachel squatted instinctively. From below came the hiss of steam. The room turned again, more gently this time, in the opposite direction.

The faint sound of the young angel's voice came from the glass sphere. *Rachel?* Once more the chamber yawed from side to side as the arconite looked around him. She saw his face reappear amongst the struggling phantoms.

"Dill, I'm not outside. I'm . . . in your head."

There was a pause, and then Rachel heard her friend whispering inside the glass. *You can hear my thoughts?* He sounded worn out. *Your voice is . . . odd.*

"Can you see me?"

I see fog, he said. *Trees down below.*

Inside the sphere the angel's lips moved, but his glazed eyes stared inwards, betraying no awareness of her.

Gingerly, Rachel touched the smooth surface of the sphere once more, but the voices in her head remained silent. "I'm with your soul," she said. "I can see it before me. It's trapped in a sphere of glass like a huge soulpearl." She hesitated. "Dill, there are other souls in there with you."

The lights within the glass prison erupted in a frenzy of gold sparkles, and then dimmed and became white again. *Twelve others,* Dill explained. *They were the people in Devon's elixir. They're angry because they don't want to be here and now they're trying to hurt me.* He paused. *Rachel, they can see you.*

Rachel realized that the other figures inside the sphere were all staring at her. Their faces moved into and out of each other, the different expressions merging and flowing between them. A young woman pressed a hand against the inside of the glass. Rachel recoiled. The phantasm appeared to smile, but there was an ugly twist of madness in her expression.

"They're not connected to this automaton in the same way that you are," Rachel said. "*You* can see through its eyes, move its limbs, but *they* can't do anything. These people have nothing but this sphere."

Can you release them?

"I don't know." Her thoughts tumbled as she stared at the jostling figures. "Dill, I can't break this glass. Not yet, do you understand?" She needed him in his current form if they were to have any chance of escaping their pursuers.

She felt the chamber tilt forward suddenly and then right itself. The automaton had nodded.

He was silent for a moment longer, and then he said, *Rachel? What's happening to the forest?*

"What do you mean? Right now?"

No . . . The chamber trembled as though Dill had started to shake his head again, but then caught himself in time. *It happened soon after we left Coreollis. The trees turned to stone.*

"What trees? Dill, I don't know what you're talking about." Anchor and Mina had made no mention of any sorcerous events taking place while Rachel had been spying on Coreollis.

The fog dissolved and the forest turned to stone, he went on. *It looked like those petrified woods we used to see in the Deadsands whenever the shifting dunes uncovered them. Do you remember?*

An age had passed since she'd last visited the desert around Deepgate. As a Spine adept, Rachel had once traveled through those thousand-year-old petrified forests, across lands poisoned after Mount Blackthrone had fallen from the sky. Yet here the forest remained verdant and alive. Was Dill confusing his memories with reality?

Or had the thaumaturge been up to something secretive and sorcerous during Rachel's absence?

Mina's calling you, Dill said suddenly. *She wants us to leave* now. *We have company.*

"An arconite?"

The room gave a sudden lurch forward.

Broken shapes littered the dark battlefield like strange volcanic outcrops. John Anchor stood at the lip of the portal, his fists on his hips, and gave a huge sigh of disappointment. "If Menoa intends to lead us into a trap, he might at least have left one of his twelve giants here as a ruse."

A ruse? Cospinol sounded weary.

"To make us believe he feared intruders. A ruse would have been most sensible!" He gazed around him but could see little in the darkness except Cospinol's fog. "It would have tired us before the assault to come. A last battle on the Larnaig Field!"

Perhaps he decided we'd see through such a ruse too easily?

Anchor grunted. "I am beginning to dislike this king. An honourable warrior is never unpredictable. He obeys the time-tested rules of combat."

The *Rotsward*'s great rope seemed to hum a melancholy note.

Anchor stared down into the depths of the portal. He had been in grimmer places, but not many. The gate to Hell looked like a lake of tar, but the stench of death that arose from it burned in his throat. How many souls now swam in those foul waters? Mist hung over the entirety of the lake and moved in layers like drab curtains dragged to and fro across an empty stage. A crust had formed around the banks, as hard and brittle as black glass. Pale unappealing lumps floated on the viscid surface.

It felt *cold*.

He judged the portal to be some three hundred yards across, and Cospinol's skyship was considerably wider than that. But the *Rotsward* was much stronger than she appeared. Whereas Ayen's sun made her vulnerable, there was no sun here, and in the darkness her ancient timbers took their strength from Cospinol's own will. The portal would expand to accommodate the *Rotsward*. If the god of brine and fog did not falter, then neither would his ship.

Are you waiting for one of the arconites to show up?

Anchor grunted again. He rolled his massive shoulders and slapped his hands together. Then he took a long, deep breath, closed his eyes, and jumped into that hideous lake.

An icy chill enveloped him. He heard the gurgle and rush of the surface waters closing over his head, until the pressure of fluid against his eardrums stifled those noises to near silence. A dull hum reverberated in the air within his own sinuses, and then Cospinol spoke:

Our best chance of success relies upon your finding the portal spine before the Rotsward *reaches the ground above you. Seek the place where Menoa's thaumaturgy is strongest. The spine should appear much denser than the surrounding liquid, like a cord or rope. Use it to pull us down through the portal opening.*

Anchor opened his eyes but he dared not open his mouth for fear of swallowing any dislocated souls. He could see little in this darkness but a faint crimson glow emanating from the depths. He curled his body and dived down, pulling at the thick waters with his massive hands. The rope trailed after him, dragging Cospinol's ship down from the skies above. His lungs cramped once in sympathy with those instincts that remained from the days when Anchor had been merely human, but he ignored the discomfort. Down and down he swam until he began to relax into the rhythm of his labours.

He descended in an inwards-turning spiral until he felt the fluid becoming thicker in certain areas. Motes of white light darted past his head. He reached for them but they shot away into the distance. He adjusted his course to take him into the denser, more central part of the portal.

After a while he spotted a black thread hanging vertically in the distance. It drifted sluggishly back and forth like a strand of kelp in an unseen current.

That's it. The portal spine. Be careful not to damage it. It's already weak and it's the only link to Hell we have.

It was twice as wide as the tree trunks in the forest he had just left, yet slippery and pliant like an umbilical cord. Menoa had woven it from souls and blood magic to form the core of his birthing channel between Hell and earth. Anchor's skin burned where he touched it—a reaction to its deeply unnatural composition. Gripping the cord firmly, he used it to drag himself downwards more rapidly.

After some time the *Rotsward's* rope suddenly jerked him to a halt.

Cospinol's great skyship had reached solid ground around the portal opening. In Anchor's mind he saw the *Rotsward's* gallows, for the lowest edges of that great matrix of greasy spars would now be lodged into the earth of Larnaig Field far above.

Anchor floated in a red gloom while he gathered his strength for the job to come. He flexed his hands, opening and closing his fingers. They felt as if he'd been using them to squeeze wasps inside their nest. Now he must drag the whole skyship deep enough down through the earth and rock to allow the portal to expand around it. The blood magic should then draw power from the dead suspended from the *Rotsward*'s gallows. It would actually feed on those damned men. Anchor smiled at the thought of his master's old army hanging up there amidst those gallows, gazing down at the fate that awaited them. Those miserable whiners would not be happy about this.

Cospinol's voice came to him through the rope. *Harper is picking up a surge of what she calls "soul traffic" on her Pandemerian device.*

Anchor paused. He had last seen Menoa's former metaphysical engineer walking the battlefield after Rys's Northmen had slaughtered their Mesmerist foes, drawing power from the bloody ground. The woman might be a corpse, but he didn't doubt her wits. Alice Harper had been the one who had first realized that the king would use his own dead to open this very portal, but it had been too late by then to do anything about it.

She thinks that something is rising *from the portal,* Cospinol went on. *Something huge.*

Another arconite? How could that be possible? The giant dived down sharply and gave the *Rotsward* a sharp tug. In all of history he had never heard of a battle fought inside a portal between two worlds. The trial to come might offer him a treasure chest of memories to savour until his dying days.

The tethered man cracked the knuckles of both his hands and then tensed the muscles in his neck and shoulders. Set, he grabbed the spine of the portal and dragged himself further down, straining against the massive rope attached to his back. The rope seemed to stretch, but here in this darkness it could not snap. Far above him, on the Larnaig Field, the *Rotsward*'s gallows would be groaning and bending as they pushed down into the earth, but they too would not break. Between the divine will of Cospinol and the unlimited strength of his slave, the only thing to bend would be nature herself.

Anchor heaved against his harness until he felt the land around the portal mouth crumble under the insurmountable pressure. Slowly and inexorably, he dragged Cospinol's great skyship down into the depths of Hell.

3

THE PORTAL

Rachel spent the night in Dill's mouth. She had curled up under a blanket with her back pressed against his molars, but she couldn't get comfortable. Air seeped in through gaps in his front teeth and turned the space into a cold, dank cave. Mina had suggested building a fire, but Rachel had snuffed *that* idea. It just hadn't seemed right. From far below she heard the constant judder of machinery and the crash of broken trees each time Dill took another step through the forest.

Living forest. Dill's vision of petrified trees could only have been a flash of memory or a dream. Since leaving Deepgate, the young angel had been thrust from one horrific reality to another, from the fathomless pit beneath the chained city to the corridors of Hell itself. It was a wonder he had maintained any of his sanity at all.

They had tied up Cospinol's stores as best they could. The stacked barrels and crates had been inclined to topple over each time Dill turned his monstrous head—prompting Mina and Hasp to leap aside in order to avoid damaging their fragile skins. Now both the thaumaturge and the debased god were slumped against the piled goods. Hasp looked twice as exhausted as Mina, the parasite in his skull having tormented him throughout the night. Only Mina's hideous little dog, Basilis, had managed to sleep easily.

Cospinol had provided them with rude furnishings: rugs, blankets, lanterns, and even an old table and chairs. The chairs and lamps had fallen over, and now stood in a heap against one side of the jaw, but the table remained where they had set it—a huge rotten old slab of wood that smelled faintly of brine.

The sky lightened. They had no view but one of fog. Occasionally Mina closed her eyes and breathed deeply of the mist, announcing the position of those arconites she could sense. Six of Menoa's twelve golems remained within the fog, following them to the south. The others were lost, somewhere beyond the reach of her sorcerous vision.

This troubled Rachel. Had those giants now gone after Anchor and Cospinol? If they had managed to stop the tethered man before he reached the portal, then all hope rested on Mina's crazy plan to attack Heaven.

She stretched her neck, then rose and peered out of Dill's mouth. Nothing but a flat greyness in the sky ahead, a bleary carpet of forest below. "How much further does this woodland stretch?" she asked.

"A hundred and twenty leagues," Hasp replied. "It once covered most of Pandemeria, but the Pandemerian Railroad Company cut vast swaths of it down during the railway reconstruction project. All that's left are the old forests beyond Coreollis. The Northmen were once woodsmen, you should remember."

"We must have covered at least eighty leagues during the night," Rachel said, "if Dill managed to keep a straight course, that is. Aren't we supposed to have reached the Rye Valley by now?"

They had decided to head for the Flower Lakes, a system of deepwater reservoirs Rys had formed by damming two of the rivers in the north. The lands around there were reputed to be the garden of Coreollis, and there they hoped to lose their pursuers. Dill's trail through the Great Pandemerian Forest was too easy to follow but, if his giant footprints could be hidden under deep water, they might yet slip away from Menoa's arconites in the dense fog.

Hasp shrugged. "I have no idea where we are, nor where to find the Flower Lakes from here." He winced and pressed a hand against his head. "No doubt Mina or Basilis has an inkling. Everything in this grey gloom seems evident to her."

Mina looked up. "The land keeps rising northwards and forms a low ridge. I can see a forest trail half a league to the northeast. It seems to have been used recently by a large number of people—refugees, I think, from an abandoned loggers' town lying to the southeast. The road runs on through a second, much smaller camp next to a sawmill, but that looks deserted, too. Just a group of workers' houses, storage sheds, and a shuttered inn. There's a huge yellow machine—an abandoned steam tractor—but it doesn't look like anyone's been working there recently."

"So, where are we?"

She shook her head. "I've no idea."

Hasp grunted. "Would that Cospinol had possessed a map."

Sabor's realm lay to the north of Pandemeria and the Flower Lakes. It was a wild, ice-blown land—a place named Herica since before man's memory. Cospinol had described it as a country of white bears and five-limbed beasts larger than aurochs. Sabor's fortress—the oddly titled *Obscura Redunda*—stood atop the summit of an outcrop of black volcanic glass in the shadow of the Temple Mountains. But not even Cospinol had known *exactly* where to find it. He'd never been to visit his brother.

None of this helped Mina, who could sense, in the minutest detail, the leagues of forest within the surrounding fog and yet couldn't explain how their immediate environs corresponded to the wider world. Without sun or stars to guide them, they were forced to rely on dead reckoning. And they were lost.

Rachel gazed down through the gaps in Dill's teeth. From this height she could see an unbroken canopy of misty trees. Acres of dismal grey forest swept by them with each of the arconite's steps. "We could stop and ask for directions," she suggested.

Hasp laughed.

It was the first time Rachel had heard the god laugh. She turned to look at him and noticed that the strain had left his eyes.

"I'm serious," she said. "In this gloom we can't even be sure if we're heading in the right direction. Mina, how close is that camp?"

Even the thaumaturge was smiling. "A few minutes away. I can't see anyone about, although there may be people in one of the houses." She looked at Hasp.

"Why not?" he said.

Rachel gazed up at the arconite's palate. "Dill? Did you hear us?"

The bony chamber tilted sharply forward and then back, causing the chairs and lamps to slide across the floor and crash against Dill's barrier of giant teeth. Hasp and Mina clung on for their lives.

Hasp let out a snarl and righted himself, his face contorting with anger. "Would you remind him to stop doing that?" he growled at Rachel. "Nine Hells, it's bad enough being trapped in this damn cave, without him almost killing us every time he nods his head." He grabbed both sides of his head roughly, then twisted away in pain and stormed off to the back of the chamber.

Rachel placed a hand against the side of Dill's inner jaw. She didn't even know if he could sense her touch or not. "Head for the settlement, Dill. Let's find someone who knows where we are."

The village hugged one edge of a broad clearing in the forest. Several hectares of the nearby woodland had been cut to provide grazing land for animals, but it looked like most of the wood had been brought in from other places via the many smaller cart tracks that radiated out from the central sawmill. Wedge-shaped piles of fresh logs waited in the fog behind a row of shacks with tin chimneys. The shuttered inn stood at one end, but Rachel did not see any signs of life. The sawmill itself was a long low shed with an overgrown sod-and-grass roof. A belt ran through the shed wall to a bright red steam tractor positioned outside, but the machine was not currently operating.

The former assassin glanced at Mina. Hadn't she said that tractor was yellow? It seemed like an odd mistake to make, but hardly an important one. Perhaps Rachel had simply been mistaken.

"It's safe enough," the thaumaturge said. "But don't take too long."

Rachel slipped out between Dill's teeth and onto his hand, and he lowered her to the ground. His four-hundred-foot-high body crouched over her, his useless wings blurring into the sky above him. As soon as he became motionless, all vestige of life seemed to desert him. He was a mountain, or an ancient and hideous piece of sculpture, as much a part of the landscape as was the settlement. The smell of chemicals and grease appeared to ooze from the scratches and whorls in his impossible bones. He had kept his skull raised level while he stooped, and the dark caves of his eye sockets now stared ahead at nothing.

She hopped down from his palm onto a deeply pocked and rutted track showing signs that a large number of people had been this way recently. Beyond the road, the row of shacks waited in the mist, their glassless windows dark. A wall of conifers stood behind them, the boles stripped of lower branches and tinged broccoli green.

Rachel approached the dwellings cautiously.

She searched three of them in turn and found nothing. They were simple one-roomed huts with bunks for six workers in each. The bedding and mattresses were missing. In the fourth shack she found a freshly cut pile of firewood beside the potbelly stove, and four human skulls lying on the floor. She placed her hand on the iron cooking plate. It still felt warm.

The inn was a larger, two-story building, constructed from heavy interconnected logs and painted grey. A wooden sign hung above the door, bearing the words *The Rusty Saw* alongside a skill-ful carving of a bowed and serrated logging blade.

Rachel walked around the building's perimeter, trying both of the locked doors and many of the small shuttered windows. After she returned to the front she banged on the main entrance door. Nothing. She kicked the door in.

A broad saloon took up most of this floor. Shelves packed with whisky bottles occupied the wall behind the bar, framing an old mirror etched with the words *Pandemerian Railroad Company*.

Rachel walked amongst empty chairs and tables, the floor-boards creaking under her boots. "Hello?" she called out. The room smelled of sawn wood, that bitter-fresh yet aged aroma of seasons past. She peered up the staircase rising at the rear of the room.

"Hello? Anybody up there?"

No answer.

The hairs on her neck tingled suddenly. She sensed a glimmer of movement at the edge of her vision, like a passing shadow, and wheeled round.

Nothing.

Her own reflection stared back from behind the scratches of the old mirror. The leather jerkin Cospinol's slaves had given her looked too bulky for her slender frame. Her hair appeared darker in this gloom, almost honey-coloured. She noted the hilt of her newly acquired Pandemerian sword protruding from its roughly woven scabbard. Unconsciously her hand had slipped down to grip the weapon.

A crack divided the mirror from top to bottom. It bisected her pale face, giving her mouth a crooked appearance. Had that frac-ture always been there? For some reason it unnerved her.

One of the two doors from the saloon brought her into a pas-sage that offered a way out back leading to the well and the privy, but also to a small kitchen through a further door on the left. This room had a water tank and a pantry still stocked with tinned food, jars of preserves, and boxes of fresh vegetables. She returned to the saloon and opened the second door. This must have been the owner's office: a wardrobe, an overstuffed chair before a desk, papers crammed into cardboard file boxes, and a narrow camp bed set against the rear wall. A pendulum rocked back and forth beneath a clock on the wall. Just as she turned away, the clock gave two brassy chimes.

Rachel heard a footfall behind her and spun round to face the saloon once more.

Nobody there.

From her position here by the office door, it looked as if she possessed two distinctly separate reflections in the old mirror behind the bar. They stared back at her from either side of the fracture. The glass must have warped, for each image appeared to have a subtly different expression. The one on the left looked . . .

Crueller?

Rachel shook her gaze away. *I must be going mad. First Rys, and now this.* Had she really seen Rys's double appear in his own bastion moments before it fell? A growing number of recent strange events troubled her, lurking in the back of her mind.

She sighed. This creepy place had let her nerves take control of her imagination once more.

Nevertheless, the footfall had sounded real enough, and such a noise could easily have carried from the building's upper floor. To dismiss it too easily would be rash.

Slowly, Rachel walked up the stairs.

Four doors led from the upper landing: three open, one closed. Gripping the hilt of her sword, Rachel edged past the first open doorway. Musty furniture filled a small bedroom: a bed, chest of drawers, rug, small stove, and grey lace curtains backed by fog.

The second room was similarly furnished.

Then she came to the closed door. "I'm not going to hurt you," she announced. "I just need some directions." She waited and then tried the doorknob.

A slender young woman in a floral dress burst out of the doorway immediately to Rachel's left and flung herself at the assassin, screaming like a witch loosed from the pyre. She hefted an axe in her raised fist. Her staring eyes and hollow, painted cheeks formed a mask of utter terror. She swung wildly, so completely wide of Rachel's shoulder that the assassin barely had to move an inch to let her attacker simply bull past. And then the woman was sobbing, visibly shaking, and turning on the landing to deliver a second blow.

Rachel could see instantly that this opponent was no warrior. "Wait!" she yelled, and held out her hand mere inches in front of the other woman's face. "What do you think you're doing?" she demanded. "You almost hurt me."

The slim woman halted, uncertain, her axe still quivering. Her lips seemed as thin as a red wire in that powdered white face. Sweat stained her dress under the armpits and across her chest. Strands of orange hair were spilling out of the loop of ribbon she'd used to restrain them, yet underneath the hideous makeup she might have been attractive. She looked at Rachel with a mixture of fear and desperation—and perhaps just a shade of hope.

"Put that down," Rachel said.

The other woman immediately lowered the axe. "Abner made me do it," she said. "It was his idea. He said since I was younger than him I'd be the best one to frighten you off. I never meant to hit you. Abner said I should…" She stopped herself and gave a small wince. "But I couldn't do that anyway. We were just trying to scare you away." Her throat bobbed. She glanced down at the axe on the floor. "Please don't kill us. There are four hundred copper marks hidden in the well. You can have them all."

"Where is Abner? Is he your husband?"

The woman's gaze darted momentarily past Rachel to the room she'd just come storming out of, before returning to the assassin. "My husband? Yes. He ran out back when the fog and the golem came. He'll be hiding in the woods somewhere. He didn't mean you no harm."

Rachel had turned so that her back was now against the landing wall. She was not surprised to spy movement to one side, a figure beyond the open doorway through which her unlikely attacker had just come.

A stout man wearing scruffy green breeches and a white shirt stood in the doorway. Abner was twice the size of his wife. His cynical little eyes fixed on Rachel as he aimed a musket at her face.

He said, "She's not getting my money."

Then he pulled the trigger.

John Anchor had carried the weight of the sea on his back before and therefore he understood pressure, but in this strange realm the fluid was becoming thinner and more transparent as he descended. He felt like he was adrift in a red sky. Hundreds of motes of light had been drawn to him, and the whole constellation sparkled and danced all around like pieces of living aether; these were souls trapped in the portal.

Anchor reached out again and again, grabbing fistfuls of cord as he pulled himself even deeper, Cospinol's great ship ploughing through the waters above him.

All the while he kept his eyes on the depths, watching out for the entity that Alice Harper had detected on her Mesmerist device.

Soon he began to perceive objects in the waters around him: physical things like Anchor himself that must surely have fallen down from earth, and other, weirder detritus that looked like it belonged below in the Maze. An oak tree floated several yards to his left, complete with roots, its twigs still bearing acorns. Three steel helmets hung suspended in the waters as though they had come together to confer. In the far gloom Anchor spotted an iron vessel, a small Pandemerian steamer of some kind. He could just make out its funnel and bridge.

And everywhere there were corpses of both men and beasts:

hundreds of the Northmen who had fallen at Larnaig; a score of dead horses like huge pale foetuses suspended in amnion; jackals and hunting dogs and countless scraps of other unidentifiable remains.

The Mesmerist refuse was even stranger: different-sized spheres composed of human bones, two figures on long black stilts—quite dead—clusters of vicious metal shapes, and dozens of vaguely humanoid warriors and flayed red men. But there was also debris that Anchor suspected had never seen the sun: broken chunks of carved black stone and arches, and entire sections of churches or temples. The lights seemed attracted to these things and looped around them in constantly slow orbits.

Opening the portal, Anchor realized, had caused a cataclysm not just on earth but also in Hell. Now the detritus from opposing universes mingled here in the limbo between them.

And then he saw something moving through the debris to his right—a long sleek shadow with a pointed head and a crescent tail. It disappeared behind a section of temple wall.

A shark?

Anchor paused his descent. Surely it was impossible for any normal living creature to survive down here. The tethered man and his master, however, had consumed enough souls over the aeons to bend the very substance of nature to their wills. Everyone else aboard the skyship, with the sole exception of Carnival, had been dead for centuries. Dead slaves, dead sailors, dead warriors hanging in the *Rotsward's* gins. Even Alice Harper did not require air to survive, simply a supply of blood.

Was *this* the creature Harper had detected earlier?

The skyship rope thrummed against his back. *What's wrong, John? Why have you stopped? Some sort of trouble?*

Anchor wrapped his legs around the spine of the portal, and then used both fists to jerk down on the rope three times in order to relay his uncertainty back to Cospinol.

Harper isn't reading anything unusual on her locator. Some ghosts nearby, but nothing that wasn't once human. The soul traffic she detected earlier is still quite far below you. I'm afraid it's much further away and larger than we previously thought. The sheer scale of it has confused her device. But the closer we get the more information she can decipher. It's certainly not an arconite, John.

The tethered man peered into the murky red waters. Human souls swarmed amongst the suspended debris like jack-o'-lanterns at play, illuminating facets of the queer drowned architecture. He looked again for the creature but saw nothing more.

No doubt it was simply a Mesmerist construct that had somehow failed to die at Larnaig. Still, he did not recall seeing such an animal on the battlefield.

He began his descent again.

Further down it grew brighter. The waters thinned and cleared, and soon Anchor could discern just how vast the debris field was. It stretched as far as he could see in every direction, men and beasts and machines and pieces of black masonry all floating in fluid as thin as air. Strange gold and crimson clouds stained the far horizon, as if backlit by a hidden sun, and from these issued an amber radiance that slanted through the fluid like evening sunshine.

The pressure had fallen to such an extent that Anchor was tempted to open his mouth and inhale. He resisted that urge. This was not air.

The rope trembled again. *John, our metaphysical engineer is obtaining clearer readings from the portal below you. There is a vast number of souls down there.* Cospinol paused. *I can't explain it, John, but this looks like another army rising from the Maze.*

An army of what? King Menoa had slaughtered his entire Mesmerist force to open this portal. He had nothing left but the arconites that walked the earth. And yet here appeared to be a second force as vast as the first. Hidden reserves, perhaps? Or had the Lord of the Maze managed to bend the souls of Rys's slain Northmen so soon after Larnaig?

Either seemed unlikely.

Then what *was* this new force?

The tethered man grinned. King Menoa had exceeded all of his expectations, a worthy foe indeed. Anchor slammed his hands together and chuckled deep in his throat. In all his long life he had not heard of another being fighting an army within a portal. Men would sing about this battle for centuries to come.

John, they're rising fast. Drag the Rotsward *down towards you. My gallowsmen have centuries of saved anger to spend.*

Anchor felt a twinge of disappointment, but he was neither proud nor selfish enough to deny his master's gallowsmen their share of sport. He gripped the portal spine between his knees and then tugged on the skyship rope. Again and again he pulled on that briny hemp, allowing a great loop of it to sag into the portal below him.

After a while the rope continued to fall past him without his aid; he had given Cospinol's skyship enough momentum to descend on her own. He looked up to see a vast dark moon burgeoning in the heavens above, the edges made ragged by countless crosshatching gallows.

And when he looked down again, he saw the opposition Menoa had brought to meet him. Not warriors. Not Mesmerists, either.

Something far worse.

Cospinol's cries of dismay traveled down through the skyship rope and into Anchor's mind. *How could he have gathered such a force so soon? Are these creatures the Larnaig fallen returned to haunt us? There are too many!*

From the depths of the portal surged a vast and ragged army of cripples. Most appeared human, or partially so, but their faces reminded Anchor of the scribbles of a delinquent child. Their twisted limbs flapped and groped at the portal waters, arms and legs that appeared to have been broken and allowed to set crooked. Rags trailed behind their torsos like bloody bandages. Many had been stretched, twisted, or punctured, as if forged by instruments of torture. Others were part beast—dog- or apelike—their toothy grins and impassive eyes mere parodies of humanity. Yet more were simply children.

Harper recognizes these creatures, Cospinol said in a weary and doom-laden tone. *She says they're known as the Failed, John. The Mesmerists broke them so badly that their minds became useless.* He paused. *Those Icarate priests abandoned them, leaving their souls to cascade down through Hell and form a river. Menoa should not have been able to recruit these creatures from their grave. They do not suffer men or gods. They can no longer be persuaded.*

Dread filled Anchor's heart. He gave up counting their numbers. There was no honour to be found here. These pitiful creatures swam in currents of madness.

He waited, a great solitary figure limned in the long amber light, clutching the portal spine as tightly as if it had been a life rope. What could Menoa hope to achieve by sending this force here to die so senselessly?

The Failed propelled themselves upwards through the debris field in ways that suggested unfamiliarity with their own flesh, their arms and legs writhing like the tentacles of strange cephalopods. Some wore useless armour made from broken mirrors or feathers stitched with colourful thread, while a few gripped weapons drunkenly by the blade or hilt or guard, as if someone had thrust unidentifiable objects into their uncertain hands. They breathed in the portal water and clutched wildly at the tiny motes of light around them, and many dropped their swords and knives in doing so.

Did they understand battle?

By now the *Rotsward* was looming directly overhead, and its gallows spanned the watery sky, its timbers aglow like gold bars in the slanting amber light. Anchor gazed numbly up at the vessel. This was the first time he had seen Cospinol's skyship without its cloak of fog. He had imagined something grander. An agglomeration of corpses and pieces of debris had snagged on the underside of her hull, and her gallowsmen had begun to struggle and kick against this refuse. Other slaves moved quickly amongst the gallowsmen, cutting them from their nooses with knives so that they might fight.

The skyship rope hung loosely below Anchor, and scores of the Failed had reached that rope and were clinging to it, some gnawing on it or hacking at it with blades. They had distinguished it as something alien amongst the floating debris and so set upon it with a common purpose.

With the lowest of the *Rotsward's* gallows still three hundred yards above Anchor, the first of the Failed swam closer. Their outstretched fingers groped for him.

The Riot Coast barbarian finally pushed himself away from the portal spine. He grabbed the first hand that drew near and pulled his opponent towards him, then broke the thing's neck and shoved its corpse away without giving any more heed to it. But the victim with the broken neck flailed his arms, turning in the clear water, and came back at Anchor again. He had bitten his tongue, and a ribbon of blood now trailed from his backwards-lolling head.

Anchor was now right in the midst of six or seven foes. Grimfaced, he set about the fight methodically. He snapped their bones and smashed their skulls with his fist, then kicked their broken bodies away with the thoughtless efficacy of a fisherman gutting his catch. The broken-necked man lunged for him again, his head lolling. Anchor grabbed the thing's jawbone and twisted the head all the way around, tearing it off.

Still it lacked the sense to die.

The headless creature swam back towards the big Riot Coaster. But Anchor was brawling with a dozen foes by now and he lost sight of the thing amidst flailing limbs. Those whom he thought he had already killed returned to fight again, while yet more swam up from the depths to join them. He broke them all and threw them back but they would not die. Three half-naked wretches set upon the decapitated head with savage blows, yet without a glimmer of thought or emotion in their bovine eyes. From the depths thousands more swam closer.

Anchor had underestimated Menoa. These foes lacked the wits to fight with any skill, yet that hardly mattered if Anchor could not destroy them. The waters all around him were already thick with fragments of them, and still more arrived with every passing moment. He could barely see through the gore. This battle was hopeless. Eventually the Failed would overwhelm him, suffocate him, drown him.

Despair filled his heart. With a powerful kick, Anchor propelled himself backwards away from the portal spine. Scores of clammy fingers fumbled over his skin, grabbed his harness, pulling him back. He closed his eyes and thrashed his arms, dragging himself backwards through the strangely airy water. He almost cried out. The desire to open his mouth and breathe became intolerable.

Cospinol's voice shuddered through the skyship rope. *Control yourself!*

And do what? Fight? Ripping this army to pieces was achieving nothing. Couldn't Cospinol see that?

The sea god must have realized his servant's plight, for he said, *Get up here, John. Swim to the* Rotsward. *We need to think about this carefully.*

Anchor bulled free from the mass of figures, propelling his huge body upwards. He swam through a detritus of broken mirror shards, fingers, and feathers. In the spinning silvered glass he glimpsed reflected a hundred calm eyes.

One of the Failed tried to pull down on the *Rotsward*'s rope, but Anchor barely noticed this. He kicked a Mesmerist bone sphere out of his way and surged up through the debris field, leaving countless outstretched hands grasping for his heels.

The skyship was still sinking towards him and he didn't have to swim far before he reached the lowest gallows. Not all of his master's dead warriors had been cut loose, yet all stopped their silent howling to watch the tethered man rise amongst their ranks. Anchor's rope grated across the timbers behind him, dislodging some of the debris the vessel had accumulated. He moved faster, pulling upon the spars to quicken his ascent, weaving through that great crosshatched scaffold like a bobbin through a loom.

By now the Failed had reached Cospinol's gallowsmen and a fight was under way. Most of the gallowsmen fled, but some remained trapped in nooses and fought; these men were soon relieved of their souls.

Anchor reached the *Rotsward*'s hull and kicked up from a horizontal joist and swooped over the drowned balustrade. The Failed were still busy with the gallowsmen and had not followed. Dragging his great rope over the midships deck, Anchor headed for a hatch in the weather deck at the stern of the vessel. He yanked it open and peered down into the dark bowels of the vessel. Which way to Cospinol's cabin? He tried to remember.

He had not been here for over three thousand years.

When he finally opened the correct door, he found Cospinol and Alice Harper waiting for him. The metaphysical engineer was drifting about a foot from the floor; her red hair floated behind her like an underwater fire. She smiled with full blue lips, then pointed up at the ceiling. The god of brine and fog floated up there, gently flexing his great grey wings to keep himself level.

Anchor and Harper swam up to join him.

The uppermost foot or so of the cabin held an air pocket. Anchor broke the surface of the water to see Cospinol's bedraggled face looking back at him. The tethered man's head knocked against a roof joist. There was a splash and then Harper emerged, too, her hair now lank and dripping.

God and slave regarded each other.

"You can breathe if you wish," Cospinol said. "The air is rank and probably poisonous by now, but I don't suppose that matters much to any of us." He gave Harper a nod. "More important, it carries sound."

Anchor coughed and spat out water, then looked around him.

"You have really let this place go, eh?" He took a deep breath, and then wished he hadn't. The old sea god was right about the air.

"The *Rotsward* still exists because *we* will it to. If it's old and rotten, then what does that say about us?"

Anchor snorted a laugh.

Cospinol smiled. "It's good to see you again after all these years, John, though I wish the circumstances were different. This battle is clearly not one you relish."

"These cripples lack the brains to know when they're dead," he grumbled. "This is no battle, Cospinol. It is butchery."

"And with little purpose," Cospinol agreed. "I'm not convinced that this enemy can be destroyed, not here at least. If all of them were present, then perhaps, but these few thousand…" He gazed down into the waters under his neck.

Anchor frowned. "What do you mean *if all of them were present?*" he said. "There are already thousands down there. That is the problem, yes? Too many foes?"

Harper shook her head. "You can't kill them," she said, "because they are not individuals. They share a common will, perhaps even a common soul."

Anchor didn't understand.

"It's like a colony of ants," she explained. "The group purpose is greater than any of its parts. But in this case, the colony is sentient. The Failed are not an army—they are a single entity, a god if you like. These crippled warriors may not even be aware that they are part of an idea that is larger and more complex than their individual selves. Destroying a handful of ants doesn't much harm the operation of the colony, and it has no effect on the *idea* of a colony. While any of the Failed remain, the idea that gives them power is unassailable."

The big man grunted. "So we must kill them *all?*" he said heavily.

"That's the problem," Cospinol said. "They aren't all *here*. Menoa's Icarates tortured these people until their minds broke. Without minds they could no longer maintain their individual shapes in Hell. Their physical bodies dissipated and dripped down through the Maze, forming a vast subterranean river. But now the River of the Failed has become sentient. It is rising again—a new god with a single mind that is able to give shape to its legion components once more. To destroy the Failed, we must destroy the whole river. But how does one destroy a river?"

Anchor felt somewhat relieved. He had shed enough blood for one day. "So what do we do?"

"Reason with it," Harper said.

Anchor grunted. "Before or after it finishes slaughtering Cospinol's gallowsmen? It hardly seems capable of listening."

"This is only a tiny part of it," she retorted. "A handful of ants separated from the colony. If we reach its source, its mind, we might be able to talk some sense into it. After all, Menoa convinced it to fight for him."

The god of brine and fog suddenly looked old and weary. "That's what frightens me. What Menoa has done here would seem to be impossible. The Lord of the Maze shouldn't be able to influence the Failed. His own Icarates ruined those people to begin with. The priests damaged them until they simply could not be damaged anymore, and now their Mesmerist techniques are useless. If Menoa has made a bargain with this new god, then he must have tricked it in some way."

"You think it is still afraid of him?" Anchor said.

"Perhaps," Cospinol replied. "If it doesn't know Menoa is no longer a threat, then we have a chance. But I'm worried it's more complicated than that." He shook his head.

A sudden burst of white light flashed under the surface of the waters. Harper lifted out a small silver and crystal device, smeared away water from its face, and then studied the readout. "They're on the decks now," she said.

"Well?" Anchor turned to Cospinol and raised his eyebrows. "One way or another, this portal is soon going to look like meat broth."

The god of brine and fog pinched his nose and then sniffed. "I will not continue to harm such a pitiful creation for no good reason," he declared. "If King Menoa spoke with the source and survived, then so can we." He looked hard at Anchor. "Break the spine of the portal. We're more than halfway down now. When it collapses the blast should scatter the Failed and throw us all into Hell."

"You don't know that!" Harper protested. "We might end up back on earth, or . . ." She wrung her lifeless hands. ". . . somewhere, anywhere in Hell. A million leagues from Menoa's citadel! Nobody has ever broken a portal before."

Cospinol looked to Anchor.

The big slave grinned. "I've no wish to kill any more of these cripples," he said. "If there's still a chance to reach Hell without further bloodshed, then I do not mind a bit of a walk at the other end."

Cospinol nodded.

This time the tethered man did not attack his foes. He met dozens of them in the *Rotsward*'s passageways and shoved them all aside. And when he finally burst out onto the *Rotsward*'s deck, twenty of the enemy erupted out into the waters ahead of him.

Anchor swam.

The portal spine had already been weakened by the passage of the arconites, so it would have torn apart before long. Now Anchor simply helped that unnatural process along. With hundreds of the Failed clawing at his back and harness, John Anchor grabbed the burning membrane in both his fists and pulled.

White light erupted from the sundered material. Anchor felt the water around him contract, a sudden momentous pressure on his flesh and bones. The force of it would have crushed a normal man.

But John Anchor had not been a normal man for thirty centuries and, when that sudden implosion reversed and then burst
outwards again, he merely clenched his teeth and closed his eyes,
suffering the blast because he had no choice in the matter. He had
long ago decided not to succumb to something as foolish as death.

In that first instant, a thousand tons of debris and bodies battered against him and threw him backwards. He felt the skyship
rope slacken behind him, and then snap taut again, slamming him
hard against his harness.

He was falling. . . .

And when at last he opened his eyes, he saw the crimson skies
of Hell churning around him. Far below, the Maze stretched to the
horizon—an endless labyrinth of gemstone-red canals and rotting
black walls. Temples and ziggurats squatted on outcrops of dark
stone or in glutinous pools. The scene was hazy with flies and hot
gusts of vapour and yet the atmosphere up here remained as cold as
frozen blood. He cast his gaze around, hoping to spy the Ninth
Citadel or the Processor from where the Icarate Prime controlled
their murderous giants.

But those structures eluded him. Menoa's fortress was nowhere
in sight. There was nothing below him but a million leagues of
Hell.

Dill heard the musket shot, a sudden crack. It rang out over the
logging camp and reverberated in the drab grey mists. The body he
occupied did not belong to him, and therefore he knew that the
pain he felt in his heart could not be a physical reaction to his distress. But it still hurt.

He reached down towards the inn on the ground below him,
but then stopped. His hand would not fit through the door without
ripping the building to shreds.

"Dill, wait!" Mina's shrill cry emerged through his teeth. "Let
us down."

Dill stared down at the shingled roof. To hell with it. He leaned forward and dug both his huge hands into the earth on either side of the inn, and lifted the whole building clear of the ground. The chimneystack leaned away from the side of the log-built wall and then fell and shattered against his thumb, but the walls and roof remained intact.

Screams came from within.

Dill held the tiny inn upon his two upturned palms. It rested upon a fat clod of earth and grass that he had scooped up along with it. He raised it close to his face and peered through one of the windows.

An empty room.

He turned the building slowly around in his hands.

"Dill!" Mina cried. "Open your goddamn mouth, and let us out of here."

He opened his mouth and then brought the building and that great lump of compacted earth nearer to his jaw. Mina and Hasp clambered across the barrier of his teeth, while mud and rock slipped through his bony fingers and spattered across the ground a hundred feet below. Hasp ran inside the building and Mina followed. Dill tilted the inn so that he could peer through the open doorway.

The Lord of the First Citadel went sprinting up the stairs from the main saloon. A sudden lurch made him growl and clutch the banister to steady himself. Mina stumbled across the sloping floor, and called out, "Dill, for the gods' sake try to keep this building level! I break too easily." Hasp had, by now, reached the top of the steps and disappeared from view.

Dill rotated the building carefully in his hands. Most of its windows were shuttered. He could not find an opening that looked in upon the upstairs landing, and with both hands full he could not flick open any of the shutters without dropping the entire inn. Its little sign flapped against the wall above the door.

He almost roared in frustration. For all his great size, he was useless.

He lifted the building again, more gently this time, and looked back in through the open doorway. Mina had halted halfway up the stairs, but Hasp and Rachel were nowhere in sight. Most of the tables and chairs had slid away, gathering like flotsam against the far wall. Dozens of bottles still rolled this way and that, spilling whisky across the floor. The smell of alcohol wafted out. The whole building creaked ominously.

Dill could not restrain himself. "Where is she?" he roared. His voice resounded across the heavens, metallic and hideously loud even to his own ears. The thaumaturge's dog began to bark frantically, still inside Dill's mouth.

Mina pressed her ears. "Try not to speak, Dill. Your voice tends to carry. Hasp is looking for her now. Hold on, I can hear…"

And then the Lord of the First Citadel came striding back down the stairs, holding Rachel's limp body in his arms. The former assassin was bleeding profusely from a wound in the side of her head.

Alice Harper sat on the edge of her bunk while the skyship plummeted towards the surface of Hell. The whole cabin creaked and whistled around her. She kept her gaze averted from the single tiny porthole, focusing instead on the array of instruments and their tiny accoutrements laid out on her narrow mattress. To keep herself occupied she made an inventory.

One Screamer. One Locator. Spare Mesmeric and parasitic foaming crystals. A knot of seeker wires in three states of agitation. Soul oil. Three phials of murderers' blood to feed the Locator and the Screamer. A silver screwtwist with a level-three shape-shifting head. Pincers and other tiny torture implements for keeping the instruments obedient. A Bael-Lossingham adaptive whistle from Highcliffe. Spirit lenses.

Her soulpearl.

Bathed in the bloody light from the window, this small glass bead seemed to emit a fierce radiance of its own—as if it could actually sense, and was reacting to, this new environment. That was impossible, of course. Only the Screamer, Locator, and screwtwist were sentient. The pearl itself was empty.

Harper clutched it to her chest and closed her eyes, listening to the winds of Hell bawling outside the skyship. A million leagues of rotten, cackling labyrinth might lie between this vessel and King Menoa's great living fortress, but she could not feel safe. The Lord of the Maze would have countless spies looking for them.

For her?

She dared not dwell on such thoughts. Menoa had previously taken a personal interest in her suffering, repeatedly breaking his promises to return her husband's soul to her.

The Locator made a tinny trumpeting sound.

Harper opened her eyes, picked up the device, and watched the silver needle dance between the glyphs etched into its metal display panel. She had instructed it to search for one particular emotive frequency—and now it was announcing its success.

"Too soon," she said. "I don't believe you."

The Locator crackled. To Harper it sounded like a tiny metallic laugh. Was the machine teasing her? She had never known it to lie before.

The needle wagged back and forth like an admonishing forefinger, then settled on a glyph shaped like a teardrop falling from a crescent moon. The Locator whined and then trumpeted again.

"Tom *can't* be here," she said. "The odds are . . ."

What *were* the chances? Harper had spent more than one lifetime in Hell searching for her husband, yet all her efforts had been in vain. To pick up his emotae *now*, at the very moment she had arrived back in the Maze, was too much of a coincidence for her to blindly accept. She sensed someone else's hand in this.

Menoa?

She shook the Locator roughly. "When did he get to you?" she cried. "Did Menoa *order* you to do this? Don't lie to me!"

The little device wailed.

Abruptly Harper stopped shaking it. With trembling hands she pressed the Locator against her cheek, feeling its warmth against her cold dead skin. "I'm sorry," she said. "I didn't mean to hurt you." She stroked the device, then sniffed. She stared down at the glyph again. Could Tom *really* be somewhere nearby?

She went over to the porthole and looked out.

Cospinol's fog had vanished. Down here there was no natural sun to injure the god or his vessel, and the skies outside burned like smouldering coals. The Maze below stretched to the limits of her vision, glistening black and red.

Harper clutched the Locator in one hand and with her other hand dragged her cold fingers across the porthole. She left neither fingerprints nor smudges on the glass. Her keen eyes, long accustomed to searching for Iolites and other transparent spies in the skies of Hell, detected something odd—vague movements, like very faint shadows flitting across the heavens.

She took the trio of spirit lenses from her bunk, shuffled through them, and lifted the darkest one up to her eyes. Seen through the tinted glass, the crimson sky became green. The vague shapes she had seen earlier suddenly clarified and became immediately recognizable.

"Shit," she said.

4

THE WOODSMEN

Shadow people crouched over her. She saw white eyes and teeth in the darkness. She feared she must be in a Spine dungeon in Deepgate's temple, because she could smell blood and she was hurting, and that meant there must be priests nearby to bless and sanction her torture.

She passed out.

When Rachel woke again, she was lying on her back on a narrow camp bed, her neck propped upon a soft pillow. Her arms and legs felt as heavy as the lumber joists in the ceiling above her. A sudden sharp pain in her head made her cry out. Gazing up at the wooden ceiling, she realized that she must now be aboard the *Rotsward*, for the whole room seemed to loll drunkenly backwards and forwards before it settled again.

"How are you feeling?"

Rachel turned her head to see Mina sitting on a chair. They were in a musty bedroom she vaguely recognized. A dim grey light filtered through the gauzy window drapes. Rachel felt so nauseous she thought she might vomit.

"This isn't the skyship?"

"What do you remember?"

"An inn... We can't stay here, Mina. The arconites..."

"They're still behind us." Mina stood up and approached the bed. "You badly needed rest, and we decided it would be more comfortable for you here."

Rachel winced as a jolt of agony split her skull. "That man shot me," she said. "Gods, Mina, I saw it coming. I tried to *focus*, but the missile came too fast. I've never..." She breathed. "I've never seen one of those weapons triggered before."

"Fired," Mina explained. "A flame ignites powder inside the musket and the explosion sends a lead ball out of the barrel, like in a cannon. We developed weapons like that in Deepgate over three hundred years ago, before the Church of Ulcis managed to stifle all the research. Abner Hill fired this one directly into your face."

Rachel tried to touch her wounded head, but Mina stopped her.

"The musket ball grazed your skull," the thaumaturge continued. "Either he has a lousy aim, or you managed to *focus* fast enough to save yourself. It's just a flesh wound, so leave the bandage alone. If it doesn't get infected, you'll probably live." She took a glass of water from a bedside cabinet and held it under Rachel's chin. "Drink," she ordered.

Rachel sipped. "Where is he?"

"Hill? He's upstairs with his wife. Hasp wanted to kill him, but I think I talked him out of it. These people know this land much better than we do. They've set us on the right path now."

"Where's Hasp?"

Mina hesitated, then shook her head. "He wants to be left alone right now. He has some issues he needs to deal with."

"And how's Dill?"

"Huge and ugly, but he'll be pleased to know you aren't dead."

Rachel pulled away the blanket and swung herself over to the edge of the camp bed. The room reeled around her. She groaned.

Her limbs still felt like slugs of metal—the aftereffects of *focusing*. The Spine technique had quickened her reactions to superhuman levels, but now her exhausted muscles were paying the price of such forced exertion. She had moved as quickly as any Spine assassin could, but not fast enough to dodge that musket ball.

"Take it easy," Mina advised.

"Sure, just as soon as I've had words with the proprietor."

Mina helped Rachel to her feet and then supported her as she staggered out of the bedroom and into the saloon. There were empty bottles strewn everywhere; an overpowering stench of whisky filled the air. Most of the tables and chairs rested in heaps against the back wall or around the base of the staircase. It looked like a squall had swept through the room.

They climbed the stairs and Mina led Rachel to one of the guest bedrooms. She unlocked the door.

Abner Hill and his wife sat side by side on the bed. The young woman glanced at Rachel and then turned away quickly and bit her knuckle to stifle a sob. Her long golden hair tumbled over her face, hiding her tearful eyes.

Rachel frowned. The woman who'd attacked her had had orange hair. She remembered it distinctly. "You came at me with an axe?" she said. "It was..." She winced as a sudden ache throbbed inside her skull. "It was you, wasn't it?"

The wife sniffed, and made no reply.

But her husband glared up insolently at the assassin. "You can't keep us prisoners in our own place," he said. "You gods-be-damned Mesmerist brigands."

He spoke with such a thick Pandemerian accent that it took Rachel a moment to be sure she'd understood him correctly, yet she did not recall that he'd had very much of an accent at all when she'd first encountered him. "We're not Mesmerists or thieves," she said at last. "You might have at least asked before you tried to shoot my head off."

"Really? And I suppose that's not an arconite outside either?"

She saw his point.

Abner Hill glowered at her. "You arrive in Westroad inside the jaw of that damn monster, then break into my property and come sauntering up my own stairs, all armed like you mean me harm. That's why you got a bullet in your head, woman." He bared small yellow teeth. "Now you say you're not thieves and yet I've sat here and watched you steal from me bold as brass."

"What did we steal?"

The man adopted an expression of disbelief. "That bullet must have knocked the wits from you. What did you steal? You stole *every* last damn thing I own. You stole my business and my gods-be-damned home!"

Rachel looked at Mina, who shrugged.

She walked over to the window. In the mists a hundred feet below, the tops of trees swept past like the peaks of waves upon a dismal green sea. Dill was still carrying the whole building.

"It's more comfortable than living in his mouth," Mina said.

The assassin hung her head. "I'm sorry," she said to the man who had tried to kill her. "I'm sorry this has happened."

Some time later Rachel was lying on her bed when Mina came in with a pot of tea from the kitchen, Basilis snuffling about her feet. The assassin must have slept for a while again because it had become much darker outside and shadows crouched in the corners of her room. Vague recollections of a dream remained, in which Rachel had been arguing with an orange-haired woman over a broken mirror, but the details were elusive, already fading. The pain in her head had settled to a dull but ever-present throb.

"Have you noticed anything odd recently?" she said, turning to Mina.

The young thaumaturge just stared at her. "We're in a building carried by a four-hundred-foot-tall golem, with twelve more giants in pursuit," she said. "Does that count?"

"Did Abner's wife change the color of her hair? I mean, since I've been unconscious."

Mina's brows rose. "Oh, you meant *really* odd things? Someone dyeing their hair?" She adopted an expression of mock thoughtfulness. "No, I don't think Mrs. Hill has been anywhere near a vanity cabinet since we met." She poured tea into two glasses. "Her name is Rosella, and she's desperately afraid of that big creep."

"I'm sorry," Rachel said. "I know how ridiculous it sounds. My head has been playing tricks on me recently."

Mina grunted. "Strange," she said. "Have you bumped it recently? Or been shot in the face at all?"

Rachel smiled.

Mina handed one of the glasses to Rachel and watched while the other woman drank.

The brew tasted strong and bitter. Rachel swallowed and then inhaled deeply of the vapours rising from the glass. "Abner was right," she said. "We stole his entire livelihood."

"Think of it as a loan," Mina said. "As soon as we've saved his life and the lives of everyone else in this world, we'll let him have his property back." She set her own empty glass down on the floor beside the teapot.

Rachel frowned at the glass for a moment. "When did you drink that tea?" she said.

"Just now."

"But..." Rachel felt suddenly confused, as if her thoughts had become knotted. She hadn't even seen Mina *lift* the glass. Rachel had barely just accepted her own drink. She glanced down to find an empty glass clutched in her own hands. It felt cold.

Had she blacked out?

"Besides," Mina went on, "Hasp pointed out that if we expect to recruit soldiers from Rys's disbanded army, then we need a base of operations. He wants to use the building to entertain our would-be allies."

Rachel was staring at her empty glass. Evidently her injury had affected her more than she'd realized. She set the glass on the floor beside the bed and then leaned back and closed her eyes. "I'm tired," she said. "I think I need to sleep."

"Finish your tea," Mina said. "It's good for you."

Rachel felt the warmth of the glass in her hand. The tea's bittersweet aroma cut through her muddled thoughts with a welcome sharpness. "What?" She opened her eyes again. "Sorry, Mina, I must have drifted off." She took a sip of the hot liquid.

Mina drank from her own glass. "Menoa's parasite won't leave him be," she said. "The last I knew he was sitting on the pantry floor with a bottle of whisky, as drunk as any man or god could be."

"Were we talking about Hasp?"

"You asked."

"Yes. Sorry, do you want me to speak to him?"

The thaumaturge shrugged. "You can try."

Rachel sighed. She seemed to have lost track of this conversation somewhere. She could hardly recall what they'd been speaking about at all. Her head continued to throb, but she felt slightly more alert now. Mina's tea had cleared her thoughts. She eased herself up against her pillow, then swung her legs out of the bed. "Thanks, Mina," she said. "I'll take him some of this tea." She topped up her glass and then stood up unsteadily.

"Are you all right?" Mina asked. "You look very pale."

Rachel shrugged. "I'm Spine."

In the cracked Pandemerian Railroad Company mirror behind the bar, Rachel glimpsed her own reflection again. She looked even thinner and more gaunt than usual, like a spectre lingering in that dark room, the ghost of some long-forgotten war. The bandage around her head had been fashioned from blue-and-white checked cloth. She brushed her fingers against the dark smear of blood above her right ear.

Somebody had cleared away all the bottles and righted one of the tables and two chairs, setting them in the center of the saloon. The building lolled gently from side to side and she heard the muted crash of trees from below. She went into the kitchen.

Hasp sat on the pantry floor with his back propped against the door frame. Four empty whisky bottles rolled back and forth across the floorboards near his feet. Clutching a half-full bottle in one fist, he raised it to his lips and drank, then looked up at her with darkly shadowed red eyes.

"A god walks up to a bar," Rachel began. "And the barkeep says, sorry, we don't serve gods in here. And the god says, why the hell not? And the barkeep says, because the last one pissed all over my begonias."

"Trying to . . . make the fucking thing drunk," Hasp said, tapping the bottle against his head. "But the little fucker is more . . . has more tolerance than I do." He lowered the bottle, sloshing yet more whisky on the floor.

"You want some tea?"

The god grunted.

Rachel downed half of her glass of tea and set it down on a convenient shelf. The drink was cold and foul-tasting, and she wondered why she'd brought it here at all. Her gaze wandered over the dusty tins and pickle jars and a box of old potatoes, carrots, and turnips. "Mina says we're following some sort of trail."

"Woodsmen," Hasp explained. "Rys's shit-head reserves. Never came to Coreollis when he summoned them." He dragged a hand across his stubbled jaw and tried to spit; a glob of saliva remained on his chin. "Probably on their way to Herica, like us . . . abandoned their settlements when the peace treaty turned sour." He grunted. "Either news of our glorious fucking defeat reached them fast, or they watched the battle at Larnaig from the cover of their forest. Cospinol's gold is only going to hire us idlers and cowards."

"It's a fresh trail, so we're likely to catch up with them soon."

Hasp sniffed. "You want me sober, eh?"

"Civil, anyway."

The god set down his whisky bottle. "I'm not..." He stared glassily into the corner of the room for a long while. "I'm no more than this fucking parasite in here." He glared up at her. "Understand? That's what Menoa has left you. If he had killed me, then there'd be nothing, but now there's less than nothing...a burden. I'm going to betray you with this fucking...little piece of Hell in my brain." He bared his teeth and slammed the whisky bottle against the floorboards. The bottle smashed, but his glass-sheathed fist remained intact.

"Easy!"

Hasp lifted his transparent gauntlet and stared at the blood flowing inside it. "Tougher than it looks, isn't it?"

"Don't test it, Hasp. We need you alive."

He snorted and wiped his nose. "Alive?" He mumbled something under his breath, then let out a sigh. "My head..."

"It'll hurt a lot more tomorrow."

"Good. That'll punish the little fucker."

It had grown almost dark by now, and the god sat sprawled on the pantry floor, stinking of whisky, his robe disheveled and his eyes hidden in caves of shadow. His neck and arms gleamed as dully red as tools from a surgeon's table. Rachel searched the shelves and then went back into the kitchen and pulled open drawers until she found some tallow candles and a taper. She looked for flints but found none.

"We need light. I'll go and see if Mina has something we can use to get a fire going."

But the Lord of the First Citadel was snoring.

The moon had risen and it glowed dimly within its own misty halo by the time Dill stopped walking. Rachel and Mina were seated before the big potbelly stove in the main saloon, eating the remains of a stew that Rachel had made for Abner and Rosella Hill, when the swaying building became totally still. Silence crept in with the cold breeze.

The inn began to rise quickly into the sky.

"He's seen something." Rachel glanced over at the thaumaturge.

Mina sniffed the air. "Refugees," she replied.

The two women set their bowls down upon the floor and picked up candles and walked over to where the arconite's great grinning face looked in at them from behind the open doorway. Rachel stepped outside and Mina followed.

Three or four yards of hardened earth surrounded the inn, as though the building had been built upon a tiny island adrift in a sea of fog. Dill's skeletal fingers curved up over the precipice, as pale as boles of dead birch. He had lifted the building close to his skull, and his eyes gazed down at them blankly, like holes in the sky itself. The inn glowed like a beacon in the night sky behind Rachel, its windows and doorway ablaze with yellow lights. The scent of the green pines mingled with the odour of hellish chemicals leaching from the arconite.

Rachel heard a woman cry out in the distance.

"Set us down, Dill," she said.

Dill did not move.

"I need to speak to them, Dill."

Mina stood to one side, frowning, then she shook her head. "They're attacking our arconite's feet with axes."

Rachel shot her an inquiring look.

"Not a chance of damaging him," the thaumaturge said.

Rachel turned back to the face in the sky. "I can handle a group of woodsmen."

The great skull tilted forward. Gold coins fell through his teeth. Then Dill stooped and lowered the building, and its earthen island, towards the ground.

A flurry of arrows greeted them as the Rusty Saw descended towards the woodsmen, their shafts hissing by in the mist. Rachel spied the refugees' caravan encamped along the forest trail ahead. A line of ten or so canvas-covered wagons had been left in the middle of the road, but scores of hide-covered tents crouched amongst the trees on either side—enough to sleep two or three hundred men. Campfires flickered amongst webs of branches and green needles, throwing shadows after hurrying men, illuminating the white eyes of horses and pack mules that snorted and struggled wildly against their hobbles.

A group of men was hacking at Dill's feet with axes—arcs of red steel in the glow of the firelight. They were as broad and fair as Rys's Northmen but wore a much simpler armour of lacquered wooden segments strapped to their torsos. Their women scattered, rushing goods and children away from the wagon train, slipping in the muddy ditches on either side of the track. Babies wailed in their arms. A horse reared against its reins tied to a running board; the wagon gave a jolt, and the animal fell in terror. Dogs barked and loped at the heels of fleeing men. Someone kicked a branch from a fire, raising a burst of sparks and embers amongst the trees.

The assassin took a deep breath. "Stop!"

A man came at Rachel with an axe, tails of hair flying behind him. She broke his teeth and then threw him, slamming his body to the ground. "I said stop!" The sudden exertion left her light-headed and reeling; she struggled to disguise her frail condition.

Mina had bitten her lip. She was backing away towards the inn doorway, muttering promises to her devilish little dog.

"Don't do it, Mina," Rachel cried. "Not here."

The thaumaturge stopped. Her eyes widened, staring beyond Rachel.

Rachel turned and grabbed a second man's upraised arm and dragged it down so as to bury his axe in the mud. She stove her elbow into the wooden panels lashed around his guts and then tipped his unbalanced body forwards. A third and fourth attacker stormed up the banks of the earthen island still clutched in Dill's hand. Rachel raised her hands. "We're not here to fight."

They grinned and reached for her, then pulled back, as if teasing. The taller of the two unwound a coiled rope lasso from around his palm and elbow. The light from the inn danced on his black-lacquered armour. His companion stroked his beard down, thrust out his tongue, and then raised his knife.

"We're here on Cospinol's orders," Rachel said. "Here to recruit those still loyal to Rys to fight the Lord of the Maze. I need to speak to your captain."

"Captain's busy," said the shorter man. His wooden armour clicked as he lunged for her with his knife. At the same moment his companion threw his rope, aiming a loop at Rachel's head. Rachel caught the rope and wrapped her arm around it and yanked hard as she sidestepped the clumsy knife blow. She kicked the smaller man off balance and pulled his companion closer. "You're wasting my time," she said. "We're not your enemies."

The tall man looked uncertain now.

But then a great murderous roar came from the door of the inn. Hasp stood there, naked but for his hellish blood-filled armour. He was blind drunk and brandishing a whisky bottle. In his other fist he clutched the same axe that Rosella Hill had swung at Rachel. He took a long slug of whisky and bellowed, "Fucking traitorous cowards! Too scared to fight with us at Larnaig!" He tottered forward down the stoop and almost fell. And then he lurched three steps sideways and looked at Rachel's opponent and lifted the axe again. "I am Hasp of the First Citadel and I'll murder every one of you bastards."

Rachel glared at Mina. The thaumaturge merely shook her head in warning. Clearly, Mina didn't think it wise to interfere with him.

The man at the end of Rachel's rope backed away from the god, his eyes wide with horror. She dropped the rope, letting him go, and turned to Hasp.

Hasp swung his axe at nothing and then staggered forward again.

"Hasp," Rachel shouted, "get inside before you kill someone and ruin any hope we've got."

"Murder them all," Hasp growled. "Bastard wood-chopping cowards." His bleary eyes focused on her. "You've hurt your head. I should protect you from these . . . foes, young lady."

"Protect yourself, you idiot. You're stinking drunk."

Hasp gave her a lopsided grin that seemed to clash with the bitterness in his tone. "I have numbed the insect," he said, tapping the side of his head. "Drank it into submission. The king's Mesmerists have no power over me here."

"These are not Mesmerists, Hasp. They're Rys's men."

"Rys?" He staggered sideways, then caught himself and looked at the fire-lit chaos all around him. "They should have fought with us at Larnaig." He sat down on the ground and stared at the axe in his hand.

Four woodsmen had now scrambled up onto the ground surrounding the inn. They wore interwoven wooden plates over banded leather and carried either iron bludgeons or strips of steel, flat-hammered and honed into rude hacking blades. They began running towards the seated god. One cried out, "I speak for Lord Rys, you fucking demon."

Rachel rushed forward to defend Hasp. "He is Rys's brother," she yelled. "Lord of the First Citadel and Menoa's only enemy in Hell for three thousand years. What are your intentions, woodsmen? If you mean him harm, then you are a traitor to Coreollis and I will fight you here."

The four hesitated.

"He's got a foul fucking mouth, girl."

"That doesn't change who he is."

The man who had claimed to speak for Rys now grunted. He was taller and broader than most of his comrades, yet as dark as a Heshette. His armour had been finely carved and painted with deep green lacquer. On his forehead ran a wide red scar, perhaps caused by the brim of a smashed helmet. He had narrow eyes, deep set on either side of a doubly crooked nose, and lines of corded black hair that fell upon his shoulders like the tails of a whip. He studied Hasp for a long time, then looked at Rachel.

"Why doesn't the arconite attack?" he said.

"Menoa doesn't control him."

The woodsman raised a hand and shouted out above the din to the men attacking Dill, "Hold off! Ricks, Nine-inch, Pace, just stop your fucking racket so I can speak."

The sound of clashing weapons subsided as the woodsmen ceased their attack and gathered around the Rusty Saw.

The man with the scar said, "My name is Oran, and this cara-van is under my protection. Who the fuck are you people?"

The woodsmen had come from a bustling town called Ferris, four leagues to the south, Oran explained. Earlier today they had passed through Westroad, the very settlement from where Dill had plucked the Rusty Saw. Now his men were much amused to find themselves in the same damn tavern once more.

"We thought we'd drunk this place dry," Oran explained. "And now we find it mysteriously restocked. That bastard Hill was hiding booze somewhere." He sat at a table opposite Rachel and Mina, star-ing thoughtfully at his glass while a score of his woodsmen roared and laughed and slammed down drinks over at the bar. Orange light from the stove lit his darkly stubbled face and scarred forehead.

"What *are* your intentions?"

Oran glanced at his men, then back at Rachel. "How much are you prepared to pay?"

"Enough to keep your people from starving," Rachel replied, "and to keep you on the right side of the war. The human side, I mean. Menoa might offer you more gold, but he'll expect your souls in return."

His brow creased as he mulled this over, his scar forming new contours. "Two hundred and sixty men won't be enough to keep those things off your back," he said. "I doubt ten thousand men could do it. Nobody has ever killed an arconite."

She nodded.

"Then we're of no use to you."

"We'll pay you anyway. Better to have allies against the unforeseen than to suffer enemies we needn't have."

He continued to frown. "Two hundred and sixty men won't be enough to keep those things off your back," he said again. "I doubt ten thousand men . . ."

Rachel felt an odd prickling sensation at the back of her neck, as if an unseen hand had brushed her.

". . . ever killed an arconite," Oran finished.

Rachel bit her lip, and stared at him for a moment. Was he just drunk, or being deliberately difficult? "You just repeated yourself, Oran."

His frown deepened. "What do you mean?"

"I said we'll pay you anyway. Everyone needs to eat."

He shrugged. "Your charity does us an injustice," he said, "but I won't refuse it." He reached a hand across the table.

Rachel hesitated. Was she reading too much into his apparent repetition? After a moment, she sighed, and leant forward to accept his hand.

As their palms clasped, the woodsman added, "We also require payment for our horses and mules. The animals won't follow this monster, nor any creature that stinks of the Maze. They'll need to be turned loose or taken to the stockyards at Himmish to await our return."

"Or butchered?"

"My men will resist that. The mules . . . that's fine, but not the horses."

She nodded. "We'll buy the horses from you. Do with them what you wish."

"And the wagons?"

Her eyes narrowed. "Don't push me, Oran."

"These wagons are all some of us have left. You can't expect families to abandon them without some recompense."

"Those who wish to stay with their wagons are welcome to do so if they think Menoa's arconites might offer them a better deal. The rest will come with us to the foot of the Temple Mountains."

Oran looked doubtful. "We're Rys's men," he said. "And Sabor will not look kindly upon us crossing the border into Herica. These two gods have respected each other's sovereignty for hundreds of years. Sabor might regard an intrusion now as an act of war. After all, you are luring Menoa's Twelve into his realm."

"The Twelve would get to Herica eventually," Rachel said. "We're going there to beg for Sabor's help while we still have a chance to achieve something. The god of clocks has been Rys's ally against the Mesmerist incursion. If he still lives, I don't believe he will view our presence in Herica in such an"—she chose her words carefully so as not to offend the woodsmen leader—"inflexible manner."

Oran did not seem to be entirely convinced. Nevertheless, he accepted her proposal.

"We can't delay here any longer," Rachel said. "Get everyone, and everything you can carry, into this inn." She turned to the thaumaturge. "How much time do we have?"

Mina closed her eyes and inhaled. She frowned, exhaled, and then took another breath, her eyes moving rapidly under their lids like those of someone dreaming. "Oh, shit," she said. "Get the people aboard now. Leave everything else behind except the weapons." Her eyes snapped open. "One of the Twelve has picked up our trail."

With the women and children taken into account, the refugees numbered almost four hundred. Despite Oran's shouted orders, they were not prepared to leave their possessions behind in the wagons. Men grabbed up tents and bundles of clothes or coils of rope and crates of woodcutter's equipment: axes, saws, and chisels. Young boys unhobbled the mounts and smacked their rumps and yelled at them to scram, while old women shouldered past with sacks of flour and meal, barrels and baskets full of salted meat or vegetables. A group of younger women stood out by virtue of their frilled lace frocks, rouged cheeks, and powdered faces, and by their apparent disdain for lifting anything heavier than makeup and jewellery boxes.

"Whores?" Rachel said.

Mina followed the assassin's gaze. "Pandemerian whores. They came here with the railroad to service the workers in Rys's logging camps."

"Don't the woodsmen's wives object?"

"Rys sent those wives to brothels in Coreollis and Cog. That way the Pandemerian Railroad made twice the profit on their services."

Rachel was aghast. "These men *let* Rys do that?"

Mina shrugged. "Men follow gods as blindly as dogs follow men. The god of flowers and knives drowned this entire land once, and they didn't object. Hasp ranted for a full hour about the situation while you were unconscious. I don't think he approves."

The older women carried hides, water skins, and pots and pans, loading them all onto the ring of open ground around the Rusty Saw, before heading down to the road for more. The whores clambered up onto the earthen island, stumbling and shrieking and chatting amongst themselves. All of the children were already inside the building and most of these were howling in distress.

"How long now, Mina?"

"Minutes only."

Rachel grabbed Oran's arm. "We're leaving now, with or without your people."

The big woodsman leapt down the bank of earth and then stepped from the arconite's hand onto the forest track below it. He grabbed an old woman who was heading away from the inn, swung her round, and yelled at her to go back the way she had come. He then shouted, "Everyone who wants to live, get into that fucking inn. We're going *now*." He moved amongst them, grabbing at the men and women who tried to return to the wagons, knocking packs of goods aside and shoving people back up towards the inn. A group of young boys took it upon themselves to assist him in this task, until Oran slapped one and bellowed at them all to get inside.

Rachel and Mina exchanged a look, then followed him down into the mob of people. They helped carry anything that could not be left behind, dragging baskets of desiccated beef and skins of water back up the slope between them.

As they reached the level part of the earth island surrounding the Rusty Saw, Mina shot a worried glance back down the road. "It's gaining," she warned.

"Can you do anything to slow it?"

"I don't know. Basilis has the real power. I just channel it. I'll need to confer with him." She pushed her way into the crowd. "Assuming these woodsmen haven't already eaten him."

"Be quick."

Oran joined the last of his people outside the Rusty Saw. There was now barely room to move amidst the jostling crowds surrounding the old building. He shouted at those near the edge to get inside, but the inn was already stuffed full of people and goods. From the upper floor issued a barrage of curses and protests, a voice that Rachel recognized.

"Abner Hill," she informed Oran.

Oran grunted. "I'll deal with that bastard later. I don't suppose he's happy you commandeered his building?"

"My concern for his feelings diminished considerably after he shot me in the face."

The woodsman laughed.

Rachel couldn't see any stragglers down on the forest track so she called out, "Get us out of here, Dill."

And the huge bone-and-metal automaton raised his hands and bore skywards the lone building upon its great clod of earth. A chorus of shrieks and startled cries went up from the frightened passengers. Several unsecured sacks slipped over the edge of the arconite's palm and fell to the ground below, but by the time the women ran to save them, the goods were already lost.

They were now moving, fast.

The Rusty Saw pitched like a raft caught in a sudden swell as it rose further up into the night sky. An ocean of dark forest rushed below the building's foundations. Cold mist broke around her wooden facade. Her joints all creaked, and her shutters slapped against their frames. A windowpane snapped in two with a sound like a musket shot. To Rachel it seemed that the heavens themselves lolled around them. The crescent moon loped through misty darkness like a swinging lantern.

Upon that cramped island it was too early yet for the conflict and arguments that must inevitably break out amongst such a crowd of people. Woodsmen positioned at the inn door herded those who would be herded inside, but the saloon floorboards were already protesting under the weight of hundreds: warriors in hand-carved armour, honing blades or waxing bowstrings; greybeards singing of past glories and clinking glasses; gamblers already at their dice and bones; spinsters and shy young women with babes in swaddle, and whores slapping and nudging and laughing with the men; young boys crowd-weaving with beakers of whisky for their fathers and older brothers, or sitting listening under tables and peering up at the girls; children running up and down the stairs and shrieking loudly on the landing, and banging doors and then running from their grandmothers' curses. The stoves had been well fed and stoked, all the candles lit and lanterns burning till the windows blazed like openings in a furnace.

"I'm beginning to understand why Abner Hill hid his booze," Mina muttered.

Rachel was trying to listen for their approaching foe, but she couldn't hear anything above the din from within the saloon. Fog shrouded much of the night beyond this tiny island of noise and light, though she spied the sheer dark cliff of Dill's torso filling the sky behind them. His forearms hovered in the gloom like vast and hellish barges made from bone.

As Oran glanced where she was looking, she beckoned him to follow her around the crowd still huddled outside the inn. A group of younger men was passing sacks of meal and bales of hide through one of the downstairs windows, while others dragged cords of firewood around to the rear of the building. Rachel slipped past them, heading towards Dill's wrist. Four whores sat on the stoop, drinking from earthenware bottles, and watched her pass.

"We need to get the rest of the women and children safely inside," Rachel said. "And we need all your men out here, sober and ready for a fight."

Oran scratched the scar on his forehead. "Won't make any difference whether they're sober or drunk," he said. "They can't fight an arconite and hope to survive. But if they have to fight, then let them have a moment of revelry first."

They reached the end of the island, where Dill's bony thumbs loomed before them like strange white gateposts. In the darkness overhead, Rachel could just make out her friend's massive jaw. She cocked her head and listened...

Regular thuds and crashes marked Dill's progress through the forest. But now Rachel could hear other sounds—like an echo of Dill's footsteps—issuing from the misty night close behind them.

Mina came and joined them. She had Abner Hill's musket propped against her shoulder, the barrel pointing skywards, the stock gripped in one slender glassy hand. "It's gaining on us," she remarked.

"What did Basilis have to say?"

The thaumaturge shook her head. "This particular foe is beyond him."

"Does Hasp know what's going on?"

"He's asleep on the pantry floor. I locked the door to stop any-one else from barging in. For their safety as much as his own."

Rachel eyed the other woman's musket. "What do you plan to do with that?"

Mina shrugged. "I wasn't leaving our only hand-cannon in a saloon full of drunken men." She shifted the weapon from one shoulder to the other. "Our guests let Mr. Hill and his wife out of their room. After screaming about the loss of his whisky, someone told Abner about the promised gold. Now he's serving the drinks himself and keeping tabs."

Rachel sighed. She had no intention of using Cospinol's gold to get their so-called army drunk, but she didn't have time to deal with Abner Hill right now. "Can Dill outrun Menoa's arconite?"

"No. He's no quicker or stronger than any of them."

Oran scratched at his stubble. "Then we fight and die here tonight," he said, yawning.

Cospinol's will determined the buoyancy of his great wooden sky-ship, while Anchor's will determined his own impossible strength. During the thousands of years of their unlikely partnership both master and servant had achieved a balance whereby they worked together in harmony. The heavier the *Rotsward* became, the greater the strength Anchor found in himself to tow it behind him.

In the confusion after the portal snapped and Anchor found himself falling towards Hell, the accustomed harmony with the skyship took some moments to reassert itself.

The rope jolted against Anchor's back in midair, bringing him to an abrupt halt before propelling him skywards again. Behind him the *Rotsward* shuddered and toppled forwards, a great mass of interconnected masts and spars. Suddenly both man and skyship were weightless. The rope snapped taut again and then slackened. Anchor heard it whining behind his ear like a living thing. The

Maze surged up to meet him at a sickening rate: the canals like bloody scrawls; the partially drowned temples, arches, and crooked steps; the mounds of rotting black masonry dumped into a crimson slough.

The vessel plummeted from the sky like some vast and ancient torture ship expelled from Heaven. Those warriors whom the Failed had not destroyed now glared feverishly about them and howled amidst the skyship's gallows. Thus exposed before Hell's fiery light they made a barbarous army indeed, blue-faced and ragged madmen plucked from so many forgotten wars.

John Anchor had slain every last one of them, and many of their souls now coursed through his veins. Corpses, bound to the *Rotsward* as thoroughly as he was. He could not gaze upon them for long before the cramps in his heart forced him to turn away.

The surface of Hell wheeled into Anchor's field of view: windows glittering in the curved side of a mound; open doorways creeping through obsidian walls; twisted iron pillars and redbrick facades; gurgling fissures; arches; stone; blood.

And then he hit.

Bloody stonework exploded under him. He plunged into a room and smashed through the floor below. Another room, another floor. Anchor gripped his knees against his chest and closed his eyes. He had the sensation of passing through pockets of air separated by parting membranes. Down and down he fell, like a cannonball dropped into a house of cards.

Deep underground he thumped heavily against a final solid surface and came to a stop.

Anchor groaned and opened his eyes.

He had fallen through twenty or more separate dwellings. Directly above him numerous layers of ragged holes formed a shaft of sorts, terminating in a distant circle of red sky overhead, where the end of the rope disappeared from sight. Each of the many levels of ruptured floorboards had already begun to bleed. Drips fell from the broken edges and cascaded down from room to room, spattering the floor around him. From overhead came the sound of moaning.

He sat up.

He was in an elegant drawing room with tall sash windows and antique Pandemerian furniture. Two identical elderly women stood looking at him, their faces white with either powder or shock. Each looked like a mirror image of the other in their hummingbird-blue high-necked frocks. Knots of tightly bunched grey hair sat upon their heads like little skulls.

"Ladies," Anchor said.

The twins looked at each other, then cupped their hands over their breasts and looked back at the intruder. "Are you the plumber?" said one of them.

"I don't think he's the plumber, Clarice," the other woman replied. "Just look at him!"

Anchor stood, brushed dust and fragments of debris from his arms, and then stepped out from underneath the shaft to avoid the cascading droplets of blood. The two women took a step back from him.

The big man grinned. "No need to fear John Anchor, ladies. I've no quarrel with you." He took a look around. "So this is Hell, eh?"

Cospinol had told him how the souls grew rooms around themselves like snails grew shells. This chamber must be one such place, a living, sensate extension of the spirits within. He nodded at the windows. Behind the glass lay a plain brick wall. "Your neighbours like their privacy, eh?"

One of the ladies said, "Neighbours? Don't be absurd. We don't have any *neighbours*. The Buntings isn't a tenement, sir. We have ninety acres."

Her twin piped up, "No doubt he hit his head in the fall, Marjory."

They shriveled their lips at him.

Anchor shrugged. He had no interest in undermining their delusion.

One twin glared disapprovingly at the hole in the ceiling. "Someone will have to repair that, you know."

"My apologies, ladies," Anchor said. "I'll go and fix it now." With that he leapt up and grabbed the bloody edge of the hole and pulled himself up.

A large bed occupied most of this next room. Propped against pillows lay an enormous woman with masses of black and white hair extruding all about her head like the tendrils of some creeping fungus. Indeed the whole room evinced decay, for tongues of patterned wallpaper hung from the walls, and black mold spattered the skirting. A smell of vinegar lingered.

"I've been hurt," she said. "Someone hit me on the head while I was sleeping."

"Sorry, madam." Anchor got to his feet. "That was me. I fell through your soul. The pain will go away after a while."

"Have you seen Dory?" she said.

Anchor shook his head. "No, madam." He jumped up and grabbed the floor joists of the room above.

"Dory said she'd come by, but I haven't seen her in ages," the woman persisted. "I don't know what's become of her."

Grunting, Anchor heaved himself up onto the next level. He looked down to see the twins still standing under the hole. He gave them a wave.

"Don't you go rummaging through the attic," shrilled one of them. "Our costumes are up there, and they mustn't be unpacked. They're very fragile."

"Who's that?" said the woman in the bed. "Dory? Is that you?"

So many potted plants filled the third room that it looked like a garden. Walls of naked brick supported trellises covered with green vines. Some old chests of drawers and wooden tables stood around the edges, but pots of yellow, pink, and red blooms adorned every flat surface and even the floor itself. At first Anchor thought the room was empty but then he spotted a young man curled up in the corner. In one hand he held a pair of shears, and he appeared to be unconscious.

Anchor walked over and crouched to feel for a pulse. Then he shook his head. These people were all dead, of course; if they had a pulse, it would be because they remembered having one and not because blood still flowed through their veins. Nevertheless he propped the young man up and gave him a gentle shake. "You all right, lad?"

The young man opened his eyes and peered at Anchor. "I must have fallen," he said. "Where am I?"

"You don't know where you are?"

"No."

"Good. Then I've done you a service."

Anchor left him alone and went back to the edge of the open shaft. He looked up to see that some of the holes above him had already begun to close as the consciousnesses within began to reassert their influences upon their environments. Down below, the twins' room was sliding away at a walking pace, underneath the bedridden woman's chambers. Those two spinsters had evidently decided to move.

"John!"

Alice Harper's head had appeared at the uppermost entrance to the shaft. Now she was looking down at him. "Are you all right?"

"This is a very strange place," he called back.

"Stranger than you realize," she said. "I need to talk to you."

He clambered up through the remaining chambers with barely a glance at the occupants within, then swung himself up out into open air. A fierce gale slammed into him. Harper waited on a nearby stone shelf, from where she could see far across the Maze. Her red hair whipped about her pale face.

From up here Anchor could see that they were standing upon the summit of a strange conglomerate of souls. It looked as if an entire Pandemerian street had been compacted together into a rude lump. But this mass of dwellings altered shape continuously, as façades stretched and compressed against neighbouring stonework. It was crawling across the surface of Hell, devouring walls under its shifting foundations. In its wake it left a shallow trench of subterranean rooms now ripped open and exposed to the flooded labyrinth surface, as streams of blood rushed into these open wounds and gurgled down through any spaces revealed amidst those smashed quarters.

Harper turned her head away from the force of the wind. "Can you hear them?" she said.

"Hear who?"

"The voices in the wind."

Anchor listened. After a moment he heard what sounded like human voices—very faint—amidst the howling air, as though the wind had carried the cries across a great distance. He could not make out what they were saying, nor even catch enough of their words to recognize the language.

Harper reached into her tool belt and took out a black circular lens. "Non Morai," she explained. "See for yourself."

Anchor peered through the lens, and into what looked like another world entirely. Seen through the dark glass disc, the crimson landscape appeared green. Winged creatures filled the skies, batlike figures with gaunt faces and red grins. They swarmed around paler yellow lights, like wisps of glowing lace, and they appeared to be herding these lights towards the surface of Hell.

He yanked the lens away, and the scene returned to normal—naught but an empty red sky. Yet when he raised the glass disc again, the winged figures and their gossamer charges reappeared, wheeling in their thousands against the verdant heavens.

"I spotted them shortly after we left the portal," Harper said. "They're steering souls here, to this particular part of Hell."

Anchor had encountered Non Morai before, but never in such numbers. On earth such phantasms often haunted scenes of violence, battlefields and places where men had been murdered. Human thaumaturges sometimes employed them to gather souls. "Why? Is Menoa behind this?"

The engineer looked doubtful. "Menoa uses Iolites for aerial work and his Icarates to collect souls," she explained. "Besides," she pointed down towards a point on the surface of Hell, "there's that to consider."

Anchor looked. At first he couldn't see what Harper was indicating, but then he spotted it. The Midden on which they stood was creeping away from a strange object on the surface of the Maze. It looked like an iron funnel rising from a crush of bloody stonework. Its huge maw, almost large enough to swallow a house, expanded and contracted continuously like a mouth. He raised Harper's spirit lens again and saw a swarm of Non Morai flitting around that opening, guiding soul lights inside.

"Why bother to travel far across Hell when there are countless souls trapped in the walls all around here?" Harper said. "These Non Morai are capturing newly arrived spirits—the souls who haven't yet become part of the Maze." She continued to watch as the queer opening consumed scores of lights. "When Menoa wants souls, his Icarates simply smash up swaths of the Maze and take them. Whoever or whatever built that funnel is being a lot more subtle. It's like they don't want to draw attention to themselves."

Anchor grunted. "Then why drag us here?"

"When the portal broke, the Non Morai would have rushed to claim all those newly released souls. We just happened to be caught up in their gale."

The tethered man lowered the spirit lens and grinned. As far as he was concerned, this could be regarded as an act of aggression against the *Rotsward,* and was therefore justification for a battle. However, he doubted that Harper or Cospinol would agree to a detour. They had bigger boars to fry. "Wouldn't take us long to go down into that funnel and have a look," he said.

She looked away, shrugging, but to Anchor it seemed that

she was feigning indifference. Did she actually *want* to go down there?

The Soul Midden jerked under Anchor's feet, and then tilted gently backwards. He peered down over the forward facade in time to see the base of the great creeping conglomerate flow up over another one of the low Maze walls. Stonework rippled, and broke into an irregular arched colonnade. The columns between these arches bent and then stepped, insectlike, over the wall, reforming into a solid facade on the other side. The Midden consumed a huge chunk of the wall and then moved on, ever further from the strange funnel.

A shudder ran through the great skyship rope, and Cospinol's voice entered Anchor's thoughts. *No, John. As confident as I am in your ability to defend us, I see no reason to seek trouble. We don't know what's down there.*

Anchor grunted. "Well, we can't ride this thing all the way to the Ninth Citadel." He stomped a heel down. "At this rate, it could take centuries, even if we could be sure we're going the right way."

"Time moves at different speeds here," Harper said. "A century here might pass as a day on earth, or an eon. But you're right about finding the right direction." She plucked one of the many silver and crystal Mesmerist devices from her belt and studied it. After a moment she looked up and nodded towards a point on the horizon, lying beyond endless whorls of black stone, broken temples, and conical ziggurats. "The Ninth Citadel lies over there."

"Then let's go." Anchor flexed his huge shoulders against the rope. "Breaking the portal gave us a good advantage, eh? King Menoa cannot even be sure we made it into Hell." He grinned. "We can catch him with his trousers down." He made to climb down the side of the Midden.

Harper stopped him. "John." She inclined her head to some point beyond him.

Anchor turned.

The *Rotsward* filled the entire sky above, like an impossible wooden city, a vast crosshatched nest of rotting timber and ropes woven around the dark heart of the skyship's hull. Cospinol's gallowsmen hung there in the thousands, their queer assortment of armour shining dully in the riotous crimson light. Many had been slain by the Failed, and some ropes held naught but heads or torsos or pieces of unidentifiable flesh. Those few hundred who had been cut loose and survived the battle in the portal now clambered amidst the joists or hung onto upright beams to keep themselves from being blown clear. The Non Morai gales formed a vortex around the mountainous vessel, a raging torrent of air that seemed to be full of fleeting shadows.

"Not what I would call relying on the element of surprise," Harper observed.

Anchor frowned. It was true—Menoa would see the *Rotsward* coming from some considerable distance away. After a moment he shrugged. "Ah... well," he said. "Let the king prepare his resistance in advance. I suppose it is only fair."

The rope at Anchor's back trembled, and he heard Cospinol's voice. *Ask Harper how deep that funnel is likely to go. Could it lead us down to the River of the Failed?*

The tethered man passed the question on to the engineer.

Harper avoided his eye, perhaps trying to hide something in her expression. "The River of the Failed flows underneath Hell," she admitted, "and any pit is going to take us nearer."

So be it, Cospinol said. *John, take the* Rotsward *underground. We're going to parley with a river.*

Anchor looked down into the gulping funnel. "It's going to be a tight fit," he said. "Much destruction in our wake." He slapped his big hands together and beamed.

Cospinol sighed in his servant's mind.

Harper slammed her Mesmerist device into her tool belt, then gestured angrily towards the surface of the Maze. "Hell is *alive*, John," she said. "You'll destroy thousands of souls if you try to drag

Cospinol's ship through its very fabric. Assuming such a feat is even *possible.*"

Anchor frowned. "Possible?" he muttered. "Strength is merely will. Anything is possible." He gave a grunt of decision. "And if Hell is alive, then it can get itself out of my way."

He leapt from the side of the Midden, dragging the great sky-ship down towards the funnel, and the living, thinking interior of Hell.

5

THE PRINCESS

O ran ordered his militiamen out of the Rusty Saw tavern, but most were already drunk, and some were off whoring and could not be found.

Oran regained order through threats and violence. He raged at them. He fought with two and broke one man's nose. His shouts of anger finally silenced the ruckus in the saloon.

"It is Lord Rys himself who commands you to stand and fight here tonight," he yelled. "I have his authority in this and all matters."

Rachel sensed resistance amongst the militiamen. Veiled glances and muttered curses passed amongst them. They had heard this speech, but clearly they did not fully accept his authority.

But they had even less liking for Rachel—and no respect. Their dark gazes evinced contempt for the assassin. After all, she had brought Menoa's Twelve upon them.

In a quiet voice Oran said to her, "They know this battle cannot be won. All of them expect to die tonight, so they would rather spend their new-won credit on whisky and whores."

They're afraid. But Rachel chose not to voice her thoughts.

The men now assembled on that cold overcrowded strip of earth outside the log building. All were armed. A few had taken up coils of ropes and the iron hooks used to scale mundane defenses, palisades and the like, but these implements did not rest comfortably in their hands. Many still drank from bottles or simply stood in the glow of the upstairs windows, gazing mutely at their own shadows.

Mina came out of the inn a moment later, clutching her dog to her chest and stroking its ears. The troubled expression on her face was enough to tell Rachel the result of her latest consultation with Basilis.

"No great plan, Mina?"

Mina shook her head. "Basilis has no power to influence this thing. Its soul is hidden from us." She hesitated, then set her dog down on the ground. "Menoa tricked us at Larnaig. We managed to free Dill because the Lord of the Maze wished us to do so—and now we face the consequences of our actions." She sighed. "He used us like puppets, Rachel. Basilis is furious about it, and yet he's reluctant to commit himself to a fixed plan of action until he understands the king's motives. My master does not want to be fooled again."

"What do *you* think?"

"I think we don't have a choice. If Menoa is steering our actions, then we risk helping him in whatever we do. But if we do nothing at all, we die."

Dill carried them onwards, the tiny island of humanity cradled in his dead hands. The smell of Maze-forged bones and metal filled the night. His gait spanned swaths of dark forest, heels pounding the earth, a deep rhythm that seemed to stir an unspoken presage in the hearts of the waiting militiamen.

Doom, doom . . . Doom, doom.

Now Rachel could hear the noise of the pursuing arconite

clearly. She turned to Mina. "We'll make a stand now. I'll tell Dill to set us down."

"Wait." Mina bit her lip. "Rachel, I think there's a way we can beat this thing. I just need to get inside its head."

"In what way?"

"Physically!"

Rachel understood. If the construction of Menoa's arconite mirrored Dill's, then they would find within it a chamber containing the trapped soul of an angel. "Shit, Mina, we'll have to get inside its jaw."

But by then they had run out of time, for Menoa's arconite was already upon them.

The automaton came crashing out of the fog. In its Maze-forged armour it was far bulkier than Dill. Dull green soul lights lingered around the edges of its bracers, cuisses, and greaves, like the remnants of some queer electric storm. It moved stiffly and unnaturally, issuing gouts of steam from its shoulder joints. Its iron-clad limbs were darkly spattered with human and Mesmerist gore from the killing field at Larnaig. Half of its skull had been burned black by some unknown inferno. In one massive gauntlet it held a steel cleaver the extent of a city wall.

Oran's men fell back cursing and gasping as the stink of the creature fell upon them: an odour of the dead, of those tens of thousands slain at Larnaig and Coreollis. The arconite brought with it the stench of war.

"Dill," Rachel cried, "set us down."

Dill turned and stooped and set the inn down roughly upon the forest track. The Rusty Saw's timbers creaked in protest. One corner of the building tilted and sank into its now-crumbling island, forcing great clumps of earth aside. Oran's militiamen leapt down, carrying ropes and axes, and spread out into the trees on either side.

Dill stood and faced the other arconite.

The automaton paused. It stood back in the fog. Its metal armour, though dark with blood, grease, and soil, was limned by a queer green radiance—like a star-festooned fortress emerged from the moonlit clouds. Its useless wings reared up behind it like great tattered sails. Engines ticked within its cuirass and scorched skull. Smoke gusted from its joints and uncurled around the naked vertebrae of its neck. With a massive shriek and groan of metal, it took a step forward and swiped sideways with its cleaver.

Dill moved to intercept.

The earth around them shuddered.

Dill met the other automaton's blow with his open palm. The concussion bleached all sound from Rachel's ears except for a shrill painful monotone. She saw men on their knees on the ground with their hands pressed against the sides of their heads. For several heartbeats she heard nothing but the sharp whine inside her own skull...

...Until she became aware of movement again, of the frenzied crunch of shattered trees and bushes, the screech of grinding metal. Somewhere in the dark skies overhead the two arconites fought. The moon vanished and then reappeared, as Menoa's great warrior grabbed Dill's neck and shoved him back. Dill retreated, his heels ramming craters into the earthen road on either side of the displaced inn. Voices cried out in the fog all around—women, howling children, all fleeing the Rusty Saw, scrambling away through mud and mist. Shadowy figures loped through the surrounding forest as Oran's men closed on the intruding arconite.

Mina tugged Rachel's arm, whispering urgently, "Tell him to bring it down."

Rachel looked up. She could make out little but vague shapes looming in the mist, the flicker of green light around armour and bone, the flash of the enemy's monstrous cleaver. Another massive concussion shook the ground. Someone screamed in terror.

"Dill!" Rachel cried over the voice, "knock the bastard's feet from underneath it. Topple it."

One huge ironclad heel thumped into the ground ten paces from Rachel. Mina stumbled and fell. Rachel grabbed her grey cassock roughly and pulled her aside as branches rained down upon them both. The assassin slipped in the mud, her wrist striking a rock buried in the clay. She dragged Mina into the darkness beneath the trees as great shadows moved across the heavens. Behind her rose a wall of blood-soaked metal. Sounds of weapons rang out from somewhere nearby, followed by another momentous clash as the arconites exchanged blows. Green lights rippled and flashed through the canopy overhead, like chemical fires.

Mina's sorcerous mist rolled and broke across the area around the track and the inn, glowing in the moonlight as though imbued with some spectral energy of its own. Rachel caught glimpses of the scene: Dill's bone limbs moving amidst columns of rank red metal, the roots of upended trees reaching from banks of wet earth, crushed bodies lying half buried in the mire or trapped under dark masses of smashed boughs. Through a break in the fog Rachel spied a score of Oran's woodsmen advancing upon the intruding automaton with ropes, trying in vain to bind its shins to trees. The great bone-and-metal limbs shifted again. She heard death cries, and then yells of rage and grief.

"What's happening back there?" Mina cried.

Rachel shoved her on, into the dark forest. "I don't know. But we need—"

A sudden clash of metal stole her words. She looked back, her ears ringing. The two giants now stood locked together, struggling in the mist. Dill's heel slid backwards and exploded through a dirt bank. Clods of earth spattered the inn and the forest canopy beyond. He turned, twisted, and thumped his foot back down. Oran's voice sounded distantly, barking orders at his men. A woman wailed somewhere to the south. The green lights in the sky moved suddenly, violently, and then seemed to *topple*.

Menoa's arconite fell.

Vast wings flashed across the heavens. A blast of dank air tore through the forest. The automaton struck the ground with such force that it threw Rachel off her feet. She landed in soft earth, mud and humus filling her mouth and nostrils. The bandage had unraveled from her head and now hung in loose loops around her neck. She spat out dirt.

Mina was now crouching against an earth embankment, panting heavily. Back in the clearing around the inn, Oran's woodsmen let out a roar of triumph. Rachel could see little through the trees but vague green lights pulsing in the mist. She extended a hand and helped the thaumaturge to her feet. "Hurry," she said. "We might only have a few moments. I don't know how long Dill can keep that big bastard down."

A strange scene greeted them as they left the forest gloom. Menoa's arconite had fallen headlong along the track, just beyond the Rusty Saw, with one arm trapped underneath its cuirass, and its vast mothy wings bent over at a shallow angle. Its huge metal cleaver rested against a nearby tree like a toppled monolith. Dill knelt on the giant's back, crushing one of its wings under his shin, while gripping its neck in his fist as he pinned it to the ground. He had forced its blackened skull down into the mud, and it lay there motionless, stinking of death and wreathed in gouts of its own engine smoke.

Enraged and emboldened with whisky, a group of Oran's men had climbed upon the arconite's back to probe for weaknesses in its armour with their axes. As Rachel hurried under the fallen giant's wing and around its shoulder, she noticed the whorls and scrawls etched in those metal plates: esoteric looping designs that again reminded her so much of the hull of the Tooth that had cut through Deepgate's chains. And yet this construct was very much from Hell.

Mina noticed Rachel's puzzlement. "Heaven and Hell have more in common than most would suspect," she advised. "Remember that Ayen and Iril were once lovers. They came from the same unknown place."

"What about King Menoa?"

Mina shrugged. "That's a more difficult question to answer. Menoa has been in Hell since the very beginning. Whether he was once human or not, I don't know, but he got close enough to Iril to betray him. I suspect there's a family connection somewhere."

They hesitated at the front of the stricken arconite's skull. Ranks of yellow-black teeth confronted them like an impenetrable wall. The colossus stared out at nothing, seemingly dead but for the hiss of steam and the tick of machinery inside its armoured torso. One of its great ragged wings twitched, but Dill held the creature fast, his own towering body looming like a great bone citadel in the fog. Fifty yards away, the enemy's cleaver slipped sideways from the tree trunk that had temporarily halted its fall, crashing to the ground.

Rachel clutched her nose. "This monster stinks worse than Deepgate's Poison Kitchens," she said. "Devon himself couldn't have concocted a fouler stench."

Mina shrugged. "It's just rotting blood."

"Lovely. So what now?" Rachel asked. "You still want to get inside it?"

"Into the skull," Mina confirmed. She examined the giant's visage for a moment, noting how the metal plates had been welded into the base and sides of the jaw. Its teeth were too closely set to permit them easy access inside its maw. "Dill, can you smash a way in?"

In answer Dill raised his free hand. The bony fist hovered in the sky for a moment, and then dropped like a boulder. He struck Menoa's warrior hard on its chin. The impact drove the creature's jawbone a foot deeper into the soft earth. A sound like a crack of thunder echoed far across the forest.

Mina shirked away from the blow.

Rachel winced and clutched her forehead as the noise of that concussion faded. The musket wound on the side of her head throbbed with renewed vigour. "Darkness take me!" she cried. "You could have warned us, Dill."

And yet Dill's attack had failed to damage the fallen warrior. Both his fist and the arconite's teeth remained unmarked.

Rachel stared at that huge blackened skull and said, "*Force* its mouth open."

Dill obeyed. This time he gripped his opponent's chin and wrenched its jaw open. A gap of several feet appeared between the columns of teeth.

Rachel and Mina approached, then stopped to exchange a glance. The assassin shrugged, and then climbed inside first.

The darkness was almost complete. Rachel stood at the inner curve of the arconite's maw, trying to see something, anything, in that miserable gloom. Almost no illumination penetrated through the gap behind her, but for a faint sliver of moonlight. The air smelled subterranean, yet as rotten as the bloodiest Mesmerist earth. She heard Mina climb through to join her and then felt the thaumaturge's cool glass-scaled hand in her own.

"There should be a crawl space at the back of the mouth," Mina said. "Somewhere on the left. It ought to lead into the soul room in the skull."

Hand in hand they edged forward. The bony floor gave a sudden lurch, and then settled once more. The air smelled of oil and scorched meat. Their footsteps echoed back from the unseen walls. Rachel realized she was gripping Mina's hand more tightly, perhaps dangerously so, given its fragility. She relaxed her grip.

After some searching they found the narrow passageway. A dank, metallic odour came from within. Rachel knelt and ran her hands over the bone lip around the opening. It was large enough for her to crawl inside. But just as she stooped to enter it, the arconite spoke.

"These are the words of Menoa's Prime," it said in a thunderous yet clear and inflectionless voice. "The Lord of the Maze commands you, Hasp, to kill the two women within his arconite."

Rachel stopped. "Shit," she said.

Mina pushed her onwards. "Hurry."

"How drunk was Hasp?"

"Not drunk enough."

Even within the confines of this strange bone warren, Rachel heard Hasp howl. His cries rang out into the night as the parasite in his skull usurped his will. Unable to resist that command, the Lord of the First Citadel would now be coming for them.

Rachel scrambled on through darkness, feeling the way with her hands. After a moment she spied a faint light issuing from around a corner ahead. The arconite's soul room? She hurried on, with Mina close behind.

The layout of the chamber was identical to the one they'd found inside Dill. A glass sphere sat amidst arcane machinery under a multifaceted crystal ceiling. Illumination came from within the sphere, where there floated the soul of an angel.

Rachel swallowed her revulsion. Unlike Dill, this thing appeared to be ancient, its flesh corrupted to the point of utter desiccation, its wings mere broken shards of bone. Some scraps of armour still clung to its fibrous muscles, but did little to cover its nakedness. It did not seem to be aware of them, but rather floated in the center of its globe and stared inwards as if dreaming.

Another terrible cry came from outside the chamber, much closer now.

"Whatever you think you can do to damage this thing," Rachel said, "do it now. Hasp will be here in seconds."

Mina placed her hands against the sphere, then recoiled abruptly. "Gods," she whispered. "Oh, god, oh, god."

"What is it?"

The thaumaturge simply shook her head. "Guard the entrance to the chamber," she said. "Try to hold Hasp *back*. Kill him if you have to."

If I can. As drunk and vulnerable as the god now was, Rachel doubted she'd be able to delay him by more than a few moments. Just buying them that short amount of time could cost her her own life.

She returned to the passageway as Mina began whispering in a low singsong voice. The thaumaturge's soothing tones filled the chamber. Another terrible howl came from outside the skull. Hasp was getting close.

Rachel drew the simple blade she had taken from a dead soldier in Coreollis. She crouched at the entrance to the chamber, listening carefully, and waited.

And waited.

After another long moment she heard a low wail issue from the night outside. It sounded more melancholy than the previous cries, but still Hasp did not appear. Rachel crawled through the passageway back into the cavern of the arconite's maw. She could just make out the gap between its jaws as a smudge of grey in the blackness. She waited again for ten rapid heartbeats, then strode over and peered outside.

The Lord of the First Citadel met her gaze with red and miserable eyes. Rachel's instincts readied her for battle, before she fully comprehended the scene, and her heart steadied. Hasp was trapped, unable to attack her. Dill had caught the god in the bone cage of his downturned fingers.

Rachel gazed up at the immense Maze-forged automaton that had once been her friend. He had shifted position, maneuvering himself so that his knees pinned down Menoa's great warrior more firmly, pushing its useless wings to one side. He still held the other arconite by its neck, but had driven his free hand down into the earth to form the prison that had snared Hasp.

Hasp slumped to his knees. He picked up a whisky bottle from the ground and poured two inches of the foul liquor down his throat. Then he crawled forward and tried to squeeze his shoulders between the bars of his impromptu cage. His cassock had parted, revealing his chest, and his glass breastplate smouldered like a furnace in the night. He tore at the ground beyond Dill's fingers with bloody red gauntlets.

"Hold him there, Dill," Rachel called out, turning away. "Thank the gods you still have your wits. Just hold him fast!"

She returned to the soul room to find Mina pressing up against the glass sphere. The thaumaturge had her eyes closed and was whispering urgently to the ghost inside. She didn't even turn around as Rachel approached.

"Hasp is indisposed," Rachel announced.

Mina held up a hand, continuing to whisper for a moment longer, then she took a deep breath and turned away from the sphere. "I can't get through to it," she said. "This angel's soul has been too badly corrupted. It shares Menoa's chaotic vision."

"Can we break the sphere?"

The thaumaturge shook her head. "These materials were forged in the Maze, so their strength isn't limited by the physical properties of this world. Their power is derived from those fragments of Iril that Menoa bound to each angel's soul. Matter thus became a consequence of will, and Menoa has simultaneously reinforced and subjugated this angel's will." She thought for a long moment. "This sphere isn't glass. It isn't even *real*. The angel's soul is little more than a vessel to hold the power Menoa placed there. To damage an arconite, you'd have to convince the arconite that it *can* be damaged. And *that* isn't going to happen, not with Menoa's tentacles lodged in the thing's mind."

"But Dill isn't like that. He has free will."

The thaumaturge snorted. "Don't go telling Dill he could be damaged. If he stops believing he's invincible, then we're really in trouble."

"But, in theory, we could free Dill's soul from its own prison?"

A dangerous smile came to Mina's lips. "Now why would you want to do a thing like that, Rachel Hael?"

Rachel said nothing.

"When we were in Hell," Mina went on, "Hasp allowed Dill to absorb power from another piece of the shattered god. Menoa used *that* fragment to transform Dill into his thirteenth arconite. Dill is far more vulnerable than this warrior, but he's stronger, too. The very fact that we're now standing in this skull is evidence of our friend's superiority."

"Because he believes in himself?"

Mina shrugged. "And because Hasp trained him."

Rachel sighed. "Well, he can't hold this monster down forever."

From behind them came a scuffing noise, as of someone moving through the crawl space located between the jaw and the soul room. Rachel wheeled suddenly and held out her arm to warn Mina to back away.

Oran crawled into the chamber, then stood, frowning at the bizarre machinery. He saw the two women. "What the hell are you two doing in here?" Then he noticed the sphere and hissed. "What is that?"

"The soul of this machine," Mina explained. "An angel of the First Citadel."

The woodsman approached. He stared at the ghostly figure floating within the glass, then at Rachel. "My men are drinking again. Is this really the victory they believe it to be?"

"It's an impasse," Rachel said, "for as long as Dill is able to restrain this thing. But we don't know how to destroy that sphere."

Oran grunted and raised his steel hack. "Stand aside and let me try."

Rachel glanced at Mina, who simply rolled her eyes.

The big woodsman took up a stance before the glass globe. He hefted his rude blade and brought it down in a ferocious swing against the glass. The impact tore the weapon from his grip and sent it clattering away into the shadows. But the glass remained completely unmarked.

Oran bent over, red-faced, wringing his hands.

"The angel knows it is indestructible," Mina explained. "Paradoxically, it's that very belief that makes it so. This whole..."

She swept a glassy hand across the room. "...construction, this machinery, the engines, they're all functionally meaningless. They exist solely to create an illusion of power and strength for the soul to adhere to. The golem sees itself and believes that this physical form requires a power source, and so Menoa has given it simple engines, pistons for muscles, and chemical blood to move its hideous limbs. None of this is actually required, and yet none of it can be physically destroyed. The whole creature is a bizarre paradox of faith and form and uselessness."

Oran scowled at her. "Your witch-speak means nothing to me, woman. My men are out there now binding the creature's limbs with rope."

"A complete waste of time."

"Then what do *you* suggest? Exactly what are you doing in here?"

The thaumaturge looked away. "I was *trying* to plant doubts in its mind, to challenge its faith in itself and thereby weaken it. I attempted to persuade it that it could be defeated." She lifted her gaze back to him. "But I failed, because its master has corrupted its will."

Oran growled, "What about its instincts?"

"What do you mean?"

He grunted. "In conflict, a warrior follows his *instincts*, woman, and those instincts are driven by naked fear and rage, not by wits or will. A charging aurochs can rout armed forces easily strong enough to take it down. The death of a leader destroys morale and hope. It all stems from *fear*. Most battles are not won by skill alone, but by the control of men's instincts." He spat at the glass sphere. "Hasp could have told you that. If you want to defeat that thing, scare it out of its wits."

Rachel nodded. "He's right, Mina. Its soul is naked before us in there, and that makes it vulnerable to fear. If it perceives danger, it might react *instinctively*. Menoa might control its consciousness, but—"

"All right," Mina snapped. "I get it." She glared at Oran. "What do you suggest, then?"

The woodsman crouched and examined the lower curve of the globe. It stood upon four small crystal pedestals. He rose and walked around it, then kicked one of the supports. Then he dragged a hand across his stubbled jaw and said, "Burn it. Cook the fucking thing in its own pot."

So his men brought jars of lamp oil and animal fat from the Rusty Saw's own supplies. They filled the arconite's mouth with firewood collected from the surrounding forest. They built a pyre under the soul sphere and drenched it with the oil and fat. And then they lit it.

Flames licked the glass. Black smoke pooled under the concave ceiling and soon began to fill the whole chamber. And within its glass globe, the arconite writhed and mouthed screams in silent terror.

Rachel watched in horror. "Can it really feel heat through the glass?" she asked Mina.

"No," she said. "It merely thinks it can. But that's good enough for us."

They retreated back along the crawl space before the air became unbreathable. Oran's men came last, piling more wood and oil into the soul room as they backed out. Soon the whole chamber blazed like the belly of a kiln. Back in the jaw Rachel stood with the others and watched the entrance to the low passageway through which they had crawled, while the fierce red glow cast their shadows high across the interior of the arconite's maw.

They climbed out into the cool night.

At Rachel's instruction, Dill released the automaton. He shifted his great bulk, moving his knees slowly from the fallen giant's back.

"It's working," Mina said. "As long as that fire keeps burning, its Icarate master can't relay its thoughts through the angel's soul. The arconite can't function."

"We're torturing it," Rachel said.

"Technically it's torturing itself. We're just giving it the means to maintain its own illusion."

Rachel turned away in disgust. "Don't even start that shit with me, Mina."

The thaumaturge laid a hand on her arm. "We need to keep it burning, Rachel, for as long as it takes to get away from here." She turned to Oran. "Two or three volunteers should be enough to keep the fire stoked. If we allow the flames to die, that thing is just going to get up and come after us again."

The woodsman chose three volunteers from the men who had assembled around them. They would be paid in gold and left with enough provisions for a week. Only after that length of time would they be permitted to abandon the fire. They asked for whisky but Oran refused to give them any. "You'll get drunk and fall asleep and the fire will die. Keep it burning until we're long gone. When we see you next, every last man of us will be buying you a glass."

The men clasped arms and Oran left them to their hellish cave, where they had promised to keep the soul of an angel in agony for the good of their fellows.

Now, with one plan under way and the majority of Oran's people returning to the Rusty Saw, the assassin and the thaumaturge turned their attention to Hasp.

The god still sat within the bone cage of Dill's fingers. Mud stained his ragged cassock and spattered his glass bracers and greaves. His coal-red eyes seemed unable to focus on anything but the empty bottle in his hand. Rachel noted with irony that he had merely passed the cheap liquor from that glass container into another. He looked old and sick, perilously close to death. Yet some of the earlier rage had now left him.

"Hasp?" Rachel said.

He closed his eyes and his head slumped forward. "Let me out," he moaned.

"We can't do that yet."

Hasp gazed down at his bottle. "I don't..." He sniffed and rubbed his forehead. "...feel compelled to do anything violent."

"How do I know that? The last order you—"

His head snapped up. "The last fucking order urged me to kill the women *within* the arconite. But you're not *inside* it anymore." He took a heavy breath and then his head fell back into his hand. "All the whisky in the world," he said, "doesn't dull the fucking thing's claws. I would have broken your necks." His fingers made vague shapes in the air and then he let out a miserable sigh. "And I would still be trying, if the parasite had any wits of its own. If you've any sense, the pair of you should kill me now."

Mina's brow creased. She looked at Rachel.

"Let him go, Dill," the assassin ordered.

Dill hesitated.

"Let him go!"

Dill lifted his hand, freeing Hasp. The god remained on the ground for a moment, then picked himself up. He didn't look at either of the women, but slouched back towards the tavern with his head held low. Ranks of Oran's men parted before him, falling silent as the glass-skinned warrior passed.

Anchor fell from the Midden and into the strange, gulping funnel. He sensed pressure on his chest as the living iron constricted around him, but then it released its grip, and he plummeted.

The spirits who had been guided here by the Non Morai reacted fearfully to the big man's presence. A gale tore at him, full of their rushing whispers. Golden motes of light and curved metal walls flashed upwards.

He dropped past windows and portholes through which he barely glimpsed rooms. They passed in the blink of an eye, like sudden memories.

Anchor came to an abrupt halt as the rope attached to his back snapped taut, a sudden jarring that tore the breath from his lungs.

Somewhere overhead the *Rotsward* had come to rest against the mouth of the funnel. The big man hung there for a few moments, gazing down at the horizontal beams of light that crisscrossed the dark shaft below. He could not see the bottom. He glanced up and spied a similar sight: Light from many windows cut across the narrow space, illuminating dust motes and lozenges of the rusty shaft interior.

He wrung his hands together, swung himself over to the side of the shaft, and smashed a fist through the nearest window. Beyond lay a room no larger than a cupboard, full of old boxes and chests. Something wailed and shuffled deeper in the shadows, but Anchor paid it no heed. He took a deep breath, then pulled himself further down the shaft, breaking more windows to make handholds for himself.

From overhead came the sounds of crumbling stone, rending metal, and screams. Anchor just bulled his muscles and dragged the *Rotsward* even further down through the living fabric of Hell. The landscape above would move, or be destroyed. He didn't care which.

After a while he began to hum an old shanty he'd once been taught by Pandemerian fishermen off the Riot Coast. The rhythm of the song matched his exertions. *Heave the anchor, pull her up*, he sang in his head, *smash that window, pull me down*. Chunks of bloody masonry from the Maze above fell constantly, battering his harness and shoulders. *Smash that window, pull me down*.

Eventually he reached the bottom. Here the shaft opened into a larger chamber below, a metal sphere perhaps fifty feet across. Anchor heaved in enough slack from the *Rotsward*'s rope to allow himself to drop down into that gloomy space.

He landed on a pile of detritus that had been shaken loose by the skyship further up the shaft. Four circular steel doors, one at each compass point, offered potential exits from the chamber, but only one of them was open. In this doorway stood a little girl.

She was about eight years old and painfully thin, dressed in a stiff black dress with white ruffs at the neck and wrists. Her huge blue eyes regarded Anchor from under a burst of blond hair. In her sticklike arms she cradled an odd-looking spear, with a glass bulb at the rear and a fragment of clear crystal at the business end. This weapon made an intermittent crackling sound, like footsteps on gravel.

"You're not a ghost," she said.

"No, lass." He beamed at her. "I'm John Anchor."

"What you doing in my ghost trap?"

"Your *ghost trap?*"

She shifted uncomfortably. "Mr. D's ghost trap, I mean. You're not even supposed to be here anyway. Why have you got a rope on your back?" She jabbed her spear at the mounds of rubble all around him. "And what's all that stuff there? Mr. D won't be pleased about *that* at all."

"Where is Mr. D?"

"Back in the shipyard, of course," she said. Suddenly she blinked. "You're not here to trade for those Icarates, are you?"

Anchor raised his brows. Had she meant *trade on behalf of the Icarates?* Or did she actually expect him to trade something *in exchange for* Menoa's priests? Was it possible that this Mr. D could be holding Icarates as *hostages?* Anchor was curious. And what did the girl mean by *the shipyard?* This whole operation clearly had nothing to do with King Menoa. "The Icarates?" he replied. "Yes, I am here to trade."

Now she looked uncertain. "Maybe I don't believe you."

Anchor shrugged. "Why else would I be here? Mr. D won't be very happy if we keep him waiting, will he?"

She bit her bottom lip and looked at the rubble again. "All right," she said. "Let's go then. You'll need to leave that rope behind because otherwise I won't be able close the *Princess*'s door."

"The rope stays," Anchor said.

She glanced back nervously, then shrugged and walked away. He followed her out of the chamber, ducking inside the open doorway, but then stopped when he saw what awaited him on the other side.

It almost looked like the interior of an airship envelope. A series of concentric steel rings ran along the inside of a long metal hull that tapered to points at both ends. Anchor was standing at one of the narrow ends. In the center of this enormous space a complex clockwork engine squatted amidst a tangle of pipes. The engine ticked steadily as its many wheels and shafts rotated. Various metal racks stood amongst the pipes, each holding what appeared to be coloured glass bulbs. Anchor shook his head. It could *almost* have been an airship. And yet the entire floor was covered in grass.

He plucked a blade of grass and sniffed it, then rolled it between his thumb and forefinger. *Grass.* A whickering sound from the front of the vessel made him look up. In the distance, just past the widest part of the hull, stood two ponies, a tan-and-white and a chestnut. The animals eyed him warily.

"What are we going to do about that rope?" The little girl was looking behind him, when her eyes suddenly widened. "Who's *she?*"

Anchor turned to see Harper duck inside the open doorway. The metaphysical engineer stepped over the *Rotsward*'s rope and looked up at the girl. "Hello," she said. "My name's Alice. What's your name?"

"Isla."

Anchor smiled at Harper. "Cospinol didn't warn me you were coming down."

"You've been blundering through one soul or another since you jumped into that funnel," she said. "I think he's worried about speaking through the rope. Too easy for someone to overhear him."

"Thank the gods for small mercies, eh?" Anchor waited a moment to see if Cospinol would respond to his jibe. When his master remained silent he grinned wildly. Finally, some peace and quiet. He'd only had to come to Hell to find it.

The little girl had noticed Harper's tool belt. "Are you a Mesmerist?" she asked. "You've got a Locator, *and* a Screamer, and what's—"

"And you have a ghost lance," Harper said, nodding at the girl's spear. "Where did you get that, Isla?"

"It's Mr. D's," she said.

"Mr. D? Is he—"

"We're off to the shipyard to speak to him about those Icarates," Anchor interrupted. "Isla is going to take us there now."

Harper nodded slowly. "Right."

Anchor stepped past the engineer and heaved the door shut behind her. The rope didn't break—but the door itself buckled. He got it closed, more or less, and forced the handle down into a bracket in the metal frame. Then, hoping that Isla hadn't noticed, he said, "All good and shipshape. This is a ship, yes?"

"She's called the *Princess*," Isla said. "And she's not a ship." She giggled, and then ran over to the massive engine, and began to pull levers. "Mr. D made her for me," she called back. "He calls her a submarine."

Anchor looked at Harper. "I've heard of buildings moving through Hell, but what's a submarine?"

She shrugged. "I've no idea."

The *Princess* was a vessel, Harper soon came to realize, able to sail through the very fabric of Hell. She moved through living stone and iron as easily as if through water, her tapered hull pushing the flesh of the Maze aside and allowing it close again in its wake. Her single engine was of a design Harper had never seen before. For fuel it burned the dead.

Before engaging the engines, Isla had connected glass bulbs containing phantasms to four inlets in the engine's housing. The terrible vessel had already sucked in the first of these souls and somehow used it to propel herself forwards. Her exhaust was located in the rear. Harper pinpointed it by listening to the screams of agony it emitted.

Her engines rumbling steadily, the *Princess* ploughed a course under the surface of Hell. As far as Harper could tell, nobody was navigating. Either the ship herself knew where she was going, or someone outside the vessel was able to direct her.

Isla didn't seem in the slightest bit concerned. As soon as the engines had started she ran to the front of the submarine to play with her ponies. The two animals ambled across the grass floor beside her, cropping.

Anchor was crouched beside the engine with his back to Harper, peering into its complex workings.

"Have you ever seen such a vessel, John?" she asked.

He didn't turn around or acknowledge her.

"John?"

She approached him, and saw that he was gripping the engine housing so tightly that the muscles in his arms looked as solid as marble. His eyes were closed and sweat glistened on his brow. "Are you all right?" she said. "John? What's the matter?" She noticed blood trickling down his forearm from one of his palms. "John! You've hurt yourself."

"No," he grunted. "Get away."

"What—"

His eyes flicked open, his neck snapped round, and he hissed, "The *Rotsward*."

Harper suddenly understood. The *Princess* lacked the power to drag Cospinol's ship on her own, so Anchor was feeding the vessel's engines with his own indomitable will. She glanced again at the tethered man's bleeding hand, and realized that it was pressed over one of the engine's intake ports.

How many souls were pouring out of him to power the ship?

"What's wrong with him?" Isla had appeared behind Harper, sitting on one of her ponies. "Is he sick?"

"He doesn't like traveling in ships," Harper said.

"Mr. D is like that, too. He never goes anywhere outside the shipyard. He never even leaves his stupid box." She blushed. "Don't tell him I said that, will you? He gets really angry sometimes."

Harper steered the girl and her pony away. "Let's give John some peace, will we? Why don't you tell me all about Mr. D?"

For the next few hours she kept Isla occupied at the front of the vessel, while Anchor remained at the engine, feeding his tremendous power into its arcane machinery. The little girl didn't have very much to say about Mr. D except that she collected souls for him, but he never liked the souls she brought back and so he always sent her out again for more. Isla thought he was looking for one soul in particular, and she thought that was sad.

And Alice Harper, clutching her own empty soulpearl, agreed with her.

The submarine finally slowed and came to a halt. Anchor released his grip on the engine housing and slumped to the floor. He smeared his bloody hand against his thigh and took a deep, shuddering breath. A slack length of rope meandered over to the rear of the hull, where it had jammed tightly between the door and its frame, but outside the vessel this same rope would form a taut line back to the *Rotsward*. For hours they had dragged Cospinol's skyship under the surface of Hell.

Anchor breathed a heavy sigh of relief. His heart continued to pound. Alone, he could have pulled the *Rotsward* for days without tiring, but this strange vessel had drawn hungrily upon his power. With trembling fingers he dug out three soulpearls from the pouch tied to his belt, and then tipped them down his throat. He felt his heart rate slow.

"We're here," Isla announced. "This is the shipyard. Come on, I'll show you. Mr. D keeps the Icarates in his shop."

Anchor got the submarine door open with a little help from his

shoulder. The skyship rope whizzed out past his feet, as the *Rotsward* took up the slack. He stepped out into a passageway lined with red brick. The *Princess's* circular hatch had fused into one wall of this corridor. Similar doors occupied both sides of the passageway, dozens of them, retreating back into darkness to Anchor's left. Evidently this dock was used by other vessels. The rope trailed away in this direction, but the skyship itself was not in sight.

To the right, the docking corridor led to a much larger space awash with green light. Through the opening Anchor could see the tops of gaslights, the source of the luminance, and what appeared to be the facade of a shabby hotel. A painted sign above the door proclaimed:

D's Emporium. Rooms for Rent. Souls Bought/Sold.

"I don't believe this," Harper said. "Renting a room in Hell is tantamount to taking possession of another person's soul."

Isla ran ahead towards the opening. "It was Mr. D's idea," she said. "He owns the hotel, and the shop, too. That's where the Icarates are."

A strange chime issued from Harper's belt. One of her Mesmerist instruments, Anchor supposed. The engineer fumbled for the device and adjusted something, silencing it. Then she set off down the corridor after the little girl.

"Are you watching all this, Cospinol?" Anchor muttered to the rope. Then he shook his head and laughed. "A hotel in Hell. I wonder how much Mr. D charges for a room, eh?" He flexed his shoulders, took up the strain, and marched on, dragging the rope behind him. From far behind came the inevitable sound of breaking stone.

He arrived in a vaulted underground cul-de-sac, where the gaslights burned with a sickly verdant hue, illuminating the crumbling facades of half a dozen tired old buildings on either side. Planks had been nailed across almost all of their windows and doors. Only the hotel at the far end looked ready for business. Its doors had been flung wide open and faced the opening through which the three travelers now passed.

Harper lifted one of her spirit lenses to her eye. "This place is swarming with Non Morai," she noted. "They're watching from the derelict buildings."

"Is it a problem?" Anchor said.

She shrugged. "You're a demigod and I'm a corpse. You can't blame the Non Morai for hiding."

"What about the child?"

"That little demon?" Harper said. "It's her they're most afraid of."

As they wandered down this unlikely underground street, Anchor became aware of a deep rasping sound from behind. He stopped, and looked back over his shoulder. The buildings on either side of the road had retreated slightly back into the surrounding walls, revealing a yard of scraped cobblestones where their foundations had been a moment ago.

"They're afraid," Harper said.

"Don't worry about them," Isla said. "They always come and go. There's only so much room for them down here, and Mr. D rents the empty spaces out. He has hundreds of customers, you see. He says Menoa...shortchanged them."

"Buildings come here to visit him?" Anchor asked.

"They come to trade," Isla confirmed, "but they're always complaining about the Mesmerists, especially King Menoa. At least, the people inside them do. So they come here and buy souls and grow stronger, and then they just slide back into the Maze. Sometimes they don't come back for ages, but you're not allowed to hurt them because they're Mr. D's special customers. He says there's going to be a revolution and he's going to be the..." she thought for a moment, "duly elected representative of the free state of Hell."

Anchor shook his head.

Harper grinned. "Hell is an endless, living, breathing city, John."

"And Menoa pissed it off, eh?"

"He's been harvesting the Maze for millennia," she said, smiling again. "I'm not surprised there's an underground resistance movement."

But a revolution? Of *houses*?

Isla leapt up three steps onto the stoop of the hotel and shouted in through the doors, "Some guests here to see you, Mr. D! They've come about the Icarates." She disappeared inside. "Mr. D! Where are you?"

Anchor and Harper followed her into the hotel. The skyship rope rasped up the steps behind them.

This level of Mr. D's Emporium had been given over entirely to the business of buying and selling souls. Shelved cabinets packed every available inch of wall and floor space, while bottled ghosts packed every available inch of cabinet shelf space. To negotiate this wooden maze, Anchor had to turn sideways and squeeze between the rows of shop furniture. The *Rotsward's* rope followed in his wake, dragging splinters from the floorboards.

"Mr. D? Where are you, Mr. D? Oh, *there* you are!"

Anchor heard a squeaking noise coming from the rear of the Emporium. He spied movement in the shadows, and then an object that he had at first taken to be a part of the furniture turned and rolled down an aisle towards them. It was a tall wooden box set on four small brass wheels. A slit, the width of two fingers, had been cut into the front panel at about chin height, but Anchor couldn't see anything inside except darkness.

The box continued to roll, of its own accord, down the aisle until it reached them. Then it stopped. A moment later, Isla padded between the rows of cabinets after it. "This is Mr. D," she said.

Anchor looked at the box. He glanced at Harper.

"Pleasure to meet you," she said.

The box remained motionless.

Isla kicked one of its wheels. "Say something, Mr. D. They've come to buy the Icarates."

A wheezy voice issued from the box: "You've been misled, Isla, dear child. These two are not soul collectors, renegade or otherwise. They are actual physical forms, substance rather than metasubstance." A soft wet *pop*, like the sound of a bubble bursting on the surface of hot soup, terminated the unseen occupant's sentence. He gasped. "They're from the living world."

"Like you, Mr. D?" Isla said.

"Indeed," said the man in the box. "You two aren't really here to buy my Icarates, are you? And you're certainly not agents of Menoa. After all, you're both still human."

"Menoa didn't send us," Harper said. "We were simply caught up in the storm your Non Morai created."

"I see," said Mr. D.

"Who are you?" Anchor demanded.

The box rolled back an inch. It creaked round to face Anchor more squarely. "I was a scientist," Mr. D replied, "and now I am a collector and a tradesman of sorts. I rent rooms and sell personalities."

"Souls, you mean?"

The box remained motionless.

"You collect souls and sell them?"

"Do you have a wife, sir?" said Mr. D. "No? A brother, then? A sister? Isn't there anyone who annoys you? Anyone you know who would benefit from a change of personality?" Another wet sound came from the box, this one like tripe slopping against a butcher's slab. The box's occupant let out a long ragged breath. "Please excuse me, sir. I am not a well man. I'm afraid I have a rather...unusual condition. But don't let that put you off. My emporium contains every type of soul. It is a simple procedure to pop open a bottle and thereby insert one mind into the physical body of another." He made a gurgling sound. "Excuse me."

"What procedure?" Harper asked. "What do you mean?"

The box squeaked back on its wheels and then rolled forward again, changing its angle so that the slit in the front now faced the engineer. "I'm talking about possession," Mr. D said. "Wholesale. Isla, fetch one of the specials for this woman. Section fifty-eight, bottle eleven, the red section."

Isla peered out from behind the box and blinked. Then she scampered away, retrieved a bottle from the back of the shop, and hurried back with it. She held up the bottle for Harper to inspect.

Harper took the bottle.

"Such a good vintage," said Mr. D. "The gentleman in this bottle was a great leader, a kind and intelligent man. He fell to his death in a terrible accident during a great battle. Somewhat older than you, and not particularly handsome, I admit, but that doesn't mean anything. Looks aren't part of the package I offer. It's up to you to find some muscled dimwit and then persuade him to drink down this soul." A slavering sound came from the box, followed by a sharp rapping noise. "Do you know what this would be worth up there . . . in the living world?"

Anchor had had enough. This boxed lunatic couldn't help them in their fight against Menoa. He was nothing more than a trader of slaves. "Let's go now," he said. "We have a long road ahead, eh?"

But Harper held up her hand. "How much?" she said. "How much to buy a soul?"

"Ha!" said Mr. D. "I *knew* you were interested the moment I saw you walk into my shop. You want the aeronaut, then? I can make you a very good deal." The box began to turn away.

"Not him," she said. "I want to . . . look around."

The box stopped. The slit in its face crept round to face Harper again. Mr. D's voice issued from the darkness within. "Someone in *particular*, is it?"

She looked at the floor.

Anchor frowned. He recalled the chime her Mesmerist device

had made when they'd first arrived here. Had she been searching for one of these souls all along? He faced Mr. D. "Answer her. How much for a soul?"

"That depends," said Mr. D, "on the soul."

"What do you want? Gold?"

"What a strange notion," replied Mr. D. "Whatever would I do with an immutable physical substance down here?" He let loose a sudden hacking cough, and the whole box shuddered on its wheels. "Please excuse me again. No, I simply require the purchaser to sign a contract, promising me certain services, and a small token to act as security, of course, just to ensure that the purchaser doesn't default on the contract."

"Tell me what you want," Harper said.

The box rolled forward. "I'd like you to kill some people for me. Nobody you know, just some old friends of mine. You've probably never even heard of the city where they come from. I doubt it even exists now."

"What city?" Anchor said.

"A place called Deepgate," said Mr. D.

"There," Monk said.

The hook-fingered boy peered through the sightglass in the same direction as the old man's pointed finger. Brands flared away down in the darkness where the *Rotsward*'s outer scaffold pressed against a towering facade. The skyship had been dragged straight down into Hell, and then pulled horizontally for many hours. Now that John Anchor had halted his progress, Cospinol's slaves worked alongside his gallowsmen with hammers and crowbars, smashing at the brick and stonework to create some more space around her scaffold ends. They broke windows and tiles, and ripped out doors and joists and lintels, passing the lot back up their ranks towards the *Rotsward*'s hull.

"They're trying to ease the pressure on the ship," Monk observed. "In case Hell decides to try and spit the whole vessel back out."

The boy lifted his gaze from the sightglass. "How do you know?" he asked. He'd taken a liking to querying Monk's assertions. "Maybe they're just looting all that stuff. Bits of souls and all that. Cospinol can boil it all down and make soulpearls."

The astrologer's face turned red. He raised a hand to strike the boy, but then seemed to think better of it. "Don't get smart with me, son," he said. "They're easing the pressure, I tell you. The Maze is *living*. All these homes might realize it's best to work together. I've seen it happen before, whole Middens crawling across the top of the labyrinth. Buildings on the move." He nodded to himself. "Aye, strange things can happen when a group of souls all get the same idea."

"Maybe we could steal some of those bricks," the boy said, "and boil them up ourselves."

Monk grunted. He unfastened his breeches, then, clinging on to the edge of the hole in the hull, he pissed down through the gaps in the scaffold. Steam rose from the arc of urine. The astrologer let out a sigh, then shook himself. "Them bricks won't give us much sustenance," he said. "We'd be better stealing a soul from inside one of them rooms. Or using the distraction to loosen the bolts on that angel's boiling pot." He refastened his breeches and turned to face the boy. "I'll bet them slaves have gone and left their prisoner alone."

"They never leave it alone," the boy said. "You're just afraid to go out there on that scaffold in case the gallowsmen get you."

"I ain't afraid of nothing," Monk said. "I'm just being smart. A few drops of that scarred angel's essence would sate you for a hundred years." He ushered the boy back inside the *Rotsward*. From the shadows under one of the bulkheads he pulled out a rag-wrapped bundle and untied it, revealing an old wrench, a hammer, and an iron spike. Monk weighed the hammer in one fist and then handed it to the boy.

"Aren't you coming, too?"

" 'Course I'm coming. Someone's got to tell you which welds to crack and which bolts to loosen." Monk grunted. "Don't want to let the bitch escape now, do we?"

6

THE RIVER OF THE FAILED

Dill removed the stricken arconite's armour while it lay immobile and took it for himself. Like all Maze-forged creations, the blood-soaked metal plates exhibited a primitive consciousness. They were fiercely reluctant to release their grip on the fallen automaton's bones. Dill persuaded them by brute force. He wrenched the sections free, revealing arrays of hooks on the undersides that writhed like cilia, and then pressed them against his own limbs and torso.

Rachel watched from the stoop outside the Rusty Saw tavern. She heard scratching sounds as the hooks attached themselves to Dill's ribs. The metal itself seemed to wail quietly. Pulses of green light raced along his newly fitted arm bracers and over his armoured chest, like a swarm of fireflies amidst the fog.

In moments, Menoa's arconite had been stripped bare. Its body formed a great dark peninsula of bone and metal upon the forest track, stinking and hissing smoke like something expelled from the heart of a volcano.

Dill picked up his opponent's massive cleaver and shook mud

loose from its blade. He then stooped and lifted the building, holding it so that its foundations rested upon that enormous blade. Rachel clung to the doorjamb for support, her hair blowing wildly about her face. More of the Rusty Saw's earthen island crumbled away and fell to the ground in dull thumps. A clamour of broken glass and shouts went up inside the main saloon as the building pitched and slid several feet across the cleaver's smooth metal surface. Rachel felt herself rising rapidly into the sky. Dill's armour-clad torso swept past her like a shower of dull green stars.

And then they were moving again, carried north in great sweeping strides.

Rachel stepped inside to find the woodsmen crowded around every table, while still more of them squatted around the edges of the room or sat on the staircase. Conversation was muted. They seemed content to brood darkly over recent events. Oran himself sat drinking beer at a table in one corner, with a whore perched on his knee. He saw Rachel and nodded to her. Meanwhile, Abner Hill leaned on the bar, glaring at his unwelcome customers while his young wife struggled through the throng and cleared glasses from the tables.

Mina approached, cradling her tiny dog in her arms, and drew Rachel aside. "They're furious at Hasp," she whispered. "They all saw how he tried to betray us." She glanced at the men around her. "Rachel, there's even been some talk of taking matters into their own hands."

"Gods, we don't need this, Mina. Where's Hasp now?"

"He's barricaded himself in the pantry," she said. "If anything, he's even drunker than before. It's only a matter of time before one of Oran's men does something foolish."

Rachel sighed. "I'll speak to Oran. We need more space, more room to breathe. And we need to keep these men busy. Will you come with me?"

Oran's eyes were glazed with drink, but he made space for the two women at his table by ordering one of his lieutenants to move. Then he pushed the whore away and told her to fetch them all a fresh jug. "Have some beer," he said, filling two cups with frothing liquid.

Rachel accepted the drink. Mina left hers on the table.

Oran raised his own cup. "To Rys," he said, "the architect of our victory." Some of the men at nearby tables joined in the toast.

Rachel hesitated, then took a sip. "I seem to have missed Rys's involvement in all this."

"The god of flowers and knives is subtle," Oran explained. "Yet his influence is apparent in all events. It's like this sorcerous fog in the way it pervades the state of Coreollis."

"You grant him omnipotence, then?"

"He speaks through me!"

To Rachel this outburst seemed unwarranted. Oran's expression had suddenly become dark, his eyes shadowed as he leaned forward. His skin looked moist and varicose, as with a man under extreme duress, while the axe scar on his forehead appeared to throb in the dim yellow light like a hot metal plate. He bared his teeth. "This is Rys's land," he continued more quietly, "and we are his agents here."

Rachel glanced at Mina. The thaumaturge was watching the man carefully.

Oran slumped back in his chair and took another long gulp of beer. "I have doubts about our destination," he said. "Why should we be seeking Sabor before we locate Lord Rys? I reckon we should return to Coreollis."

Rachel was losing patience with him. She was just about to explain that Rys had, by all reasonable accounts, died in Coreollis, but Mina preempted her.

"Cospinol told us that Lord Rys trusted Sabor and Mirith to find a way back into Heaven," the thaumaturge explained. "While Rys fought the Mesmerists in Pandemeria and Skirl, his brothers explored more...esoteric options. If we agree that Rys destroyed his own palace as a ruse to trick King Menoa, then it's likely he's left Coreollis entirely." Her glass-sheathed hand now curled around her cup. "The battle has moved from the city of flowers, Oran. We'll find Rys at Sabor's castle in Herica."

The woodsman gave Mina an indignant look. "You think *you* can guess our Lord's intent?" he growled. Then he spat on the floor and moved his face very close to hers. "Listen to me, witch. Rys sent you here in answer to our prayers. The arconite carried you from his own city. Do you think that was merely coincidence? Now, why shouldn't we simply take your gold and use it to execute *his* will?"

Basilis growled.

Oran started to speak again, but was interrupted by the arrival of the tavernkeeper's wife.

Rosella Hill set a fresh jug of beer upon the table. Her golden hair had spilled out from its ribbon, and white makeup smeared her powdered forehead and the back of one wrist. Avoiding the eyes of everyone present, she began mopping up spills from the table with a cloth.

Oran stared up at her with hot glazed eyes. "All things are sent to us by Rys," he muttered. Then he drained the last of his cup, set it down on the table, and grabbed her wrist. "*You* know what I'm talking about?"

Rosella said nothing. She wouldn't even look at him.

The tables around them grew quiet. Rachel could sense the tension amongst Oran's men. She glanced over at the bar, where Abner was now busy scrubbing the polished counter, his full attention fixed on the task at hand.

Oran maintained his grip on the woman's wrist. With his free hand he lifted the jug and refilled his cup. "If Rys intended that you serve me," he said to her, "or that you sit and drink with me, how could we argue with *his* will?" He pulled her towards him and breathed heavily through his nose. "Stay here a while. The witch will give you her seat."

Rachel stiffened, but then she felt Mina's hand clutch her knee under the table—a warning gesture. The thaumaturge slipped out of her seat, and said, "Thanks for your time, Oran," then, "Rachel, would you help me find some blankets? We should sort out bedding for all our civilian guests."

Oran gave them a dismissive wave.

Rachel felt heat rise on her neck, but she followed the thaumaturge back through the crowded saloon towards the rear door. The militiamen watched them go, except Abner Hill, who was still furiously scrubbing at his bar with one white-knuckled fist.

When they reached the back hallway, Rachel whispered, "I should just kill him."

"And all two hundred of his men?"

The assassin snorted. "I know how to make it look like an accident. I could do it tonight."

"No."

"We're losing control, Mina. Oran is trying to usurp our authority, and Hasp is so fragile he could snap at any moment." Her voice rose. "We've got two hundred men and a drunk of a god all locked up in a fucking inn."

Mina shushed her, opened the back door, and urged her outside. A gust of wind cooled Rachel's face, but then the stench of death filled her nostrils. It was still hours before dawn, yet Dill's stolen armour illuminated the building and its earthen island and even the surrounding forest in soft green radiance. She heard the distant thud of his footsteps crashing through the vegetation below.

There was little space left. Two yards of compacted earth were left to form a ledge along this side of the inn, although firewood stacked under the eaves took up most of this area. Dill's fleshless fingers curled up over the edge of the mud foundations like the remains of white stone arches. The hilt of his giant cleaver extended into the night air like a battered metal bridge.

Mina set Basilis down, and the dog padded away to urinate against the woodpile. "The remaining arconites now know where we are," she revealed. "I can sense nine of them within the reaches of my fog: six to the south, one east, and two west of here. They're converging on us." She looked out into the night as though she expected to see imminent evidence of their approach. "Those nearest are holding back and waiting for the others. It seems they won't challenge us singly."

Rachel felt a headache creeping up on her. The wound on the side of her head irritated her. She looked back up at Dill, at his vast and uncertain form in the mist. How could such a giant be so vulnerable?

"But we're nearing the Flower Lakes," Mina went on. "I can sense a large settlement just north of here, a lakeshore trading town built around a harbour. It looks like they export timber and coke. And it's well guarded, too. There's a palisade wall manned by local militia."

"*More* locals?"

"These soldiers vastly outnumber our current friends. Recruiting new forces would dilute Oran's influence and provide us with the makings of an army."

"Or start a war between their two factions," Rachel said. "Besides, where are we going to put all these people?"

Mina smiled. "We need to steal a bigger building."

"Not a chance, Mina. If you intend to—"

The thaumaturge's smile abruptly withered. She squeezed her hands against the sides of her head and let out a sudden wail of pain.

"What's wrong?" Rachel reached over to comfort the other woman, but Mina shook her away.

"Didn't you *feel* that?" she said.

"Feel what?"

"There was a... an earthquake? Gods, I don't know what it was! Like a crack appearing in the fog, a crevasse that ran from one side of the world to the other. Everything *jolted*. Every-thing—"

A sudden uproar came from the inn. Rachel heard the sounds of smashing glass and heavy objects being thrown to the floor, men shouting and cursing—and, above it all, Hasp roaring, "Cowards!"

"Oh, god," she said, turning back to the inn. "Stay here, Mina."

There had been a scuffle inside. Tables and chairs were over-turned. One of Oran's men lay unmoving on the floor, blood seep-ing out from his gut. Two more were rising to their feet not far away, while most of the remaining warriors huddled back against the walls. The Lord of the First Citadel had discarded his robe and stood stark naked in the center of the saloon. Blood pulsed through the transparent etched scales and metameric plates across his body, and stumps of muscle and bone visible under glass protrusions on his shoulders indicated where the Mesmerists had removed his wings. In one fist he gripped an axe.

Hasp wheeled and staggered sideways. He lifted the axe and swiped at the air. A few of Oran's men laughed. The warriors who had risen from the floor circled around the glass-armoured god to flank him. One of them carried an iron-banded club, while the other gripped a long knife.

Oran remained seated at his corner table, with one thick arm around the innkeeper's wife standing beside him. Rosella Hill looked flushed and disheveled, her skirts lifted around her thighs. She suddenly pulled away from her captor and Oran let her go.

Rachel drew her own sword. The Coreollis steel was heav-ier than the layered Spine weapons she was used to, but it was sharp enough to open throats. "What's going on here?" she demanded.

Oran's gaze fell upon her naked weapon, then he eyed her without apparent interest. "This abomination killed one of my men," he said.

"You provoked him?"

The woodsman picked up his blade from the floor and rose from his seat. In that dark smoke-filled corner of the saloon he looked as filthy and feral as a wild man. Mud spattered his banded leather armour and clotted his wild grey hair. His eyes smouldered with a feverish light. The scar on his forehead seemed to throb. "Rys sent Hasp to Hell for a good reason," he said. "He should have had the decency to remain there."

Hasp's full attention was now focused on Oran. The god was grinning like an imbecile, ignoring the two men now edging towards him from either side.

Oran made a subtle gesture with his head.

As Rachel heard a simultaneous intake of breath from Oran's two soldiers, she *focused*...

...and the world around her stopped.

A dead silence encompassed the saloon. Candle flames and oil lanterns abruptly ceased to flicker. The light dimmed and yet intensified, becoming simultaneously tarry and harsh. Black particles of smoke waited, perfectly motionless, in the air. On either side of Hasp the two approaching woodsmen were just preparing to lunge. Rachel detected the tiny motions that evinced the coming changes in the stance of each: the slow curl of the lips, the tightening of tendons in their necks as their shoulder muscles began the process of lifting their weapons.

She considered Oran. The militia leader, too, was primed for violence, and his stance suggested that he might throw the heavy blade he wielded. There were plenty of other weapons around him to replace it.

Three targets. Forty paces between them. Rachel didn't know

if she could move that far while *focusing*. Any exertions she made now would leave her collapsed and vulnerable afterwards, at the mercy of every able-bodied fighter in the saloon.

The assassin had little choice.

She moved. Ten careful paces towards the first attacker. As Rachel walked, she kept her body as fluid as possible, considering every muscle, the position of her arms and shoulders relative to the stance she wanted to achieve. At this speed, abrupt motions might injure her, while halting was dangerous. Her target had not yet fully raised his club. He was powerful, heavy, burdened by layers of banded armour. She pressed her shin beside his leg and took hold of his club and turned, lifting the weapon gently while easing her body into his bulky shoulder.

He began to topple.

Rachel let go of the club. She could not hope to wield it at this speed. His fingers released their grip on the weapon. Now the heavy baton crept upwards through the air. Rachel nudged it twice with the back of her hand, altering its trajectory so that it would crush his skull when he finally hit the ground.

He continued to fall. The club was still rising, turning end over end. Its bulky iron tip swung through a layer of smoke and began to descend towards the warrior's head.

Rachel's heart gave a long slow beat. She had not stopped moving. Her body flowed on beyond her defeated foe and then past Hasp. The Lord of the First Citadel stood frozen in the center of the saloon, his black eyes fixed on Oran. Cracked lips framed his yellow teeth. Rachel noted the tiny glass veins within the breastplate of his hideous armour, the stubble on his naked jaw. She took another two steps and reached her second target.

This warrior was leaner and quicker than the first, and his eyes simmered with rage. He had already lifted his knife to the height of his shoulder, bunching his muscles to cut down diagonally. The steel shone white-yellow behind his fist. A thread of saliva extended from his jowls, and his lunge had already gathered significant momentum. Rachel could not steer his body from its course without considerable risk to herself.

She broke his arm instead.

A chop to his wrist shattered the carpal bones there. The assassin then gripped the man's knife between her thumb and forefinger, and pulled it back in the opposite direction of the intended swing. She sensed his tendons and muscles rip. The agony would not hit him for another few moments, not until after he realized that the blow had missed.

The assassin felt her heart beat again, and again, and then suddenly quicken to a crescendo.

Oran still posed a threat, but for Rachel time had run out. Her heightened perception returned to normality with a crash. She lost control of her limbs and collapsed. A barrage of sound assaulted her, disjointed cries and groans and the pounding of boots. Oran yelled for order. Somewhere a woman screamed.

Rachel lay on the floor, her nostrils full of the smell of wood and dirt. Saliva dribbled from her slack lips. From here she could see the woodsman whom she'd first disarmed. The heavy club had landed precisely where she'd intended, crushing his skull. Now he lay in a pool of expanding blood.

She felt hands upon her.

A woman's voice cried, "Leave her alone!"

Mina? I told you to stay outside.

Rachel felt herself being turned roughly onto her back. A savage visage loomed over her, its cheeks and neck clad in bloody glass, its eyes as black as the abyss. Hasp bared his teeth, and his whisky breath spilled over her. His expression was one of rage and desperation and misery. "I don't want your fucking help," he growled. And then he drove a fist hard into her stomach.

The assassin doubled up in pain, gasping as she felt the wind rammed out of her. Mina was yelling somewhere nearby; men were laughing and shouting. Hasp snarled. He punched her in the guts again, and again, then raised his glass fist above her face, piling all the strength of his upper body behind the coming blow.

Rachel closed her eyes.

"We are not killers for hire," Anchor said.

Mr. D's strange wheeled box rolled back a few inches along the aisle, and knocked against one of the cabinets packed with bottled souls. Glass clinked together. The box's occupant spoke through its dark mouth slit: "I think you should let your friend decide that. After all, she is the would-be purchaser."

Anchor could see Harper's mind working. Worry creased her brow; her eyes frantically searched the floor as if an answer to her dilemma might appear there. She was actually *considering* Mr. D's indecent offer: one of his bottled souls in exchange for the murder of two strangers.

"For my own security the contract must be signed in blood," said Mr. D. "I find that purchasers are much less likely to renege on the deal when such a document remains in the hands of a thaumaturge. The threat of vengeful blood magic tends to keep people focused on their side of the bargain."

Harper said, "Gods help me . . . I'll do it."

Anchor was shocked to see her fall apart so quickly. This woman was no murderer. She didn't even yet know whom Mr. D expected her to kill.

He recognized desperation when he saw it.

"Excellent!" said Mr. D.

"Hell, no," Anchor said. "I won't let you bully her."

"She has agreed, sir."

Anchor faced Harper. "Whose soul do you want to buy?" he asked. "Is it family? A lover?" He saw from her pained reaction that he had struck upon the truth. "A husband, eh?" He turned to the nearest cabinet, flung open the doors, and dragged out two fistfuls of soul bottles.

"That's robbery, sir." Mr. D's wooden enclosure rumbled forward in a threatening manner. A strange glutinous slopping sound came from within. "Do you know who I *am?*"

Anchor thrust the bottles towards Harper. "Use your mesmerist devices. Find him."

She sobbed and shook her head weakly. Her gaze moved back and forth between Anchor and the proprietor.

"Do it," Anchor said.

Harper fumbled in her tool belt. She took out one of those odd silver contraptions, a slender device packed with crystals and covered in etched glyphs. It made a sharp, tinny noise, and then started to whine. The engineer shook her head. "Not those," she said. "But he's here in this place somewhere."

"Your husband?"

"Tom. His name's Tom."

Anchor uncorked one of the bottles and brought it to his lips. A tiny amount of liquid dribbled down his throat...

...and then the memories of the soul contained in that liquid rushed into him.

A stage... Gaslights and applause... Sitting on the edge of a bed watching a dying woman... The smell of sweat, the weight of a man lying on her back... Wheeling downhill on a heavy wooden bicycle...

Mr. D laughed. "Now you've gone and done it. You've just consumed another person's soul." His box squeaked forward on its wheels. "Your own mind, such as it was, is about to disappear."

Anchor grunted, and then upended two more bottles. He felt strength pouring into him, even as fresh memories assailed him.

... Alone in a desert watching a campfire... A wailing woman, her face bleeding from his blows... Maggots squirming in the body of a dead dog...

The tethered man threw the empty bottles aside, and grabbed more from the shelves. "What about these?"

Harper scanned them, shook her head.

"He's not changing, Mr. D," Isla said.

. . . shooting gulls with arrows . . . a rowdy tavern . . . a brother's hug . . . watching a small boat set out across misty waters . . .

"I can see that, Isla. Please unlock the Icarate cages."

"But Mr. D . . ."

"Do it, child."

Empty bottles rolled across the floor. Anchor kicked them aside and wrenched open another cabinet. Mr. D's box retreated down the aisle, its little wheels squawking. Isla scampered ahead of it, disappearing through a curtained doorway at the rear of the emporium.

Harper was staring at her device. "He's here, John."

Anchor was drunk with power and memories that did not belong to him. His thoughts spun. . . . *a pier ablaze . . . an old man crying . . . gutting a rabbit . . .* He wheeled around, then staggered over to the cabinet beside Harper and ripped its door clean off its hinges. The *Rotsward's* rope followed after him, snagged on the doorjamb, and then wrenched it clear off the wall.

Harper withdrew one of the bottles from the cabinet.

Anchor blinked and shook his head. The emporium was spinning around him. . . . *kissing a girl dressed in a steel suit . . . sex in a moss-green gazebo . . . a knife clutched in bloody fingers . . .* He grabbed the bottle from Harper, uncorked it, and lifted it to his mouth.

"John!" she cried.

He stopped, with the bottle resting against his lower lip. He could almost taste the first drop of cool liquid.

"Sorry." He lowered the bottle, and handed it to her.

Harper replaced the cork.

Behind you! Cospinol had remained silent for so long that the god's sudden outburst in Anchor's head startled him. For an instant he thought that the warning had come from one of the souls he'd just consumed, before he recognized Cospinol's deep tone. *The madman's loosed his Icarates.*

Two of Menoa's hellish priests were shuffling through the curtained doorway at the rear of D's Emporium. They wore queer armour composed of bulbous ceramic plates like pale fungi spattered with darker rot. Green sparks dripped from these protrusions, bursting against the floor around their white boots. Uncertain buzzing sounds issued from their copper mouth grilles. Their black eye lenses were broken, but nevertheless fixed on Anchor.

"He can't be controlling them," Harper said. "Icarates answer to no one but Menoa." She backed away, sweeping her scanner across the approaching enemies, and then added, "John, their minds have been replaced. He's implanted new souls within them."

Anchor stepped in front of her and folded his arms. "Go back," he said to the Icarates. "I am in no mood to fight more cripples."

A maniacal laugh came from the other side of the curtain. "No mood to fight? Do you think these souls will *parley* with you? These creatures have the minds of murderers and rapists, you big dolt— the very worst I've found during all my time in Hell."

The tethered man grinned. "Now I am in the mood to fight." He strode forward and grabbed the first Icarate by its neck and groin, hoisted the bulky armoured figure over his head, then turned and threw it out of the emporium window. The glass panes exploded outwards, as did a substantial part of the surrounding brick wall. The Icarate flew far across the cul-de-sac, spraying sparks, and came to a rest in a crumpled heap two hundred yards away.

The second Icarate hesitated.

Anchor seized it by the neck and picked it up with one hand.

Its pale gauntlets crackled and fizzed and groped wildly at his arm, but he paid the thing no heed. Still hoisting the Icarate up before him, he ducked through the curtained doorway and stepped into the room beyond.

It was completely dark for a heartbeat, and then a flash of green light illuminated the room.

Mr. D's box stood before a semicircle of at least twenty cages stacked overlapping one another like two rows of bricks. Two of these enclosures had already been opened, and were now empty, but the remainder of them held hunched, bulky forms. Motes of green light burst from extrusions in their warped armour, intermittently dispelling the darkness within this windowless chamber. By this flickering light Anchor saw their copper mouth grilles, crusted with verdigris and red rust, and those dark circles of glass that served them as eyes.

Isla was wrestling with a key, trying to turn it to unlock one of the cage doors.

"Leave that be, lass," Anchor said.

She glanced uncertainly at the tall box in the center of the room.

"He won't hurt you."

Isla released the key. Mr. D's box remained completely motionless, its thin mouth slit facing Anchor.

Anchor realized he was still holding the struggling Icarate. He pitched it away, and heard it thump against the rear wall of the room. The priest's armour blossomed with a sudden cascade of green scintillations, before the whole suit dropped from sight behind the cages and went dark.

"What *are* you?" said Mr. D.

"John Anchor," the tethered man replied. "I will make you a deal, yes? You give us Miss Harper's husband, and the little girl." He paused for a moment and then nodded to himself. "So, do you agree?"

"*Agree?* Agree to *what?* What do I get out of the deal?"

Anchor frowned. He made a show of examining the room, and then the floorboards. "Ah," he said at last. He slammed his heel down into one of the boards, shattering it, then picked up a fragment of wood. "You get this piece of wood."

"Is that supposed to be funny?"

Anchor grinned. "It is my best offer."

Mr. D snorted. "I don't know what sort of demon you are, but you can't threaten me. The body within this box cannot be harmed. Nor can you make me suffer more than I already do. If you leave, I will pursue you. I will bring Menoa's Iolite spies down upon you. I will—"

Anchor took hold of the box, turned it upside down, and set it back on the floor so that its wheels pointed at the ceiling.

"What?" Mr. D cried. "Turn me the right way up or—"

"John." Harper was standing over the hole Anchor had just kicked in the floor, scanning it with her Mesmerist device. Her other hand still clutched the bottle to her chest. "I'm picking up the same signal we received in the portal, but it's much stronger here. We're right above the River of the Failed."

"The ants' nest?" He peered down through the gap in the floor, but couldn't see anything except darkness. A faint meaty odour filled his nostrils. "Good," he said. "We can smash our way down. Will you take the girl to her ship, Miss Harper?"

"Can't I come with you?" Isla said.

Harper crouched and hugged her. "It's too dangerous, sweetheart. Come on—" She stood up and took the girl's hand. "Why don't we speak to the other ships? I think there are better places in Hell for you all than this one."

Isla glanced back at Anchor, who beamed at her. Reluctantly, she stepped over the *Rotsward*'s rope and followed the woman out of the room.

As soon as they'd gone, Anchor said, "That little girl is powerful, eh?"

The great rope trembled at his back. *Powerful! Nine Hells, John, that girl had more collected matériel in her vessel than any human ought to. It actually resisted you. I suspect that even Hasp's castle pales in comparison.*

Mr. D snorted. "She's powerful because of her proximity to the River of the Failed. Why do you think we're down here? If you want to discuss this properly, please turn me the right way up."

It makes sense, Cospinol said. *Millions of lost souls, all heading for the sewers of Hell, converge here. That sort of power could be trapped and utilized by a strong will. Indeed, desperate souls might find such a will attractive, might latch on to it. That demonic little girl must act like a magnet for them.*

"Are you listening to me?" Mr. D sighed, and then made an attempt to sound reasonable. "Listen, I promise not to pursue you if you turn me the right way up."

What are you going to do about him?

"Nothing," Anchor replied. "He can rot here."

"Who are you talking to?" said Mr. D.

"My master," Anchor said.

"Your master? Where is he? I want to speak to him."

Anchor grunted. He crouched over the hole in the floor and began to widen it by ripping up more boards. After it was wide enough for him, he stopped and peered down into the darkness. A chill breeze blew up from below. He could not guess how deep the chasm went.

"Anchor?" Mr. D said. "I demand an audience with your master."

The tethered man sighed and lowered himself into the gaping hole. It was utterly dark down there. He felt a lattice of iron beams around him, jutting from brick facades, but there was enough space to climb down between it all. "An audience?" he called back, flexing his shoulders as he took up the strain of the *Rotsward's* rope. "It is no problem. Cospinol will be along in a moment." Then he gripped an iron strut and began to drag himself down into the abyss.

Eventually John Anchor ran out of Maze. The girders and facades he had been using to drag himself down terminated suddenly. He broke through a floor and found nothing below but air. So he pulled in a mile or so of slack rope, and then jumped.

He fell for a long moment and landed in at least four feet of thick, cloying liquid. His head went under and then he came up again, spitting and gagging. He wiped his eyes, but could see nothing but a red blur. The stink of fouled meat filled his mouth and nostrils, and he spat repeatedly to try to remove it. The floor underneath the waters felt as smooth as skin. He heard echoes of his own coughs and gasps, the slosh and gurgle of fluid.

When he stood up again, the liquid flowed sluggishly around his belly and seemed to tug him in several directions at once. He rubbed sticky fluid away from his eyes, and then blinked them open.

He was in a space without walls, an immense gap underneath the twisted iron and redbrick roots of Hell. The base of the Maze formed an impossible ceiling overhead. Without any obvious means of support, the leagues of cluttered stonework and metal filled the heavens like a massive bank of thunderclouds. Rays of light fell from countless windows in the dwellings overhead, dappling the surrounding landscape.

The ground beneath was uneven and treacherous. Narrow channels of crimson water looped and spiraled and twisted back on themselves in an endless scrawl. Ribs of raised fleshy material separated the waterways, and in the patchy gloom, the swamp seemed to stretch to eternity. From all around came the constant sound of dripping, as the blood trickling down through Hell reached this open space and fell like rain.

A beam of harsher light flashed across the waters just to the left, revealing their dark, bloody colour, before vanishing once more. An instant later the same light reappeared overhead as Harper climbed down the *Rotsward's* rope. She was lowering herself down through a rift in the ceiling, and a wandlike crystal device gripped between her teeth proved to be the source of illumination. She stopped, dangling a few feet below the ceiling, and then shone the wand around her.

The Icarate cages had fallen nearby, and most of the twenty enclosures had toppled over and now lay on their sides, partially submerged, while four still stood upright on the raised banks. Long shadows reached out from the bars as Harper swung the light across them.

Every one of the cages was empty.

Anchor looked around for Mr. D. The proprietor had probably fallen somewhere nearby. After all, most of his collapsed emporium lay scattered around here. Cabinets and bottles bobbed in the red waters. A moment later, a smile came to his lips as he spotted Mr. D's strange wheeled box rolling across one of the raised banks, heading away into the darkness.

The metaphysical engineer swept her beam beyond the cages. The circle of light caught flashes like sparkling rubies, illuminated pockets of rippling water, and veins throbbing within a low, muscular bank. Falling droplets flashed in the gloom. And then the beam settled somewhere behind Anchor.

Harper let out a startled gasp. "John," she said quietly, "we've found our ants' nest."

Anchor turned to look.

They were standing in the water. Wet red figures like rude sculptures of men had risen up from the shallow depths and now stood motionless and glistening under the glare of Harper's wand. Anchor estimated there to be a hundred or more of them. He couldn't detect any eyes in those faces, but he noticed mouths and teeth.

Harper called down, "The waters are sentient. These creatures are not individual souls. They're extensions of the river itself, parts of the god of the Failed."

Anchor faced the figures. "Hello."

The figures spoke together in one fluid whisper. "Are you an Icarate?" Echoes hissed through the conduit like a breeze, so that it seemed like the air itself had spoken.

"Do I look like one?" Anchor replied.

They hesitated. "What do you want here?"

The rope at Anchor's back thrummed, and his master's voice sounded in his head:

Don't mention Menoa, Cospinol warned. *This is treacherous ground. Ask it to grant us passage under Hell to the Ninth Citadel. We're seeking the source of the Icarate infestation.*

Anchor relayed his master's words.

The figures were silent for a while. Finally they said, "You bring me food."

Anchor frowned. He couldn't be sure if this was a question or a statement—or what it referred to.

"I think it means the gallowsmen," Harper said. "If it can sense all the souls aboard the *Rotsward,* it would certainly regard them as sustenance, a veritable feast." She untangled her legs from around the rope and slid further down. A foot from the surface of the water she hesitated and tightened her grip on the soul bottle clamped to her breast. Then she let go, plunging into the river up to her chest.

She faced the big man, her expression full of awe. "A river of disassociated dead," she muttered. "John, this is vaster than I ever imagined. It could become *anything.*"

She cupped a hand in the water, raised it to her lips, and took a sip.

Anchor grimaced at the sight.

Cospinol spoke through the rope: *It can have the damned gallowsmen if it lets us pass. Tell it we want an alliance. Tell it we're its friend. It ate those bloody Icarates we brought down with us, for god's sake. We need to spend time with it, and talk to it.*

Anchor relayed the message.

The figures waited for another long moment. Finally they said, all together, "Follow me."

The tethered man watched as, one by one, those glutinous figures slowly sank back into the River of the Failed. "Follow you where?" he inquired, but in that vast darkness only the echo of his own voice answered.

But then the currents eddying around him *shifted* and strengthened in one mighty surge. The channel in which he stood began to flow purposefully in the opposite direction.

Harper stumbled, but Anchor grabbed her and held her firm. She clutched the bottle and light wand to her chest as the crimson waters bubbled and frothed around her shoulders.

Carried by this new force, the empty Icarate cages slid away into darkness.

Anchor pulled the engineer close to him. "Don't lose your bottle," he said.

She laughed. "Was that supposed to be a joke?"

He frowned. "The water is very high. Your bottle might go whoosh"—he made a sweeping gesture with his hand—"and then you will lose your husband's soul."

"Never mind," she said.

Anchor began to heave the *Rotsward's* rope down towards the hungry river. "These gallowsmen aren't going to like this," he said. "Nobody likes to be eaten. I know this from experience."

But Harper wasn't listening to him. She was hugging her bottle and crying.

They waited in that same cramped crawl space above the boiling room for hours, until the slaves finally finished their shift at

Carnival's brazier, only to watch in frustration as four more slaves appeared to take their comrades' places.

Monk crawled away from the hole and then dragged the boy close to him so that he could whisper in his ear. "Gods damned waste of time," he said. "Why didn't you tell me they never leave her alone?"

"I did," muttered the boy. He thought it rather unfair that Monk was putting the blame on him. The whole thing was the old man's idea in the first place.

The astronomer stretched out his legs and winced. "You'd think they'd be too busy smashing up Hell to stay at their brazier." He drew a hand across his stubbled jaw. "What we need," he decided, "is some sort of diversion."

"Like what?"

"I don't know! Ship isn't moving, is it? Gives you the chance to slip outside and do something unexpected. Take an axe to the hull—that'll soon get the bastards running."

"You can't break the hull," the boy replied. "No matter how rotten it gets, you can't break it, not even with an axe. I know that much."

Monk frowned. He seemed ready to argue, but then the whole vessel gave a sudden lurch and began to creak and groan. "We're moving again," he said. "They've eased the pressure on the hull. We're going deeper into Hell."

In the chamber below them, Cospinol's slaves toiled at the brazier, shoveling coke and working the bellows and checking the contents of the condensing flask. Ghost lights whirled inside that glass tube and gave off a fierce illumination. Dull thuds continued to issue from the cooker as the scarred angel kicked at her tiny iron prison.

Hidden in the crawl space, the two conspirators waited.

After a while the hook-fingered boy heard the old man snoring. He had fallen asleep again. Lying there on his side in that confined wooden space, he looked like something that truly belonged in a coffin. His forehead was the colour of ancient bone, and tufts of wild hair sprouted from his cranium like scraps of dry moss. The boy thought about piling him down through the hole. It would be fun to see the slaves grab him and string him up again. Gallowsmen were supposed to stay outside the *Rotsward*.

But Monk was interesting in his odd way. The boy liked it when he talked about Pandemeria, the battles with the Mesmerists, and the first great automaton. And Monk knew how to get that pressure cooker open. The boy decided to wait until after he'd drunk some of the angel's essence.

He left the old man sleeping and crawled back through the skyship's maze of conduits. Once he reached the outer hull, he slipped out through one of the many gaps in it and onto the great scaffold that surrounded the vessel.

Now that the fog had gone, he could see the gallowsmen clearly. Most had moved to the outer reaches of the wooden matrix, ready to break down Hell's facades. The boy scuttled along one long spar and then leapt onto another one. He jumped again and his metal fingers gripped one of the empty nooses. He swung, let go, and landed next to a huge vertical timber that acted as a support column. Numerous ropes dangled around him, but these were for hoisting up debris and he couldn't risk using them, so he climbed down the timber itself. The *Rotsward*'s hull diminished above him.

He wanted to see exactly where the ship was going.

In no time at all he neared the lower edge of the skyship's scaffold. The whole vessel sat atop what looked like a huge crushed labyrinth. A vast network of rooms with torn-open ceilings stretched away into the gloom on all sides, the scene illuminated in places by gallowsmen with flaming brands. The *Rotsward*'s lowest spars had pierced the floors below, and many men were working down there, moving through the rooms or ripping up great chunks of stone, tiles, and wood, and loading it into baskets to be dragged up to the skyship's decks. They would squeeze the living energy from this detritus and manufacture soulpearls to feed the god of brine and fog.

Crunch.

The scaffold jerked and sank further into the maze. The boy heard men and women howling. He climbed down even closer and saw that most of the rooms were occupied, but the gallowsmen were not loading the people up. They were butchering them instead.

Crunch.

Another jolt, and the *Rotsward* descended again. Floorboards shattered. Walls toppled. Scores of dwellings crumbled down into the ones below. Cospinol's slaves were working flat out to save as much matter as possible, but they could only recover a fraction of it. The rest simply dropped away, falling upon the unwitting denizens below.

The armoured gallowsmen moved over this devastated landscape like a swarm of strange metal insects, entering houses through corridors wherever possible and climbing over debris where the damage was too great. They used their eclectic armaments against any souls they encountered. An old woman sitting at a loom turned when a metal-suited soldier leapt down beside her. She smiled and then died on his sword, before he put his boot to her chest and slid her corpse free.

Crunch.

Two warriors suddenly reacted to a new breach in the floor of a large stone dwelling. A young man in rich finery looked up in time to see their spears fall before his twitching body left red stains across his tiled floor. Four others were meanwhile dragging a screaming woman from her tiny brick cell.

These men were the dead from a thousand armies, the corpses of those warriors Anchor had slain since the day he first hitched the *Rotsward*'s rope to his harness. No two were alike. They wore battered mail, plain plate, or enameled armour in bright yellows, greens, and blues—mercenaries and woodsmen in banded leather; archers with bone or yew bows; knights in steel, wearing colourful plumes; thieves, hooded gangers, and way-trappers. Some fought like brawlers with iron fist spikes; others used skinny blades in exotic flowing styles that the boy did not recognize. Blue-skinned and distended from years in their gins, these butchers moved in force through the steadily crumbling labyrinth.

Crunch.

Why were they killing these people in the Maze? Could these souls not be better used by Cospinol? The blood of those slain was now being wasted. Their essence mingled with the blood from the walls and floors, and leaked down into the depths of the Maze.

To where?

The slaves harvested scraps of living stone and wood, but they would not touch the corpses. The whole bloody scene felt like a giant *sacrifice*.

Crunch.

The scaffold dropped again. But this time something unusual happened.

The ground gave a sudden rumble, and great sections of it simply fell away. Several gaping chasms appeared amongst the network of interconnected rooms, corridors, and rows of brick partitions. The *Rotsward* appeared to have broken through into a vast cavern. The boy could see nothing down there except impenetrable darkness, but he heard the unmistakable sound of rushing water.

There was a pause.

And then John Anchor heaved on the rope again.

The *Rotsward* broke her way through the base of Hell. The network of gallows shuddered and groaned, and then suddenly dropped twenty fathoms. The lowest spars struck something solid, and the whole skyship came to an abrupt halt.

At that point, had the boy not shaped his own fingers to grip his environment, he might have lost his hold on the wood and fallen. Cospinol's gallowsmen were not so lucky, however. Dozens slipped from the greasy timbers and plummeted. To the boy's surprise, most of them landed in water.

It was an entire maze of waterways separated by low, greasy banks. Its layout reminded him of the old spiral patterns that the ancients had painted on rocks back in Brownslough: a single line looping back on itself again and again, to form a labyrinth. Like the lines of a finger, the channels did not intersect each other. They were all part of the same river.

Debris rained down, sending up thick gouts of liquid. Islands of rubble formed quickly. The waterways were shallow, not even reaching as high as a man. Brands fell from the scaffold and hit water, fizzling out, or else landed on banks and islands and threw wildly flickering shadows across the landscape. By the light of these torches, the boy saw that the watercourses were as thick and red as blood.

A sacrifice?

A great cheer went up from the gallowsmen. Those still left on the scaffold were now climbing down towards these subterranean shallows. Even the slaves abandoned their baskets of debris to join them. Those warriors who had already fallen splashed around and roared and laughed and drank their fill of the waters. Some of them climbed upon the islands to reclaim brands, their armour darkly stained and dripping. They hollered and clashed blades against their own armour, and then knelt on the shore to sup. Evidently Cospinol had promised them a feast.

The boy glanced up.

In the torchlight, the base of Hell looked as gnarled as the thickest forest. Around the rift created by the skyship, twisted iron girders extended like black roots through the brickwork.

The *Rotsward*'s main hull sat lower than this ceiling, but her upper scaffold still remained lodged in the Maze above. There was not enough room here to fully contain her great size. Bloody streams still trickled down through her joists and spars, and also from the edges of the well John Anchor had made by dragging the skyship down here.

The boy returned his gaze to the shallows, hoping to spot the tethered man. Torches moved over the waters and over the islands between the skyship's masts, but the spaces between them remained dark. Anchor was nowhere to be seen, so the boy looked for the great rope instead.

It had curled around one of the scaffold's lower joists, a few hundred yards away, and was tightening, drawing in slack as Anchor pulled on it. The boy peered in the direction of the rope and spied a faint aura of white light receding in the distance. The *Rotsward* would soon be moving horizontally again.

He had to tell Monk. This celebration might be the distraction they needed. While Cospinol's gallowsmen and his slaves feasted, they could sneak into the boiling room.

But just as he was about to turn and climb back up the scaffold, he spotted the red figures rising from the water below.

She was drowning and had been drowning for months or years or perhaps even centuries. Carnival could not remember how long she'd been trapped in this hell. Scalding water filled her eyes, her mouth, and her lungs. It flayed her skin. Her wings and legs had been broken once, but now they had healed, though the bones had reset themselves in awkward positions. That made kicking at the inside of her prison difficult.

But she kicked again anyway, as there was nothing else for her to do. The pain gave her strength. She savoured it and used it, compressing the agony up inside herself and then releasing it with another vicious blow to the walls of her container.

She felt, however, that she was growing weaker by degrees. The scalding water seemed to sap the very life from her. She wondered if she would die. On one level the idea of an end to her suffering was appealing, as it offered her some consolation, a hope of peace. At the same time it enraged her. Someone had put her in here.

And so she lashed out again.

This time she felt the wall of the container give.

7

UNDER HELL

The River of the Failed was quick and cunning and carnivo-rous. In its many disparate parts it tore the fallen gallowsmen to pieces. Columns of lamplight dropped from windows in the base of Hell and lit up the scene. Red figures rose from the bubbling wa-ters and set upon their foes with no weapons except their newly forged hands and teeth. Their hardened liquid forms could be mu-tilated and scattered by blades and spears, yet the Failed them-selves remained immune to death, for the river was their common flesh.

Anchor turned his back on the slaughter as the screams of Cospinol's warriors filled that vast emptiness underlying Hell.

They fought with increased desperation but ultimately they fought in vain. The river learned from its mistakes, and it adopted new tactics to trick its foes. Giants rose in places where the smaller constructs were destroyed, great brutes with clubs for fists that ter-rified the gallowsmen and caused them to flee. Long muscular shapes with fins and jaws lashed through the water. Red threads reached up and wound themselves around the gallowsmen's weapons, entangling them. Vortexes chewed at their shins, forcing them to retreat to higher ground. But the red river swelled around them and hardened itself into walls that funneled its victims into pens where they could be murdered more efficiently.

For a brief time it rained upwards. The tiny droplets were as cunning as their source and trickled up across the warriors' skin and into their mouths and eyes. So afflicted, a knight in blasted-steel plate rushed blindly through a frothing channel and scratched at his eyes and cried, "Teeth, teeth!"

Downstream from him a short, wiry way-ganger clung to his useless bow as he struggled against the red threads that tried to pull him under.

Three warriors clad in coloured enameled armour stood back to back atop one of the larger islands, driving spears into the crimson shapes that crawled up the rubble towards them. Before long this trio became the only effective resistance that Anchor could see. The river seemed to have momentarily neglected them, but then the waters receded suddenly and surged back over the warriors' island, knocking them into the surrounding channel.

As Anchor walked away, he felt a chill in his heart. He dragged a hand through the fast-flowing waters around his midriff. Surely no army could defeat such an amorphous foe. Here was the antithesis of Iril—brute power without any structure that could be dominated by physical force. How could one fight absolute chaos?

Anchor carried Harper, his large hands grasping her waist. She had stopped supping the fluid. "The river would have taken the gallowsmen anyway," she declared. "Cospinol had no choice but to sacrifice them. By doing so, he has gained its favour."

"For now," Anchor said. "We are still at its mercy, I think. If it decides to eat us, I do not know how to stop it."

"Then let's try not to do anything to upset it."

"How do you upset a river?"

"The river is a god, and this god is a child. Anything might cause a tantrum."

After some distance the *Rotsward*'s rope tugged at Anchor's harness and he felt the familiar pull of the skyship against his back. He took a deep breath and bulled forward. The skyship felt so much lighter than before. He hardly noticed as, behind him, the great wooden vessel shifted and scraped across the drowned floor of this subterranean realm. The upper part of the scaffold remained buried in the base of the Maze, but its timbers would not be broken by mere bricks and iron.

"This is a very strange place," Anchor said.

"You get used to it," Harper replied. "Hell, I mean. I don't know if this place down here can still be called Hell. The Maze ends up there." She slipped the luminous wand behind her ear, and nodded at the ceiling. "That was my home for a very long time."

The big man grunted. "The way you speak . . . I think you miss it."

"I do. Your soul imposes its own order on its surroundings. You become a world amongst many others, but still joined. If it wasn't for overcrowding and the Mesmerist threat, it would be paradise. Imagine the sex."

He laughed.

"It's when others impose their will upon you that things become difficult." She looked at him meaningfully. "Wouldn't you agree?"

"I chose to become a slave."

"But you regret it now."

He chose not to answer. "Do you think Heaven is like the Maze?"

"Not while Ayen remains dominant. She expelled her own sons just to maintain order. *Her* version of order. If there are still any souls left in Heaven, I doubt they're at all free." She gazed up at the ceiling. "No, Heaven is for sheep, and Hell is for—"

"Goats?"

"Wolves, John," she said. "Wolves."

The fierce current made walking difficult, but Anchor held her firmly and caught her when she slipped. She kept Tom's soul close to her heart, and imagined she could feel the warmth of it through the glass. In this unnaturally engineered state, he would not be aware of anything around him. His spirit was trapped in a suspension of some esoteric fluid, an elixir like those rumoured to have been distilled in Pandemeria before the war. In such a form he would merely be dreaming.

Removing his soul from the liquid wouldn't be difficult. She could simply find a man—living or dead—to drink the elixir, and thereby become host to her husband's personality. Yet that person wouldn't *physically* be Tom, not as she remembered him.

Nevertheless, a return to any physical body was infinitely better than an eternity spent in a soulpearl. This way she wouldn't just *possess* her husband's soul. She would have Tom back.

If she could find a man to act as host for Tom's spirit, she and her husband could finally be together again. A couple, a home. In time they might even create a nice apartment in Hell, something far from the Ninth Citadel, something with a view.

But who would be the host?

The crimson river continued to rush past them, urging them on to their destination. Drips fell from above and bloodied their skin and clothes. They followed a path as twisted and tortuous as a deathbed scribble, but when they tried to leave the waters to cross one of the many adjoining banks, the currents sucked at them, urging them back into the center of the channel. Harper's light bobbed ahead, glistening on the waters, while in the darkness far behind, the grounded skyship scraped a terrible gouge through the ceiling of this thin realm.

Finding a hale physical form down here wasn't going to be easy, Harper realized. As far as she knew, in all of Hell there was only one such body available. And John Anchor wasn't about to give it up.

Before long the Failed reappeared again, rising from the waterway as though they had been submerged all this time. Thousands stood in the main channel and in all the surrounding ones. Harper shone her light around, revealing more of them everywhere. They had become more defined, Anchor noticed. He could now discern features in their faces—mouths and noses, yet none of them had yet developed eyes. Many now resembled the gallowsmen they had so recently butchered. Their wet red skins had the appearance of armour, and they carried blades, bows, and spears.

Anchor and Harper halted.

As the Failed spoke, a single voice issued from many mouths. "What is that object you drag?" they said. "There is food within."

"The *Rotsward* is my master's ship," Anchor replied. "There's no food aboard."

One figure stepped closer. It was larger than its neighbours and appeared to be wearing red plate armour, yet the steel panels of its suit did not move in the way layers of metal should. This armour was merely an affectation. "There are many souls inside the *Rotsward*," it said, and the group chorused its words. "Souls everywhere." It tilted its head and seemed to be studying the pouch of soulpearls tied to the tethered man's belt. Then it reached out towards them.

Anchor stepped back. He felt Harper's grip tighten on his arm. She hissed something urgent in his ear, but he couldn't make out what she had said.

The figure crouched there in the waterway, dripping and sniffing the air. Then an angry voice cried out from all directions at once. "You have food."

This time Anchor heard Harper whispering clearly. "Give it everything it asks for. You can't fight this thing."

Anchor hesitated. Without those soulpearls he would soon lose his strength.

"Do it," Harper urged.

An urgent shudder ran through the skyship rope. *She's right.* Cospinol sounded wary. *We need to build up trust. We can't anger it now. Give up the pearls, John. I have many more.*

Anchor snorted. "Then you should get used to walking, Cospinol. If it takes these, it will only want more. How much power are you prepared to give up?" The river heard him, but Anchor no longer gave a damn. "It's broken one deal already. There's no honour in it, just hunger."

Right now its hunger is the only part of it we can communicate with.

The figure tilted its head again. A thousand voices whispered, "Where is the person who speaks through the rope?"

"He's in the ship," Anchor retorted.

John! What's the matter with you? If I didn't know you better I'd say you were afraid of this thing.

The tethered man clenched his jaw. "Afraid?" he said. "The river should fear *me!*" He untied the leather pouch and emptied the glassy beads into his cupped palm. The soulpearls emitted their own weak light, the ghosts inside sparkling in the darkness. Anchor tipped the lot into his mouth and swallowed.

Then he grinned. "Now I've eaten them all," he said to the dripping figures. "No more souls. You've had enough today already."

The Failed threw back their heads and howled. The air filled with their furious cries. The waters rose and quickened to a torrent, buffeting against Anchor and Harper. Red foam rushed past. The current threatened to rip the engineer from the tethered man's side, but he held on grimly.

"Enough!" he shouted.

The voices dwindled to a chorus of wails.

"I said, *enough!*"

The Failed fell silent. The river torrent slowed to a more gentle flow. Every one of their heads was now turned towards Anchor. In the surrounding darkness they shifted uncomfortably.

Anchor rested his hands on his hips and studied them. "Now take us to the Ninth Citadel like you promised," he yelled. "You get nothing more from me until after we arrive. You understand?"

Abruptly, the figures dissolved back into the waters, disappearing as quickly as they had appeared. After a moment there was no trace of them, no sound but the incessant drip of blood from the Maze above.

Harper squeezed his arm. "John, that was..." She paused. "I don't know if that was stupid or brilliant. How did you know to do that?"

"Stupid, maybe," Anchor said. "You said this god was a child, and it behaved like a child. But I had children once; I know what they are like. It is bad to spoil them, yes?" He grunted. "Bad to give them all the things they want."

"*You* have children?"

He shook her off him. "Had," he said. "I do not want to talk about it." He rolled his shoulders, took up the strain of the rope, and then marched forward. From far behind came the rumble and crash of Hell being further destroyed in his wake.

How many times had Rachel woken in agony? For a Spine assassin, she thought, it had been once too many. She raised herself onto her elbows and groaned. Her muscles felt like beaten strips of leather. It was dark and foggy, and she didn't know where the hell she was. The whole room seemed to be swaying.

"Do you want the good news or the bad news?"

Rachel recognized Mina's voice, and then she recognized her surroundings. *Caskets of coins, an old table and chairs, a rug.* The room was indeed moving, after all. She was inside Dill's mouth again. A wall of teeth separated her from the grim daylight outside, and the crump of his great footsteps sounded far below. Mina sat with her back against the leftmost incisor, her glass-scaled face floating, hazy and red, above the shoulders of her robe. She was stroking her devil pup, Basilis.

Rachel winced. Her jaw felt bruised and tender. She lifted a hand and touched it gingerly and located some swelling. "The good news, please."

"You're alive."

"That's the best you could come up with?"

"Sorry," Mina said. "I tried to think of something better to off-set the bad news, but there really wasn't anything else."

"Don't tell me the bad news," Rachel said.

"Okay."

Rachel sighed. "What is it?"

"Hasp tried to beat you to death. Then when Oran's woodsmen realized what you'd done to their friends, they tried to kill you, too. And that just pissed off Hasp even more. We're only alive because I dragged you out while they were hurling abuse at each other. Now this miserable cave is the only safe place left. Oran is threatening to burn the inn if we don't come down to face their justice. He won't do it, though, because it's the only shelter they have. But he'll probably find some other leverage soon enough. The whole situation could get quite messy."

"How did I get up here?"

"I asked Dill to intervene. He lifted the building rather quickly, and we made our grand escape. Your head made really weird knocking sounds as I dragged you down the inn's front steps."

"Thanks."

Mina looked down at her hands. "I'm afraid I had to kill one of them . . . Well, Basilis . . ."

"*You?*" The assassin shook her head, and then regretted it immediately, as she groaned again. "I don't want to know. Needless to say, you're now an outlaw, too?"

"The bastards fired arrows at me."

Rachel got to her feet and moved over to peer through the arconite's teeth. Down below she glimpsed the tops of evergreen trees sliding past in the mist. The inn still rested on the cleaver Dill had taken from the fallen arconite, but its log walls looked even more lopsided and battered than before. Part of one eave had fallen away, and the timbers comprising it now rested on the automaton's huge bone wrist. The earthen island on which the building sat had all but disintegrated. A ribbon of smoke rose from a hole in its shingled roof. Nobody was outside.

She faced the thaumaturge. "You said Oran would probably find some new leverage soon? I assume that's why we haven't just told Dill to abandon those bastards in the forest. We don't *need* Abner's inn that much."

Mina nodded. "Hasp is still down there."

Now Rachel understood. The woodsmen might use the Lord of the First Citadel as a hostage, as soon as Oran figured out that Rachel didn't actually want Hasp dead.

Or did she? The bruise on her jaw throbbed evilly. "That glass bastard deserves to be used as a hostage. Why did he react like that? I was only trying to protect him."

"He's not himself." Mina let her dog jump down from her lap. "Hasp can't come to terms with what Menoa did to him. The parasite in his head will force him to betray his friends, and for an archon of the First Citadel there can be no greater crime. When the king's arconite attacked Dill, it became brutally evident to Hasp that he couldn't resist its influence. He thereby lost his honour, and turning on you was just a reaction to that loss. I think he deliberately angered Oran's men because he truly wanted to die. You denied him that escape by intervening. In his eyes, you diminished him."

Rachel sighed. "Spine have never been very good at reading people," she admitted. "I really should just stick to murdering people in dark alleys."

"There aren't any dark alleys here."

The assassin grunted. "I think I need to speak to Dill." She left the rest of her thoughts unvoiced. She needed to speak to someone human and, absurdly, Dill's voice was the most human one she knew.

A dark blue radiance filled the inside of the skull chamber. The tiny motes trapped within the crystals set into the ceiling appeared to be unusually active. Agitated, Rachel reckoned. She eased her body between the banks of shining machinery, leaning for support against a metal panel as the chamber lolled like a ship at sea.

Dill's ghost still shared the glass sphere in the center of the room with thirteen others. The phantasms floated through each other and shoved and brawled silently. White light pulsed faintly inside that huge bauble, occasionally erupting into glimmering fits that seemed to correspond to moments of conflict between its gauzy prisoners.

She laid her hand against the sphere.

. . . back . . . she's back . . . Murder on her . . . Don't let her see your thoughts . . . The agony . . . I was once within a room and then . . . Stop screaming! Who are you . . . ? . . . in that place . . . men in the river . . . Shush . . . Quiet, quiet, quiet . . . Who . . . ?

"Dill?"

The voices faded, then she heard her young friend. *Sorry, Rachel.*

"Sorry? For what?"

They almost killed you.

She pretended to laugh, but failed even to convince herself. She shook her head, thinking their situation was already dire enough without Dill's angst. "You got us out of there, Dill. Now Oran and his would-be avengers are in the palm of your hand. I'm actually pleased you've resisted the urge to crush them."

Not entirely. Mina yelled at me to stop once I started to squeeze. I think I cracked one of the walls. He paused. *They were so fragile. Everything seems so fragile now.*

"But you're not."

Tell that to the other eleven arconites. The big ones.

This time she gave a genuine laugh. "That's one fewer than there were two days ago. Who taught you how to fight like that?"

Hasp.

Hasp? Ayen's youngest son remained an enigma to Rachel. The goddess's other sons had adopted grandiose titles for themselves: the god of chains, the god of clocks... But not Hasp. They knew him only as the Lord of the First Citadel—ruler of a mere stronghold, a human position—and now he seemed to have wholly embraced this comparatively diminutive status. He was currently as drunk and suicidal as any mortal man.

That meant he'd given up.

Mina had once informed Rachel how Hasp had gone willingly to Hell. While his brothers raised armies and harvested power from the world of men, Hasp accepted the role of looking after the dead. The First Citadel belonged to mortal archons, the bastard descendants of gods and men.

Rachel. Dill's voice interrupted her thoughts. *I've been seeing more strange things . . . Visions, or waking dreams. I don't know exactly what they are, but they're becoming more frequent.*

She recalled his nightmare of the stone forest, soon after they'd left Coreollis. "What sort of things?" she asked.

A crack appeared in the world, stretching all the way from one horizon to the other. It was full of . . . emptiness. *Not darkness, but emptiness, as if something fundamental was missing from the world.*

Rachel frowned. Mina had experienced a similar vision, she recalled. And Rachel herself had witnessed a number of strange happenings since leaving Coreollis: those two identical versions of Rys inside his bastion, moments before it fell; the inexplicable change of the steam tractor's and Rosella's hair colour; Oran's strangely repetitive conversation. As isolated incidents, she had dismissed them as nerves, dizziness, or confusion. But now that she thought about it, couldn't these glitches, when put together, be the result of some greater force at work?

"Thaumaturgy?"

The whole chamber swung violently to the left, then to the right, and then left once again.

Rachel heard an abrupt yell of protest coming from the crawl space behind her. "Stop shaking your head, Dill," she said absently. "Mina's skin is made of glass."

I don't think this is thaumaturgy, Dill went on. *It feels . . . bigger than that. It's like we're walking through a ghost world, as if the whole of creation is somehow wrong. I can't explain it. The closer we get to Sabor's castle, the more powerful the feeling becomes.*

Could the god of clocks be responsible?

Mina cried out again, from somewhere nearby.

Rachel turned to find the thaumaturge poking her head into the room. The blood inside her glass-scaled cheeks looked hot and angry. "Dill," she yelled, "are you aware that you've just killed two men and sent another fleeing for his life?"

Abruptly the chamber stopped moving.

What men? Rachel heard the angel's reply through the glass, but Mina remained oblivious to it, because Dill had not spoken aloud. The assassin repeated her trapped friend's question for her.

Mina said, "He just trod on a watchtower."

"A manned watchtower? Where?"

The thaumaturge nodded. "An outpost belonging to the settlement I told you about, the town on the shore of the Flower Lakes. They didn't even have time to light their warning beacon. There are two really flat corpses lying back there, while the lone survivor is now riding for the main settlement."

Rachel let out a long breath. "How soon until he reaches their palisade?"

"His horse's legs aren't as long as Dill's," Mina replied. "If our giant friend just moved now, he could catch up and crush him."

The chamber lurched to one side again, quite suddenly. Mina grabbed the side of the passageway to stop herself from falling.

I see the horse, Dill said. *The rider . . . he's only a child.*

Rachel glared at Mina. "You didn't mention that."

The other woman shrugged. "You didn't ask. Does it make any difference? When that lad tells his people what bonehead has done, it might just cast a shadow over our attempts to parley with them."

Rachel raised her hand. "Dill is not killing anyone else today. And certainly not a child."

"I could—"

"No, Mina!" the assassin cut her off. "You're not going to do anything. Let the boy go. We'll face the consequences of this mishap if we have to." She hissed through her teeth. "Either we avoid the place entirely and leave its populace prey to Menoa's arconites, or we try to ally with these people. We've nothing to lose by speaking to them. They pose no threat to Dill."

The bloody scales on Mina's face transformed into a smile. "Fine," she said. "Then you can handle the negotiations. I'm sure the town militia will listen to you, since you're so good with people."

The hook-fingered boy scrambled back up the *Rotsward's* scaffold. The sudden emptiness of those timbers chilled him more than he had expected, for he'd never seen the skyship without her complement of gallowsmen. When he reached the hole in the hull he ducked inside, swinging Monk's sightglass on its tripod, and looked around. The old astronomer was probably still asleep above the boiling room. He'd obviously missed the whole battle.

The boy set off through the narrow skyship passageways, heading back towards the boiling room. All around him, the interior of the vessel shuddered, clicked, and groaned. These noises seemed much louder since Anchor had started dragging her sideways again, and he could feel the wooden boards bending under stress. The *Rotsward* sounded like she was falling apart.

But she wasn't. The old vessel was as indestructible as she'd ever been.

One more bend before he reached the crawl space above the boiling room, the boy suddenly became wary. Something was wrong. Something—he couldn't put his finger on it exactly—sounded *different*.

He stopped, lying on his belly in that dark and narrow conduit, and listened hard.

The bellows had stopped working.

He shuffled forward again, more quickly now, suddenly angry. What if Monk had decided not to wait for him? What if the old man had spotted an opportunity while the gallowsmen were being slaughtered? Where were Cospinol's slaves?

"You'd better not have taken a sip of her without me," he muttered. "Better not, better not." They were supposed to have *shared* the scarred angel's essence.

Dragging himself around that final bend in the passageway, his worst fears became realized. There ahead was the hole in the floor above the boiling room, the roof of the crawl space flickering overhead with the brazier light.

Monk was nowhere to be seen.

"Rotten, rotten..." The boy rattled his metal fingers against the wood and then clawed his way up the crawl space towards the hole.

And then he peered down, and stopped dead.

She crouched there, glaring up at him, her eyes as black as the scorched bulkhead behind her. The iron cooking pot had been wrenched from its vice above the brazier and now lay in one corner, heavily dented. The angel's body was misshapen, too, crooked as a scare-for-crows, her arms and legs and wings all bent at odd angles. The leathers she wore had rotted and burst open in places, revealing patches of scarred white flesh beneath. Blood covered her mouth, jaw and neck. Thin lines of red extended upwards from this gruesome stain and wrapped around her eyes and crosshatched forehead.

Scars.

Pieces of Monk's corpse lay scattered around her feet amidst shards of glass. She had broken the condenser flask. Carnival coughed, regurgitating water.

And then she threw her head back and screamed—a cry of such desperate fury that it froze the boy's wits. No creature should have been capable of uttering a sound like that. He tried to move, but his muscles would not respond. He simply stared down at her.

Her cry subsided. Her eyes met his again. She tried to step forward, but her leg buckled and twisted horribly underneath her. One tattered wing flapped. One arm hung limply at her side; the other remained at her chest, as gnarled as an old root. She moved again, dragging her body closer to the hole in an awkward shuffle. Then she gave a snarl that tapered into a wail of frustration.

"Break my bones," she said.

The boy continued to stare.

"Break my bones."

He said nothing.

Her chest rose and fell in rapid motions. "Get down here and help me or I will rip open your throat." Her white teeth flashed suddenly in the red mess of her face. "Help me!" she cried, the pitch of her voice seesawing. "Help me!"

Before he even knew what he was doing, the boy obeyed. He gripped the edge of the hole and then swung his body through it, heels over head. In one quick somersault he dropped to the floor in front of her. His left foot slid sideways an inch across the slick boards before he recovered his balance.

The room smelled of fire and meat. The brazier still burned

bright red in that confined wooden space, turning the scarred angel's body into a demonic silhouette. Her crippled wings shuddered.

"The hammer," she said.

He spotted the tool lying amongst pieces of offal. An old man's hand still clutched its handle. The boy stooped and picked it up. He peeled away Monk's hand and let it drop.

"My arms," she said.

The boy hesitated. "I don't—"

"My arms!" she screamed, dragging herself a step nearer. Her terrible shadow loomed over him. Scars slid under the scraps of leather that still clung to her. "Break them at the elbow and the wrist, the shoulders..."

The whole process happened in fits, so he could hardly recall it afterwards. He remembered the weight of the hammer, the momentum as he swung...Pauses between the sounds of snapping bones in which he wiped sweat from his brow...Carnival's voice, growing steadier as time passed. *The hands. The knees. This foot. My wings. My spine.* She did not scream again. She stumbled occasionally. Once she collapsed. Scars flared like lines of fire around her eyes. He remembered her eyes, at least.

The boy couldn't say how long they spent together in that room, but when it was finally over the scarred angel rested on the bloody floor, her back pressed against one of the bulkheads. Her leathers hung in tatters about her wiry body, her muscular thighs and small hard breasts. Carnival was barefoot, and for some reason, the boy thought that strange.

"Your name," she said. "What is it?"

He shrugged. "Don't know." Then he thought about it. "Maybe John. After my father."

"Okay then, Maybe John." Her voice was barely a whisper. "Leave here while you still can."

"I don't see Cospinol's slaves coming back anytime soon."

"Get out." She said this through her gritted teeth. The anger was building inside her again. "You stupid, ignorant...get the hell out of here!"

The boy fled. He rushed to the door and pulled it open and ran through, leaving it to slam against its frame. Now he was in one of the ship's main companionways, but he didn't recognize it. He was used to the *Rotsward's* darker spaces, the cramped tunnels behind the bulkheads and between the decks. But nobody was about to see him. Where were all the slaves?

He skidded around a corner and ran straight into Cospinol.

The god of brine and fog occupied the whole of the passage. His sagging grey wings stretched from wall to wall. His lank hair fell over the shoulders of his crab-shell armour, that cracked and useless suit that still stank of distant oceans. In one fist he held an axe.

"You!" the god said.

The boy turned to run away, but Cospinol grabbed him. Instinctively the boy's skin began to morph. It became pliant and slippery. He felt claws extend from his feet to give him greater purchase on the floorboards.

"Oh, no, you don't." Cospinol struck him across the back of the head. "You'll keep that mangy shape, you little demon." He wrenched the boy around to face him. "What have you done?"

The boy realized that Cospinol's hands were trembling.

"What have you done?" the god repeated. "Slippery little Mesmerist shit. I heard her *screaming.*"

"Nothing," the boy wailed. "I didn't do anything."

"Is she in there?"

"Let me go."

"Did you let her out?" Cospinol shook him roughly. "Where is she?"

A female voice answered, "Here."

Carnival hovered at the end of the companionway. Her wings were smaller than Cospinol's and very black. But she stood taller than before. Her limbs had reset and now looked almost normal.

Her attitude evinced litheness and power. Only her tattered armour and pallid flesh spoke of her months-long ordeal in the boiling room. Countless wounds burned fiercely red against her pale skin. The blood around her lips had darkened and dried, and now cracked when she spoke.

"Cospinol," she said in a low and even voice.

Cospinol released the boy. "I am Ayen's eldest son," he said in a tone that managed to sound both defensive and indignant. "Heaven's shipwright. I am the god of brine and fog . . ."

She walked towards him. Her eyes were dark and devoid of any recognizable emotion, as unknowable as those of a wild beast.

She stopped just beyond the reach of his axe, and stared mutely at him for a long moment.

And then she killed him.

The attack came so fast that the boy did not see it. Carnival's wings flickered like a passing shadow. Cospinol had no time to raise his weapon. By the time the god's instincts compelled him to flinch, the scarred angel had ripped off his jaw. He gaped at her incredulously as she dropped the bloody chunk of bone. Then she rushed forward again. It seemed to the boy that she embraced the god, held him close as a lover would. It took him a moment to register that the snap he heard was Cospinol's spine. Carnival buried her teeth in her victim's neck. He spasmed once, but the life had already left his eyes.

She was a long time drinking.

When she was done, she let the old god's body crumple to the floor. She then turned to face the boy, staring at him without recognition, her eyes seeming unfocused. Blood sluiced down her neck and arms. The clawed fingers twitched at her sides.

"You killed a god," he said.

"A long time ago."

"What? No, I mean Cospinol. Him! You killed him."

She glanced at the corpse, then back at him. Awareness tightened the corners of her eyes, and her expression became suddenly suspicious. "I know you?"

"Yes," he said. "Don't you recognize me?"

She continued to stare at him as her bloodied chest rose and fell rapidly, her breaths coming in quick rasps. For a moment she looked uncertain. Her hands twitched again. A drop of blood fell from her fingernail and hit the floor. Finally she said, "Maybe John."

"That's right."

"After your father."

"Please let me go."

The scarred angel lifted her eyes and gazed into the far distance. She licked the palm of her hand and then licked her knuckles. Then she turned around and walked away, leaving the boy alone with the corpse of the *Rotsward*'s master: the god whose will had bound the rotten skyship together . . .

"Oh, no," said Maybe John, suddenly realizing.

The first beam broke before he had even scrambled to his feet. A mighty crash sounded somewhere overhead, and the companionway ceiling collapsed as heavy timbers plunged through the thin wainscoting. Clouds of dust rolled into the narrow passage. Coughing, the boy shuffled away—on his knees and elbows—from this scene of collapse. A section of floor gave way behind him and he was pitched backwards down a steep wooden ramp.

He struck solid boards again inside one of the *Rotsward*'s many crawl spaces. Overhead, the ceiling joists snapped and a mass of rotten wood and dust crumpled into the companionway he'd just vacated, filling it entirely. Now trapped in the gloom of the narrow conduit below, Maybe John glanced around. Debris blocked both directions. There was no way out.

He changed his human form for another, more suitable, shape, though shape-shifting had never come naturally to Maybe John. He had resisted the Mesmerist implants all along, and the priests in turn had almost given up on him. They'd threatened to put him to work in the Ninth Citadel simply as a door, before he'd finally stopped fighting them. He hadn't liked the idea of people walking through him. He'd told himself that it would be better, after all, to become a shiftblade.

He clasped his hands and stretched out his arms, allowing his skin, muscles, and bones to flow together into a long ribbon. His metal fingers twisted around each other and became a slender cone. He forced the rest of his body to tighten and elongate behind that cone, becoming serpentlike. As an afterthought he grew metal scales along his back for protection.

Finally transformed, Maybe John slithered through gaps in the rubble and thus cleared the crawl space blockage. Around a bend he found another conduit, similarly congested, but this likewise proved to be no problem now. All the while, the skyship continued to break apart around him. Great booming noises issued from somewhere outside the hull. The *Rotsward*'s gallows? Insects scurried everywhere, shaken out of the rotten wood. The boy spotted a tiny hole that seemed to lead in the right direction, and squeezed himself through. He slipped down between decks and reached what was left of the outer hull. Here dozens of the heavy gallows crossbeams had punctured and crushed the skyship's skin as if it were paper.

The boy coiled around one such timber and slipped outside through the narrow gap surrounding it.

Nothing recognizable remained of the vessel he had known. The shafts of light that fell from the lowest windows of the Maze revealed dark tangles of broken wood and knotted rope scattered over the River of the Failed. Curious souls peered down through the squares of glass above, as though from portals of a far grander vessel than the *Rotsward* had been. Cospinol's ship had ceased to exist in any true sense. Stripped of his protection, she had simply disintegrated.

The boy resumed his human shape. A few yards to his left, a huge pile of debris shifted suddenly, and then collapsed. The great rope that had pulled the *Rotsward* slithered across one of the raised banks between waterways, and then it stopped.

Far across the flooded landscape John Anchor stood beside a woman with red hair. He still wore his harness, but now his rope connected him to nothing but debris. Then the boy saw movement close by. A small winged figure was pushing through the waters in the direction of the tethered man.

Anchor didn't notice the skyship's demise—probably because destruction had always followed in his wake. He had learned to tune out the sound of devastation. And he didn't immediately become aware of the slackening pressure against his harness because the weight of the *Rotsward* was not something he had ever paid much attention to.

It was Harper who noticed it first.

He was grimly trudging through a warm current when she suddenly grabbed his arm and whispered urgently, "John."

"What?" He turned, and then frowned. The rope lay slackly across the mire behind him. He stared at it for a long moment before lifting his gaze to the scene beyond.

The *Rotsward* was in pieces. Debris covered the flooded ground for half a league behind him. Wafers of hull sat half submerged in the red channels. Thin lines of rigging rope stretched from one patch of detritus to the next, linking odd arrays of items: clothing, furniture, window frames, painted crockery, a horsehair mattress, several unidentifiable iron drums, and a silver tea tray.

The air remained still and silent. Nothing moved out there.

"He's dead," Anchor said. "My master is dead." A surge of panic came over him, although he could not say why. He stared at the rope and then he looked at the wreckage again. Had anything survived? He scanned the horizon, searching for larger parts of the *Rotsward*'s hull. There was nothing to be seen but broken wood.

"Cospinol is dead," he said again. He felt numb from head to foot. For the first time in years he noticed the weight of the harness on his back. He also noticed that his mouth was dry. "I'm free," he said. But the words had a cold ring to them. They sounded odd to his ears.

Harper straightened up. She was gazing across the wreckage, as if looking for something. Her fingers tightened on his arm.

Anchor saw her, too. He wasn't surprised. From the moment he'd seen the broken skyship he'd known. She was now wading towards them through the bloody waters.

"She's an angel," Harper said.

"Her name is Carnival."

8

BURNTWATER

Rachel allowed the watchtower rider to escape—a decision that threatened their plans and placed them all in greater danger. From the airy heights of their vantage point behind Dill's teeth, she watched the horseman disappear into the fog-shrouded woods. The assassin, however, didn't get much chance to dwell on possible outcomes, for their immediate situation suddenly became a whole lot worse.

"Stop this march or we kill Hasp."

A small group of woodsmen waited on the stoop of the Rusty Saw tavern in Dill's hands, looking up at them. Oran himself had barked the demand. He'd finally realized the leverage he held over his exiled employers.

"Well, it was only a matter of time," Mina said. "I suppose we could tell Dill to rip the roof off that building."

Rachel shook her head. "It's too late now," she muttered. "I'd have risked it before, but we don't know what's going on in there right now. One blow could break Hasp's armour." Her jaw still ached from the punch Hasp had delivered, and the musket ball wound above her ear continued to gnaw at her. If she'd been think-ing clearly, she would have told Dill to free Hasp before the woods-men ever thought of using him as a hostage, but she had hoped that they weren't smart enough to consider such a plan. After all, Hasp had tried to kill Rachel and Mina, so he must have seemed as much of an enemy to the two women as a friend.

She shouted down to them, "Kill the bastard if you like. I'd do it myself if he wasn't Rys's brother."

Oran laughed at that. "I know my lord's will," he said. "In this case, I'd be doing him a favour."

"Nice try," Mina said, "but he has a point. Our glass friend is a liability to his living kin. If Rys survived Coreollis, he'll be more likely to reward the man who slays Hasp."

Rachel rubbed her head. This whole land was beginning to grate on her. It seemed backwards and hostile, and she hardly knew who to trust anymore. She had also sustained more injuries from her supposed allies than from her enemies.

She stepped back from the wall of teeth and considered their situation. Oran knew he could not attack the arconite himself, and his threats to burn down the Rusty Saw had been nothing but blus-ter. Rachel and Mina had the gold, and an ally powerful enough to crush the soldiers at any moment, should they choose to do so. And yet they were prisoners up here.

Oran had Hasp.

"I'm surprised at you, Mina," Rachel said. "You haven't ever suggested we let them kill Hasp."

Mina pouted and gave a look of indignation. "I *like* Hasp."

The assassin sighed. "The whole point of recruiting help was to prevent Menoa from using them against us. And now I've turned these bastards against us anyway. The Mesmerists couldn't have done a better job of it if they'd tried."

"Hasp put you in a difficult position."

"He put himself in a difficult position. And now I have these bruises to thank me for getting him out of it. How long until we reach this settlement on the lake?"

"We're moments away, although it would seem entirely sensible to avoid the place altogether. We're not likely to find any friends there now." She shrugged. "Should I also remind you that we now have eleven arconites in close pursuit of us? Or would that just be confusing the issue?"

Rachel leaned against the inside of Dill's incisor and peered out through one of the gaps. The air smelled fresh and cool. The sun had risen behind them in the southeast, and filtered through the white mists ahead, where branches laced the fog like gossamer. The forest was mostly deciduous here and had been thinned recently. There were still signs of recent logging: stacks of freshly cut logs and piles of smaller branches. Wide trails crisscrossed the grey-green earth underneath the cradled tavern. A reflection flashed across the steel blade of Dill's cleaver. Down below, one of the woodsmen on the stoop moved suddenly.

An arrow struck the edge of the incisor, glanced off, and hit the roof of Dill's mouth. It dropped, landing just inside the row of huge teeth.

Rachel flinched. She heard laughing from below, and then Oran yelled up: "You have until we finish this to come down." He held up a bottle of whisky. From up here Rachel was unable to tell how much drink was left in the bottle. "And then we're going to start peeling the glass armour from your drunken friend." They moved back inside the inn.

A second arrow struck the edge of the incisor and ricocheted off. But this time there were no archers around to fire it. All of Oran's men had gone back inside. The arrow bounced off the roof of Dill's mouth and fell in exactly the same place as the first one.

Rachel stared down at the thin wooden missile. There was only one arrow there. "Mina?" she said. "Did you see one or two arrows hit the roof?"

The thaumaturge was sitting further back, her head resting against the inside of Dill's jaw. She yawned and stretched out her arms. "Two, why?"

"Because there's only one here now."

"What do you mean?"

"I mean two arrows flew up through that gap, but there's only one here now. And it's not just that. I've been seeing strange things for days now...memories that don't match up with reality, moments in time that repeat themselves. They're like *defects*, as if reality...or even time itself has somehow become fractured." She watched the other woman frown. "Dill experienced the same vision you did—of the world cracked open."

"That was...odd," Mina admitted.

"Something strange is happening," Rachel said. "Thaumaturgy, or..." She waved her hands. "I don't know. Something to do with what happened to Rys's bastion in Coreollis...or else something involving the god of clocks. Doesn't Sabor study time?"

"He observes time," Mina said, "but what you're talking about sounds like the *manipulation* of time itself, and that's impossible."

"The same arrow came through that gap twice. The *same* arrow. And just before Rys's bastion fell I saw two versions of the god of flowers and knives. One Rys on the balcony and another Rys inside. I'm sure of it now."

Mina considered this for a long moment. Finally she said, "I experienced something odd, too. When Dill pinned down that arconite...for an instant it seemed to me that it was Dill lying on the forest floor, and Menoa's warrior holding him down."

"Why didn't you say anything?"

Mina came over to join Rachel. "Sometimes our minds play tricks on us. I didn't dwell on it at the time." She picked up the arrow and turned it over in her hands. Then she shrugged, and turned her attention to the view outside.

"What must we look like?" Rachel said. "The settlement militia is going to attack the very moment we heave into view."

Mina smiled. "Just look at us poor women," she said, "held hostage inside a demon's mouth, our hapless friend, Hasp, imprisoned and hideously tortured by a gang of ruthless mercenaries."

"Ruthless mercenaries?"

"They look like mercenaries to me," she said. "Don't you think? I mean, just look at all this gold. The Mesmerists must have paid them well."

Rachel turned slowly to face her. "Oh, Mina..."

"It explains why this ghastly automaton is cradling them so gently, and why it shows them so much respect. Clearly these woodsmen are leading Menoa's assault against this land." She gave an abrupt nod. "Local knowledge, you see—that's what conquerors pay for. You knock out the scouts and the watchtowers before you attack. I'll bet this arconite attempts to keep those traitorous dogs out of harm's way once the settlement defenders begin firing arrows."

"Firing arrows at *them*."

"Yellow Sea pirates used to do the same thing. They'd fly the flags of their enemies during attacks on merchant vessels. The merchants blamed the attacks on the pirates' enemies."

"That's terrorism."

She grunted. "We've little choice. Oran knows us too well. If he killed Hasp, would we crush his people in a bloody act of revenge? Murder all those women and children? He doesn't regard that as much of a gamble. But if he found himself caught amongst an angry mob, thousands of people who would readily kill him to protect their town... then the ensuing violence no longer becomes our responsibility. Our position changes from one of potential avenger to potential saviour. In such a situation, he might be more amenable to bargaining."

Rachel smiled. "You're really quite fiendish, Mina."

"You have to be," the thaumaturge replied, "when you have a devil for a master."

If this was Hell, as she suspected it might be, then she found it sat-isfying to think that the gods might well have created this realm with her in mind.

A *river of blood*.

Carnival waded onwards through the thick red waters. Her rage felt like a cold fist in her gut. It had reached an extreme where it could no longer remain in conflict with her soul. Hatred, pure and simple, controlled her every thought. She was going to kill a lot of people.

She thought she recognized the dark-skinned giant up ahead, but couldn't remember where she'd seen him before. He wore a cumbersome wooden harness attached to a heavy rope that floated limply in the river behind him. The line seemed to have been pre-viously connected to the vessel now scattered across this bloody landscape.

A pale, red-haired woman in a grey uniform was held in the big man's arms. Carnival studied her, but nothing stirred in her mem-ory. The woman had a small wand tucked behind her ear that emit-ted harsh white light, and she held a bottle in the crook of her arm while she manipulated a silvery device with both hands.

As Carnival walked towards the couple, she felt odd currents tugging at her legs. It was almost as if the river was *examining* her. She heard a splash, and turned sharply.

The boy from the airship was following a short distance be-hind. Realizing he had been noticed, he ducked behind a mass of broken timbers. Carnival ignored him. She strode up out of the water, across one of the low banks between channels, and then back down the other side. The river embraced her again her like a lover.

"I do not wish to fight you," the tethered man shouted. "Choose another path, angel."

Carnival continued straight for him.

"You are free of the *Rotsward*," the man said in a steady voice. "But you are not free of Hell, eh? We are here to fight the Lord of the Maze...to save our world...your world. Come with us. We'll leave this place together."

Carnival made no reply. She was within twenty paces of him now.

"I am not afraid of you," he said. "You hate me, yes? But I do not hate you. Violence between us makes no sense."

She heard the boy splashing through the river behind her, but she didn't turn around this time. Her full attention remained fixed on the huge warrior. He was now urging the red-haired woman away from him.

"I beat you once before, angel," he said. "And I can do so again—but you need not fight me. You wish an apology? Then I am sorry. My master sent me to fight you and I obeyed him."

Carnival stopped. A memory surfaced: a glade in a stone forest, a place where every branch and thorn had been coated with colourful poisons. She remembered fog, too. "You," she said.

He nodded grimly.

She felt the blood rush into her scars. Her muscles tightened, making her rotted leathers creak. Instinctively, her wings angled backwards as she prepared to pounce.

The giant reached around behind his back, where the end of the great rope had been split into strands and woven into the latticed harness. He grabbed a fistful of hemp and tore it free, then repeated the process. He was tearing the rope loose.

Carnival waited.

One strand at a time, the tethered man ripped the mighty rope from his back. When he was finished he rolled his shoulders and stepped forward. "I am ready now," he said.

She leapt at him.

He sidestepped with remarkable agility, bringing one huge fist round to bear on her like a mast hammer.

Carnival twisted and ducked under the blow. Putting her knee behind his own, she grabbed the rear of his harness to pull him downwards.

He remained standing.

She might as well have just tried to pull down a mountain.

His punch had swung wide, but now he tried to loop the crook of his other arm around her neck. Carnival bowed out of this attempted maneuver. They wrestled for a heartbeat, their shins splashing through the sucking water, until she found an opening and threw a vicious punch at his neck with enough force to kill any normal man.

He released her and backed away.

They faced each other again.

The warrior rubbed his neck, looking at her for a long moment. "You have improved," he said, nodding. "You are much quicker than before, eh? Much stronger now. That is good."

His red-haired companion was still studying the silver contraption in her hands. "She isn't an angel," she announced. "I don't know what she is. The locator won't probe her. It's *terrified* of her."

The big man laughed uproariously. "Impressive," he said. "If she can terrify Mesmerist silver, then she can terrify the walls of Hell itself." He cricked his neck and then crouched, holding out his arms as though he meant to catch her. "Now let me see that move again."

She flew straight at him.

His arms closed around her.

She made a savage downwards kick at his knee and vaulted up out of his embrace, lashing her wings to gain height.

He grunted in pain.

Carnival flew up, twisted in midair, and dived down on him.

He was ready. He swung at her.

Her wings snapped out, stopping her descent. She allowed his fist to pass an inch from her face and then wheeled and kicked him in the jaw with the back of her heel.

His head snapped round, but he turned his huge body in time to save his neck from breaking. He groaned and then jerked around again to look up at her. "You are stronger than—"

Thrashing her wings to keep airborne, the scarred angel spun again, aiming her foot at his neck.

The big man ducked, moving his body at incredible speed. It wasn't nearly fast enough. Her heel connected with the side of his mouth, knocking him sideways.

He gasped, his huge chest heaving within its wooden harness. Sweat sluiced down his dark cheeks and mingled with the blood now leaking from one corner of his mouth. He backed away from her, pressing two fingers against his swollen lip. Then he withdrew his hand and stared at the blood there.

He gave her a bloody grin. "You are the first one ever to make me bleed." He slammed his enormous hands together and growled. "Come on, then."

Carnival flew at him again.

As soon as she was within range, her opponent launched a ferocious flurry of blows at her, aiming at her face, her chest, her neck.

She blocked them all. She saw him reach over her shoulder, grasping for her wing, and punched upwards into the base of his jaw. The blow connected with a loud crack. He grunted, but didn't otherwise react. He had a grip of her wing. Muscles in his shoulders bunched as he pulled.

Carnival sank her teeth into his neck. She tasted blood.

"John!" the red-haired woman screamed.

They were locked together. He huffed and grunted, his huge greasy body engulfing her as he wrenched at her wing. She smelled his sweat, the spicy odour of his skin. His muscles slid across her own. Her shoulder gave a sudden crack, and she felt the bone jerk loose from its socket. A spike of pain. She ignored it, tearing at his flesh with her teeth. Hot blood flowed over her jaw.

"Leave him alone!"

This cry had come from somewhere else. Carnival recognized the voice of the boy. For a heartbeat she hesitated, relaxing her grip on the giant.

With a roar, the huge warrior pushed her off.

Carnival splashed backwards through the shallow red waters, but remained standing. A dull throb had taken root in her broken shoulder.

Her opponent looked in bad shape, too. He took an awkward step backwards, sucking in great breaths of air through his nose. He had one hand clamped against his bleeding neck.

The boy was standing in the river, ten paces to one side of the giant. Red water coursed around his thin chest. He held his hands clasped together under his chin as if in prayer, the metal hooks splayed outwards like fans. "Please don't kill him," he said.

Carnival returned her attention to the giant warrior. Her dislocated wing hung slackly against her back, the feathers trailing in the river. She clenched her teeth, reached behind her back, and pushed the bone back into its socket. She barely noticed the pain. Flexing her rapidly healing wing, she strode forward to finish off her enemy.

"No!" The boy rushed over and put himself between Carnival and her opponent.

"Get away from me, lad." The giant grabbed the boy's upper arm and started to shove him to one side.

The boy *changed*.

Carnival halted as the child's skin began to flow like tallow from his bones. He closed his eyes and his head seemed to melt down into his shoulders. His flesh was re-forming around the thin muscle of his upper arm where the giant held him, shrinking and changing colour. His bones clicked and cracked. In two heartbeats the whole of the boy's body had altered shape, hardened, and taken on a metallic lustre. He had ceased to exist in his previous form.

Instead of a boy, the warrior now clutched a sword.

A humming noise came from the device in the red-haired woman's hands. She glanced down at it. "It's a shiftblade, John," she explained. "That child is a Mesmerist demon."

John? Carnival looked at her opponent. They had given him another name in the poison forest, she now recalled. *Anchor.*

John Anchor frowned at the weapon in his fist. He swung his arm to cast the blade away, but threads of metal spun out from the grip and wrapped themselves around his wrist.

Anchor growled and tried to shake the sword loose. The metal threads tightened. It would not leave his hand.

"For the gods' sake, John," the woman cried. "Sod your ridiculous principles and just use the damn thing!"

The big man ignored her. He seized the weapon's hilt with his free hand and tried to prise it loose. "Let go of me," he growled. "This is not the way I fight."

The shiftblade turned into a spear.

Anchor shook the long weapon furiously. He slammed it down against the water and put his sandaled foot halfway along the shaft and tried to snap it.

The demonic weapon let out a shrill cry. It changed from the spear to a short, fluted mace with elaborate silvered flanges and a grip cord of woven gold that coiled around the warrior's wrist like a serpent.

Anchor roared. "No swords, no spears, no bludgeons! I will not carry you."

Carnival watched him struggle with the weapon. No matter how hard he thrashed his arm around, it would not release him. It changed shape again and again: to bows and clubs and punching shields. Each new weapon was more elaborate, more beautiful than the last, but Anchor would accept none of them.

He yelled at the red-haired woman, "Why is it doing this? Shiftblades feel pain. Since when do they choose to fight? Since when do they *force* themselves upon others?"

"Maybe it likes you, John."

Carnival thought she understood. She recalled the boy's words in the skyship. *Maybe John, after my father.* The child did not look like the man, but then that child was a shape-shifter.

The shiftblade had stretched itself and become a broad steel shield with a sumptuous floral design in green and blue enamel that seemed to shine in the crimson gloom. In the world of men, such armour would have cost a presbyter's ransom, but Anchor simply beat at it with his fist, denting the brightly coloured metal until the shiftblade finally gave up. It released its hold on him.

The giant let out an angry roar. He wrenched the offending shield from his hand and threw it far across the River of the Failed. It spun away, flashing through the shafts of light descending from above, before disappearing into the distance.

The scarred angel looked at Anchor, and then she turned and gazed out in the direction where the shield had vanished. She tested her wounded wing, thumping it slowly, before she took to the air. And then she left the warrior and his red-haired companion and set out across the red river.

Ahead of her lay all of Hell.

Evidently the escaped rider had been quick to raise the alarm, for the entire local army awaited them when they finally reached the settlement.

From Dill's mouth Rachel watched as they reached the northern fringe of the great forest. The lakeside town appeared out of the fog; a brown ribbon of timber buildings ranged along the shore and was hemmed within banked palisade walls on its three landward sides. Mists hung over the waters like puffs of cotton. A hundred yards out from the harbour, Rachel could see manned barges loaded with mounds of coke and logs. Yet more sailors were steering empty vessels out from their jetties to join them, leaving only a cluster of smaller fishing skiffs at the quayside. It seemed that the merchants had received enough notice to try first to protect their fleet.

Long lines of soldiers stood atop the battlements, while others peered out from watchtowers set at regular intervals around the perimeter. Most of these men were bowmen; it seemed the settlement lacked any of the heavy ordnance—the catapults and scorpions—Rys had employed at Coreollis.

Dill paused, turning his jaw slowly from side to side as he helped them survey the scene before them.

"They don't seem *very* keen to listen," Mina observed. "But it's hard to tell with these provincial types. Does Dill know what he has to do?"

"Yes."

"It has to be convincing."

"He understands!"

Mina shrugged. "Then let's hope our friend Oran hasn't already killed Hasp."

"With all that free-flowing drink, they're not exactly on top of things. They haven't even noticed the town yet."

Mina inclined her head. "That's about to change."

Dill was moving again, now coming within range of the bowmen. A shower of arrows flew up from the battlements, closely followed by a second, smaller barrage from the streets immediately behind the wall. They whined through the misty air. Most of the missiles clattered harmlessly against Dill's armoured shins, but a score or more thunked into the log walls of the Rusty Saw tavern.

There was a pause.

One of Oran's men appeared at the entrance of the inn. He clung to the edge of the doorway, swung woozily for a moment, and then stared across at the town with its defenders massed upon the walls. He shook his head, and looked again. Then he bolted back inside.

Mina smiled. "Here we go," she said.

A second volley of arrows lanced up at the arconite. Gripping the cleaver in both hands, Dill raised it—and the entire tavern that rested upon it—high above his head, as if to protect the building. He roared.

"Nice touch," Mina said to Rachel. "I can imagine how someone would find that menacing."

Rachel yelled, "Don't overdo it, Dill."

The huge automaton had reached the palisade. Rachel heard cries from below and yells from Oran's men overhead. She caught glimpses of the woodsmen peering down through Dill's fingers. In the settlement below, defenders scattered in both directions along the spiked embankment. Groups of men began assembling in the adjacent streets.

Dill lifted his foot and brought it crashing down upon the timber defenses. The wooden spikes and part of the embankment collapsed. Arrows pinged off his armour as bowmen attacked from both flanks. He raised his foot again, leaving a deep trench full of crushed wood, and stepped inside the town.

He was standing at the top of a long mud track that continued all the way down to the lakeside wharfs. The air was crisp, and thin lines of smoke rose directly from chimneys above the shingled rooftops. Pale faces gazed up from windows on either side of the street. Had the townsfolk not been given enough opportunity to flee? Didn't they fear for their lives?

Angry voices came from below. Two groups of town soldiers converged on the arconite and attacked his ironclad ankles with long poles.

Dill swung around and inclined his head to look down, causing Rachel to topple against the inside rim of his teeth. She held on to the upper edge of a huge smooth incisor as the automaton lowered the tavern again and now clutched it against his breastplate like a baby. One gable cracked, and two of the Rusty Saw's windows shattered. Dill lifted his foot as if to crush the attackers.

Those men immediately under the shadow of his heel broke and fled, before Dill slammed his foot into the ground with hideous force. Even up here, Rachel felt the jarring blow in her bones. Her head throbbed. She watched as Dill raised his foot again, revealing nothing but a muddy crater below. No one had been injured.

"Good," she shouted. "Now on to the lake."

Cradling the tavern and the enormous stolen blade against his chest, he set off down the slope towards the lakeshore. Scores of Oran's woodsmen had appeared at the Rusty Saw's windows to watch these unexpected events unfold. The tavern's back door burst open and their leader himself emerged. With three of his men he ventured out to the very edge of the building's foundations and from there gazed down into the streets. Oran was far too absorbed by the scene below to look up.

Rachel could still hear the defenders yelling orders and curses behind them, but the streets below were now deserted. All around clustered two- and three-tiered timber houses with diamond-paned windows under the canopied eaves of their bark-shingle roofs. In a dozen steps Dill reached the lake, where low wharfs crowded the shoreline amongst timber warehouses and boatsheds. Huge, three-beamed stanchions overhung the water, supporting ropes, chains, and pulleys for hoisting cargo.

All of the larger vessels had been maneuvered out into deeper waters, but a number of smaller craft still occupied the shallow moorings. Dill crouched by the waterside, leaning closer to examine one.

Rachel experienced a sudden rush of vertigo as the arconite stooped and the whole of his skull tilted forward. She pressed her hands against the cold enamel of his teeth as the wooden skiffs rushed closer. But then the alarming motion stopped. She heard a creaking sound.

Dill picked up a boat with his free hand, then swung round to face the streets again.

Some two thousand men of the town militia were marching down the main thoroughfare towards them. They were armed with poles, bows, or spears, but now many also carried flaming brands. Wisps of orange tar fire jigged between the leaning buildings on either side, while a pall of grey smoke followed the vanguard, trailing over the helmets of those behind.

A horn sounded.

Rachel shot a glance at Mina. "Arconites?"

"No, that's local," the thaumaturge replied. "A rallying call. We still have time."

Dill threw the boat at the advancing forces.

The vessel was barely twenty feet long, so he could have thrown it right into the midst of the defenders—or half a league beyond the settlement—if he had chosen to. It spun mast over hull and hit the main street well short of the town militia, bursting into planks. The soldiers cheered and quickened their pace towards the arconite.

Dill roared again. The engines inside his breastplate thundered and blew gouts of hot black fumes out through the joints in his armour. He backed into the lake, smashing one jetty and three more boats to driftwood. In another three steps he had retreated up to his shins in the water. He reached down to pick up another vessel . . . and froze.

For a long moment he remained quite motionless, crouched over the harbour as though his joints had seized. He then shuddered and let out a mighty groan.

Slowly, he sank to his knees in the harbour so that a great wave surged right across the docks, lifting boats and depositing them on the ground beyond. Water burst against the shorefront warehouses, washing barrels and bales of goods aside, before slowly draining back into the lake. With agonizing slowness the huge automaton slumped forward onto his elbows, holding the tavern balanced on its huge blade out before him like a wounded man trying to save a child—or like an offering of penance to the advancing horde. He bowed his neck, lowering his head until his jaw settled in the mud of the shorefront street.

"Now that," Mina said, "was bad acting."

"Give it a chance," Rachel muttered.

Many of the town defenders hesitated, apparently suspecting a trap. Their giant enemy had shut itself down for no apparent reason. But others cheered and rushed towards the fallen arconite. Oran's woodsmen remained trapped in the upheld building, still

fifty feet above the ground. She hoped they would have the sense
to stay there.

"You do it," Rachel said to Mina.

She snorted. "No way. It was my idea. You do it."

"I'm not going to scream."

"Well, neither am I."

The assassin looked at her. "Mina, I don't want to argue with
you. It'll sound more convincing coming from you. I'm not used
to—"

The thaumaturge raised her hands and walked back towards
the crawl space in the rear of the jaw. She stooped to pick up
Rachel's sword from the rug. "I'll be in his skull," she said, "doing
murderous things with an assassin's blade. I'll see you in a moment." Basilis barked and ran after her.

Rachel peered out between the gaps in Dill's teeth. She could
see the town defenders gathering on the opposite side of the
flooded street, edging forward with their weapons ready. "Gods
damn you, Mina," she muttered.

She swallowed, and then cried out for help.

It wasn't the dramatic scream Mina had insisted on. Rachel
couldn't even be sure that she sounded like someone in distress.
But it was enough to give the town defenders pause.

Lying prostrate on the shore of the lake with the inn still raised
before him and his chin resting upon the muddy ground, Dill must
have looked defeated. Or so Rachel hoped. The defenders were
bound to be suspicious. All Rachel had to do now was allay their
doubts.

"In here," she called.

She saw boots and mud-spattered breeches moving about outside the jaw, the flashing steel of spear tips and blades. She heard
hoarse cries and barked orders coming from amongst the men. A
face appeared between two of the arconite's teeth—a young man
looking in at her along the blade of a short knife.

"Help me out," she said. "Please."

"Who are you?" the young soldier asked.

"A prisoner," Rachel replied. "Please get us out before Menoa's men regain control of this monster. We can't keep the arconite disabled for long."

He frowned at her. "How many of you are in there?"

"Two of us. Mina is in the back." She tried to sound pathetic. It helped that she felt pathetic. "The men in that tavern forced us in here. They've been guiding Menoa's arconites since the battle at Coreollis. They even have Rys's brother hostage."

"Did you say Rys?"

A deep voice behind the soldier intervened. "Who is it?"

"A woman," he replied. "She's trapped in there."

The young man moved to one side, and an older soldier peered through in his place. This man wore a beard and a metal skullcap over braided hair. "How the hell did you get in there?" he said. "What's happened to this golem?"

Rachel took a deep breath and repeated her story. The old warrior listened, but continued to eye her with obvious suspicion.

He waited until she had finished before asking, "Mercenaries? You mean the woodsmen trapped up there inside that building?"

"King Menoa paid them in gold." She picked up a handful of the coins strewn everywhere and shoveled them through the gap. "There are whole caskets of it in here."

The man glanced at the coins but left them where they had fallen. "He paid them to lead this brute here?"

"Eleven more are on the way," she said. "But we know how to stop them. Please get us out; we don't have much time."

He moved away. A third face peered in, a man of age with the first soldier. His eyes opened in surprise, and then he, too, withdrew. Rachel spied movement outside, torches flickering. She heard the first two men conversing in hushed tones. Finally the old soldier returned to the gap. He was holding a long pole. "Get back," he said. "We're going to have to force it apart."

She watched as the man inserted the pole between Dill's teeth and pushed down at one end. On cue, Dill opened his jaw.

"Thank you." Rachel started to climb out.

"Hold it there," the old soldier said. "There's not one thing about you I trust yet. Get back from its mouth." He waited until she had retreated, and then he climbed into the jaw beside her.

He was a short, stout man with powerful shoulders and arms, and eyes as brown as his bulky leather armour. His nose had been broken at some point in the past and reset crookedly. Framed by his steel cap, it looked unnaturally large and ugly. In the scabbard at his belt he carried a short sword, and on a loop around his shoulders hung an enormous hammer. He peered around the gloomy bone chamber for a long moment before returning his attention to her. "More of these are coming, you say?"

She nodded.

"We spotted two of them near Harwood a short while ago." His gaze traveled the length of the dim chamber, pausing on the piles of caskets and the scattered coins. "And we've heard no word today from the watchtowers on Wycke Road and Boulder. No birds sent, nothing. Now you'd better explain to me why Menoa's giants are heading this way. Those woodsmen and their women in the tavern are crying out for assistance, too. They claim *they're* the prisoners."

"Lies," Rachel said. "The arconite has been protecting them all the way from Coreollis."

"So you say," he muttered with a complete lack of conviction. His brown eyes stared at her intently. "Some of those woodsmen are familiar to us. Oran Garstone is well known to me. You're still alive only because I know exactly what sort of a man he is." He paused. "But don't think that makes us friends. *You* aren't yet known to me at all, and I'm too good at smelling a lie to believe much of what you've already told me."

"We're from Deepgate," she said. "Ulcis's city. Cospinol brought us here to fight with Rys at Coreollis. We slaughtered the Mesmerists, but then Menoa released his arconites. Rys ordered us—"

"Your friend is inside now?"

"She's back through there." Rachel pointed to the crawl space at the rear of the jaw. "We found a way to disable the arconite. Let me show you." She beckoned him towards the crawl space.

The soldier grunted. "If I climb through there, am I going to find her with a blade poised at this giant's brain?"

Rachel said nothing. That was eerily close to what he would find. Mina would be standing over some critical link in the machinery, apparently ready to strike down the evil arconite if it failed to obey her commands. "What's your name?" Rachel asked.

"The men call me Iron Head."

"You run this town?"

"Burntwater, it's called. I captain the town militia here."

"Rachel," she offered. "The woman in the back with the knife is Mina."

A sudden verbal row broke out between the Burntwater militia and two of Oran's men trapped in the uplifted tavern. Insults flew both ways. Oran's men kicked clods of soil down upon the soldiers below. One of Iron Head's men laughed derisively.

The captain yelled for order and then turned back. "So what's the truth, Miss Hael? Why did you kill two of my lookouts and yet allow the third lad to escape? Why come to Burntwater at all? What was the reason for that ridiculous boat-throwing charade? And how did you come to be traveling with my brother in the first place?"

"Your *brother?*"

"Oran is my brother."

Rachel sighed. If Iron Head was willing to listen, she saw no reason now to continue the charade. "Can I get out of here now?"

He offered her his hand, and helped her out.

She told him everything: their plan to reach Sabor's castle; the decision to recruit an army of men along the way; Dill's fight with the arconite in the forest, and its subsequent effect on Hasp. She admitted that she had killed two of Oran's men in the Rusty Saw's saloon in order to protect the glass-skinned god. And, after a moment's hesitation, she even told the truth about the watchtower Dill had destroyed.

"You have made a lot of mistakes," Iron Head said.

"This is only my second war. I'm learning."

The old soldier scratched his beard. "I have good reason to believe that Sabor escaped Coreollis unharmed," he said. "We'll take you to his castle at once."

"How far is it?"

"The Obscura? No more than an hour by boat and another two hours' march," he told her. "The realm of Herica lies directly across this lake. My family came from there originally." He nodded privately to himself as though deciding upon the elements of a plan forming in his mind. "The vast majority of them still work for Sabor—and have for decades now."

"Sounds like a large family."

"You could say that." He gave her an enigmatic smile. "Thanks to Sabor, I'm fortunate enough to have the largest family in the history of the world." He grunted. "Of all my brothers it's a shame you met Oran first."

He peered into the back of Dill's massive jaw. "Might I see the giant's workings for myself?"

"You'd better let me warn Mina."

But the thaumaturge yelled from within: "I heard it all, Rachel. My ears might be covered in glass, but I'm not deaf. Hold on, I'm coming out."

She crawled out of the low passageway, holding, as always, her demonic dog. Iron Head's brows rose when he saw her, but he made no comment. He stepped on past the thaumaturge, and peered into the crawl space. "Please wait here," he said. And then he got on his hands and knees and shuffled into the narrow passage, the shaft of his hammer knocking against the roof.

Mina watched him disappear. "I'm going to charge him a copper double when he comes back out," she said. "This is too creepy. It reminds me so much of my freak show days."

"You will *not* charge him."

"I ought to," Mina replied. "Why on earth would he want to look inside *there*? That's provincial types for you, Rachel." She walked over to Dill's open jaw and peered out at the Burntwater militia. "What's the matter with you lot?" she yelled. "Haven't you seen a skinless Mesmerist witch before?"

They looked like they were about to flee, but then the young man whom Rachel had first seen broke through their ranks. "Where's the captain?"

She jabbed her thumb behind her.

The soldier ducked his head between the giant teeth. "Trouble, Captain," he shouted. "The rest of these big bastards have just arrived."

Carnival did not know why she flew after the shape-shifting boy. She felt nothing for him, and nothing for the boy's father. No hunger troubled her here in Hell. Neither did she dwell on John Anchor's reasons for casting the strangely persistent weapon far across the subterranean river. She just didn't care.

Nevertheless, of all the paths she could have taken, her instincts drove her to follow one that would bring her to the boy.

The boy who called himself Maybe John was guised in human form again, sitting alone on one of the fleshy banks separating the waterways, his elbows supported on his knees. The shins of his breeches were drenched in blood. He looked up as Carnival drew near.

She landed ten yards away in ankle-deep shallows, still uncomfortable to be in his presence and altogether unsure of her reasons for seeking him out. For a long moment she just stared at him. Perhaps she had come here out of simple curiosity? After all, she had never seen anything like him. Or perhaps the darker part of her heart had an altogether different motive?

"I can't remember what I used to look like," he said suddenly. "That's maybe why he didn't recognize me." He held up one finger before his face and watched as the flesh turned into a thin metal spike. The spike then curled around itself like a child's doodle. "And don't say I should just have told him. No point in doing that until I know for sure he's my old man."

Carnival said nothing.

"I can't remember much before the Icarates got me," he went on. "The Mesmerists work like that. They persuade you that you're something else, and you believe them." He lowered his hand and stared into the waters. "I'm not really a shiftblade. They just convinced me I was." He paused. "Did you have to kill Monk?"

The scarred angel made no reply.

"He only tried to loosen the bolts," the shape-shifter continued. "We was all hungry on that ship, but you didn't have to kill him." He looked up at her. "Are you going to kill me, too, now?"

Still she said nothing.

"Or did you want a sword? Most people want a sword. You learn that pretty quick. The Mesmerists gave me to a nobleman on Cog, but his wife died of Early Cough and he killed himself on the edge of my blade. I made myself really sharp for him, like he asked me to."

All of the boy's fingers suddenly became knives. They glittered in the uncertain light. "Good swords are difficult," he said. "Hammers are easier, but it hurts more when they use you. If you need a weapon down here, you need me."

"No," she said at last. It was the truth. Down here the dark moon didn't pluck at her nerves. Whatever vengeance her heart had demanded had been satisfied. She felt no further desire to kill. She gazed up across the vast reaches of the Maze, at the millions of souls trapped together, and she felt suddenly cold. The red river seemed to tug insistently at her ankles. She bent down and scooped some up in her hand, lifting it to her lips.

It tasted dead.

The boy watched grimly as she emptied her hand. "I don't think that was a good idea," he said. "It won't like that at all."

The river?

She felt it suddenly in her throat, a strange sensation of pressure as the liquid she'd sipped crawled back up towards the back of her mouth. She coughed and tried to spit, but the fluid seemed to have a mind of its own. It flooded the passages behind her nose and then burst out of her nostrils in guttering spasms.

Carnival gasped.

The boy stood up. "They're coming now," he said quickly. "Take me away from here. I can be useful to you."

The angel drew in a breath. She spied movement at the edge of her vision, and turned.

Something strange was happening. The waters bubbled and frothed.

"Please carry me out of here," the shape-shifter pleaded. "You have to leave now, before it's too late. Take me with you."

From the myriad waterways all around rose an army of red warriors, hundreds of them, all clad in glutinous armour and clutching dripping weapons. Carnival wheeled, watching as more and more of them emerged above the surface of the river. Their faces looked roughly human, but like rude sculptures, without detail. Yet their weapons looked sharp enough.

The boy grabbed her hand, having elongated his arm to reach across the ten paces between them. "They're dangerous!" he cried. "Fly!"

She snatched her hand away from his, aware of the tricks he had used to attach himself to the tethered man. She lashed her wings and took to the air.

The boy yelled at her, but his words were drowned out by a much deeper voice that seemed to emanate from everywhere at once. "Come back!"

The men in the river had spoken as one.

Carnival's instincts drove her to fly higher. Her heart thundered in her chest. Her skin crawled with sensations emanating from countless old wounds, filling her with a sudden rush of hatred and anger. Twenty yards above the river, she paused and looked down.

Something massive was forming in the seething waters. It looked like a huge bubble, but as the angel watched, it swelled and took on a new shape. Shoulders appeared on either side of the initial protrusion, then arms and eventually hands. Even as Carnival thrashed her wings to lift herself even higher, the crimson thing burst upwards like a geyser.

For a heartbeat the giant, incomplete figure lolled drunkenly in the gloom before her, a thing of bone and sinew and layers of sluicing liquid. It seemed to Carnival that it might collapse, but then its hands reached out for her.

She thumped her wings, but not quickly enough. Red fingers closed around her leg and pulled her sharply down. In the instant before she hit the water, she caught a glimpse of the creature looming down on her. Wings had sprouted from its back, while its eyeless face was now etched with scars.

She closed her eyes and mouth as the waters slammed over her. The river was shallow; her back struck something soft and pliant. She struggled, tried to rise, but remained trapped in the grip of the giant.

Drowning . . .

Carnival thrashed violently, using her nails to tear at the hand holding her down. She felt its skin shred, the hard knuckles underneath, so much harder than the surrounding waters. Her fingers closed around something round and solid. She wrenched it sideways.

The giant eased its grip.

Carnival broke the surface of the river. She sucked in a breath of air and staggered to her feet.

The creature had roughly assumed the shape of an angel. It towered over the river, clutching the back of its hand as if in pain. Dark crimson wounds crisscrossed its bright red arms. It swayed on its long legs, as though it had not fully learned how to use them.

The warriors in the river had no such infirmity, however. They were fast closing on Carnival, their liquid-forged weapons ready. The nearest of them drew back his spear...

Carnival felt a small hand grab her own. The shape-shifter boy was by her side, though only his head remained above the frothing water.

"Let go," she cried, turning fiercely away. A spear lanced past her shoulder. She glanced over to see another spear growing in the hand of the river man who'd thrown it. The replacement weapon flowed from the warrior's own fist. Cold fury bucked inside her. Her gaze snapped to his wet red throat and she crouched to pounce.

"You need a weapon!" The shape-shifting child was still clutching her hand. And as she looked he began to change. His body diminished, twisted itself into a new form. She saw the glint of steel.

The river spoke to her again, its voice as soft as rain. "Join me." Overhead, the unsteady giant leaned over her, its hands grasping for her neck.

Carnival swung the blade.

The sharp edge met with little resistance. She severed the tips of two of the giant's fingers, and brought the weapon back for another strike before they had yet fallen to the water. Her second blow split the thing's palm along the middle. Red droplets spattered her face. She felt them tighten on her skin... and *move*.

Complete rage overcame her.

She unleashed a furious attack, hacking at the giant's arms and at the hands of river men who groped for her. She split open a dripping skull and, striding forward, reached the giant's knees and plunged the blade in deep.

The thing collapsed.

The river howled.

But the lesser warriors continued to advance. And Carnival threw herself amongst them, hacking and thrusting, her demon blade a whir of steel. There were many of them, and wherever they fell others rose to take their place. Carnival could not kill them all, but neither could she stop her slaughter. The sword danced to her fury.

The waters tried to suck her down, but she would not be dragged under again. It formed walls before her and she cut through them. Red weapons lunged for her on all sides and she chopped them down and returned the men who wielded them to the waters that had birthed them.

In relentless waves they came. With her dark eyes shining murderously under the lamplights of Hell, Carnival waded onwards through the bloody river to meet them. She had given up any thought of escape. Rage filled her soul entirely. If this endless river had limits, then they would be tested here.

John Anchor watched the disturbance in the distant gloom. It looked like a red storm front moving across the surface of the waters. "That looks about where I threw that shiftblade," he commented.

Harper glanced down at her locator and then back at the horizon. "It's Carnival," she said. "My locator is too afraid to search for soul traffic in that direction. It coped with the river, before, but not with her. I don't even know what she is, John."

The big man beamed. "You need to discipline Mesmerist tools, eh? Or do you just give them a hug now and then?"

"Cuddles only embarrass it."

He laughed, then rested his fists on his hips and let out a long sigh. "We are in a pickle, yes? The river has turned its attention to the angel now." He moved one foot through its limp waters. The currents that had been pushing them towards the Ninth Citadel had stopped. "And we do not know which way to go. The god of the Failed has become distracted."

"By the look of that cloud," Harper said, "that's a good thing."

Anchor turned away and gazed back over the wreckage of the *Rotsward*. Little of the skyship or its contents remained identifiable—no large pieces of its superstructure, no bodies.

No soulpearls.

He had eaten them all, and without more, his strength would soon fade.

"A very big pickle," he repeated under his breath. And then he smiled again and turned back to the engineer. Unconsciously he glanced at the bottle she held cradled against her heart, the container that held her husband's soul.

The waterlogged street had become chaotic. On Iron Head's orders, Rachel instructed Dill to drop his pretence of submission and deposit the Rusty Saw tavern by the wharf side. She called to Mina, who met her outside just as the town defenders were hurriedly regrouping. Glances flicked the thaumaturge's way but didn't linger, as the Burntwater militia was given orders by its captain.

"This is an evacuation," Iron Head yelled. "Women and children to the barges and skiffs. Holden, signal the pilots. Spindle, take your men—you already know what to do. I want twelve units, four to the east and four west of Hoggary Row. The third group, take up position at the junction of Ashblack and Green Darrow, or as close as you can get. Bernlow, Malk, Cooper, Geary, Wigg, someone else—you, Thatcher—keep the attackers divided, and away from the wharfs. Harry them and then retreat, but don't let those bastards step on you."

Basilis began to bark. Mina tried to shush him, but he wouldn't be silenced. The ragged little dog struggled against her grip, his eyes fixed somewhere to the rear of the crowd.

"What's wrong with him?" Rachel asked.

Mina peered into the crowd. "Nothing's wrong with him. He's just barking at you."

"Me?"

The thaumaturge seemed distracted, and it took her a moment to respond. "What? No." She turned back to Rachel, shaking her head. "I don't know... I suppose one of the militia must have startled him."

They were interrupted by a door banging.

Oran came barging out of the tavern, red-faced and full of raging accusations, but stopped short when he saw Iron Head. "You're not actually *parleying* with these bitches?" he said with a contemptuous jerk of his scarred head towards Rachel and Mina. "We've been—"

"Shut up, Oran," the captain said. "Look there." He gestured with his pole towards the southern perimeter of the settlement, then turned away as a group of his soldiers came running up. "Fire the bales and coke in the warehouses," he instructed the men. "Tar them first if there's time. Another two units... Weatherman and Block, go find them and spread the word. I want the whole dockside burning right *now*."

"Captain?" The young lieutenant frowned.

"Smoke, man, smoke. They're too big to take down, so we need cover and confusion. This mist's too thin to hide us."

"Aye, sir."

Oran had finally spotted the enemy beyond the palisade wall and now stood there with his mouth open.

Six arconites loomed over the town, their armour pulsing faintly in the fog, their great skulls turning slowly as they peered down at the streets underneath their ironclad boots. Behind them, great translucent wings shimmered in the gauzy light like pale auroras.

Iron Head seized his brother's arm. "Your women are going on the barges. Your men are going to fight with us. Give Hasp over to these two, but keep him covered up. I don't want the arconites to spot him."

"You don't have the right—"

"Do it or I'll have you killed." The captain beckoned another of his lieutenants over, and ordered this man to ensure that Oran obeyed. The woodsman snarled and stormed off back to the Rusty Saw with Iron Head's lieutenant close at his elbow.

"What can we do to help?" Rachel asked.

"Trust breeds trust," Captain Iron Head said. "Or at least I hope it does. Can your arconite defeat any of these others?"

"They can't be wounded or destroyed," she replied, "but if Dill brings one down, we can get inside its head and disable it with fire. Against any one of them he has a chance, but he can't fight all six at once."

"Then tell him to remain here and help with the evacuation. He can ferry people and goods over to the barges, and defend them if he has to. That'll earn us some time to get our families out onto the lake." He turned back to his troops, but Rachel halted him.

"Captain, we have another problem."

"Yes?"

"Hasp is compelled to obey any Mesmerist orders. They'll order him to kill as many of us as possible."

"Then confine him in your arconite's jaw." The captain turned away abruptly and strode over to where three units of his men were waiting for further orders. In moments he had dispatched them all and turned his attention to an approaching commander of yet another unit.

Rachel stood beside Mina, the pair of them watching as men rushed to and fro. Three short blasts of a horn sounded over the town of Burntwater, followed by another long single note: the evacuation signal, Rachel assumed. Some units were already marching back up into the main thoroughfares, while others ran into side streets, yelling and knocking on doors. Old men, women, and children were already making their way towards the lakeshore, carrying bundles of clothing, water, and food. Oran's people, too, poured out of the Rusty Saw. Meanwhile a blaze erupted with a roar against the wall of a warehouse over to the east. Other soldiers were busy rolling barrels along the jetties or dashing between the warehouses with flaming brands held aloft.

"Those civilians look like they were all actually *ready* to be evacuated," Mina pointed out. "Either that or they packed remarkably quickly. A careful observer might think that's odd."

"It never occurred to me," Rachel said.

"What?"

"To confine Hasp in Dill's jaw."

"Let's only hope Hasp agrees to it." Mina indicated the Rusty Saw tavern, where eight of Oran's men were carrying the glass-armoured god down the sloping earth of the building's ruined foundations.

At first Rachel thought the god was unconscious or dead, but then she saw that he was still gripping an empty bottle. His arms moved as he tried feebly to resist his bearers.

Rachel winced as the woodsmen deposited their burden roughly on the muddy ground in front of the two women. They all glared at the assassin with murder in their eyes, but then left without as much as a word. They had, after all, witnessed her fight.

A quick check revealed that Hasp's glass armour remained intact. Rachel could smell the harsh spirit on his breath. He had drunk enough to kill a normal man, and his red eyes rolled wildly, as if staring into a fever dream. He tried to stand, but slipped and fell back in the mud.

The assassin and the thaumaturge hoisted him up between them and helped him over the uneven ground towards Dill. Rachel called up to her giant friend, who, with a hiss of pistons and creak of metal, lowered one of his dead hands and allowed them to climb aboard.

Maneuvering the drunken god into Dill's jaw needed the combined efforts of both women. Though Hasp seemed unaware of his surroundings, he retched and spat and cursed them under his breath. After they had finally bundled him inside, he lay down upon a rug amidst scattered coins, turned over, and threw up.

"To think people used to worship him," Mina remarked.

"What people?"

"I don't know," she replied. "He's a god, so somebody, somewhere, must have worshipped him. Otherwise what use would he be?"

"Look after him, Dill," Rachel said.

They left Hasp lying there and climbed back outside. From this height, Rachel could see Menoa's arconites clearly. Six great simulacrums of angels towered over the palisade walls, their armour still scorched black and bloodied from the battle at Coreollis, smoke pouring from their Maze-forged joints. Thin wings disturbed the fog, their white bones shifting constantly through the veiled atmosphere. Slowly and steadily they were surrounding Burntwater on its three landlocked sides. And then, with a sound of crashing metal and shattered timbers, they broke through the town's useless defenses.

By now the streets below were crowded with people fleeing towards the wharfs. Units of Iron Head's men hurried in the opposite direction, heading towards the approaching enemy. Many of the town's defenders had already taken up positions at key intersections, but for all their bravado it seemed to Rachel that they would accomplish nothing.

"The fog is getting thinner," she said, as they began to descend.

Mina had her arms tightly wrapped around Dill's thumb. "It isn't easy to maintain," she protested. And then she fell silent, and did not speak again until they had stepped safely back onto solid ground.

"I'm doing my best, Rachel."

"I didn't mean to suggest you weren't." Rachel now realized

how the other woman's glass-scaled face disguised her exhaustion. The thaumaturge had been conjuring this fog ever since the battle at Coreollis. She could not keep it up for much longer.

Shouts came from the nearest wharf, where a throng of soldiers and civilians stood waiting for an approaching barge. The vessel bumped against the dockside, whereupon scores of men and women began clambering aboard its long low hull. Burntwater militiamen yelled orders to the pilot, and gestured to the captains of two more vessels further out.

By now, fires had taken firm hold of the nearby warehouses, and dense black smoke churned overhead. Frightened children howled and clung to their mothers, as militia pushed their way through the jostling crowds. Four armed men hurried along a lengthy wharf, rolling a huge barrel before them, while nearby an old man leaned against a mooring post and smoked his pipe and casually watched it all. Others raced back towards the town, clutching flaming torches, long poles, bows, and swords.

Rachel looked for Iron Head, but couldn't see him anywhere. She heard a distant scream and then a series of dull concussions originating from somewhere to the south. That meant Menoa's arconites were destroying buildings inside the walls.

"There's not enough time." Rachel looked up and yelled above the surrounding clamour, "Dill, help these people get onto the boats!"

His great skull swung down to face the lake, the ground shaking under him as he moved forward. Another step took him into the churning waters, till the metal columns of his legs straddled the shoreline. Engines drumming, he stooped and picked up a barge in each hand and lifted them, dripping, out of the lake. As he moved, his wings swung across the heavens like some vast carousel. The refugees screamed and broke away all around him.

Dill set both vessels down on the promenade. Their hulls landed with heavy thuds and then tilted to one side. He turned back to look for more.

In the confusion, the town's refugees didn't know what to do. Many ran to the shore and tried to board the vessel now moored there, but it was already overloaded. The surging crowd pushed many unfortunates into the lake. Others clung to the sides of the moored barge and were dragged aboard by its passengers. Desperate cries filled the air, only to be drowned out by the sound of destruction increasing from the streets behind.

Rachel tried in vain to shout instructions, but the panicking masses ignored her. She spotted three of Oran's men shoving two whores towards the western docks, before a unit of town militia ran in between and blocked her view.

She grabbed a passing soldier. "Get your people onto *those* barges." She jabbed a finger at the recently grounded vessels. "They're going back into the water as soon as they're loaded."

The young man gaped at her and then at the grounded barges. And then he shouted over to his colleagues. Moments later they set to work herding the civilians up onto the sloping decks. Once the vessels were filled, Dill lifted them back into the water.

The warehouses were blazing furiously by now, smoke and embers billowing right above Rachel's head. She dragged Mina into the lee of a loading stanchion, and they crouched as low as possible to breathe some cleaner air. Booming sounds continued to resonate across the streets behind the dockside, where secondary fires had by now taken hold. Torrents of ash spiraled above the stricken settlement, and in that turmoil Rachel saw vast shapes moving, bones and metal limned in tremulous green auras. Most of the soldiers here had already boarded the town barges, and Dill was nudging those vessels out into deeper water. But she saw no sign of the men who had gone to confront Menoa's angels.

Even from here, Rachel could see that Iron Head's diversionary tactics had failed. The six giants had not deviated far from their initial paths through the settlement. They now stood still, in a half-circle around Dill, no more than two hundred yards from the water's edge.

One of them spoke. "King Menoa wishes to negotiate a truce, Dill. His conditions are generous, and you need not join our cause. The Lord of the Maze simply wishes to avoid more bloodshed, and to prevent you from coming to harm. Your own free will makes you vulnerable to our attack. King Menoa would speak with you, if you will listen."

Rachel tried to shout a warning to her friend, but her voice got lost in the chaos. In the same way that the *Rotsward* drew its strength from linked will of Cospinol and Anchor, so Dill drew his from his own convictions. Doubting his abilities would begin to corrupt those abilities.

Dill took a step backwards into the lake. He crouched and gently nudged one of the barges closest to him. A score of vessels now floated in the lake behind his knees.

"These people will not be harmed," Menoa's angel went on. "Look around you. Have the king's warriors harmed any who tried to flee? Have they hindered this evacuation? Have we used our influence over Hasp? The king desires peace, Dill. He asks only that you listen." The automaton's gaze moved over the shoreline, and then it lifted its head again. "All will be pardoned, Dill. All differences can be resolved. We will even repair the weakness in your construction, allowing you to function without the fear of breaking limbs and corrosion. We have no desire to cause further harm or distress to anyone."

Dill dragged his cleaver out from underneath the Rusty Saw. The hammered metal blade was twice the size of any of the barges. Reflections of flames flashed across its scoured metal surface. He flipped it menacingly from one hand to the next.

"Observe the scratches on that blade," Menoa's angel said. "The weapon lacks the will to maintain its own purity of form, a flaw that is also evident within you, Dill. If you fight us you will be destroyed."

Rachel yelled up at him, "Don't listen to it! It's trying to plant doubt in your mind. You've already beaten one of these bastards."

From the corner of her eye she glimpsed movement, as six of Iron Head's men came running around the corner of the Rusty Saw tavern, closely followed by the captain himself. They looked bloody, beaten, and exhausted, but they ran like men with witches at their heels. As they neared the wharf, the captain spotted Rachel and Mina, and signaled wildly to them.

She stood and spread her arms. "What is it?"

". . . back," he cried. "Going to blow!"

"What's going—?"

There was a loud crackling sound, and then a series of tremendous booms. A chain of orange flashes erupted in the streets behind Menoa's giants. Tons of debris burst skywards, pounding against the armoured figures. For a heartbeat they were entirely enveloped in thick grey smoke and grit. And then a second barrage of explosions shook the air. Enormous pillars of dust spiraled over Burntwater.

The concussion hit Rachel like a physical punch. Her ears rang. She stared in disbelief as two of the six arconites toppled backwards, arms flailing, into the mass of houses. A third giant lurched sideways and crashed into another, and both fell towards the earth. The ground shuddered under Rachel's feet.

Iron Head skidded to a halt beside her, and adjusted the position of the hammer on his back. "Coke and saltpeter," he explained. "Sadly not enough sulphur, but we used whatever we had."

A hail of grit peppered Rachel's hair, as she gazed up at the rising funnels of ash and smoke. "When did you prepare *that?*" she said. "That must have taken—"

"After we heard about Coreollis, we installed the powder kegs as a precaution. Didn't particularly want to use them, mind you, but they were there if we ever had to flee . . . Our sappers nearly set one off under your friend Dill, and I'd have let them if he hadn't behaved so strangely." He frowned grimly at the devastation and shook his head. "Not nearly powerful enough to do them much harm, though. These bastards are tough."

He was right. Despite the blasts, two of Menoa's arconites remained standing, and the four who had fallen were already rising to their feet. Soot caked their armour and their massive blades, but they otherwise seemed entirely unharmed.

Iron Head suddenly waved his arm and shouted, "Here! Spindle!"

Soldiers appeared all along the promenade as scores of Iron Head's men left the smoke-filled streets and retreated towards the wharfs. Grey dust now covered their faces, boots, and armour. Barely half of the men who had gone off to fight the arconites now returned.

Spindle stood a foot shorter than his captain, and dust and soot caked every inch of him, so much so that he carried a thin grey aura of the stuff around him. He hurried over to Iron Head, smacked powder from his gloves, and sneezed. "Not enough sulphur, Captain," he confirmed.

"We're pulling out, fast as you can. You know what to do."

"Aye, sir." Spindle turned away and began bawling orders at his men. Soldiers from other units were still moving towards the wharfs, helping wounded comrades along, then unlashing the mooring ropes of the smaller skiffs and climbing aboard. Others had converged on a pyramid of barrels stacked under a loading stanchion. They were lifting them down and rolling them across the wooden decking, spreading them out.

Iron Head turned back to Rachel and Mina. "Can we rely on your big friend to cover our retreat?" He raised his chin towards the towering figure of Dill, still standing in the shallows. "That blade of his looks like it could do some damage."

"I don't think you need ask."

Evidently Dill had witnessed the soldier's efforts on the water's edge, for he now strode forward to meet the enemy. He stepped carefully over men and boats, and up onto the promenade, landing with a massive metallic clunk. Torrents of water sluiced from his armour and rushed across the boardwalk. His head turned slowly as he studied his six opponents.

"Good man," Iron Head muttered, then led Rachel and Mina towards a smaller vessel moored to the dockside. Many of the other skiffs were already moving out onto the lake. The three now crossed a gangplank onto the tiny pitching boat. The thaumaturge's little dog sniffed at the dockside one last time before padding after them.

The voice of Menoa's leading arconite resounded through the heavens once more: "Surely you see the folly of this, Dill? Why die here in defense of this wooden town? Look at what this violence has already accomplished. The town is in ashes, yet we six remain unharmed." The arconites had all regained their feet and once again stood motionless amongst the boiling smoke. "We have attacked no one here," the leading angel continued, "yet you continue to reject our attempts at diplomacy. Should we crush your bones right now, or will you stand amongst us and hear King Menoa's terms?"

Dill took two giant strides forward and buried his massive cleaver in the automaton's neck.

The sheer force of the blow drove the massive warrior to his knees. Its armoured shins obliterated the burning remains of two houses.

Dill smashed his knee in the automaton's face, hurling it backwards into three rows of houses. The ensuing shock wave reduced the surrounding buildings to powder. He flipped the cleaver over, turning it sideways, and swept it sidelong across the broken rooftops. The end of the blade struck another arconite, clashing against its armoured thigh with a hideous peal. Its leg buckled and it toppled too.

Now dust and smoke obscured the battle. Amidst this turmoil Rachel caught glimpses of vast wings moving, monstrous shadows, and geysers of spinning debris. She heard thunderous booms and gut-wrenching metallic bangs, as Iron Head's men worked the oars and their little boat withdrew further into the mist.

"He can't beat them," Rachel muttered.

Iron Head raised his head from the tiller. "What was that?"

"Menoa's warriors can't be destroyed," she said. "They lack minds of their own, and so they are incapable of losing conviction in their own invincibility. But Dill is different." She gazed back into the fog. "He can fail if he loses faith in himself."

"Just like any other soldier," the captain replied. "Confidence is good armour." Then he grunted. "Pandemerian steel is better, of course, but who can afford it, eh?"

Rachel sat on a creaking bench between two militiamen with her arms wrapped around her knees. Mina's plan had fallen to pieces. Dill was supposed to have attacked the gates of Heaven, thereby provoking the goddess Ayen to destroy *all* of the arconites. Yet now they had no choice but to abandon him here and hope he bought them enough time to reach Sabor's castle. Everything now rested on the god of clocks.

How long could Dill keep fighting?

The town militia heaved at their oars, and the flotilla of skiffs moved out into deeper waters towards the waiting coke barges. Soldiers aboard these larger vessels were busy stoking the air-engine furnaces with shovelfuls of fuel, and the deck-mounted fly-wheels spun faster as the temperature differential increased. Black smoke trickled from tall funnels and looped over the heads of the women and children who squatted upon the loaded decks. Amidst the rasp and scrape of the militiamen's shovels and the hum of the flywheels, the refugees watched in silence as the ashes rose from their shattered homes.

Behind her, Rachel could see nothing now but Mina's sorcerous fog. The boats drifted in their own grey world that seemed suddenly so far from land. Even the crash of battle from the lakeshore sounded muted and dreamlike.

As the two fleets rendezvoused, skiffs and barges jostled in the cold waters under a canopy of coke fumes. Wet lines were thrown and snatched from the air and tied off. Tamping engines rattled decks and planking.

Iron Head's men helped some of the refugees from the more crowded vessels clamber across to the smaller craft, amongst them Rosella and her husband, Abner. In the fibrous gloom Rachel spotted scores of Oran's men and the Rusty Saw whores seated together upon other barges, and she gave silent thanks to the Burntwater troops for keeping the woodsmen away from the innkeeper and his wife.

Within moments the motored barges had attained full power, their air engines thrumming jauntily as they altered course. Iron Head's men strained over their oarlocks and struck a new path around the flanks of the larger boats. The whole clutter of vessels maneuvered into a surprisingly regular formation, and then set out across the lake.

The air stirred, as an unseen object whoomphed through the mists overhead. Rachel heard it splash into the lake in front of them. Low waves rolled out of the grey distance and set the boats pitching.

Calls rebounded between the leading barges.

"What was that?"

"Looked like a chunk of the sea wall."

"You see anything else?"

"Nothing."

Silence descended. The men bent to their oars again. For a long time they continued in this manner: the vague dark shapes of the barges like bruises concealed under veils of grey, the steadily rattling engines and the rasp of shovels, the knock of wood on wood and the constant slosh of the lake water. Lines strung between the vessels tightened and groaned. Hulls shifted to compensate.

In time the noise of battle faded behind them.

A man shouted up ahead, his voice strangely calm and unconcerned: "Hericans...Hoy! Who's that? We're steaming down on you."

Rachel raised her chin from her knees and looked over at Iron Head for explanation.

The captain shrugged, causing the shaft of his hammer to rise and fall behind his back. "Fishermen from across the lake," he said. "I'd be surprised if they've come to help. These Hericans don't interfere with us much, beyond occasional trade."

"Friendly sorts?"

"Decent enough folks, but not the sort to take up arms and rush into a scrap. Not unless it's over fishing rights." He stood at the tiller and peered into the gloom. "And probably not even then..."

But then the voice ahead called back again. "Captain, there's something strange here."

"What do you see, man?"

"Rafts."

And then Rachel saw them, too, as first one, then two of the simple craft drifted into view. They were indeed rafts, constructed of nothing more than lashed-together logs, and floating low in the water. Both were unmanned, each empty but for a thickly smoking cauldron fixed squarely to its center. Tar or some other additive had been applied to these pot fires, for they emitted foul black vapours.

Basilis gave a low growl. Mina cuddled the tiny dog to her chest.

"Another three to port," yelled the unseen sailor. "These ones have fires burning on sheet tin. And two more ahead, nor'west if I'm reckoning right."

"A trap?" Rachel asked.

Iron Head frowned. "Looks more like a diversion. You'd assume the Hericans are trying to aid our flight by confounding our pursuers. You'd think that, if you didn't know Hericans." His frown deepened. "Then again, they're not the sort to cause trouble, either."

The unseen sailor called out into the fog again. "Hoy! You there! Make yourself known." There was a pause, and then he shouted. "Captain, it's a woman. She's coming over."

"What kind of vessel?"

"Rowboat."

An interminably long pause followed, before the sailor raised his voice again. "Captain, she wants to speak to Rachel Hael."

Me? Rachel straightened in her seat. No one could possibly know she was here. She strained her eyes, trying to discern something in the mist. Nothing but vague shapes.

"Send her over," Iron Head called back.

They waited another moment. Eventually the sailor answered, and this time his voice sounded more relaxed. "She's just one of Miss Hael's family, Captain."

Grinning, Iron Head turned to Rachel and whispered, "I have a confession to make, Miss Hael. I've been expecting this. Your sister's here."

Rachel just stared at him. "I don't have a sister," she said. "My family is all dead." She waved her hands in frustration. "I *never* had a sister. Don't trust this woman, Captain. She is *not* who she claims to be."

The captain chuckled. "I have every reason to believe she is exactly who she claims to be," he said. "Her presence here is a very good omen for all of us. You, Miss Hael, are about to meet someone who has walked through the labyrinth of time." He pointed ahead. "She's approaching. You will soon see for yourself."

The impostor who claimed to be the assassin's sister was using an oar to push her tiny boat away from one of the barges up ahead. She nudged her vessel into open water, altered course, and then rowed quickly towards them. She was facing away, bent over the oars, but wore leather armour strikingly similar to Rachel's own.

Three burner rafts drifted in the fog behind her, disgorging clouds of inky fumes.

Finally the impostor's boat knocked against the bow of their skiff. Iron Head moved forward, extended a hand, and helped her aboard.

The woman turned to face Rachel.

And Rachel's heart froze.

A moment passed in which nobody spoke.

"I can see the resemblance," Mina said.

Rachel couldn't speak. She was staring into a face she knew intimately. The woman who had claimed to be her sister could easily have been Rachel's identical twin: the shocking green eyes, the gaunt face, the fair hair tied back so severely. The Spine leathers were not just similar, but practically indistinguishable from Rachel's own. A partially healed wound traced a line above the woman's ear—exactly matching the path Abner's bullet had scoured through Rachel's flesh. Even the twin's jaw was swollen, still bruised from the punch Hasp had delivered.

"You were right about Sabor, Rachel," Mina said. "Clearly he's been meddling in Time. This woman is *you*... returned to us from the future."

Rachel could spot only one difference between herself and this mirror-image woman. The twin had an extra bruise—a soft yellow smudge under her left eye. That single blemish was the only thing that differentiated them; without it, a stranger might never manage to tell the two apart.

"You're me?" she asked, incredulously. "A future me?"

The twin narrowed her eyes. "Hardly," she said. "I'm the original. *You*, little sis, are the earlier version of *me*. About ten hours earlier to be exact. I stood where you are now and said exactly the same things you are about to say."

"But this can't be..."

"Yes, that's more or less what I said."

Rachel's thoughts tumbled wildly. "No... I won't... You *can't* be me. You're an impostor, a fraud. The bruise on your face..."

The twin snorted. "They told me it was necessary to help me understand. It's called a paradox, and this is how it happened." And then she lashed out a fist and punched Rachel hard under the left eye.

9

IN THE CASTLE OF THE
GOD OF CLOCKS

The rafts had been built with the help of the Hericans, the *future* Rachel explained, to act as a distraction and so confuse their arconite pursuers. Iron Head had apparently given this alternate Rachel the idea, after he'd first seen the craft used here today. Not that she could explain that paradox, either.

"Sabor's castle bends logic," she said. "He claims it allows temporally distinct versions of a person to exist in the same moment." Then she sighed. "I don't completely understand it, but Sabor says it has something to do with collapsing universes. You can ask him yourself shortly."

"We're that close?" Rachel asked.

"It's not far from the shore, sis." She pointed.

A beach of metallic shingle had appeared out of the fog. Conifers crowded the bank behind it, tightly spaced and so dense as to seem impenetrable, while white boles of some long-dead deciduous variety—perhaps the remains of an earlier forest—bent over the silver-grey grass of a bank rising abruptly behind the beach. After a moment Rachel perceived a track partially hidden by this sun-bleached wicker. It divided the pine forest as precisely as a knife cut.

Iron Head's men beached their boats all along the shore, the hulls scraping the pebbles with a sound like growling cats, and soon the entire party had disembarked. There were more than forty craft of all sizes, their dark shapes strewn along the water's edge. Rosella and Abner stayed close to the captain, Rachel, and Mina, but Oran and his woodsmen herded their people over to one side, evidently to maintain a structure of authority amongst their own.

The thaumaturge let her dog jump down onto the beach, and then strolled over to where Rachel's temporally removed twin stood peering into the mists that shrouded the Flower Lake. Dark patches of smoke lingered here and there, wherever the rafts drifted.

"You didn't have to hit her, did you?" she said.

"She had it coming, Mina."

"How?"

The twin shrugged. "A future version of her got me into this whole mess. Or maybe it was a past version, I don't know. Trying to unravel these paradoxes gives me a headache. I haven't slept, and I just spent the last ten hours up to my knees in the freezing lake, lashing logs together with the bloody Hericans." She snorted. "We built every single one of them by hand—and for what? Did you see any arconites back there? They're still slugging it out on the other side of the lake. All that effort wasted, and it's *her* fault. Or another version of her self's fault. There was no reason for me to come back here at all." Her eyes met Mina's. "I'm sorry for striking her; I was annoyed at myself, I suppose. Now you're going to tell me that I gave myself this bruise."

"Well, you *are* her," Mina said. "Ten hours from now."

"She's *me*," the twin insisted, "ten hours ago. *I'm* the real Rachel...the definitive one. I left your side less than half a day ago... or I *will* leave your side—gods, this is confusing—and now you look at me like I'm a stranger."

"You're both the same person."

The assassin shook her head in frustration. "I don't like the idea of there being two of me. It's creepy. And she has a job to do. Apparently, now she needs to go back into the past and do all the pointless backbreaking labour I've just done before she'll really become me..." She ground her teeth together. "At least I think so... You see how mad this situation is? I should have ignored Sabor altogether."

"I'm itching to see this castle of his."

The future Rachel grunted. "It isn't quite what you think it is. It surprises you, and it disappoints you—I remember that well enough. Time travel is much harder work than you'd expect, because it involves a hell of a lot of walking." Then she hissed in frustration and turned to stride up the beach. "Come on!" she exclaimed. "The castle is this way." She stole a glance back at Rachel. "And don't ask how *I* found my way there in the first place. I simply followed *me* after *me* socked me in the eye... and that makes no sense whatsoever. Paradoxes! Just thinking about it is enough to drive you insane. Let the god of clocks explain it all again!"

Mina opened her mouth to speak, but Rachel's twin lifted her hand and, without even looking round, said, "Sabor will explain that too, Mina. We can travel that far back, but there are problems, as you'll see."

Rachel caught up with the thaumaturge as the party climbed the loose gravel bank behind the beach. "What were you going to ask her?"

"I was going ask you why Sabor, or an agent of his, couldn't simply travel far enough back in time to prevent the battle at Coreollis. If we'd stopped the slaughter, the portal would never have opened. Then the king's arconites would still be in Hell."

Rachel just shook her head in confusion. The logic was entirely unfathomable to her, and she began to understand her future self's miserable mood. But did she *really* have to return and confront herself again? What if she elected not to?

The Burntwater refugees slowly moved in single file along the narrow track. Dense woodland hemmed them on either side, and hoarded a deep grey silence that seemed entirely devoid of life. The ground rose steadily before them, till soon the group was climbing between well-worn boulders. The air became cooler, fresh now with the scent of mountain rain.

Rosella and Abner Hill stayed close to Iron Head's soldiers, while Oran's militia followed some distance behind. This latter group seemed content to sulk silently, but their whores muttered and complained. Despite the family ties between Iron Head and his brother, the two men and their respective troops had little contact with each other. No one spoke outside their own party. Even Rachel's temporal twin kept her head down and her mouth shut.

No more than a quarter of a league into the forest, the track came to another shoreline, with a similarly pebbled beach. It seemed they had traversed a narrow peninsula and thus arrived at an inlet on the other side. Here the waters were mirror still, for this part of the Flower Lake formed a natural harbour. A number of small metal boats lay grounded upon silver shingles, beyond which stood a cluster of simple wooden houses and sheds.

The Hericans waited for them at the edge of their settlement. They were small, tough-looking people with weathered faces not unlike those of their Burntwater neighbours. Evidently they had been busy felling trees, as there were a great number of ragged stubs behind the waterline. Iron Head shook the leader's hand. "I appreciate all the work you put into those rafts, Kevin."

The man barely raised his hooded eyes. "The lady promised Sabor would pay us. Same weight in copper for all the iron we sacrificed to make those burners," he said. "We've not an oil pot left in the village, and there's still sixteen hundredweight of candlefish to be processed before they rot. So you have your brother Eli remind Lord Sabor which Hericans in which timeline he's supposed to pay, and sod his paradoxes. We've heard that excuse too often."

"You have my word on that. I'll speak to Eli myself."

The other man nodded.

Iron Head peered over at the other villagers and the tiny group of buildings behind them. "You got plans to avoid those arconites?" he said. "They'll probably head this way eventually."

Kevin yawned. "Hide in the forest, I suppose. What are they going to do? Conquer Kevin's Jetty in the name of Hell?"

"Fair enough. We'll leave you in peace, then."

Kevin yawned again. "Hide in the forest, I suppose," he said. "What are they going to do? Conquer Kevin's Jetty in the name of Hell?"

Iron Head frowned at him. "All right, Kevin. We'll leave you in peace."

Rachel and Mina exchanged a glance.

Mina whispered in her ear, "There must be consequences to time travel. Sabor's probably gone and broken some part of the universe."

"Great."

Mina leaned over and whispered again, "There must be consequences to—"

"Mina!"

The thaumaturge smiled. "I'm sorry. I couldn't resist it."

Rachel's twin led the group on through the village. Kevin's Jetty was a dismal little settlement where the slatted timber dwellings had been rubbed with grease or oil as weatherproofing. The whole place stank of fish. From the opposite edge of the village the path continued around the narrow bay and climbed a headland beyond. Rachel sensed someone at her side, and turned to find Rosella and her husband, Abner, there.

"We're staying here," the innkeeper's wife declared. "The Hericans have already agreed. We can hide with them when the arconites come."

Abner just glared at her.

"I'm sorry for everything that's happened," Rachel said. "I should never have involved you."

"No, you shouldn't have," Rosella replied. "You should never have come and kicked down our door." She hesitated. "We lost everything: our home, our business, our stock—even our savings that were buried in the ground outside the Rusty Saw."

Rachel didn't know what to say to that.

"Abner thinks maybe . . . maybe you should compensate us. You have all that gold, after all."

The assassin sighed. "The coins are in Dill's mouth," she said. "I'm sorry, Rosella, we've got nothing to give you."

"Nothing?"

Rachel shook her head.

The couple turned away and walked back towards the Hericans.

"Oh, you're not going to let that depress you?" Mina was stroking Basilis with one glassy hand. "I've never seen you look so miserable. It's war, Rachel. Stuff happens." She gave a half frown. "And didn't she attack you with an axe? I can't remember . . . was that before or after her husband shot you in the head?"

"She was only defending her property."

"And you were exercising your right to seize that property."

"My right?"

"By executing Cospinol's grand vision for our freedom, the god of brine and fog granted you the right."

Rachel felt utterly miserable. "What gives him the authority?" she said harshly.

"He's bigger than us, so he can crush us mere mortals under his salty thumb. Relax now. That's the beauty of war. Utter subservience to one's leaders absolves a soldier of the consequences of her actions. Shift the blame, Rachel. It makes it easier to sleep at night."

"Stop it," Rachel snapped. "You're just doing this to annoy me. *I* made the decision, not Cospinol. I fucked up, and now I've ruined that woman's life because of it. Knowing we're at war doesn't make it any easier."

Basilis barked suddenly. Mina looked down at the dog and then smiled. "He thinks you're a lousy Spine assassin," she said, "but a very good soldier. Remember, the Adepts that Deepgate's Spine used to create by chemical torture are severely limited. Those assassins cannot develop their talents further once the Spine have finished raping their brains. But you can. Just think of war itself as a more gradual tempering process. You can let it break you, or change you." She ruffled the dog's ears. "He's glad you weren't wasted under the Spine needles."

Rachel grunted. "What would he know? He's just a dog." She strode on ahead of the thaumaturge.

Irritated and thoroughly depressed, Rachel just wanted to be left alone now. Rosella's departure had left a shadow in her heart. Rachel had hardly spoken to the woman, didn't know what sort of a person she was, and until very recently hadn't actually cared. Had she spoken even once to the woman's husband?

Oran stepped in front of her, interrupting her thoughts. Ten of his men stood behind him. She'd been so preoccupied that she had hardly noticed them approaching. "You owe us wages," the woodsmen's leader said in a hoarse whisper. "And blood money for the two of us you killed."

Rachel glanced back along the path. Iron Head and his men were only just leaving the outskirts of Kevin's Jetty, so none of them had yet noticed this confrontation.

"Your wages are in Dill's mouth," she said. "Go get them if you want."

Anger flashed in his eyes. "Look at her," he growled. "Her legs are still shaking. She's too weak now to pull another stunt like the one in the tavern." He reached out for her.

Rachel sidestepped him easily, then backed away, her misery rapidly turning to anger. Oran and his men spread out to surround her, but she had no intention of allowing herself to become trapped. She was fully alert now, ready for any move they might make.

A hand on her shoulder startled her. She hadn't heard anyone sneak up behind her. She turned...

...and looked into the eyes of her twin.

The future Rachel said, "My legs aren't shaking, Oran. Tell your men to stand down. You saw what I did in the Rusty Saw. Now imagine what two of me could do to you right here and now."

The woodsmen halted, and dark looks passed amongst them. Oran opened his mouth to speak, but was interrupted by a shout from further down the path.

"What's this, brother?" Iron Head was quickly approaching. "You wouldn't be picking fights with women, would you?" He laughed. "That's not like the man I used to know."

"Stay out of our business, Reed," Oran growled at the Burntwater captain. "Two of my men died defending Lord Rys's honour."

"Rys's honour?" Iron Head replied contemptuously. "Since when did the god of flowers and knives appoint *you* his champion? Did I miss your appearance at his court?"

"It was a fair fight until *she* stepped in."

The captain grunted. "I heard about the last fair fight of yours," he said. "A family on the Deepcut road, wasn't it? Strapping seventeen-year-old lad and his old grandfather."

"Poachers," Oran snarled. "Lord Rys charges us to uphold the law in his forests. This is *his* land, *his* deer and fowl—not yours, Reed. Those who steal from him deserve what they get."

Iron Head had reached the group by now. He hadn't drawn either of his weapons. "Aye, they told me all about it," he said. "But

I forget, Oran, how many sparrows had that boy and the old man stolen from Rys?"

The scar on Oran's forehead reddened. He wheeled, gesturing angrily to his men, and they moved back into the forest.

Iron Head turned to the two Rachels. "Stay away from him," he said. "He'll put a knife in your back any chance he gets."

The future Rachel said, "We reach the castle safely, Iron Head. I remember that much."

The captain shook his head. "Don't count on it, Miss Hael. This may or may not be the same past that you remember. We've all witnessed a lot of... unusual events recently. Around these parts, history has a habit of changing when you least expect it to."

Rachel's twin just grunted and walked away.

Ahead the land rose steadily. In a long single file they climbed the narrow trail up through the forest and over the rocky headland behind the bay. Uncomfortable in her future self's company, Rachel slowed her pace, allowing her twin to walk on ahead with Iron Head. Something about that woman unnerved her. Perhaps it was in the glances they shared, the terrible intimacy and understanding she saw in her twin's eyes, as if at that very moment they both knew each other's thoughts with utter certainty. It was like they were gazing warily into each other's souls.

One soul, or two?

Rachel didn't want to think about the metaphysical aspects of the situation. It was enough to know that the other woman felt just as uncomfortable. They both considered themselves to be the *real* Rachel Hael, the *only* Rachel Hael, and neither wanted the other casting doubt upon that belief.

As she turned to look for Mina, a shaft of sunlight lit up a patch of ground over to her left so that, for a moment, yellow lichen blazed brightly against the grey rocks. Rachel glanced up and saw the sun now shining overhead. The fog that had followed them from Coreollis was finally dissipating.

Mina was struggling up the trail below—her hooded figure

moved slowly, pausing to rest every few steps, while Basilis bounded across the rocks ahead and then turned and waited for his mistress to catch up.

From this vantage point, Rachel could see a great expanse of silver water and the curve of the bay sweeping round to Kevin's Jetty. The mists had now retreated far across the Flower Lake and formed a grey haze in the distance, intermingled with filthy plumes of black and ochre smoke from the Hericans' rafts. Wind or current had now carried those rude vessels much further to the east. She looked for Burntwater on the opposite shore, hoping for a glimpse of Dill, but the settlement remained hidden by the last of the fog.

Here the skies were rapidly clearing. Warm sunlight bathed the green forest and the pebbled beaches along the lakeshore. Birds chittered and whistled amongst the trees. It was the first time Rachel had seen real colour for a long while, she realized. There was no sign of Oran or his people, so she sat on a rock and waited for Mina to join her.

"At least it's a nice day," Mina said, when she finally caught up. "I'd almost forgotten what the sun feels like." She paused, rested a hand on the rock, and took a deep breath. "There was a limit to how long I could maintain the fog, and I fear this is it."

"You did well," Rachel said. "We're nearly there."

Mina nodded towards the smoke clouds rising from the lake. "Those rafts aren't going to be a distraction for very much longer. Menoa's arconites will soon spot them for what they are."

"They never were a real distraction," Rachel said. "All that effort was a complete waste of time. Making those rafts didn't help our escape, and they didn't help Dill. *She* should have crossed the lake and warned Iron Head to expect us. Without those delays at Burntwater we'd have reached Sabor's castle by now. Dill and Hasp would then be safe."

"I don't know," Mina replied. "Isn't it best not to alter what has already happened if you can avoid it? Our present situation could be a lot worse." She gazed at the smoke-filled horizon. "I think you should do exactly what she did when it's time for you to return. Enlist the Hericans, build these rafts"—she smiled—"and don't forget to punch yourself in the face."

"I'm not doing anything," Rachel said. "If we reach the castle safely, I'm staying there until we can figure out a way to reach Heaven. We have a job to do. Why would I want to come back here?"

"You *did* come back here. Right now you're a hundred yards further up this same trail."

"She's not me."

"I'm sorry, Rachel, but she absolutely *is* you."

The assassin snorted. "Well, then, *she* can travel back in time again. I don't see the point of any of it."

Mina gave her a sympathetic smile. "Maybe you will...given time."

The trail passed over the headland and then meandered down into a shallow valley before the landscape began to rise ahead of them again. For another hour they climbed up through dense, centuries-old pine forest. On either side of them the thick canopy sheltered verdant, cathedral-like spaces carpeted with mats of brown needles. The path itself had been cut into steps to form a steeply sloping ravine between the trees. Rachel did not find the going particularly taxing, but Mina continued to struggle. She accepted Rachel's arm with gratitude.

Despite the brightening sun, the air became steadily cooler. Eventually they crested a rise and stepped into the teeth of a mountain gale. Here the forest ended at a plateau of blasted rock. The landscape beyond soared to vast heights in a bleak vista of glassy black bluffs and sheer cliffs, all fractured as if by some terrible cataclysm. Tumbles of obsidian scree glittered like anthracite in the mountain fissures.

And there, on a ragged promontory in the center of the plateau, stood the castle of the god of clocks.

It was like no fortress Rachel had ever seen: a maze of interconnected blocks, square towers, and spheres all extending up and outwards from its massive rock foundation. These queer extrusions appeared to be entire buildings in themselves, clamped to the main mass in an ad hoc fashion so that the whole structure had the look of a bizarrely geometric tree. The castle had been built from the same local obsidian that was strewn around it, though inset with metal girders and lozenges of brightly blazing glass. It was truly monstrous in size, and yet its exact limits defied explication, for the surrounding air blurred and shimmered as if the gales that howled around its structure were bending the very light itself.

A chill ran through Rachel as she watched parts of the great dark castle evanesce and then clarify. Whole towers and facades existed and then ceased to be. Sudden bursts of red, pink, and mauve scintillations trembled around its edges. Then it shrank... and, in utter silence, the structure became brutally massive again. It towered over them, vapourous and uncertain, like some hideous desert mirage.

Rachel's twin grimaced and clutched her stomach, then she hurried towards an arched portal in the front of the fortress.

But Rachel herself hesitated to follow. For all its dazzling colours, the fortress exuded a deeply disturbing aura. Its impossible facades induced a feeling of vertigo in her, while its gemstone lights irritated her eyes and froze her skin like liquid aether. The surrounding air tasted unnatural, strangely glassy, as though devoid of some element whose absence distressed Rachel's lungs. All of her senses felt oddly jumbled, somehow *askew,* as if her nerves had been subtly rerouted.

Unable to gaze upon the shimmering fortress any longer, she turned her eyes away.

"The sensation goes away once you get inside," Iron Head said. "You're probably feeling it doubly in the presence of another one of yourselves."

"What's causing it?"

"The castle's engines warp the space around it. It exists simultaneously in different pockets of time, which means that the building must be here *and* elsewhere in space, and that cannot be permitted. Sabor requires massive amounts of power to keep it rooted to this mountain." He beckoned to her. "Come on, Miss Hael, let's get inside quickly."

The castle's engines?

Rachel stole another glance up at the building's delirious facades. The stonework blurred like ten thousand storm-blown flags, a riot of colour that contracted and then expanded to such heights that it seemed to reach beyond the surrounding mountains themselves.

The god of clocks dwelling within now expected her to enter his domain and, by some temporal trickery, travel back ten hours to meet her own self. And then? To force another Rachel to return here once more? To travel back through those same ten hours? Would some part of her soul remain forever trapped here in a loop of Sabor's devising? Rachel's head spun with the consequences of it all. She felt angry and tired and sick.

She swallowed hard and followed Iron Head inside the massive building.

The River of the Failed would not be beaten, but neither would Carnival. She dragged her wings through its bloody waters and used her demon sword to hack down the foes it raised against her.

There was no end to them.

They came at her in endless waves, thousands upon thousands: simulacrums of Cospinol's gallowsmen, warriors from unknown continents and ages past, crimson giants and angels made after her own image, and queer bestial things of the river's own devising. They shrieked and howled. They bullied and taunted her and tore at her with claws and teeth and bloody weapons formed of the crystallized fluid itself. She should have flown above their reach and smashed her way back into Hell.

But she didn't. She stayed in the river because the butchery was here, and her rage would not otherwise be sated.

She fought tirelessly, not knowing or caring if she truly damaged the river, for those she slew died shrieking, only to rise again and confront her in new forms. They were cunning and fast, but Carnival was faster and more treacherous than all of them. She murdered with a terrible efficacy honed by aeons of survival.

Yet their numbers were vast, and sometimes those watery blades nicked her flesh. The scarred angel was well used to that pain and returned tenfold the wounds she sustained.

She fought just for the sake of the battle, without any motive other than a desperate and unquenchable need to hurt the world around her. Cold rage steered her hand, but she had no final destination in mind. In the grip of war, she strode wherever the river currents took her, and murdered everything she encountered in her path.

Hell loomed above, like a sky of brick and iron and glass, and through its myriad bright windows the souls of the damned watched her pass below. She glimpsed them shudder and turn away, but felt nothing for them. The damned did not concern her.

How long she fought she could not say. It seemed like many days and nights. The river was endless, the creatures it birthed uncountable. This army had no limits, and neither did the angel who walked amongst them.

But the demon sword began to fail.

A low wail issued from the weapon. The shape-shifter was tiring, his steel edge growing dull. Carnival put more muscle behind the cuts she made. She didn't question or demand more from the sword; she simply fought harder. Her anger rose to meet the demon child's failings. And the red figures fell in even greater numbers than before. She drank in their screams as she carved through them.

Soon she noticed changes in her opponents. Now the great majority of her foes had assumed winged forms. Was this done in mockery of the scarred angel herself? Carnival didn't understand the river's motives, nor did she care. Her own brutality exceeded any violence these crimson forms could inflict, and so she used them as a necessary anathema toward which to direct her thirst for destruction.

In time the sword lost its edge entirely. The shape-shifter had reached his limits, and he could no longer sustain the sharpness such a blade required to cut through flesh. The metal moaned woefully in her fist. In mortal hands the failing weapon would have now merely broken bones. Carnival simply put more of her strength behind each blow. The sword cried out in agony, but Carnival ignored it. A million enemies still waited to be slain.

By degrees the attacks against her lessened. Her winged opponents hesitated. Often they held back entirely, reluctant to be the next to meet her blade.

Carnival's fury bucked again inside her, and she threw herself amongst them. If they would not bring the fight to her, then she would take it to them. She leapt at them and spun, and hewed them down. Arcs of blood followed her wailing sword. Dragging her wings through the weakening currents, she moved ever onwards, now grinning desperately as she tried to incite bloodlust from her reluctant foes.

Suddenly they stopped altogether.

She rushed at them, and they collapsed back into the bloody waters. She wheeled and threw herself at new foes, but those also dissolved into nothing.

"Fight me," she cried.

But they would not. The myriad figures around her returned to the bloody river. The waters receded, draining into nearby channels as they drew back from her thighs. Soon Carnival stood alone on a slick red riverbed. "Fight," she insisted.

But the River of the Failed had rejected her.

She felt the sword tremble. The demon weapon sighed and then flowed out of her fist, as the shape-shifter resumed his human form.

He became a child once more. He crouched by her feet, seemingly unable to stand. He looked boneless, partially dissolved. His thin metal fingers splayed across the moist ground. One of his eyes swiveled round to meet her gaze. The other followed a moment later. "It was testing you," he said.

Carnival just stared at him.

"Why else would it keep fighting?" he added. "It can't be destroyed. You can't even really hurt it. It was just testing you."

"Why?"

The shape-shifter appeared to shrug, but his shoulders moved in odd directions. "Cospinol said the river was an infant," he said. "He said that it doesn't know what it is, that it is still learning what to become. I reckon that's why it formed itself into all them angels. It was trying to copy *you*."

Carnival gazed out across the subterranean realm. Twenty paces away the red waterways flowed all around, but they came no nearer. Standing in this shallow depression, she had the impression that the river was waiting for something.

"I'm tired," the boy said. "I want to go home." He leaned back and closed his eyes.

The scarred angel grunted. Her heart continued to hammer, as her scars writhed and itched. The battle with the river had not been enough, and she still hungered for war. Her dark gaze dropped to the demon child, and a sudden knot of rage tightened in her gut. It took all of her will to stop herself from ripping out his throat.

She needed a blade desperately.

Mercifully, the shape-shifter hadn't noticed her anger. His face had paled and he was staring up with wide eyes. "No, no, no," he said. "Not here."

Carnival looked up.

Overhead the sky looked different. Instead of the usual cluttered mass of brick and iron, a series of black iron conduits led up into the Maze from here. The stonework around these pipes appeared smooth and uniform, apparently the result of some grander design than simply the chaotic crush of countless souls. This looked *ordered*, like the foundation of one single structure.

"Not here," the boy wailed. "I won't go back . . . I won't!"

"What is it?"

"The Ninth Citadel," he sobbed. "This is where they made me!"

"*Who* made you? What's up *there*?"

The boy sobbed, and rubbed tears from his eyes. "King Menoa is up there," he said. "The Lord of the Maze and all his armies and his Icarates." He sniffed and rubbed his nose. "The river brought you here to meet its father."

Iron Head led the party into a tall stone gatehouse and, while his men waited there, he took Rachel and Mina on through a massive copper door and into the heart of the castle of the god of clocks.

Whatever Rachel had been expecting, this wasn't it. Iron Head put his shoulder to the metal door behind them, and it swung shut with a resounding boom. The subsequent echoes gave the sense of an immense chamber, yet Rachel could see little in this darkness except for a single shaft of light that fell upon a circular table fifty paces ahead. From all around came the sound of ticking, whirring clocks—the *thunk-thunk* of heavy cogs, tinny metallic chimes, and the dull brassy peals of larger bells. Underlying this orchestra Rachel could just discern a faint hissing sound, like trickling sand.

Her future self stood waiting beside the god of clocks. Sabor was grey-haired and grey-winged and clad in a suit of dull chain that lent him an air of stiff authority. He frowned at the table before him and did not look up as the three newcomers approached. Then he reached under the table and tugged at some unseen mechanism.

Rachel heard a clunk.

"Garstone," the god of clocks called out, "please refocus lens number six hundred and twenty-three on level ninety-two—the Buttercup Suite should now be situated seventeen minutes ago, but something seems to be causing a distortion. Did you clean the window glass in there, Garstone? Did you check the timelock lens seals?"

Out of the darkness overhead replied a chorus of many droll voices. "The windows are pristine, sir . . . One of me shall attend to the lens seals forthwith . . . However, I fear it is already too late . . . The Buttercup Suite is about to end its current cycle." The hidden speakers had uttered their words in complete harmony.

Iron Head began, "Greetings, Sabor. Here—"

"A moment, please, Reed," Sabor cut in. He withdrew a book from under the table, thumbed through it quickly, and then called out again in a raised voice, "Wait until the suite completes its cycle before you change the seals, Garstone. It's due to slip backwards nine weeks, three days, ten hours and . . ." He turned the page. ". . . three minutes. That's night time."

"Yes, sir," the voices called down.

Sabor closed the book, and returned his attention to the circular tabletop.

As Rachel drew nearer, she could see the object of the god's scrutiny more clearly. The table was actually a shallow basin made of white ceramic, and upon its smooth surface moved tiny figures. The god of clocks was studying a moving image: a bird's-eye view of streets and houses all wreathed in smoke.

A camera obscura?

Rachel had heard rumours of such devices. In theory they were simple to construct. A series of lenses and mirrors, set high upon a tall building, projected an image of their surroundings down into a darkened room.

Sabor glanced up at the newcomers. His gaze settled on Iron Head, and he called up into the darkness. "Your brother Reed is here, Garstone. No doubt he wishes to speak to you."

"I am aware of that, sir," replied the many voices. "One of me will attend to him."

"There's really no need, Eli," Iron Head replied. "I can see you're busy."

"One of me always has time for you, brother," the multiplicious speakers replied. A pause followed, and then a single voice said, "I'll be down forthwith."

The captain grimaced.

Rachel gazed down in wonder at the ceramic depression. The image there was warped and blurred in places, yet she recognized the scene instantly.

Burntwater.

Fire consumed the entire wharfside, sending billowing mountains of black smoke into the air. The neighbourhood beyond lay smothered in dust, but she could see that it had been completely destroyed. Here and there, a few smaller, isolated fires had taken hold. The remains of hundreds of buildings lay open to the sky, their roofs staved in and their walls smashed apart. Piles of rubble clogged every street. But there was no sign of Dill, or the other giant automatons. The settlement was utterly deserted.

"Where's Dill?" Rachel asked, grabbing the edge of the table.

Sabor made an adjustment to some hidden mechanism beneath the table. Rachel heard wheels turning. The projected image gave a sudden lurch, and then scrolled rapidly across the tabletop. Rachel caught a glimpse of the shore flying past her fingers before the view moved out over the lake. For several heartbeats she saw nothing but water, but then the image settled again on the opposite shore—*this* side of the Flower Lake. Rachel's breath caught in her throat.

An arconite was dragging itself out of the water and up into the forest beyond. Rachel's heart screamed at her that this wasn't Dill, that it couldn't be him—that it *had* to be one of Menoa's angels. But her head told her that this wretched thing was indeed her friend. His wings and armoured back plate had been ripped off, exposing his naked spine to the sky. The shattered vertebrae trailed behind his neck like a broken chain, barely held together by a tangled assortment of pipes. One of his legs was missing entirely; the other ended at the knee. His left arm had been crushed in three places and flailed pathetically in the muddy shore behind him. His jaw was gone, and his skull had been smashed open, revealing the machinery and gleaming crystals within. Chemical blood leaked from the engine in his chest and stained the waters black.

But he was still alive.

With his one good arm, Dill pulled his broken body further into the trees above the waterline.

Seventeen minutes ago?

The image vanished, leaving nothing but the plain white surface.

"What happened?" Rachel cried. "Get it back."

Sabor raised his head and yelled up into the darkness above. "Garstone?"

"As I feared, sir," came the chorus in reply. "The room's cycle has now finished. It is currently recharging."

The god of clocks nodded. He glanced at Rachel and then at her future self. "That particular view has ceased to be."

"This happened seventeen minutes ago?" Rachel said. "But that means Dill is down there now. We have to go back." She spun to face the Burntwater captain. "Iron Head, I need your help."

"Wait," Sabor said.

Rachel stopped.

"There isn't time," Sabor went on. "The suite that returns you to this morning will complete its own cycle shortly. You must go back now or lose this opportunity."

"No." She turned to go.

"Light the lamps," Sabor yelled.

Far overhead a light flickered and brightened, immediately fol-

lowed by another, and yet another. In moments the whole chamber became illuminated.

Rachel felt suddenly giddy.

The interior of the castle resembled a twisted cylinder or vortex, much like the spiraling body of a whirlwind. It consisted of
hundreds of levels, each with a multitude of inward-facing doors
set around its circular gallery. Stairs of curlicue metalwork connected one level to the next, all canted to follow the crooked
walls. The towering room terminated far overhead in a glass hemisphere, from the center of which descended a complex optical array of interconnected brass tubes, mirrors, lenses, and cogs. Rising
above their heads, its burnished metal columns formed a towering
spine in the center of the room, from which many more links extended sideways to disappear into the surrounding walls. This
queer arrangement of glass and metal occupied most of the space
between the galleries. The image of Dill had issued from its lowest
tube, suspended mere yards above Sabor's viewing table.

The god of clocks straightened. "Please forgive my discourtesy, but
we simply do not have time for arguments or discussion. Miss Hael,"
he inclined his head towards Rachel, "you *must* go back to the past, in
order that the rest of us might deal with the issue of your giant friend.
If you refuse, and choose instead to leave my castle now, you will en-
danger all that we have achieved, and will subsequently achieve."

Rachel glanced over at her other self, and was startled to see
the fear in the woman's eyes. Her twin caught Rachel's inquiring
look and said, "Just listen to him."

"She's right," Mina said. "Rachel, we'll look after Dill."

"I can't just leave him," Rachel said.

"You *aren't* leaving him," her future self said. "I'm here, and I'm
you. For the gods' sake, just go and let us do this."

"Go where?"

"This way." Sabor beckoned her over to the nearest staircase.
"Hurry—I'll explain as we go."

Rachel glanced at Mina, who nodded.

The small party hurried after Sabor, who led them up a metal-work staircase that curved towards the first tier of his castle.

"This fortress," Sabor said as he ran up the stairs, "offers one the opportunity to explore paths back through Time." He indicated the many doors situated on the tiers of galleries above him. Iron steps rattled under his feet. "Each of these doors leads to a timelock, and behind each timelock is a suite. And each of those suites exists in a separate moment in the past: whether one hour ago or three hours, two days in the past, a year, a month—it all depends on the suite's current cycle. The Obscura's engines keep the whole thing ticking." From a pocket under his mail shirt he withdrew a chart, quickly unfolding it to many times its original size. "Each room's temporal reach changes with the passage of Time. They cycle through various set permutations. It has been my life's work to map them all." He stabbed a finger at the huge sheet of paper. "Right now, for instance, the Larollen Suite on the thirteenth floor looks out upon the new moon of four months ago. But when it finishes its cycle, a year from today, it will only be able to take a traveler back five days."

They reached the first gallery. A walkway with a smooth dark wood banister encircled this level of the giant chamber, with a second staircase then rising up to the next gallery. A dozen or so doors led off this platform, each one boasting a round glass window like a ship's porthole as well as a tarnished gold dial similar to the locking mechanism found on a safe. Some of the portholes were dark, while light shone through others. Tubes from Sabor's camera obscura ran into the adjacent walls.

Here were the clocks Rachel had heard from downstairs. On the walls between doors hung every sort of timepiece, from the modest to the ostentatious. Hands ticked around faces in short halting steps past numerals and dates and diagrams of suns and moons.

As they hurried past the first door, Rachel glanced through its porthole. Beyond the timelock she glimpsed a comfortable room full of many more clocks, handsome furniture, and bookcases stuffed with ancient tomes, cabinets of astrological instruments, and an enormous brass device set upon a tripod before the exterior window. This, she thought, must be one extension of Sabor's obscura, and it was currently looking out through an outer window upon a dark and starry sky.

"How is that possible?" she said.

Sabor glanced back at the dial on the door, and then checked his map. "That particular room exists forty years ago," he said. "The temporal register appears to be in accordance with the clocks inside. This therefore remains part of our current timeline, our actual history." He raised his head. "Garstone? Where are you, Garstone?"

Rachel gazed back at the porthole in awe. "So stepping through that door would take you back forty years?" She found herself racing to catch up with the others again. "Why don't you go back and change the past, stop the portal from opening at Coreollis?"

"It's too late for that," Sabor replied. "This castle was intended to be an *observatory*, not a vehicle for would-be time travelers. One can safely journey back to the dawn of Time, so long as one remains inside the castle. But the moment you set foot outside these walls, you threaten the natural order of Time. Then every action you take, no matter how small, might alter history and thereby create a parallel universe. Time would split, like a fork in a branch. Thereafter, that room would become a junction, a crossroads between two realities—the one you left behind and the one you created *yourself*." He glanced at his pocket watch. "Faster—the cycle change is due any moment."

"If it's so dangerous, then why am I going back?"

Sabor threw up his arms. "Because our own timeline has already been corrupted," he cried. "It's failing, rotten. The universe outside these walls is dying a slow death, and nothing we do now is going to make it any worse. It might last another hundred years—

or ten, or a thousand—but the cancer has already spread out of control. All we can do is hack at it with a knife and try to buy ourselves some more time. Right now, you are that knife."

Just as they reached the second staircase, one of the doors on the first level flew open and a stooped old man, wearing a garishly striped brown and red suit, stepped through it. He had his nose buried in a book, but when he noticed the group he nodded to Sabor and then to Iron Head before disappearing through the neighbouring door. A heartbeat later a third door on the opposite side of the circular gallery opened, and the same old man stepped back onto it. This time he was wearing a plain blue suit and scribbling notes in his book. He spotted the group again, nodded two times more to the captain and the god of clocks, and then vanished through an altogether different door.

"Who were they?" Rachel said.

Iron Head grunted. "That's my brother, Eli. Just call him Garstone. He's the only one of us who still uses our old man's name."

"Indeed," Sabor concurred, glancing at his pocket watch again. "However, that is not the version of Garstone I was looking for. For the work to come we require a much younger man."

"But how can he be two different ages?" Rachel enquired.

"Not just two ages," Iron Head said. "Travel back ten minutes in this place and you'll meet yourself before you step into the timelock you've just used. And if there's no longer any reason for your original self to step inside the timelock, then there's suddenly two of you. My brother is every age from now until his death. He keeps overlapping himself."

"Garstone winds the clocks," Sabor added, "but it's becoming hard to keep track of him all."

The god of clocks now urged them up the next set of steps, to the second gallery. It was identical to the first in every way except for an even greater variety of clocks set upon the walls. Garstone was here, too, albeit in greater numbers. Rachel counted three separate versions of the stooped old man, all winding clockwork, opening and closing doors as he moved between different rooms. He went about his business quietly, frowning over the books he carried, but with unfailing politeness, for each copy of him nodded to Sabor and Iron Head—and even to his other selves—in passing.

"How many of him *are* there?" Rachel asked.

"There must be several billion of him by now," Sabor replied. "He has worked here, in this labyrinth of Time, for more than thirty of his own years." He shot another glance at his pocket watch, and then quickened his pace. "Three minutes until the cycle change."

Rachel stared after him in confusion, but then Iron Head took her arm, urging her on. "That's how long we have until the particular window you need to take into the past ends," he explained, as their boots rattled up the metal stairs. "All these rooms change their positions in Time. They reorder themselves to allow for the celestial movement of this planet."

Somewhere below, a large timepiece began to chime, its loud clangs resounding throughout the vast chamber. Several smaller clocks answered with a chorus of silvery notes, like songbirds responding.

"Too much stress in space-time would tear the fortress apart," Sabor called back over the ruckus. "Thus, to maintain balance in the cosmos, the Obscura's engines make constant temporal adjustments to certain rooms—cycle changes. You!" He halted, and made a gesture at one of the galleries above. "Come down here at once."

A head appeared over the banister of one of the levels high above them, peering down. This version of Garstone appeared to be much younger than the others. "Me, sir?" he replied. "I'm on my way, sir."

"Two minutes," Sabor said to the group. "Hurry. We have one more level to climb." He ducked under a brass lens tube and set off again around the curve of the gallery, one of his wing tips brushing the banks of ticking, whirring clocks against the wall.

Rachel felt dizzy and uncertain now, suddenly unable to decide if she was doing the right thing. The whole group seemed intent on shoving her back into the past for no good reason. *To build rafts?* Those rafts hadn't helped Dill escape. Even Rachel's future self had admitted as much. Wouldn't it be more sensible to stay here and protect Dill now?

But then she realized how foolish she was being. This was an opportunity to be seized, a ten-hour window during which time she could alter the course of recent history.

She might still be able to save her friend.

"What else do I need to know?" she said to Sabor.

"You need to know how to chop wood and lash logs together," the god replied.

"No, I mean about Time . . . about this castle."

"Nothing."

"You called it a labyrinth in Time, which means that there are hundreds of doors back into the past. If one plan fails, can't we simply try another?"

"Do not deviate from the current plan," Sabor said. "It is the best way to limit the damage already done. Every single time we step outside the Obscura Redunda there are consequences, unforeseen paradoxes, and further stresses on the whole continuum." He consulted his timepiece yet again, and frowned. "You must understand: The Obscura itself is eternal and indestructible—it cannot exist solely in one point of Time. At any given moment, large numbers of its rooms are in the past. So if the castle exists at time X, other parts of it also exist at time X minus an hour, or X minus ten years. And because those rooms lead back into this very chamber, the whole fortress carries the entire history of its own existence wherever it goes."

"He just means," Iron Head added, "that it's older than it looks."

"Older?" Sabor grunted. He had reached the third staircase, and now raced ahead up it. "There are paths in here leading back through the vast emptiness of the cosmos," he said over his shoulder, "to times long before the birth of this galaxy. These are routes impassable to humans, which are traveled solely by the gods. Several copies of myself are currently attempting to map them. Other gods, too, no doubt, from aeons past. Countless billions of explorers! And because the castle existed at the birth of the multiverse, then one must be able to move it, eventually, to every point in space. My observations lead me to believe that space is collapsing in upon itself, and the multiverse is shrinking. At one point it may indeed have been no larger than this fortress itself, which begs the question: Were all possible universes created inside this castle?"

He reached the top step and glanced around him. "This way!"

"But if that's true, then *who* created the castle?" Rachel asked.

"Ayen did."

"After the...multiverse was already created!"

Sabor looked at her with an expression of faint distaste. "The lower orders have trouble wrapping their heads around that paradox. Ayen is, as you say, part of the universe, and yet by creating the castle she may well have created the very reality she now occupies. This castle is a singularity. Unfortunately it is *this* truth that will make it so difficult to reach Heaven."

"You know why we're here?" Rachel asked.

"Of course I do. You told me earlier, or later." He waved a hand in frustration. "It hardly matters now. Here is the timelock we seek, the entrance to the Greengage Suite!"

He strode over to a nearby door and examined the dial below the porthole. "Less than a minute left," he said. "We made it with scant time to spare." He pulled down a huge brass lever and swung the timelock door open. "This will take you back ten hours before now."

Rachel just shook her head in confusion. "I still don't understand," she said. "You said the universe around us is failing, but the castle is eternal and indestructible. Why can't you use it to reach a time before Ayen sealed the gates of Heaven?"

"Thirty-two seconds," Sabor said. "I don't have *time* to explain. You need to go *now*."

Rachel's thoughts were still spinning. She looked from Iron Head to Mina, and then at her future self. She felt suddenly afraid. "What happens to me?" she said.

"You end up standing on this very spot trying to persuade your past self"—she pushed a finger into Rachel's chest—"to step through a sodding door."

Sabor glanced at his watch again. "Twenty seconds."

Rachel peered inside the timelock. It was a small cylindrical chamber with an identical door and porthole on the opposite side. Through this she could see a library with its own extension of Sabor's pipe-work obscura and a window overlooking a dull, misty landscape. By the texture of the light, she judged it to be early morning outside, rather than late afternoon as it should have been.

Just as Rachel was about to step inside, her future self said, "No offense, sis, but one of me is quite enough."

She shoved Rachel roughly into the timelock, and then slammed the door shut behind them both. Air hissed. Immediately, her twin threw open the other door and pushed Rachel through.

The assassin landed on her backside on the library floor. She scrambled to her feet, and spun round.

The twin had already closed the library door behind her. She waved once through the porthole, and stepped back out of the timelock.

And then she vanished.

The outer timelock porthole was empty. Mina, Sabor, and Rachel's future self had disappeared. Nothing but an empty landing. A version of Garstone strode past, carrying his book, and gave her a polite nod.

Rachel went over to the window and pressed her hands against the chill glass. Fog blanketed the mountain outside, forming a bleak tapestry of black and grey that reminded her of a coal quarry. She could not even see the lake from here. Low in the east, the sun glimmered as faintly as a brass penny.

She turned away from the window, angry that her other self had denied her the right to make her own decision, and resolved to find Sabor. She stormed across the library and threw open both timelock doors.

Garstone stood on the landing. "Good morning, Miss Hael," he said. "I am so sorry I missed you later this afternoon. Sabor required a younger me than those older replicas of myself that were available at the time."

And indeed this version of Sabor's assistant *was* younger, though not nearly as youthful as the figure who had peered over the banister a few moments ago. This Garstone looked middle-aged. A creased brown suit hung about his shapeless shoulders. The chain of a pocket watch dangled from his breast pocket. From his hand-wringing posture to his watery blue eyes, everything about him exuded meekness. He stood there on the gallery surrounded by the tick, clatter, burr, and chime of countless clocks.

"How did *you* get here?" Rachel asked. "You weren't in the room."

"No, miss. I missed your departure by just moments, so I was forced to travel here by an alternative route."

"An *alternative* route?" Rachel's anger rose. There *had* been another way to get back here after all. All that rushing around had been merely to get her out of the way quickly, to consign her to a menial task that Sabor had deemed to be a necessary part of whatever grand scheme he'd concocted.

"An initial leap of ninety-four days through the Lavender Suite," Garstone said, "after which I stepped back four more days, and then six months more before I rediscovered the correct timeline. Then all I had to do was wait—a refreshing sojourn in the main Obscura Hall. Thereafter I picked up the path again via the

Farthing Suite." He bowed his head. "The entire journey took me no more than fourteen years."

"Fourteen *years?*"

He looked peevish. "I did miss one connection, which cost me eleven days. I'm afraid I'm no longer the youthful version of myself that Sabor had enlisted for the task."

Rachel studied him. "How many different timelines are there now?"

"It's hard to say, miss. There are two main lines, as it were, but changes made recently in each of those have created many smaller branches. Temporal corruption is rife throughout the whole continuum. Excuse me, but you *are* Miss Rachel Hael, are you not?"

She nodded. "And you're really Iron Head's brother?"

"His given name is Reed, miss. Reed Garstone. I disapprove of that vulgar moniker used by his men. But, yes, as you say, he is my brother. Older by one year, three months, nine—"

"Okay," she said impatiently. "How do I get back to Burntwater? I'm going to need a boat to take me across the Flower Lake."

"Burntwater, miss? But we are to proceed no further than Kevin's Jetty. I was led to believe that that was all explained to you. Upon our arrival I shall endeavour to negotiate a contract with the Hericans for the construction of a flotilla of small craft. After which—"

"Yes," she said through her teeth. "I know all that, but I'm not doing it. Building those rafts was a waste of time."

"If you deviate from the plan, you will change history," Garstone said. "Sabor's calculations have been quite meticulous. We need to build—"

"His original plan changed history," she cried, "and accomplished nothing!" She couldn't shake the image of Dill from her mind, dragging his shattered body from the lake. Right now she had a chance of preventing his destruction.

"But . . . Miss Hael, in our future those events have already happened. We are here to ensure that they *do* happen, that they con-tinue to have happened, if you will. If we stop those events from occurring, the multiverse will create another new branch to ac-commodate our failure, and the entire continuum will be further weakened as a result."

"Where is Sabor?" she demanded.

"I have some drawings of the proposed rafts..." Garstone went on, with evident distress. "If we—Miss Hael, where are you going?"

She was going to find the god of clocks. It was bad enough that they'd forced her back here without even waiting for her consent, but now they expected her to adhere to their ridiculous plan. The more she thought about it, the more it seemed that her bitchy twin had forced her into the timelock simply to get her out of the way. It was the sort of thing Rachel herself might have done.

I ought to have punched that woman!

Rachel halted, and touched the bruise under her eye. A bitter smile came to her lips. *I'll bet you're laughing now, sis.*

She didn't halt again until she reached Sabor's camera obscura table. The god of clocks was nowhere to be seen.

Garstone hurried to catch up with her. "The master is indis-posed, miss."

"*Where* is he?"

"Not so much where, but *when*, miss."

"*When?*"

"This appears to be one of those pockets of Time that Sabor has not yet experienced. He prefers to keep himself moving between critical or interesting moments in Time. The Obscura Redunda al-lows him to skip the more...mundane stretches of Time entirely."

"So he's avoiding me?"

Garstone looked at the floor. "My master will arrive before you return to the castle this afternoon. He must do so; otherwise you'd never have met him."

The assassin grunted and stormed towards the door. She wasn't about to wait around for Sabor to appear, and she certainly wasn't about to spend the next ten hours chopping wood to build rafts. She had time to reach Burntwater before Dill, Mina, and her other self arrived there. Now all she had to do was think of a way to stop the forthcoming battle and save them all.

John Anchor and Harper picked through the wreckage of the *Rotsward*, searching for soulpearls. Little now remained of the huge wooden skyship. The mental link between Cospinol and his slave had been the real source of the vessel's strength, but Cospinol's death had severed that link. The ship had become nothing more than timber.

Harper swept her Locator over a tangle of ropes and broken planks. The silver device in her hand made a keening sound.

Anchor looked up.

"Nothing," she said. "The environment is confusing my Locator—all these dislocated souls. It's hard to find something as small as a soulpearl amongst all this...gore."

"But there is less blood than before, yes?" Anchor replied cheerfully. "And less with every passing moment. So we still have hope."

The River of the Failed had moved on. Its myriad waterways were still draining away, even now, in the direction Carnival had taken. The river was *following* her.

In its wake it left a red wetland of low banks, ankle-deep arroyos, and refuse. The sinking waters uncovered more wreckage with each passing heartbeat. Anchor found scraps of armour and weapons left by the gallowsmen. Sodden beams lay piled everywhere like the beginnings of bonfires. He found bent lumps of iron, hinges and nails, and even pieces of furniture. But there were no bodies. The departing currents had consumed all of those.

The rope that had once tethered him to the *Rotsward* stretched far across the landscape, like the corpse of some vast serpent. He stooped and picked up a section of it, and then let it drop. Strange that it seemed so heavy now.

Instinctively he reached for the leather pouch at his belt, but of course he had swallowed the last of his soulpearls. An odd feeling of irritation came over him, but he shrugged it away. He would just have to make do until he found some more.

"John, look up."

Anchor followed Harper's gaze. Overhead loomed the Maze in all its hideous glory. Shafts of lamplight fell from countless windows in the uneven brickwork. A huge gouge existed where the *Rotsward's* upper scaffold had been dragged through the underside of Hell. The buckled iron and shattered facades around the edges exposed whole apartments, now ripped open and bleeding profusely. A few figures lingered on the brink of the chasm, peering down into the queer realm below.

"Aye, I would be curious too," he admitted. "They have not seen such a thing in Hell before. I suppose."

Harper pointed more urgently. "No, look there."

Anchor lifted his eyes again. This time he noticed a blunt, cone-shaped object jutting from the shattered rooms at one side of the rent. This odd protrusion was dull grey in color and looked out of place amongst all the red brick and black iron. On a ledge below the object stood a little girl. She was waving at them.

"Isla?" he said.

"That vessel of hers might be able to take us out of here," Harper replied.

Anchor frowned. "I need to find Cospinol's stash of soulpearls," he said.

"Forget that." Harper made a dismissive gesture. "The river consumed them all." She waved back up at the tiny distant figure, then held up both her hands to tell the girl to stay where she was.

"No," Anchor insisted, "my strength will fail without them.

We must keep searching." He picked up a huge cross-section of gallows wood and flung it to one side. There was nothing underneath but more of the fleshy red terrain.

"You don't need your strength any longer," Harper argued. "We can't stay here, John. We must get back to Hell."

He wheeled to face her, suddenly angry. "Did you not hear what I said? I need more souls! Now use your damn Locator to find me some, before I . . ." He growled, and kicked at a pile of planking, sending the fragments spinning in all directions.

The engineer just stared at him. "John, what's wrong with you?"

"Nothing," he muttered. He strode away from her to search through another likely mound of debris. In truth he could not remember feeling this way before. It took him a moment to understand what the pangs in his stomach indicated.

Hunger.

When he reached the debris he set to work shifting aside pieces of wood and knots of rope. Curved fragments of a large iron pot lay half buried underneath. Then another warrior's helmet, a length of lead pipe, and a bow. Anchor examined each in turn and tossed them away. Useless, worthless rubbish. He instinctively reached down to his belt again, before he remembered that the pouch was empty. He gave a snort and bent to his task more quickly. Sheets of tin, splintered decking, a pot, planks, planks, and more bloody planks. He heaved it all over and stood gasping.

Something huge fell from the sky and smashed into the ground a hundred yards away. It had been a section of brick wall. Blood rain spattered down after it.

Anchor lifted his gaze once more.

The base of the Maze was cracking and breaking apart as a huge, tapering metal object pushed downwards through it at a shallow angle. Huge lumps of iron and masonry shuddered free from that weighty sky and fell all around him. Glass cascaded down in sparkling showers. Loose bricks fell amongst clouds of dust. The hull of Isla's ship trembled, but ultimately broke free from the stonework. Clear vapours streamed from vents at the rear of its hull, blurring the atmosphere around it.

Turning slowly, the submarine began to descend towards them.

Anchor took one deep breath and then another. The muscles in his jaw felt unbearably tense. His teeth hurt. He stood rock-still and watched the vessel drift down from the sky, wondering what— if anything—there was to eat aboard.

10

CHANGE OF PLAN

Garstone harried her heels. "Sabor has given us clear instructions. Miss Hael? The rafts must be built to assist your own escape across the Flower Lake. Failure to adhere to the plan will have unknowable consequences."

Rachel wrapped her arms around herself against the cold. She kept her gaze firmly on the path ahead to avoid looking back at Sabor's strange ethereal castle. "The rafts weren't necessary," she said. "It was Dill who kept Menoa's arconites off our backs, not your pathetic diversion."

"Are you quite certain of that, Miss Hael? In the fog, I mean—"

"Enough, Garstone. We're doing this my way."

She was still furious with the others for forcing her into this position, but she had resolved not to act on that anger. Another version of her was currently inside Dill's mouth with Mina, heading for Burntwater even now. What good would it do to allow the events to unfold as they had done? Sabor expected her to enlist the Hericans at Kevin's Jetty, construct this foolish diversion, and then row out into the lake, where she would meet herself and give herself the bruise that now throbbed under her eye. But even if she did all that, the arconites would still destroy Dill. There had to be a better way.

After an hour's descent along the misty trail she and Garstone reached Kevin's Jetty. Greasy smoke billowed from every chimney pipe, and thickened the air around the shacks and the old jetty itself. The heady smell of boiling fish permeated everything. A mud track ran between the buildings, deserted but for a scraggy white cat.

Rachel had no trouble stealing a boat.

She selected a small but sturdy-looking craft from those beached upon the shingle strand behind the settlement. She bent against the vessel's prow and pushed. The hull scraped a few feet closer to the water. Garstone checked his pocket watch and then glanced back towards the houses, seemingly unsure what to do. "Please, Miss Hael..." he said. "Sabor devoted several hours of study to developing the original plan. He believes that it was the best solution to keep the timeline stable."

"Help me with this thing."

"Consider the consequences of what you are doing, Miss Hael. This rash decision will cause Time to split once again—you are creating an entirely new universe whose future we cannot predict."

"It can't be any worse than the last one."

"You don't know that, Miss Hael. At the time of my departure, Menoa's arconites had not yet reached the Obscura Redunda. Your friend Dill was wounded, but alive. There yet remained hope of finding a way to reach Heaven."

Rachel panted as she heaved at the boat again. It grated another foot closer to the mirror-still lake. "What hope?" she gasped. "Did you see what Menoa's arconites *did* to Dill? How could he have possibly stormed the gates of Heaven in *that* condition?"

Garstone shrugged. "I don't believe Sabor intended to use your friend in an assault," he said. "He has been working on his own solution to the Mesmerist problem. At least..." He closed his mouth.

"At least *what?*"

"Nothing, miss." He consulted his pocket watch. "We still have nineteen minutes to begin negotiations with the Hericans. It isn't too late to change your mind."

With another shove the stern of the boat sloshed into the water. Rachel pushed the vessel further out and then climbed in, over the prow. "Are you coming, Garstone?"

"Miss?"

The boat began to drift. Rachel dug an oar into the lake bed to halt it. "If I'm going to change history," she said, "I could use you with me to help ensure that I change it the *right* way."

Sabor's assistant gave his pocket watch yet another fretful glance. "I fear you have already changed history," he said. And then he slipped off his shoes and socks, rolled up his breeches, and waded into the lake after her.

Rachel didn't know exactly how to reach Burntwater amidst this fog, but she recalled that the lake had not been particularly wide, and she had about eight hours remaining before Dill arrived in the settlement. If she struck out directly away from shore, she ought to reach the other side before long. From there she could follow the water's edge.

She rowed, while Garstone leaned against the stern and frowned at his timepiece. "Twenty-three minutes have passed since you were supposed to have contacted the Hericans," he said. "Actually, it's closer to twenty-four."

"You're not going to keep this up all the way to Burntwater, are you?" Rachel muttered.

He gave her a look of reproach. "We are no longer in our former universe, Miss Hael. *You* have created this particular branch of the multiverse yourself. Even now it is careening wildly down an uncharted path. If we returned to the Obscura now, we might be able to predict some of the future events you have just set in motion." His eyes flicked down. "Twenty-four minutes and ten seconds."

"You want to *return?*"

"It is the most sensible thing to do now."

"We're not going back."

Garstone's gaze returned to the pocket watch. He opened his mouth to speak, but Rachel cut him off.

"I don't care what time it is!" she cried, heaving at the oars. Other than those gentle splashes at either side of the hull and the steady creak of the oars in their locks, the Flower Lake remained utterly still and silent. Fog smothered the boat in a soft grey veil that seemed to stifle all other sounds. No birds called. No breeze stirred the lake surface. The air smelled of pine and the cold metallic tang of water.

They traveled onwards in silence for a long time.

Eventually Rachel discerned trees in the mist ahead, and before long a rocky shoreline materialized. The forest encroached upon the water's edge, a barrier of dense shadow stretching in both directions. She brought the boat to a halt and sniffed the air. The merest scent of woodsmoke might have told her where the settlement lay, but she couldn't detect any such odour. She listened hard, but heard nothing at all.

"Right or left?" she said to Garstone.

"I do not know, Miss Hael." Another glance at his watch. "We have spent forty minutes and ten seconds aboard this boat. It might be too late to change the course of events in this universe, but we can still abandon it and flee back to the Obscura. Once there, we might find a pathway back through the castle to an altogether earlier time. It might only take a few decades of travel within the labyrinth of time to find a route back to this morning. To speed things up, you could create more versions of yourself—"

"No," she said. "There are too many of me already."

"Another Rachel Hael might be more amenable to working with the Hericans. Sabor's plan could still be implemented."

"Forget it. I'm going left."

No sooner had she made the decision than a voice called out from the shore: "The current dragged you east of Burntwater. You need to turn right, little sis."

Rachel's head snapped round.

On a boulder by the shore sat a woman wearing a white shirt and tan cotton pants. She was much older than Rachel, a decade or more, but Rachel nevertheless recognized that pale face and those bright green eyes. Once more Rachel found herself looking at a temporal version of herself.

"Gods damn you!" Rachel cried. "You followed me here!"

"No," the other Rachel said. "Well, yes, but not in the way you think I did. I'm not the woman you've just left behind."

Garstone raised his eyes to the heavens and sighed. "The complexities of the Obscura Redunda..." he muttered. "This is not a good omen. Am I also with you, Miss Hael?"

The older Rachel smiled sadly. "Not this time, Eli. I came here on my own."

"To avert disaster, I presume?"

"Perhaps."

Rachel sat in the boat and stared at the newcomer. She had aged reasonably well, she supposed. Her bruises and wounds were gone, but she noticed wrinkles across the other Rachel's brow and around her eyes. Her hair had suffered, too; her skin looked tired, her breasts...

Rachel sighed.

"Don't be angry with me, sis," the older Rachel said quietly. "I've walked a long, long way to be here. You really need me to be with you now."

"Why?"

The older woman shook her head. "The less you know, the more chance we have of success. I need events to run as closely as possible to the way they did in *my* universe. There might be a moment when I can affect a change, but I don't know exactly when that moment might be. Much depends on it, though. That's all I can tell you."

"But something must have gone wrong...something terrible. Otherwise you wouldn't be here." Rachel's anger left her suddenly. She sensed an aura of sadness, even despair, coming from this older woman. *As if she's harbouring painful secrets.* "I fucked up, didn't I? By changing history I've only made things worse. The Hericans' rafts must have actually made a difference."

The other woman said nothing.

Rachel swallowed and said, "Okay. What do we do to fix it?"

"You can start by giving me a lift."

The three rowed west in gloomy silence. Rachel kept glancing up to find her older twin staring at her. Their gazes met often, but always parted.

"Isn't there *anything* you can tell me?" Rachel said.

Her other self smoothed the front of her white blouse. "I'd love to tell you a thousand things," she said, "but I just can't risk it. Let's not corrupt this timeline any further. Let me just watch what happens. I'll know what to do when the time comes."

"You can't even tell me if we manage to find Heaven and stop Menoa's arconites?"

The other woman thought for a long moment. "There are lots of universes," she said, "and many possibilities are played out. But right now I'm only concerned with this one, sis."

"Sis?" Rachel grunted. "Somehow that word doesn't seem as insulting coming from you. But why do you care what happens to this world if there are better outcomes elsewhere?"

"You know why."

And Rachel did. If the decisions she made today led to immense suffering in this world, then wouldn't she try to come back here and prevent it? "Look at me," she said, "the Spine's only philanthropic murderer."

This world?

She had already begun to think of this place as a mere corridor in a much larger Maze: *The labyrinth of Time*, Garstone and Sabor had called it. She hoped this particular passageway wasn't a dead end.

"At least tell me how Sabor escaped Coreollis," Rachel said. "I didn't get a chance to ask him."

The older Rachel looked uncertain.

Garstone said, "He didn't escape, Miss Hael. Rys, Mirith, Hafe, and Sabor all died that day."

Rachel frowned, but then she understood. "They must first have made temporal replicas of themselves?"

"Only Rys and Sabor have ever existed as multiple versions in one place," Garstone replied. "Hafe and Mirith simply believed that they were replicas of their real selves. Sabor convinced them of that over supper one night. In fact those two gods were unique, the only two of their kind in the whole universe. They are quite as dead as their brother Rys, and will remain so unless Sabor returns to pluck them from history."

"I'm surprised that even a *copy* of Rys agreed to sacrifice himself."

Garstone smiled. "An astute observation, Miss Hael. A temporal replica believes himself to be the real person, the definitive one, and of course in a sense he is. They all are. Rys was not at all the magnanimous type—a character trait shared by his own replica—and each of them was quite incapable of sacrificing his life for the benefit of the other." He reached for his pocket watch, but stopped himself. He smiled again. "My master found a way around the problem, however. On that fateful day, *both* temporally distinct versions of Rys were inside the bastion. Each schemed to betray the other, and thus secure his own escape. Sadly, the collapsing building killed them both while they fought each other inside."

Rachel laughed. "I knew I'd seen two of him in there. There's more to your master than meets the eye."

"He is used to thinking in parallels, Miss Hael."

At last they reached Burntwater. Jetties and wooden buildings loomed out of the grey air. They tied up against a wharf at the easternmost end of the settlement and clambered up onto the muddy promenade flanked by old shingled houses. This waterfront street ran all the way to the warehouses at the center of the town's dock area. Rachel recognized the buildings from the earlier battle that had taken place there...*would* take place there. The fight, the mass evacuation—none of it had happened yet.

"You have a plan," Rachel's older self said.

"I did, but now I don't know what to do. Anything I try might destroy the future."

"Stick with your plan. I'll be watching for the instant that something may go wrong."

"But you don't know what my plan is."

"You intend to meet with Iron Head and warn him about what's about to happen. You'll plead with him not to attack Dill—and to keep all of this a secret from the version of yourself now approaching. And then you'll get him to pass a message on to Dill himself, so our giant friend knows exactly how to escape his enemies."

Rachel gaped. "How did you know *that?*"

"Because it's exactly what *I* did."

"But...you stayed in Herica and built decoys. You were never *here.*"

The other woman nodded. "I put the Hericans to work on their rafts, but did you really think I'd stay with them and merely chop wood when Burntwater was only an hour across the lake?" She lifted her blouse and withdrew a short knife hidden there. She examined the blade and then stuffed it back into her belt. "No, sis, while the Hericans laboured, I rowed across here and did exactly what you are about to do now. I was waiting here in Burntwater before you ever reached the town. Didn't you think it strange how Iron Head used your surname before he could have known it?"

So what's the truth, Miss Hael? Rachel recalled the captain's words.

"And didn't you wonder why he wanted to crawl inside Dill's skull?" the other Rachel added. "He was delivering the same message you are about to give him. He told Dill how to escape from Menoa's arconites." She paused while Rachel took this in. "When you met me there on the lake," she said, "I was actually on my way back to Kevin's Jetty."

Rachel's thoughts spun. She felt somehow betrayed. "So now it's *my* turn to do what you did?" she said. "Except the only difference this time round is that *I* didn't contact the Hericans. There are no decoys out on the lake. You could have met me at Kevin's Jetty and just told me the truth. Why didn't you do that?"

Her older self said nothing.

"What are you hiding?"

She shook her head. "I'm sorry, sis."

Garstone checked his timepiece. "Ladies, might I suggest—"

"I know!" both women said at once.

Rachel took a deep breath. "Where do we find Iron Head?"

"I can't say. Who knows what else I might change if I told you? You'll find him, sis."

So Rachel walked up to the first house in the street and banged on the door. After a moment the door opened and an old woman peered out.

"Where do I find Captain Iron Head?" Rachel asked.

"Captain who?"

"Garstone," Rachel said. "Reed Garstone, the captain of the Burntwater militia."

The old woman scrunched up her eyes. "On the wall, of course. Where else would he be at a time like this? Ask them at Headquarters. They'll know exactly where he is."

After a short march up the main thoroughfare they found Headquarters located beside Burntwater's southern gate. A squat, rectangular log building, it was barely large enough to contain forty men standing shoulder to shoulder. Lean-to sheds set against two of the walls held pigs and chickens. The entrance had been left unguarded, so Rachel simply barged in. Her older self chose to remain outside. *To preserve the integrity of the timeline*, she explained.

Nevertheless, when Rachel opened the door she was relieved to find Iron Head himself seated at the room's only table. The captain had removed his cap, revealing a lank mop of dark hair, and hung his sword and hammer on hooks on the wall behind him. He looked up from the map he was reading and frowned at her. "Can I help you?"

Rachel opened her mouth to speak, but then realized that she hadn't exactly thought through what she intended to say. However she put it, the news she was about to divulge would sound like the ravings of a madwoman.

And then Garstone walked in.

Iron Head's brows rose. His gaze flicked to Rachel, and then back to his brother. "Eli!" he said. "Long time, no see."

Garstone consulted his pocket watch. "Technically, Reed, it's less than a day since—"

The captain raised a hand. "Don't bother, Eli. It's the same old thing every time we meet. It's always disconcerting when you recall conversations with me that haven't happened yet." He grinned at Rachel. "He never remembers my birthday, though."

Rachel felt a surge of relief. "I have something...odd to tell you," she said.

Iron Head leaned back in his chair and put his hands behind his head. "It wouldn't be the first time," he replied.

King Menoa was seated in his newly formed library at the top of the Ninth Citadel when the whole fortress began to howl. He set down the book he had been reading and said, "Enlighten me."

The walls and floors within his fortress, like the very books in this library, had each been adapted from Hell's dead to serve whatever purposes Menoa required of them. But, unlike his Icarate priests, these simple constructs had limited intelligence. Unable to define the exact cause or nature of its distress, the floor simply gibbered nonsense.

"Word from the foundations!" it yelled from a single grey mouth in the very center of its tiled expanse. "Subsidence and fire! A presence. The citadel is flooded. There has been an earthquake, my lord. Lightning struck the clock tower. Your precious library is burning to ashes."

"The library is not burning," King Menoa replied. "Such a thing is impossible here."

But the books moaned and trembled nervously upon their shelves all the same. Menoa wondered briefly how many of their stories might have changed in that instant of panic. Fear was too often the source of misrepresentation, and the dead lied no less than the living. He approved of change—chaos suited his nature—but did not condone the unknown event that had caused *this* particular change. Surprises irritated him.

"A star has plunged through the guts of the fortress," the floor wailed, "and left us vulnerable to intruders."

The king rose from his chair. "What intruders?"

"A great army is within, my lord."

"There is no such army in Hell! Has the Ninth Citadel lost its mind? Send a witchsphere to me. Order my Icarates to attend."

Perhaps he had allowed this building to grow too quickly too soon. It now contained three thousand and three levels, and so afforded him a striking view across Hell. But, by forcing such growth, had he also stretched the building's capacity for rational thought?

"Slaughtered, all slaughtered," the floor howled, "their minds sucked out by the red water."

The red water? A sudden chill gripped Menoa's heart. Had the River of the Failed breached his fortress? From where had it acquired the courage and the *wits* to do such a thing? He growled at the floor, "Stairs, down."

The surface of the floor rippled suddenly and then melted away, forming a square spiral of steps that descended to the lower levels of the Ninth Citadel. The king snapped his fingers and torches flared all the way down in that well, suddenly bathing the library ceiling in their shifting light. He moved to throw his book away, and then stopped and glanced at the final page.

. . . formed a staircase down to the lower levels of the king's magnif-icent fortress. His Glorious Majesty, the Lord and Ruler of all the Maze, swung his arm to cast the poor, frightened—although loyal—book aside, but in his wisdom he stopped and stole a glance at the final page.

Useless thing. It was now trying, in its own fawning manner, to describe the events around it. He tossed the offending tome hard against the library wall, and then stormed down the stairwell he had just made, wondering how the book would interpret that re-sponse.

All the rooms below were equally agitated. The king strode purposefully down the shaft leading through the heart of the citadel, past writhing walls of eyeless constructs that held the very slabs of stone he now used as steps. Others raised yellow lanterns to light his way, or simply reached out towards him like beggars. Menoa bent the shapes of those who dared come too close. He cre-ated doors wherever he felt like it and portals so that he might gaze into the rooms beyond the walls. The steps quivered under his boots, while the blind figures in the walls moaned and cowered. These constructs were terrified, but not of him.

Not of him!

Anger was not something the Lord of the Maze had much ex-perience with. He found that it clouded his vision. He preferred to detach himself from his emotions, for only then could he analyze them and alter them to suit his purposes. But now his glass mask changed to form new and feral expressions, almost against his will. He endeavoured to calm himself.

Could the River of the Failed actually have entered the most powerful fortress in Hell? It certainly had the strength to do so, but he doubted it possessed the desire. Despite its power, the river was merely a child. Since it had learned who its father was, Menoa had taken swift steps to discipline it. He could not harm it, but he could make it respect him.

The king paused on the stairs, as a splinter of doubt entered his mind. What if Cospinol had somehow managed to turn the river against him? After all, there had been no sign of the sea god's vessel since the portal broke. Had the *Rotsward* gone *underground*?

Menoa willed the walls to cease their moaning. Hundreds of voices fell silent, though the lanterns still trembled in their grips.

For the first time since his rise to power, the Lord of the Maze felt fear. He gazed up at the vast spiral he had made through the building's heart, the myriad doors he had unconsciously created around the shaft's perimeter. Why had he done *that*? He looked down into the hazy depths, where a hundred levels stood between him and the citadel's dark foundations.

Where were all his Icarates? They ought to have responded to the building's cries of distress.

He faced the wall and made a gesture with his hand. The constructs parted with a soft rending sound, allowing the king to step through.

This led him to an unattended suite in which items of old furniture, left for aeons without a guiding will, had crowded together into one corner as though trying to escape. The king waved a hand and returned them to their rightful places. He opened another portal in the wall beyond.

A moment later he reached the outer facade of the Ninth Citadel. Here he willed the stonework to blister and form a balcony, which he stepped out upon.

His glass claws gripped the fresh bones and tendons of the balustrade he had just constructed. From this height he could see far across the canals of Hell. Temples and ziggurats of rotten black stone crouched amidst the red haze like huge dead spiders.

Heavy barges plied the soul routes to every corner of the Maze. The skies were unusually busy with Iolite movement, he noted abstractly.

And then he looked down.

His Icarates were indeed responding to the citadel's pleas. Great numbers of them massed around the huge pyramidal Processor, driving dogcatchers and Non Morai and every other sort of demon and spectre before them. Thousands more of the king's creations were pouring into the citadel itself.

A flash of light drew his attention back to his own level. One of Menoa's many spies, an Iolite in the shape of a glass-winged lizard, alighted on the balcony. Its transparent feathers clashed and glittered, and then in a calm and pleasant voice it said, "The Ninth Citadel is under attack, my lord."

"From whom?" Menoa asked. "Is it the river?"

"The river accompanies her," the lizard said. "It hounds her heels like a dog, consuming the demons and Icarates that fall under her sword."

"Her?"

"She is an angel, my lord."

Menoa's glass mask assumed the visage of a frowning human. "Is she from the First Citadel?"

"She is not dead, my lord."

Realization struck Menoa. A warrior *hidden* aboard Cospinol's skyship? Perhaps he had underestimated the old god . . .

But who was she? Where had Cospinol found someone powerful enough to attack the greatest stronghold in the Maze—*by herself?*

"Are you quite certain she is not from Hell?" he asked.

The Iolite snapped its beak impatiently. "She is *alive.*"

King Menoa's mask began to change again, its glass mouth turning upwards into a cold smile. He strode back into his fortress and further descended the central shaft without a tremor of hesitation in his pace, for Cospinol had just given him an unexpected and wonderful gift.

"We don't have any explosives," Iron Head replied, as he adjusted his steel cap.

"But you must have," Rachel insisted. "You said they'd been ready since the battle at Coreollis. They were put in place before the enemy arrived."

"Clearly I lied, then. How many did you see?"

"How many *bombs?*" She tried to recall the sequence of explosions that had destroyed the town. "I don't know . . . at least twenty, I suppose."

The captain thought for a moment and then nodded. "That sounds about right," he said. "We ought to be able to scrape together that much powder before the Red King's automatons arrive. We've enough coke and saltpeter, although we're low on sulphur."

Garstone clicked shut the cover of his pocket watch. "If the original Miss Hael—which is to say the version currently approaching this town in an arconite's jaw—is to reach the Obscura Redunda in time to return to this moment, we must evacuate Burntwater by sixteen minutes past three this afternoon."

Iron Head nodded. "So we have about four hours." He rose from his seat and plucked his scabbard and hammer from the wall behind. "I'll make the necessary arrangements. Miss Hael, will you show one of my lieutenants exactly where to place the powder kegs? I'd like to position them as closely as possible to the locations where you saw them explode."

Rachel agreed.

Outside, she wasn't surprised to find that her older self was nowhere to be seen. She exchanged a glance with Garstone, who pressed a finger to his lips. *Maintaining the integrity of the timeline.*

No doubt the other Rachel was still watching events unfold from somewhere nearby.

The captain gathered a group of his men together and issued his orders, and soon the whole settlement began making preparations for both the battle and the evacuation to come.

Burntwater became a labour camp for the next two hours. Rachel wandered the streets with Garstone and one of Iron Head's soldiers, a studious young man who scribbled notes on his slate with a piece of chalk. They chose the locations for the powder kegs to match, as precisely as possible, the places where Rachel had witnessed explosions going off. Armoured soldiers ran between the stockpiles, laying fuses. Sailors and fishermen readied their boats for a sudden departure. Citizens were informed of the evacuation plan and told to pack food and water, but nothing more.

Later in the afternoon, the same watchtower lookout whom Rachel had allowed to escape arrived in town. She was already waiting with the captain and Garstone outside Headquarters when the young man reined in his mount. Iron Head's lieutenants helped him down from the saddle.

Barely older than a boy, and dressed in oversized leathers, he spoke in breathless fits. "An arconite . . . Captain, it destroyed our tower . . . killed Bennett and Simons. It was huge . . . Captain . . . Armed with a blade as big as a barge. It's coming this way."

"It's all right, son," the captain said. "We've been expecting just such an attack since Coreollis fell. Get yourself down to the docks and report to Cooper. He'll get you onto a boat." He turned away, but then paused and looked back at the boy. "You did well, son. You've given us plenty of warning."

Once the boy had gone, Iron Head said to Rachel, "We're manning the walls now, Miss Hael, so if I were you I'd make myself scarce. I suggest you take your boat out onto the lake and wait for me to turn up with your other self."

"You can't let her know about all this," Rachel pointed out.

"I'm supposed to be the one who explains things to her." *And punches her.* Rachel suppressed a wince. She now found herself in almost exactly the same position as the future twin she had met out upon the lake.

Almost exactly.

"Don't worry, Miss Hael. I've never met you before. We'll fling our arrows at the monster, and dodge the missiles he throws at us."

Rachel nodded. She needed to find her older self now, though with any luck she wouldn't require her help after all. The powder kegs were all set, and her approaching self would be kept in the dark about all the preparations made here today. The whole situation looked set to replicate the events she remembered.

And perhaps she could still save Dill.

"One more thing, Captain," she said. "How deep is the lake?"

"About a hundred and fifty fathoms. Why?"

Deep enough. Rachel felt a surge of hope. "Not long after I first met you," she explained, "you climbed inside Dill's skull. I mean . . . this all happened in the battle that's about to come. You said you wanted to look inside the arconite for yourself. I couldn't understand why at the time, but now I do. You were giving Dill a message from me."

"What's the message?"

"In all the smoke and confusion to come, he might have a chance to escape from Menoa's giants—"

"If he submerges himself underwater and walks across the lake bed?"

Rachel's eyes narrowed. "Have I told you this part of my plan before?" Had yet *another* version of herself already been here?

"No, Miss Hael, it just seems obvious to me. Your giant friend doesn't need to breathe, after all." He scratched his beard. "If Dill is going to flee under the lake, the best place for your friend Hasp is likely to be inside the air pocket in the angel's skull."

Of course. It made perfect sense to Rachel. Hasp would be able to breathe for a short time while Dill escaped. She could save both of them.

The captain added, "I'll tell you to put Hasp there before the king's arconites arrive. Until then, we'll let your plan to foil Oran run as planned."

A horn blared from one of the watchtowers atop the Burnt-water walls. Iron Head turned to go, but then paused. "These automatons have engines, don't they?" he asked Rachel.

"The engines are just an affectation, a device used to reinforce the Mesmerist conditioning enforced on the soul. They're not functional; therefore, water won't affect them."

"No," Iron Head replied. "I mean they produce smoke, and a trail of smoke rising from the water will betray your friend's position to his enemies." His brow furrowed again. "If we had more time, I'd have worked on some way to disguise that trail. Some sort of diversion, perhaps."

The watchtower horn blared a second time. "Time for me to begin the charade, Miss Hael," the captain said. Hurrying away, he called back, "I look forward to meeting you soon."

Rachel felt numb. The Hericans' rafts had not been constructed to disguise the Burntwater vessels' own smokestacks. Rather, they had been designed to mask Dill's engine fumes as he fled under the lake. But now, without such decoys, her friend would be exposed. There was no way he could escape by submerging himself under the lake.

And Rachel's older self must have known that.

A voice behind her said, "I know what you're thinking, but you're wrong, sis."

The assassin's temporal twin stepped out from under the eaves of a nearby building.

Garstone gave the older woman a smile. "There you are, Elder Miss Hael."

"You can stop that *Elder* thing right now, Eli," she replied.

"Sorry, Miss Hael."

The older Rachel walked up to her younger self. "We could never be sure how much of an effect the Hericans' rafts might have had on the fate of this universe," she said. "The outcome Sabor witnessed here was too...extreme for us to take any chances. Building those rafts might have altered what we had already perceived, and confused events to such an extent that we wouldn't know exactly when to step in and fix the problem."

"So you've been keeping this world running the way *you* perceived it, because you've already figured out the exact moment to intervene? You know *exactly* what you're going to do."

Her elder self said nothing.

"And you can't tell me?"

"Not without risking everything."

Rachel spread her hands in exasperation. "But if it wasn't just the rafts...then what do I do to fuck up so badly?"

Her other self gazed down towards the docks. "You need to keep doing whatever you are planning to do. I'll stay close by, unless I feel that my presence will badly affect the course of events."

"I was planning to get out of here."

"Let's go, then."

They had only just reached Burntwater's waterfront when Dill began his fake attack on the settlement. Rachel heard a dull crashing sound and spun around to see the giant automaton approaching the palisade wall. The plates of Maze-forged armour glowed unearthly green in the fog, and his great tattered wings encompassed the sky. In his hands he clutched the Rusty Saw tavern, much battered now and listing to the side. He hesitated, leaking black fumes from his shoulders, and surveyed the town's defenses with empty eyes.

Had Dill paused like this the last time? Rachel couldn't remember. Her mind spun with vague recollections and countless possibilities. Something was about to go very wrong, an event she herself would cause to happen. She stared up at the automaton's grinning maw, from which another Rachel now peered out, the same woman she had been so recently.

Arrows lanced upward from the town defenses as bowmen let loose. A second barrage followed a moment later. Dill raised the tavern above his head, and roared.

"Don't overdo it, Dill," Rachel muttered.

Transfixed, she watched the pretend battle unfold. Dill crushed the palisade wall and roared and stamped craters into the ground, careful not to hurt a soul, while unbeknownst to him the Burnt-water militia acted out their own charade. They fought back convincingly, loosing their arrows freely because they knew Dill could not be harmed. Events, as Rachel remembered them, unfolded precisely as they should have.

Garstone tugged at her arm. "Miss Hael, I don't think it's wise to remain here. The automaton might decide to head this way."

"He does, Garstone. He's coming straight for us."

"All the more reason for us to depart."

They ran for cover in a dead-end alley round the corner of a nearby house, just as Dill came thundering down the main thoroughfare. He stopped at a wharf, scooped up a small boat from the lake, and then turned and threw it at the advancing forces.

"It's all happening the way I remember it," Rachel said. "Nothing's different." She glanced over at her older self, but that woman was too busy watching the lakeside to respond.

Dill roared again and retreated into the lake, his massive iron-clad boots smashing boats and jetties to splinters.

And then he froze, let out a terrible groan, and slowly toppled forward to his knees. The resulting wave pitched boats up out of the harbour and slammed them onto the dry land beyond. Cold water sprayed Rachel's face, and she heard Iron Head's men cheering as they rushed forward.

And then she heard a cry for help coming from within the arconite. To Rachel's ears it didn't sound particularly convincing.

Garstone apparently agreed. "I believe that attempt at distress came from you, Miss Hael," he said. "It is fortunate that you didn't actually *need* the cry to sound authentic."

Iron Head and his men played their parts well. They gathered nervously around Dill's jaw, gaping at the fallen giant with genuine awe. A moment later Iron Head himself came forward. Rachel could not hear much of the conversation that took place between the captain and her former self, but those snippets she did manage to catch sounded more or less as she remembered them.

A runner broke through the ranks of the Burntwater militia, calling out for his captain. In the moments that followed, all hell broke loose.

"This is it," Rachel said to her two companions. "Menoa's arconites have arrived. This is where the fake battle becomes a real one."

Garstone snuck a glance at his watch. "Perhaps this would be a good time for us to head back to the boat," he said. "If you are going to meet yourself on schedule, we do not have much time left."

Rachel had to agree, and yet she was reluctant to leave. Her former self had just stepped out onto the promenade. Mina followed a moment later, cradling her dog in her arms. Basilis immediately began to bark.

"This is an evacuation," Iron Head yelled. "Women and children to the barges and skiffs. Holden, signal the pilots. Spindle, take your men—you already know what to do. I want twelve units, four to the east..."

Rachel shrank back against the side of the building. Mina's dog had spotted them. Even now he struggled against his mistress's grip, his little eyes fixed on the three intruders.

"...Bernlow, Malk, Cooper, Geary, Wigg, someone else—you, Thatcher—keep the attackers divided, and away from the wharfs. Harry them and then retreat, but don't let those bastards step on you."

Rachel didn't know what to do. She recalled Basilis barking

like that after they'd stepped outside. Still, nothing had noticeably changed. She glanced back.

Mina was staring directly at her. Their eyes met for an instant, and then the thaumaturge looked away. She said something to Rachel's other self.

Nothing's wrong with him. He's obviously just barking at you.

Mina! You knew I was here all the time.

The scene continued to unfold exactly as Rachel remembered it. A series of great crashes came from the south. On the opposite side of the promenade Dill set the Rusty Saw tavern down upon the ground. Oran stormed out to argue with his brother. Soldiers were running back up towards the Burntwater defenses in response to the new threat. Three horn blasts sounded the evacuation.

And on it went. Transfixed, Rachel watched herself and Mina carry Hasp up onto Dill's open palm. She watched as Dill raised his hand up towards the heavens. When he finally lowered his hand once more, only Mina and Rachel's other self stepped down.

"We've just put him in Dill's mouth," Rachel explained.

Garstone gave a gentle cough. "Fascinating," he said without a mote of conviction. "Shall we retire to the rowboat now, Miss Hael?"

"I'm supposed to do whatever I feel is right," she reminded him, "otherwise I might corrupt this timeline. Well, I want to see this." She turned to the older version of herself. "*You* must have lingered here, too, because that's what I would do. Hell, it's what I'm doing now. We'll leave as soon as the explosions go off. It leaves me plenty of time to get out onto the lake and meet myself."

"Very well, miss," Garstone said.

A thought occurred to Rachel. "*You* weren't in the boat," she said to Garstone.

"Wasn't I?"

"No. I was alone on the lake."

Garstone made a sound of surprise. "I suppose this version of me must have died, miss. After all, this is a particularly dangerous environment."

She looked at him. "Perhaps you just decided to stay here?"

"I don't think that's very likely, miss. I have no intention of leaving you behind. Sabor would never approve of that."

"You might have been injured."

"That is certainly possible, Miss Hael. Although it would have to have been a severe injury to cause me to abandon you. If one cannot walk, one crawls, and if one cannot—"

"Well, what if you were unconscious?" she said. "You couldn't follow me then. You wouldn't even have to be particularly badly injured."

Garstone glanced at his watch. "Yes, no doubt that's it, Miss Hael," he huffed. "It explains my absence from the boat perfectly."

"Yes," Rachel said, "it does." She struck him hard on the side of the head, knocking him out cold. The small man crumpled to the ground in his faded brown suit.

Rachel grabbed him under his armpits and hoisted him up. "Help me carry him onto one of those boats," she said to her other self.

"You know I can't interfere, sis. Not yet."

Rachel groaned. "When I become you," she said, "don't expect any help from me." She thought about that for a moment, and then shook her head. "Forget I said that."

She dragged him backwards to the opposite side of the alley, away from Dill and the Rusty Saw, and propped him up while she surveyed the promenade. All of Oran's men and their whores had by now alighted from the stricken tavern. Hundred of refugees were already converging on the harbour. She spotted Rosella and Abner Hill, and felt a pang of regret. Would she be able to grab some gold for them now, while she still had a chance?

No, she couldn't risk it. Any decisions that affected the future, as she knew it, might trigger the events that led to the end of this world.

Her older self hung back, watching carefully.

"This can't be where I fuck up," Rachel decided. "Any version of me would have done exactly the same. None of us would have left him here to die."

Crowds jostled along the waterfront as the town barges steamed in from deeper water to dock against the wharfs. One unit of Burntwater militia was already herding people onto smaller boats, but most of the other soldiers now raced back into the town or began to fling burning torches against the dockside buildings. Fire crackled and leapt up the walls of the nearest warehouse.

Rachel waited until a group of refugees hurried past the mouth of the alley, and then dragged Garstone's unconscious body out across the promenade after them. One of his shoes fell off. Panting heavily, she reached one of the gangplanks where a queue of refugees waited to board.

"Can you take him across for me?" she said to an old couple at the front of the queue. The husband was old enough to be her grandfather, but tall and lean, and he looked strong enough to manage. He was already carrying a huge shoulder sack.

"Excuse me?"

"Take him," she insisted. "I need to go back and find my children."

The lie worked as she had intended. The old man tossed his sack onto the waiting barge, then slung Garstone's arm around his shoulder. With the help of a large woman already on the barge, they managed to hand the unconscious figure across the gangplank.

Now all the nearby warehouses were ablaze. Dill backed into the water and lifted two empty barges up onto the promenade to be loaded. Overhead, the massive wings of Menoa's arconites shimmered amongst the fog and smoke. Their armoured legs stood amidst the streets like war-blasted towers of steel. Sounds of battle came from the south, and then Menoa's arconite spoke: "King Menoa wishes to negotiate a truce, Dill..." Rachel ran back to the mouth of the alley to where her older self waited.

"What the hell is this?"

The voice belonged to one of Oran's men. A bearded giant, he stood at the corner of the alley entrance between two of the Rusty Saw's whores, each of them clinging to one of his arms. They looked disheveled and drunk. The woodsman's large dark eyes stared at the two Rachels for a moment before he glanced over at the promenade, where Rachel's former self still stood beside Mina. Then he shrugged the whores aside and drew his sword.

"Sisters, eh?" he said to Rachel. "What you doing sneaking about back here?" He shoved one of the whores away. "Go tell Oran what I caught here." The woman scowled at him, but then lifted her skirts and ran off in the direction of the Rusty Saw.

Meanwhile the voice of the arconite continued to boom: "...Have the king's warriors harmed any who tried to flee? Have they hindered this evacuation? Have we used our influence over Hasp?"

The remaining whore raised a tin flask to her lips and took a drink. "Twins, I'd say," she said. "That one's her spitting image. Look, she's even got the same cut above her ear."

The woodsman grunted. "What are the chances of that? Looks like mischief to me."

"Mischief," his companion echoed.

Rachel exchanged a glance with her older self. *Is this the moment you were waiting for? Is this the moment where history goes wrong?* The other Rachel must have understood the unspoken question, for she lowered her eyes.

The powder kegs exploded.

The concussion blew the roofs off the buildings on either side of the alley. Rachel dropped to a crouch as a great cloud of grit and spinning shingles rushed out over the entire promenade. Something struck her head, knocking her forward. A tinny whining sound expunged her thoughts.

But instinct took over.

She pushed herself up.

"Stay down," the woodsman growled. A fist grabbed her hair, forcing her head into the muddy ground. Dirt filled her nostrils. She glimpsed the edge of a blade.

And then the man suddenly released her. Rachel looked up to see his body slam against the side of the alley. Her older self now stood over her, lowering her leg from the kick she had just delivered.

Rachel gasped, "You intervened."

"Yeah."

"What about the future?"

"I'm changing it." She grabbed Rachel and hoisted her to her feet. "We need to run now, before..." Her voice trailed away. She was looking beyond Rachel towards the mouth of the alley.

Oran and a large gang of his woodsmen blocked their escape. There were scores of them, armed and angry and smothered in grey dust. The whore who had gone to fetch them sat on the ground nearby, blinking and staring vacantly at her hands.

The militia leader sneered at Rachel. "Sisters?" He laughed and shook his head. "But I know the truth. Your other version doesn't even know you're here, does she? She hasn't yet *been* to Sabor's castle to become you. What's the difference in time between you and her? A couple of days? And at least twenty years between you and *her*." He jabbed his sword at Rachel's older self. Then he turned to his men and said, "Take them."

Rachel's older self stepped back, her eyes darting between the approaching soldiers, *calculating the odds*. Rachel didn't even know if the older Spine assassin could still *focus*. A supernaturally fast attack right now might slay five or more of the enemy. *Leaving fewer than forty for me*.

She'd faced worse odds in her time.

But her other self made no such move. She simply lowered her head and stepped forward, allowing Oran's men to seize both women.

With all the chaos going on around them, nobody noticed

Oran's men steer their captives away from the docks. They marched away from the lake and turned into an empty street running parallel to the promenade. Here the houses on the landward side had been all but obliterated by Iron Head's powder kegs. One of Menoa's arconites filled the dusty skies above, while Dill's own vast form towered behind them. Oran yelled, urging the group to hurry on between the two giants.

A voice rang out across the heavens: "... continue to reject our attempts at diplomacy. Should we crush your bones right now, or will you stand amongst us and hear King Menoa's terms?"

Rachel knew what was coming, but it still made her jump. Dill buried his massive cleaver in the other automaton's neck, driving the huge warrior to its knees. Its shins burst through the rubble mere yards from their fleeing party. One of Oran's men cried out and fell, buried under a collapsing wall. The others covered their heads with their hands against the spewing dust.

Now prostrate, but looming directly overhead, Menoa's fallen creature had noticed the humans underneath it. Its vast dark eye sockets seemed to stare into Rachel's own soul.

Oran was yelling up at it, "... Menoa to form an alliance. We have—"

Dill slammed his knee into the arconite's face and sent it pitching backwards. He turned suddenly and his cleaver flashed across the sky over their heads, disappearing towards the east. The ensuing gale whipped up dust from the street. The blow struck its target several blocks away with a mighty *clang*.

"... speak to him," Oran finished shouting. He growled with frustration, and then ordered his men to head deeper into the stricken town.

Rachel found a chance to whisper to her other self. "I hope your moment is still to come, sis," she said. "The brakes are off this universe now. We're well and truly careening down the road of the damned."

"I know."

"Can you *focus?*"

"Yeah."

"Well, that makes one of us. I won't be quick, but I'll back any move you—"

One of her captors shoved her forward. A dozen of his fellows followed behind, as battered-looking and ashen as earthquake survivors. They coughed and spat and constantly dragged leather gauntlets across their eyes. Whirlwinds of embers scorched the heavens behind them. The group moved on, turning south again at another intersection, while overhead the battle amongst the giants raged.

She could not now tell where they were, since nothing recognizable remained of Burntwater. She wondered if her former self had escaped with Mina by now. They would cross the lake under the cover of fog, but Rachel herself would not now be waiting in her own boat to meet them and guide them to Sabor's castle. She would not now punch her former self in the face.

Rachel lifted a hand to touch the bruise under her eye. The flesh there still felt tender and sore. How could she have sustained the blow when she had not been there to deliver it?

But of course that had all happened in a different universe than this one. *This* world was the one where everything went wrong, where the future would become so unbearable that Rachel herself would come back from another time to try to fix her own mistake. She turned to face her older self and said, "What are the consequences of all this? Does it really matter if you tell me now?"

The other woman hesitated, and then said, "Dill loves you. He'd do anything for you. Even if it meant his own death. Even if it meant the end of this world."

"I don't understand."

"Don't let the Mesmerists take you alive."

Rachel nodded. Now at last she understood.

An order to halt came from ahead, and the party drew up before a steep bank of rubble. Oran was standing amidst rising vapours on the summit of this obstruction, his hands cupped around his mouth as he shouted up against the great clamour of steel from the skies. Fuming clouds of smoke obscured all else.

But then Rachel spied something huge and metallic stir in the murky air behind the militia leader. The sounds of battle ceased. A shadow fell over her.

Her older self cried out and shoved Rachel hard to one side. But she wasn't fast enough. Five monstrous bone fingers descended and closed around the two women, the tips gouging deep furrows in the earth. The ground rocked, and Rachel fell against her other self.

She felt herself being lifted up rapidly into a cloud of choking dust. Below, Oran continued to shout, but she could not decipher his words. "Dill!" she cried. "Dill, is that you?"

But then a thundering voice came from very nearby: "I am told the name Rachel Hael holds meaning for you." A pause, and then the arconite spoke more gently. "Is this she in my hand, Dill? We will not harm her. The king has always desired peace between us."

Rachel's heart thundered in her chest. She struggled to breathe. "I hope you haven't missed your moment, sis," she said, rubbing tears from her aching eyes. "The future isn't certain yet."

She felt a hand squeeze her own. "No, it isn't."

Through a break in the dust she saw Dill's skeletal face. Or was it him? She couldn't tell anymore. The arconites were all around her now. She could hear the massive crash of their feet, the rumble of their engines. She smelled the Maze in every quivering breath she took.

"Kneel," Menoa's warrior commanded.

And then she saw him. He lacked expression—for that bone visage could muster none—but she knew it was Dill when he sank to the ground amidst the smouldering remains of Burntwater.

"Put down your weapon," the arconite demanded.

Dill set his stolen cleaver down upon a row of rooftops. The partially destroyed buildings collapsed beneath it.

"The king is pleased," the arconite said, "but he remains cautious. As a gesture of goodwill and submission, he requires that you permit us to return Lord Hasp to the Maze. We need his assistance to deal with a small matter there. Do this for the king and you have his word that Rachel Hael will not be harmed."

Rachel threw herself against the automaton's fingers, and cried, "No!"

"If you agree," Menoa's warrior went on, "you need only lower your head."

Rachel cried out again, but she couldn't stop what happened next. Dill lowered his head. Menoa's arconite raised its blade and brought it crashing down upon the top of his skull.

Dill's jaw slammed into the ground with the force of a rockslide. The resulting dust cloud billowed out over the whole settlement.

Rachel watched in horror as the dust settled. The stream of doubts Menoa's warriors had been planting in Dill's soul throughout the battle had successfully weakened him, for she could see that he was injured. A deep fissure now ran from the top of Dill's cranium down to his jaw. He managed to raise his head again. Blood flowed freely between Dill's teeth and down across his chin.

"Hasp?" Rachel cried.

"This is the moment, sis."

Rachel felt a hand on her shoulder. She turned to see her older self slipping her knife out from her belt. She looked tired, much older now than the two decades that separated them.

"What happens if you don't do it?" Rachel said.

"A lot of people suffer."

Rachel took a long slow breath. "I wonder if we missed another opportunity—if I had only done *something* differently."

"This was always the only way for us to be sure. It's too dangerous for either of us to exist here." She turned the blade over slowly in her hands. "I'll make it quick. Neither of us will suffer."

"But the Rachel on the lake manages to escape, doesn't she?"

"Dill won't stop the arconites' advance now. He doesn't know that that Rachel escaped, because you are here. As long as Menoa has one of us hostage, he'll obey the Lord of the Maze. This time-line is a dead end for us."

"But we must survive elsewhere?" Rachel insisted. "The universe where I met myself out on the lake ... that still exists, doesn't it? That other version of me is still in Sabor's castle."

The other Rachel nodded. "She's you," she agreed. "And she does survive, and grow older. And one day she realizes that no world deserves to suffer, not even a doomed one." She smiled sadly. "Doesn't make it any easier, does it?"

Rachel rubbed tears from her eyes. "No," she said, "it doesn't."

"Good-bye, sis."

"Good-bye."

11

CARNIVAL AND MENOA

Rachel felt finally relieved. The room into which her former self had stepped was now empty. The Greengage Suite had undergone another temporal shift, and now looked out upon a different Time altogether. She peered through the porthole to see a moonlit room.

A younger version of Garstone appeared, wearing a crushed brown suit. He tilted his head to his brother Iron Head, and then to Sabor. "You asked for me, sir?"

"You're late, Garstone," the god of clocks replied. "I needed you to accompany Miss Hael ten hours into the past, but you've missed your opportunity. She's already gone."

The small man took out a map from his inside jacket pocket and unfolded it. "Ten hours, sir? Hmm . . ." He frowned. "That does present us with a little problem, doesn't it?"

He scratched his head and then sighed. "There *is* a route, but I'm afraid I shall be fourteen years older by the time I rendezvous with her."

Sabor raised his nose. "Fourteen years is nothing. You'll still be fit enough when you emerge. Ah, thank you..." He snatched an envelope from the hand of a second, much older, Garstone, who just *happened* to be passing at that very moment, and gave it to the younger assistant. "Here are your instructions, along with some drawings of the decoys we'll build to ensure our friendly arconite eludes his pursuers. You have fourteen years to read them and less than ten hours to execute them."

"Those decoys were a waste of time," Rachel said, "and we're wasting even more time here. Dill needs our help right now."

Garstone accepted the documents from his master. "Thank you, sir. Now if you'll excuse me, I'd better be going. The first suite fails in"—he glanced at his timepiece—"fifty-three seconds." He hurried away and disappeared into one of the many doors.

Clocks chimed all around them as if in celebration of his departure.

"Now let's go." Rachel turned away without waiting to see if the others followed. Too many minutes had passed since they'd crowded around Sabor's obscura table and witnessed Dill crawling from the lake—an image that had already been seventeen minutes old. Anything could have happened to her friend since then.

The group assembled beside a glassy basalt outcrop at the edge of the plateau surrounding the Obscura Redunda. A freezing wind shrieked past their ears, while the walls of the castle flickered and throbbed behind them. From up here Rachel could see for leagues in each direction along the Flower Lake's northern shore: peninsulas and crescents of silver beach; the smudge of smoke over Kevin's Jetty; the green wooded hills rising up in banked mounds from the water's edge to the dour Temple Mountains; and, half a league further down the slope below, the arconite Dill.

He was using his one good arm to drag his huge body up through the forested slopes. A clutter of pipes and bones and wire-snagged machine parts scraped along the ground behind his broken pelvis. In his wake he left a trench full of oil and broken trees.

Rachel ran towards the path that would take them back down the mountainside, but Sabor called after her, "You can't help him."

"I have to help him," Rachel replied.

"He's too big," the god of clocks said. "You can't carry him up here, and you can't repair him. He has to make it on his own."

"He might have to drag himself," Rachel said, "but that doesn't mean he has to make the journey alone." She wheeled away and sprinted down the track.

She had barely covered two hundred yards before Iron Head caught up with her. She heard his leather armour creaking, and the thud of his boots behind her, and looked back to find him grinning.

"You gave Sabor a lesson in compassion," he said.

"I've never met a god who didn't need one," she replied. "Except for Hasp, and he tried to kill me."

A yelp came from somewhere behind. Rachel glanced back up to see Mina struggling down the steep trail a short distance away, her glass-sheathed feet slipping in the loose dirt, while her little dog sauntered along beside her. There was no sign of Sabor—apparently he had decided not to come.

They remained on the path for an hour before Rachel heard the arconite's enormous body smashing through the forest. She turned in the direction of the sounds and led her two companions through densely packed trees. All was silent except for the regular crunch of the canopy breaking up ahead, and the rhythmic thud of bone striking earth.

He stopped moving when he saw them. His massive arm collapsed to the ground with one final crash, and his jawless skull simply settled upon the hillside and lay there, staring.

Rachel burst into tears. She scrambled over to his skull and pressed her body against it. The dead bone felt coarse and hard under her hands, utterly cold. The arconite's great skeleton stretched far down the slope below in a mess of twisted metal, pipes, and ribs.

Rachel felt a hand on her shoulder and turned to find Mina standing beside her.

"He can't speak," she said. "Let's find his soul."

The narrow passageway leading into Dill's soul chamber had been left exposed by his missing jaw, and they had little trouble finding it and crawling inside. The chamber within remained gloomy, only partially illuminated by dim shafts of daylight falling through holes in the arconite's cranium. In the very center, the glass sphere containing the angel's spirit rested amidst piles of broken machine parts and blue crystal shards.

A hooded figure was slumped on the floor with his back against the sphere, an empty whisky bottle in his hand. He looked up and groaned.

"Hasp!" Mina shouted, rushing towards him.

The Lord of the First Citadel clutched his head in his hands and groaned again. "Stay away from me, thaumaturge," he said. "I don't know where I am or what I might do. It seems I've been in a battle, but I have no recollection of it."

"You're hungover," she said.

"That, too." Hasp tilted his head back and closed his eyes.

Rachel stepped over debris and placed her palms against the glass sphere. The ghosts inside drifted through each other like dreams, passing in and out of Dill's own spectre. Their voices assaulted her mind:

Too late . . . too late . . . It is dying . . . He should not have fought, and now . . . Killing us . . . Too late, the blow from above . . . withering . . . Such pain, and dust, and darkness . . . Leave us alone . . .

"Dill?"

His voice sounded faint. *I was coming to meet you at Sabor's castle.*

"It's not far now."

He was silent a moment. *This hill nearly finished me.*

"Are you in pain?"

Some.

She pressed her face against the cold glass. "But you got away from them. You made it here."

I lost the cleaver.

"That doesn't matter." A tear ran down over the smooth surface of the sphere and broke against her hand. She didn't know what to tell him. They couldn't heal him, and they couldn't take him inside Sabor's castle. If he managed to crawl to the top of the mountain, he would have to remain there while the rest of them went inside.

Mina pressed her hand to the glass an inch in front of Rachel's face. "Do you realize how much of a mess you're in, Dill?" she said. "They've completely destroyed you."

Mina?

"Mina!" Rachel glowered at her. "Do you have to be so fucking insensitive all the time?"

"Well, just look at him," the thaumaturge said, "or what's left of him. He's got no legs, one arm, and the rest of him looks like crawling scrap. He's not even going to make it to the Obscura."

"He'll make it," Rachel said.

"And then what?" the thaumaturge retorted. "He'll lie outside and rust. There's nothing left of him, Rachel, nothing here we can salvage."

A crack sounded above them, and a table-sized chunk of Dill's cranium fell down and smashed into a mound of shattered crystal at one side of the chamber. Hasp twitched and clutched his head.

Rachel grabbed Mina by her shoulders and wrenched her away from the sphere. "What are you doing?"

Mina's dark eyes narrowed. She leaned her face forward and whispered in Rachel's ear. "I'm telling it like it is, Rachel. He can't survive like this, and I think he should know that." She straightened again, smiling coldly. "Use your head, Spine."

And suddenly Rachel understood. Menoa's warriors had weakened Dill by planting doubts in his mind. This huge bone-and-metal body was only as strong as Dill believed it to be, so the other arconites had made it vulnerable simply by convincing Dill that he *was* vulnerable. Now Mina was trying to finish the job for them. If they weakened him enough, they might be able to break the sphere and release his soul.

Rachel glared at the other woman. "What happens to his soul if we can free it?"

"Most spirits can survive for a short while on this earth," she whispered, "and Dill is a lot more powerful than your average phantasm. When he was in Hell, he consumed a fragment of Iril, a piece of Hasp's soul, and . . ." She smiled. ". . . a little bit of me."

"How long could he exist outside this body?"

Mina shrugged. "He's a rather uncommon person," she said, "even for an angel. Why don't we get him out of here and see what happens?"

"Are you sure about this?"

"No," Mina replied. "But do it anyway."

Iron Head swung his hammer at the glass sphere. It connected with a loud crack. He examined the tiny white scratch he'd made on the smooth surface, shook his head, and then hefted the weapon once again. On the second blow the glass shattered.

Thus liberated, the ghosts from the sphere tore around the walls of the chamber in a vortex of vapourous hands and eyes and teeth. Rachel staggered as they howled past her face, grabbing at her, buffeting her, and she heard their cries in her mind.

Not in Hell . . . freezing . . . there's life, warmth . . . look at the glow . . . so cold . . . treasures . . .

Mina remained at the back of the chamber, her eyes closed. She was stroking her little dog and muttering something under her breath. Then she opened her eyes and allowed Basilis to jump down from her embrace.

The dog padded forward, growling.

"Stay out of my friends," Mina warned the spectres. "Possess any one of us here, and my master will drag you back out again and send you somewhere you really don't want to go. Do you know what a Penny Devil can do to a soul?" She smiled grimly. "If you thought Hell was bad, just wait until you see Basilis's house."

The spirit wind rose, shrieking, into a tighter spiral of twisting, gauzy figures that raced up towards a hole in the arconite's skull. In a heartbeat, they had departed, leaving one last ghost behind.

"You got your wings back," Rachel said.

Sort of.

His translucent feathers seemed to glow faintly blue in the gloom. He looked much stronger and taller than the angel Rachel remembered from Deepgate all that time ago, but he was dressed in the same tattered old mail shirt and breeches and carrying the same old blunt sword his ancestors had used. A few lines now etched his brow, but his eyes radiated calm confidence. He lifted a hand up in front of his face and looked straight through it, smiling.

I'm thinner, too, he said.

Hasp threw open the huge copper doors of the Obscura Redunda, and bellowed, "Sabor! Where are you? I'm sore, hungry, and in need of a drink."

The god of clocks eyed his younger brother with obvious disdain. "Welcome back from Hell, Hasp," he said. "You've lost your wings, I see. And your skin."

Hasp grunted. "That bastard Menoa got the better of me. He

only sent a million demons, mind you, but it had been a tiring week."

Sabor raised his chin, regarding his brother coolly from under half-closed eyelids. "I'm sure the battle was tremendously impressive."

They continued to converse, but Rachel stopped listening. She was watching Dill carefully from the corner of her eye. The young angel stood between Mina and Iron Head, gazing up in awe at the array of tubes and lenses packed within the high chamber. Had his body become more translucent, or was she just imagining it? It seemed to her that he faded in bright light, only to solidify once more when he stepped into the shadows.

"I don't suppose ghosts eat," Hasp said, "but the rest of us are starving, brother. We've had nothing since Dill abandoned the Rusty Saw."

Sabor sighed. "I'll have Garstone prepare supper."

Rachel turned to face him. "Do we have time for this?" she said. "There are still eleven arconites out there somewhere"—she pointed back towards the main doors—"and now we have no way of defending ourselves against them. We've no plan, no idea where Heaven is, and no way to provoke Ayen even if we could reach her."

Sabor merely raised his eyebrows. "Time?" he said, incredulously. "You ask *me* if we have time?"

They sat down to dinner in a sombre wainscoted and darkly paneled hall that, mercifully, existed in the here and now. The adjoining kitchen, however, bounced backwards and forward in time by as much as half an hour, which meant that the main courses arrived before the starters and the pudding appeared three minutes before it had been ordered.

Dill stood a little way back from the table, glowing faintly and with a half-smile upon his lips, content to watch the others eat.

Not one of them could fault the fare, however. Garstone cooked and waited on all four of his guests simultaneously, edging past alternate versions of himself as he carried plates to and from the dining hall. He walked through Dill constantly, but apologized unfailingly.

"The doors to Heaven," Sabor said between mouthfuls of roast lamb, "lie within a temple at the summit of this very mountain."

Rachel started. "Here?"

Sabor nodded. "However, knowing their physical location does not help us. The doors cannot be opened." He chewed thoughtfully. "Ayen removed us, her lawful sons, from Heaven after our uprising against her failed, but she expelled this fortress for an altogether different reason."

Iron Head drained his cup. Garstone hovered close by, trying to pour him more wine from a carafe, but Iron Head snatched the vessel from his brother's hands and filled his cup himself. "I won't have you serve me, Eli," he declared. "It isn't right." Then he turned to Sabor. "She couldn't allow the castle to exist in Heaven?" He paused. "With all these doors leading into the past, and who knew how many multiple versions of yourself living within, she would never feel safe."

"Precisely," Sabor said. "She moved the Obscura Redunda into this world, and by doing so moved the entire history and future of the castle out of her realm. It no longer exists in Heaven, nor has it ever existed there."

Hasp hunched over the table, ripping meat from a bone with his teeth, then rubbed one of his greasy glass gauntlets against the tablecloth. "Took a lot of power," he mumbled.

"The effort exhausted her," Sabor explained. "In that one instant of fury, she created a door inside her earthly temple, and through it she expelled every hint of our presence from Heaven. Our armies, our archons, our weapons—all were expunged from her sight. We had no idea she could summon up so much... *wrath*."

"But why?" Rachel asked. "What did you do to anger her?"

Hasp snorted into his wine cup.

The god of clocks smiled thinly. "We are her lawful sons," he said. "Ulcis, Cospinol, Rys, Hafe, Mirith, Hasp, and myself, all born of Ayen and her husband, Iril. By rights we should have inherited Heaven." He took a sip of wine. "But she never loved us. Never doted on us like she did her favourite child."

"Ayen had *another* child?" Rachel said.

He nodded. "A bastard, a half-human boy conceived after Iril had already taken our mother as his bride. She betrayed our father in the most unconscionable manner. She bedded a *mortal*, and you can imagine how Iril reacted to *that*."

Hasp gave another snort of derision, and then held out his wine cup for one of the Garstones to fill.

"Not well, I take it?" Mina said. She sniffed at her cup. "Is this wine off?"

Two Garstones appeared beside her at once. "I am terribly sorry, Miss Greene. It is so hard to keep track of the vintages in our cellar. Please let me replace it." One of him snatched the offending cup out of her hand and drifted away with it, while the other disappeared to find a fresh bottle.

"Not well," Sabor agreed. "Iril slew our mother's mortal lover and ate him. He would have murdered the bastard son, too, if she hadn't hidden the child away. Our father demanded that she give the boy up, but Ayen refused. And so began the War in Heaven."

"So the child lived?" Rachel said.

"For a short while," Sabor said. "Ayen was vulnerable after the war, you see? She had used every scrap of her power to expel us. So her bastard son left Heaven, sacrificing his own life to seal the doors behind him. He damned himself to Hell just to protect her."

Iron Head grunted. "Some folks might regard that as a noble gesture."

Sabor and Hasp both shot him a dark look.

"*Some* folks," Iron Head added. "Fools and traitors and such."

"But Iril ruled Hell," Rachel said. "What happened to the bastard there?"

"Our father had never seen Ayen's illegitimate son," Sabor explained. "None of us even knew his name. By the time we discovered the youth's identity it was already too late. In Hell the bastard rose through the ranks of Iril's followers. He distinguished himself, becoming one of our father's elite. But all the time he was plotting Iril's downfall." The god's lips thinned to a grim line. "Ayen's eighth, and favourite, son is Alteus Menoa, the creature who now calls himself Lord of the Maze."

A hush fell upon the room, only to be broken a moment later by the arrival of one of the Garstones from the kitchen.

"Pudding!" the small man announced.

"We didn't ask for any," Mina said.

"You will, Miss Greene, once you've tasted it."

They ate in silence for a while, but then Rachel had a thought. "If the doors to Heaven are impenetrable," she said, "why don't you just go back in Time and stop Menoa from sealing them in the first place?"

Sabor simply glowered at his pudding.

Hasp guffawed, and drained more wine.

After a long moment, Garstone said, "Shall I tell them, my lord?"

The god of clocks nodded.

Garstone turned to Rachel. "That has already been attempted," he said. "Lord Rys used the labyrinth of Time to return to the exact moment Alteus Menoa left Heaven. He tried to prevent the bastard from killing himself in his mother's temple."

"He failed," Sabor said. "But by leaving this castle, Rys corrupted our timeline and put the whole cosmos in danger. His meddling with history gave birth to a second universe running parallel to this one."

"And now both of them are failing," Garstone added. "You can see the evidence of it everywhere—glitches and bubbles in Time wherever the two streams overlap." He shrugged. "We've made adjustments here and there to try to keep our timeline from collapsing entirely, but the damage was done three thousand years ago."

"You don't get out of debt by borrowing more money," Sabor muttered. "I tried to explain that to Rys, but he wouldn't listen. The fool wanted to return to the source of the problem a second time, to try to capture Menoa *again*!"

"So you killed Rys?" Rachel said.

The god of clocks grunted. "The farther back one travels into the past, the more profound the consequences of one's actions. A third attempt to stop Menoa could destroy the entire cosmos."

Mina frowned. "Is the Lord of the Maze aware of all this?"

"Yes and no," Sabor said. "In this timeline, Menoa was not accosted when he spilled his blood in my mother's temple. But in the other timeline—the one Rys created—he understands what has happened. In that universe, his arconites have already reached the Obscura Redunda. If he conquers us *there*, he'll gain access to the labyrinth of Time, thereby allowing him to wander through both his own past, and ours."

Garstone cocked his head suddenly. "Did anyone else feel that?"

Rachel had felt it too: a tremor through the floor. No sooner had it passed, than another, stronger, vibration succeeded it. And then another.

For the most part, Hell's Ninth Citadel seemed to be constructed of people. There were no doors or windows here. Mouths set into the floors and ceilings shouted at her, and the walls...a mass of grey eyeless torsos reached out from those walls. They gnashed their teeth and groped at Carnival's wings, mewled and sniggered and spat at her, before she began to kill them.

After that they howled. Screams of terror and panic ran through the whole mad fortress as Carnival butchered a path through the writhing figures. Her demon sword flashing, she broke through into a second room, and then a third and a fourth...

The naked figures clawed at each other in their frantic attempts to flee, but they were already so knotted together that escape was impossible. And so they gibbered and died under the scarred angel's blade. She hacked off arms and heads and carved out chunks of flesh to make the openings through which she passed.

In this manner she reached a much larger room where the brawling figures reached to dizzying heights above. Many clutched slabs of pale stone that formed a rude and crooked stairwell arranged around the interior void of this tower. Others waved tin lanterns, bathing the scene in shifting yellow light.

Was this the center of the citadel?

She heard a trickling, rushing sound and turned to see the River of the Failed seeping up through cracks in the floor behind her. It quickly filled the rooms she had previously occupied, but it did not come any closer. Defying nature, the wall of water trembled at the rough-hewn entrance to this larger chamber, as though waiting for Carnival to proceed.

Carnival couldn't have explained why she was here. She had merely followed the river's current. But reason or motive did not matter while the blood in her veins screamed for battle. Everything around her had become an enemy. She needed to *hurt* this place.

The figures within the walls hissed and wailed. And then a terrible ripping noise issued from all those massed bodies. They parted in places, forming portals in the three undisturbed sides of the room.

Carnival raised her sword. She felt it tremble with fear.

The things that rushed, lurched, creaked, and hobbled into the tower were unlike anything the scarred angel had seen before. She rolled the blade in her hand, testing the weight of it. And then she dived in amongst them.

... warriors in pale ceramic armour that crackled and dribbled sparks upon the floor, and skinless figures with skulls full of teeth, and winged shades that could only be seen out of the corner of the eye, and human men bolted inside brass carapaces, and clattering wheels of bone or steaming machines full of spinning blades, and black jackals and aurochs and ragged howling priests on metal stilts, and dwarves with mirrored eyes and iron limbs, and swords, spikes, maces, pikes, bludgeons, whips, spears...

Carnival slaughtered them all.

And still they came, until she stood atop a mound of corpses and hacked at them from above. Her scars burned with the pleasure of the battle, as her hair clung to her face in a bloody net. Carnival snarled and laughed and spun in circles behind her demon sword, gutting and slicing, painting the walls with blood. She inhaled the dying breath of her foes and exulted in the taste of it. And the blade in her fist only wailed in agony.

The horde stopped.

And a soft male voice called down from above: "Those souls within your veins... are they *all* unbroken?"

Carnival looked up.

A tall warrior sat upon one of the steps some twenty feet above her. He wore darkly sculpted glass armour bristling with spikes and extrusions like wind-blasted ripples of ice. His opaque mask had been fashioned to resemble the face of a young man with arching cheeks and a narrow sloping chin, but Carnival imagined she saw another, even more beautiful, face behind it. *Golden eyes peering out through the glass?* There was something odd about the way the light fell on him, as if his translucent garb altered reflections in subtle ways.

"I can see through you," he said. "My Icarates should have

known better than to pander to your desires. You came here deliberately looking for slaughter, didn't you?"

Carnival just stared at him.

"Not one for conversation, are you?" the man said gently. "I am Alteus Menoa, son of Ayen and destroyer of Iril, and," he paused, "father to the river god that brought you here." He raised his gauntlet, indicating the flooded chamber below her. "The poor thing loves me like a puppy dog, but I see it is fond of you, too." He let loose a burst of bright, musical laughter. "All Hell is mine," he said, "and you are *most* welcome here. Will you stroll with me upon the citadel balconies? The view is extraordinary."

Carnival stood knee-deep in gore upon a mounded summit of her victims, her heart thundering. The stink of death filled her nostrils, and her bloody leathers hung in rags about her. She couldn't drag her gaze from this strangely compelling figure. *Something about him . . .* She became suddenly aware of her scars, and shifted awkwardly in a pointless attempt to hide them from him. The demon sword shuddered in her grip and wept.

"You've used that shiftblade badly," Menoa continued kindly. "By the way it's trembling, I'd say it is unaccustomed to the demands you've put upon it. Allow me to forge you a better one, a sword with purer memories of war."

"It cuts," Carnival said, and felt immediately ashamed of her own voice. What was *wrong* with her? Her own self-disgust fueled a fresh surge of anger. She lashed her wings and snarled, "Come down here and I'll show you just how well it cuts."

The sword let loose a terrible wail.

Alteus Menoa stood up. From greaves to helm his armour warped and rippled before settling around his body once more. Had he grown in size? He seemed at once more imposing than a moment ago.

He removed his mask and helm.

The face beneath *was* extraordinarily beautiful. Arched cheeks and eyebrows framed almond-shaped eyes that shone like gold. His skin was pale, faultless. He tossed his head, and hair like polished silver cascaded upon his glass gorget and shoulder guards. He smiled at her.

"All souls arrive here naked," he said, "freed of the natural constraints that so limited them in life. In your world they existed merely to survive, but such order is crude and animalistic. Nature has no other purpose than the continuation of itself." He swept a gauntlet across the disparate demons that still surrounded Carnival. "Observe these constructs. They have been given a *higher* purpose, one only possible because of Hell's nondeterministic nature. Your own sword is more beautiful than you in every way. Its purpose is granted by divine will, whereas yours is not."

He made a gesture with his hand.

Carnival's heart stopped beating. She felt the muscles in her arms and legs twitch. Her fist opened and she dropped the sword. Her scars tightened and seemed to crawl across her flesh. She fell to her knees and exhaled sharply. But her lungs would not draw in another breath.

"All those souls in your blood may empower you," Menoa said, "but they have never been in harmony with you. They are trapped in the hell that is *you*, but what can you offer them except rage and murder?" He shook his head. "Yet now that they are here, I can offer them so much more."

Carnival tried to breathe, tried to scream, tried to move. But her own body refused to obey her demands. Her hand made a claw in front of her eyes. She couldn't open her fingers. The ancient scars writhed upon her wrist and palm like thin red worms. Her flesh seemed to turn pale and crystallize.

She was changing into something else.

Another vibration. Sabor whipped the map from the obscura table and called up to the many Garstones on the balconies overhead,

"Lens zero, please, and snuff the lights. Show us what's happening outside *now*."

The lights dimmed. In the darkness Dill's vapourous form cast its own blue light. A series of whirrs issued from somewhere overhead, followed by a clunk. Rachel, Mina, and Iron Head gathered around the table, on which a blurred image was forming. Hasp stood back from the group and downed another cup of wine, while his brother Sabor reached under the table and cranked a handle around. The image on the table became suddenly sharper.

It was a view from somewhere high up in the castle. Yellow evening light slanted across the blasted mountainside, leaving shadows as black as the rocks themselves. A great expanse of green forest swept down towards the Flower Lake, from where the waters stretched on to a brooding, storm-racked horizon. Dill's huge, shattered corpse lay at the top of the trench he'd scraped through the trees. Someone had lit an enormous bonfire beside his skull, from which rose clouds of grey woodsmoke. Rachel could see men throwing more branches onto the flames.

"Oran," Iron Head said grimly. "He's made a signal fire."

To signal whom? Dill asked.

Rachel pointed at one edge of the image. "To signal them," she said.

Nine arconites were emerging from the frothing waters of Flower Lake, reeds clinging to their dripping wings. They advanced towards the shoreline, crouching low, dragging their massive blades through the surface of the lake. Torrents of water rushed out of the spaces between their steaming armour and their bones.

A hundred yards further out, the lake suddenly bubbled as smoke rose from its depths, and two more enormous skulls broke the surface of the water.

"That makes all eleven," Rachel said.

Hasp glowered at the image for a moment, and then said, "Tell me you have a plan, brother."

Sabor stared at the obscura table for a long time, his hands gripping each side. He glanced over at Dill, who stood nearby, his ghostly wings shimmering in the gloom, and then he returned his attention to the image on the table before him. "Phantasms," he muttered. "Phantasms..."

He suddenly straightened up. "We're going back," he said. "Right now. Back to the moment when Ayen's bastard sealed Heaven."

"Didn't you say that another attempt to stop Menoa could destroy the whole universe?" Rachel pointed out.

Mina yawned. "I remember him saying that."

"We no longer have a choice," Sabor said.

Hasp roared up into the darkness, "More wine!"

Sabor spread his map across the obscura table. The paper was old, and heavily inked with many lines and circles and miniature tables of dates and numbers. "This map details all the routes we've found that access the previous three months," he said. "But many of those now lead into the bastard universe, and so must be avoided whenever possible. As we proceed further into history we'll have to fetch additional maps."

"Where are they?" Mina asked.

"In the cellar," Sabor replied. "But there are far too many to carry with us. We shall simply take them as and when we need them."

Rachel stared at the complex patterns in awe. They were about to walk back three thousand years—to the very moment when Ayen expelled her sons from Heaven—in order to save the life of Alteus Menoa, the enemy who was even now trying to destroy them.

Sabor had crossed out many of the circles on the map before him. Those, he claimed, led to what he called the *bastard uni-*

verse—the second, parallel world Rys had created when he'd traveled back in Time to confront Menoa and thereby changed the course of history.

The air suddenly resounded with the chimes of countless clocks.

"That's the cycle change we need," Sabor said. "We must go. Garstone, I'll need every self you can now spare. We might as well generate some extra manpower while we travel. Do the Burntwater militia know what to do?"

"Iron Head will bar the castle doors as long as he can," the small man replied.

"Good," Sabor replied. "Then follow me." Holding his map, he led Rachel, Mina, Hasp, and Dill up into the castle galleries. They crossed balconies and climbed stairs, higher and higher. Each version of Garstone they passed joined the party, so by the time they reached the appropriate door on one of the higher levels, there was a crowd of twenty assistants in tow.

These made an unlikely following of quietly shuffling men dressed in an eclectic mixture of tatty suits. Rachel wondered where they found their clothes, and if they tailored them themselves. They were of various ages, from the middle years onwards, although each Garstone wore the same bland smile.

Hasp glowered at them.

Sabor led them all to the door of a suite, then checked his map again. "As expected," he said, "the Grenadier Suite is now fifteen days ago. This is a decent start." He opened the timelock door and beckoned everyone inside.

It was a squeeze, but the entire party made it into the chamber beyond in three shifts. The Grenadier Suite was a rather small chamber with walls draped in worn green velvet. A brass obscura tube extended out from the interior wall, terminating at a fat lens just inside the window. The view outside was of a dull grey afternoon.

As soon as the last of the Garstones shut the door behind him, all twenty of them adjusted their pocket watches. One Garstone wound the standing clock against the wall, while another opened the timelock door again.

"Onwards," Sabor announced.

Mina nudged Rachel. "Three thousand years of *this?*" she whispered. "Gods, Rachel, I don't know if I can take it. When do you think we stop for supper?"

"Where's Basilis?"

The thaumaturge drew back her robe. The little dog's head peered out of a deep pocket within. "Always near," Mina said.

The dog growled.

"He'd better not piss himself," Hasp grumbled. "He makes you smell bad enough as it is."

Mina merely smiled, and drew her robe back around herself.

Rachel soon lost track of the number of suites they visited. The views outside the castle's many windows changed from dawn to night to dusk in no particular order, as Sabor consulted his map frequently. They stopped for supper in the dining room after six hours of such time travel, whereupon the god of clocks announced that they were now two years earlier than the day they had begun.

Hasp sat apart from the group at one end of the table, drinking heavily. When Garstone approached the god for the umpteenth time to refill his wine cup, Hasp snatched the carafe from the little man's hands, shoved him away, and roared, "Leave it here, you bloody imbecile! How many times do I have to tell you?"

Sabor stiffened in his chair and remarked, "Whatever Menoa did to you in Hell, brother, pales in comparison with what you've done to yourself."

"What's that supposed to mean?"

"You are no longer the god I remember."

Hasp grunted. "Then kill me like you did the others, Sabor. At least *my* hands are clean."

New Garstones had regularly joined the party, while others elected to stay and wait until future times when new suites would become available. By doing so they could return to the past again, thereby increasing their numbers. Already the castle was teeming with replicas of Sabor's assistant—the further back in Time the party traveled, the more Garstones appeared to occupy the castle.

After supper they resumed their progress into the past. This time Sabor ordered only one of his assistants to accompany the party, leaving a multitude of others to remain here and join them earlier in Time if possible. He hurried Rachel, Mina, and Dill on up to the highest level, whereupon he announced they would leap back a full four years by stepping into what he called the Tansy Suite.

Hasp trailed behind, cursing gruffly to himself.

No sooner had Rachel stepped out of the timelock than she knew something was wrong. This room looked much more unkempt than the others. Spiderwebs softened the plasterwork cornicing. The rotten, worm-riddled furniture evinced an aura of long neglect, and even the nail heads in the floorboards had rusted. But a richly pungent stench indicated something far more sinister than a lack of housekeeping.

Here, Rachel.

Dill was standing next to an old horsehair couch, his wings floating behind him like pale blue auroras, and pointing down at a body lying on the floor.

It was a version of Garstone dressed in the remains of a dark blue suit. It had been dead for a long time, Rachel realized, for the flesh remaining upon its bones had partially mummified; the hair was dry and brittle. Deep indentations in the skull spoke of terrible violence. This poor man had, she supposed, been beaten to death.

One of the Garstones took the pocket watch from the breast pocket of his own dead replica and examined it. Then he looked up and said, "This is most unusual."

Sabor frowned. "When was he killed?"

Garstone compared the reclaimed timepiece with his own watch. "He stopped winding this six months from now, yet the state of his body indicates that he died long ago in the past. Either this corpse was carried here for us to find or..."

"He forgot to wind his watch?" Mina suggested.

Garstone shook his head. "No," he said with complete conviction. "That is impossible. I *never* forget." He thought for a moment. "I believe I did this deliberately—as a message."

"Wouldn't a note have been easier?"

"A note might have been removed from my corpse, Miss Greene. But who would bother to adjust or even look at a watch?" He nodded. "If I ever found myself confronted by an enemy within this castle, I would undoubtedly wish to record the time of that encounter in some subtle way. Furthermore, if I thought that my life was in danger... yes, now that I think about it, I would do precisely this."

Sabor stood grimly over the corpse. "Are you saying that this version of you found an intruder six months from now, and fled back in time to warn us?"

"I believe so. Unfortunately, whoever I encountered seems to have followed me."

"And now he's further back in history than we are?"

The assistant nodded. "Which implies that he's taken a more direct, and dangerous, route. You see, in order to get ahead of us, both this version of myself and his pursuer must have traveled through the bastard universe."

Hasp spat on the floor. "This is all bollocks," he growled. "I don't understand a word of what you're both gibbering about. If there's a faster way into the past, then why aren't you taking it?"

Sabor stared at his brother for a long moment. Finally he said, "The bastard universe is dangerous because the version of Menoa who inhabits it is aware of our plans. In *his* world, Rys appeared from the future and tried to capture him. Since he knows the Obscura Redunda as a threat, he will have sent his arconites and other agents here directly."

Hasp's eyes narrowed. "Then this whole castle could already be infested with Mesmerists?" he said.

"It's possible."

The Lord of the First Citadel slumped down upon the couch and let out a deep sigh. He held his head in his hands as, quietly, he said, "Fetch me whisky."

"That isn't going to help," Mina said. "It never has."

"What the hell do you know about it?" Hasp growled.

Rachel stepped forward. "This arguing is pointless. We don't know who killed this particular Garstone, and we don't know if we'll run into him, but we *do* know that the aggressor was most likely human. An arconite simply can't fit inside this castle, and other Mesmerists require bloodied ground to survive."

"She has a point," Mina said.

Hasp sighed wearily. "All right." He nodded. "All right."

Back in the main Obscura Hall, Sabor spent a few minutes bent over the viewing table in search of the safest route for them to follow. "We must avoid suites that have become junctions between the two universes," he said, "for it is through such rooms that our enemy may find his way into this timeline."

Garstone dimmed the lights while his master operated the machinery underneath the table. Sabor pulled levers, cranked wheels, and threw switches. His voice echoed through the towering galleries above:

"Lens nine-zero-four... The Foster Green Suite... Cycle through one to seven... Two days back, Garstone... We've lost that morning for good, so lock and bar the door."

In the gloom overhead there seemed to be a million men at work. Garstones ran between suites, winding clocks, fetching maps, opening timelocks, slamming doors, reading from dials, and sliding lenses into fitments as their master adjusted the huge brass optical device.

The views upon that circular white table flicked from one scene to another. To Rachel's horror, she saw mostly destruction. Image after image of burning forest and arconites flashed across the viewing table.

Sabor wore a look of grim determination. "These are not from our world," he explained, "but are visions of the bastard universe. The parallel version of Alteus Menoa has breached this fortress *somewhere* in the future. And now he is using the labyrinth of Time to return to his past. He's making changes, allowing his arconites to reach the Obscura Redunda sooner and sooner. He has traveled further back in Time than we are currently, so now he is ahead of us. We must hurry if we are to catch up."

A sudden rumble shook the building. The moving image projected from the obscura lens went out, plunging the castle into darkness. A moment later, small flames flickered and brightened overhead as dozens of Sabor's identical assistants lit candles on each of the galleries. Under these weak shifting lights, the optical mechanism in the center of the chamber loomed like a huge brass skeleton. The uppermost third of it was now wreathed in smoke.

"Something is here," Sabor said.

"Mesmerists?" Hasp growled.

"I don't know, but whatever it is, it isn't from our world."

"I like to think that in some other world all this would have been different."

The echo of the man's voice faded to silence, and white linen sheets came into focus. As Carnival's eyes grew accustomed to the light, she found herself lying on a clean, soft bed. A shaft of red light slanted down through the single window to form a hot slab on the white tile floor, but otherwise the walls were starkly whitewashed, illuminated by an unseen source. She spied a dresser, a tall mirror, a table, and a chair, all white, too. She was alone.

The room had no door.

She rose from the bed. Her body felt strange, somehow lighter. And indeed her old leather armour had gone. Instead she had been dressed in a simple linen frock, its fabric as pale and smooth as the skin on her wrists.

Carnival stared at the back of her hands for a moment before she realized what was wrong. A terrible numbness crept into her heart.

She had no scars.

She yanked back the sleeve of her frock and stared at her slender, supple arm, at the unblemished white flesh. She noticed how the hair hanging down over her shoulders was black and silky smooth.

"Such an improvement, don't you think?"

Carnival spun around, but there was nobody there. "Where are you?" she snarled.

Silence.

She leapt off the bed, and her bare feet pressed against cold white tiles. She felt suddenly giddy, unbalanced, and tried to spread out her wings for support. Her efforts resulted in nothing but a sharp feeling of panic.

She *had* no wings.

Carnival stood there for a long moment, completely disoriented, her heart galloping. She looked back at the window, at the fiery oblong it cast on the floor. Her gaze moved to the tall mirror in one corner of the room. From here she could see nothing in the glass but a reflection of the opposite wall. Fear gripped her more intensely.

"You know it's only a matter of time."

She recognized the soft, lyrical tones of Alteus Menoa. His voice had seemed to emerge from that far corner of the room, from . . .

She stared at the mirror again.

Cautiously, she approached it.

He was waiting for her behind the glass, in place of her own reflection. He had now discarded his glass armour for white breeches and a white padded doublet. His golden eyes and silver hair shone as he smiled. "Most souls adapt fairly quickly to new forms," he said, "but your soul is much older than most. The shock of seeing the face I have given you would be... traumatic."

"Show me."

The son of Ayen raised his brows. "No threats or fury—just a simple request?" He laughed. "You keep surprising me, Carnival. So much of you still remains hidden, buried under an ocean of anger and insanity. Even the souls trapped in your blood know little of you beyond your name. And even that, I suspect, is a lie. Who are you really?"

Carnival said nothing.

Menoa shrugged. "We'll reach the truth by degrees." He raised one slender hand, and an image began to form in the glass before him. It was of a human girl with coal-black hair and vivid blue eyes, small and slender and dressed in a plain linen frock. She was the most beautiful creature Carnival had ever seen, but why had Menoa conjured this phantom if not to make the revelation of Carnival's own appearance all the more hurtful? This other young woman stood before Menoa's own reflection, her head at the height of his chest. The Lord of the Maze leaned forward, bringing his lips close to the phantom's ear.

Carnival felt his breath upon her neck. And this time, when he spoke, she knew exactly where he was. "Do you approve?" he whispered into her ear.

Three thousand years of instinct activated the angel's muscles before her heart or mind could respond. She spun fiercely, lashing a fist round at him...

There was nothing behind her but air.

She turned back to the mirror, certain that the beautiful reflection had soured, that she would find her own hideously scarred face glaring back from that polished surface. She expected to see madness and pain.

But the same fair visage met Carnival's gaze. The Lord of the Maze had vanished from the glass, leaving the slender blue-eyed girl alone. Now, flushed and panting, her reflection gazed out at Carnival with a look of frightened awe.

Menoa's soft voice filled the room like music. "There is nothing for you to kill here," he said, "and no one to judge you. There is no longer any reason for you to carry scars."

A sob burst from Carnival's throat. She kicked the mirror savagely, shattering it. Then she snatched up one of the shards and drew it frantically across her arm, again and again. Blood welled in thin lines. The pain shocked her, but she welcomed it with a sort of wild desperation. She fell to her knees, dropping the shard, and groped for it again with slick, bloody hands. She picked it up and drove it into her thigh, crying out in pain.

Again and again and again.

Menoa's voice returned, now hardened by anger. "This is not your creation to destroy," he said. "Do you understand me? *It is not yours to destroy.*"

But Carnival was lost in her own pain and terror, driven by a compulsion that she couldn't fully understand. She needed her scars; her own soul required them. And so she used the glass knife until her frock hung in tatters and the white walls of Menoa's room were painted scarlet with her blood.

Smoke billowed from one of the uppermost suites of the Obscura. A sudden flare illuminated the high ceiling with ripples of red and yellow light. One of the Garstones called down for the others to fetch water, and then mildly added, "There appears to have been an explosion in the Camomile Suite."

Scores of Sabor's assistants rushed down to the kitchen to fetch pails, pans, and carafes of water, carrying them back to the upper galleries. Hasp looked fearfully up at the growing fire, until Sabor announced, "Explosions are the work of men, not Mesmerists. Is it possible this attack has come from our future? That this is merely cannon powder from Burntwater?"

"There wasn't any powder left in Burntwater," Rachel observed. "Iron Head's militia used it all."

"Then our enemies simply took it before you used it," Sabor replied harshly. "Stop thinking that every cause must precede its effect. Who knows how many universes now branch from this present moment? Menoa's forces are now in our future *and* our past, and they *know* where we are. We must leave this part of Time immediately." He whipped open his map and frowned at it.

The massive double doors to the Obscura Hall boomed suddenly, almost leaping from their hinges.

The nearest Garstone to Rachel jumped. "I believe that was a battering ram," he said, glancing at his pocket watch. "Our enemies must be outside."

Rachel stared at the door. *What manner of enemies?* Without the camera obscura, they had no way of safely observing.

A second concussion hit the doors, and the cross balk cracked. Dill drew his phantom sword and positioned himself before the door.

Could such a ghostly weapon even harm the living?

Sabor scrunched up his map and set off, beckoning the others after him. Dill turned his back on the main doors and joined the group as they hurried up three floors and stopped outside the fourth timelock along the gallery. Garstones ran past them, heading in one direction with various water-filled containers, passing other versions of themselves who were returning with empty vessels towards the kitchen.

Another boom sounded below, and wood splintered.

The god of clocks peered into the suite beyond the timelock. "An eleven-year jump," he said. "Unfortunately this suite appears to have been recently occupied."

Rachel cupped her hands around her eyes and pressed her face against the glass. In the gloom beyond the two opposing windows she could just make out a stuffy lounge, the usual antique furniture faintly lit by starlight falling through a tall window. But then she noticed the blackened wainscoting and wall panels, the scorched shelves of a bookcase. A fire had been lit here, but had failed to take hold.

"Is there a better route?" she suggested.

From below came the sound of smashing wood.

"None with such a long reach through Time," Sabor replied. "Nor any that is safer. The bastard universe has claimed most of the suites here, but this...this one should be untainted."

"Get in there," Hasp growled. "The castle's main doors are kindling. They'll be through them in a heartbeat."

Rachel pressed up against Mina and Hasp as Sabor closed the inner door behind them. Dill hovered in the air in front of her, his translucent form partly absorbed by Mina's body. Sabor opened the outer door, and the sour smell of smoke assaulted Rachel's nostrils.

Mina covered her mouth with her hand as she hurried forward to look out of the window. "It looks peaceful. There's no sign of... anything."

And indeed the whole castle was now silent. Rachel could no longer hear the commotion that had been so audible outside. They were in a cold, empty room smelling of fire damage.

Hasp glared at the singed furniture. "We could burn this place properly," he said, "and stop those bastards from following us back here."

It was quickly agreed.

They left the suite and moved back into the castle's Obscura

Hall. Now all appeared normal here, with no sign of the damage that would come later. Looking over the balcony, Rachel reassured herself that the main doors were intact. Sabor called over the six Garstones working on that particular level and gave them instructions, and within minutes the rumple-suited assistants were dousing the suite with lamp oil.

Standing outside, Mina looked thoughtful. "Could this fire we're about to light be the source of the damage we saw in that suite?" she asked.

Sabor was now studying a different map that one of the Garstones had handed him. "No," he said. "Not unless we did so further back in Time. The damage is apparent *now*." He looked up suddenly from the map. "Garstone!"

Two of them appeared at once.

"Yes, sir?"

"Find a suite to take you back a few hours, and light the fire *then* rather than now. Let's preserve the integrity of this timeline if we can."

"Right away, sir." The pair disappeared again.

Rachel still found it difficult to wrap her head around these constant paradoxes. Those two assistants would return to an earlier Time to light a fire that would be out before they arrived here, all to keep things as they should be and prevent this doomed universe from deteriorating any faster than it already was. And yet Hasp had only had the idea *after* they'd seen the aftermath of that fire.

Time, as Sabor had said, need not be linear.

Soon smoke wafted out of the Camomile Suite, but as a result of which fire Rachel did not know. Had these flames been lit moments ago, or much earlier?

Either way, the results were as expected. No pursuers came through the timelock and, for the moment at least, the castle appeared to be secure.

The views from the camera obscura, however, were grim. Nineteen of the rooms now looked out upon the bastard universe. They watched giants striding across blasted, war-ravaged lands: the Flower Lake was polluted, its waters copper blue and streaked with ochre, its shores rimmed by glistening black trees. Soul Collectors' caravans and gangs of human road agents traversed crimson trails that looked like wounds cut into the ash-grey plains. Cages of bone squatted amongst the dust of Burntwater, each silhouetted against a pale yellow sky. In every silent image Rachel imagined she could hear screams.

"The universe outside these walls is no more spoiled than before," Sabor announced. "Yet even greater numbers of the Obscura's windows now look out onto parallel worlds, as the Lord of the Maze continues to meddle in the past. Each time he makes a change, he creates yet another universe for his agents to infiltrate." He tapped his fingers against the viewing table, and then he made some adjustments to the mechanism underneath. A cool blue dawn appeared before them, the forest lushly green and holding pockets of mist. "Our own timeline appears to be safe for now," he added with a nod. "The previous attack must have come from one of our local futures."

He ordered his assistants to bring him as many of the local Time maps as he'd be able to carry and, thus armed, the party hurried further back into the past again.

Three hundred fewer years had elapsed by the time they stopped to rest and eat. The god of clocks even ordered his castle doors thrown open, so that they might take in the sunset while they supped.

The sunlight turned green where it bled through Dill, so that the young angel seemed to glow like an emerald against the amber sky.

From the castle steps they could see all the way down to the Flower Lake. Kevin's Jetty was no longer there. It would not exist for another two hundred and ninety-two years, Sabor explained. The forest had changed, too. Gone were the mass of evergreens they would later walk through to reach the Obscura. Instead, these trees were ancient and deciduous.

"The last pockets of wildwood," Sabor commented. "This is an arm of the Stoopblack Forest, or what's left of it. It extended all the way to Brownslough, where Hafe and I used to hunt together. These trees died out when the world cooled."

"Cooled?" Rachel asked.

"Our expulsion from Heaven affected this whole planet," Sabor explained. "Aethers poured out from Ayen's domain, forces malignant to this world, so whole lands were poisoned, skies burned, seas rose, and the earth cracked to its core. The clash of incompatible matter damaged the very fabric of this universe. We armoured ourselves in sheer will, and fell as stars do." He gazed into the long golden rays of sunset. "We arrived weak and naked, so vulnerable. There was a time when this alien light would have killed us all."

They didn't belong here, Rachel realized. None of them. This world was so alien to them that the land itself had rejected their presence. "But you acclimatized," she said.

"We became more human."

By consuming human souls. And now we're going back into the middle of your baptism . . .

Rachel craned her neck round to look up at the great building, blurring like a fevered dream as it clung to this one point in Space while joining countless other moments in Time. This castle did not belong on this earth, either. It was as much of an abomination as the gods themselves.

And now it was their only hope.

Carnival woke again in the same bed in the same pristine room. Even before she opened her eyes she knew that the Lord of the Maze had removed her scars again. She felt a complete absence of physical pain, but a whole world of anguish inside her heart.

There was no mirror this time.

The white room was bare but for the bed and the single red window. She got up and walked over to it.

There was no glass.

Beyond lay a scrawl of red swamps and canals divided by endless low walls. Barges slipped in and out of locks on seemingly pointless journeys, while batlike winged figures cut across the sky. Carnival leaned out and looked down.

She was near the summit of an impossibly high tower, surrounded by oddly shaped buildings made from the same obsidian stone that dropped sheer below her window: inverted pyramids and vast windowless blocks with rows of leaning funnels. Giants lurched like cripples along the thoroughfares between these structures, weaving through crowds of smaller figures and clouds of green specks that darted to and fro like flies.

Carnival had no wings to hinder her as she climbed out on the window ledge. She sensed the touch of an unnatural sun on her skin, cold and vaguely unpleasant. A light fuel-scented updraft stirred her hair, perhaps fumes from the strange industry so many thousands of feet below.

She jumped.

"The year 442, by the Herican calendar," Sabor announced, opening the outer door of the timelock. "Or 1603 in Deepgacian terms. We are now almost fifteen hundred years before the time we set off. Here Rys has freed himself from our mother's earthly yoke, and his great Pandemerian civilization is now flourishing. Ulcis gazes up in hunger from the pit under his chained temple. Hasp here commands Hell's garrisons, while Hafe still broods in his world of Brownslough tunnels. Mirith and Cospinol at this time are traveling: Cospinol in his ghastly ship, and Mirith in a bathtub upon the Strakebreaker seas. And I..."

A stern voice answered from the Obscura Hall below the balcony. "I welcome myself and my new companions to a castle crushed by war."

Rachel peered down over the gallery balcony to find a replica of Sabor looking back up at her from the center of a group of half-naked savages. These men were as dark-skinned as John Anchor, equally powerful in stature, but painted with whorls of ochre. They wore knee-length skirts of a green and blue cross-hatched pattern, adorned with bone fetishes at their broad waists. They appeared to have been in conference with the god in their midst who, from boots to hauberk to cape, wore entirely black raiment. He seemed no younger or older than his other self, and yet his hair appeared greyer. "Crushed by war?" Sabor called down.

"There are now hundreds of new universes around us," his other self replied, "and almost all of them are burning. Even this one has come under attack. We've been forced to mount recursive sallies in order to keep the enemy from our own doors. Tell me, brother, what *have* you dragged through Time behind you?"

Sabor slapped his open palm upon the banister. "We are pursuing *them*," he said. "We chase the forces of Alteus Menoa."

"*Our* foes are human men," the other Sabor said.

The god of clocks frowned at this, and said nothing more until they had reached the lowest level. Rachel and Mina negotiated a path through the dark-skinned giants, gaining the attention of more than twoscore curious stares. Many of the warriors made quick gestures against their chests when they saw Dill. Hasp regarded them with approval. "Riot Coasters," he announced to the resident Sabor. "If I were besieged, I'd want men like this by my side."

Sabor now faced his other self. The pair almost made a mirror image, but for the color of their hauberks. "You are certain these attackers are men?" he said.

"The Sombrecur," the other said. "The same Pandemerian sect who razed Rys's temples at Lorn and Logarth in 411. They do not know for whom they now fight, only that this battle fulfils what they believe is an ancient prophecy."

"Then the lands here are not bloody enough for Mesmerists? Menoa simply planted a lie in the Sombrecur's past and then allowed events to unfold."

The other god nodded. "The land has not yet been drenched with enough dead blood to allow the king's hordes through. My Riot Coasters will not use blades against the Sombrecur, but we are outnumbered and Hulfer's warriors must fight time and again without respite. I have tried to quench this false prophecy, but to no—"

Just then the double doors creaked open. A gruff hail issued from the antechamber beyond, and a second, smaller band of Riot Coasters entered. These new arrivals showed their exhaustion in every movement of their limbs. Sweating and huffing, they limped into the hall on tired legs, greeting their waiting fellows with handclasps and back slaps. Bloody wounds on their flesh told of recent battle. A great number of them eyed Hasp with evident awe.

Hulfer's warriors? Rachel recalled the story from one of John Anchor's songs. *A hundred men against five thousand Sombrecur . . .* There were far fewer than a hundred here.

Sabor's resident warriors searched eagerly amongst the newcomers, as though looking for friends.

But then Rachel realized the awful truth of it. Those who had waited and those newly arrived were both versions of the same men. The battle-weary fighters were greeting themselves. *Returned from the past?* Rachel now understood what Sabor had meant by recursive sallies. *The warriors who have been in the god's company since*

I first looked down . . . Were they now about to travel back in Time to fight the same battle their other selves had just returned from?

It made sense in a twisted sort of way. And yet not all of the warriors *had* returned.

Ten of the Riot Coasters did not find themselves amongst the returning survivors. The grim knowledge of this shadowed their expressions.

Oh gods, those men know they're not coming back.

"Garstone," cried the dark-caped Sabor. "Let's do this quickly."

An older version of the multiplicious assistant appeared, wearing round-rimmed spectacles and a faded green suit. He bowed to his master and then ushered the original Riot Coasters further up into the castle, towards whatever door would lead them to the battle.

Amongst the warriors who remained below, one raised his head to those who now marched away, and shouted three words in a language Rachel did not recognize.

The warriors on the gallery laughed. One replied in a single harsh word that Rachel took to be repartee, for his battle-weary colleagues now joined in the laughter of their departing selves.

Once the warriors had gone, a bleak silence fell upon the hall. For several moments the resident Sabor conferred quietly with another of his Riot Coasters, then he turned to his temporal brother. "Hulfer died bravely," he said. "His men have sworn to avenge him as soon as they are rested."

"How many times have these men gone back to fight?" Rachel enquired.

"Twelve times."

"Against men?" Hasp growled. "I'll join the fight and even the odds. Menoa's parasite can't take orders from *these* foes."

"You can't," Mina warned. "If you fight along with the Riot Coasters, you won't come back. Look around you! You *haven't* come back."

Hasp made a dismissive gesture. "That hardly matters."

Mina stared at him for a moment longer. "If you go, then I'm coming, too."

Rachel turned to her. "Mina!"

"I won't allow it," Hasp said. "Use your own logic, thaumaturge. Do you see yourself here amongst these survivors?"

One of the Riot Coasters spoke in his own language to the resident Sabor.

"He says Hasp fought like a god of old," the dark-suited Sabor said. "He killed many Sombrecur. The women and the phantasm, too, proved their bravery on the battlefield. Without their help, the Obscura would surely have fallen."

Rachel felt a chill in her heart. She hadn't actually planned on returning to fight, and certainly had no intention of sacrificing herself during the next few hours. Their path lay elsewhere. She was determined to reach Heaven at all costs.

The Riot Coaster had continued to speak.

The resident Sabor translated. "He says you were delayed at the lakeshore, because one of the Pandemerian holy men had intelligence relevant to your mission. He then says the first boats were successfully repelled, and the Sombrecur are regrouping across the lake. You are no longer in danger, and you have promised to return before nightfall."

"You see?" Hasp said. "It's evening now. I'll be back with you in less than an hour from now."

"We'll all be back," Mina confirmed. "Rachel? What do you say?"

But Hasp became suddenly angry. "You two are staying here," he insisted. "I'm going on my own."

"But history—"

"To hell with history," he growled. "I don't need or want a couple of frightened girls with me. You'll just get in my way and slow me down." He stormed away, roaring, "Garstone! One of you show me which godforsaken door I need to take."

Mina hurried after him. Rachel exchanged a glance with Dill, and they both followed. They caught up with the Lord of the First Citadel just as he was about to step into the timelock.

"We were *there*," Mina protested. "So you know we're coming back with you now."

"You are *not*."

"What's the matter with you, Hasp?"

He opened the timelock door. "Just get the hell away from me. If you try to step in here beside me, I'll murder all three of you myself." With that he disappeared into the timelock and slammed the door behind him.

Rachel peered through the porthole. She saw Hasp reach forward to open the outer door beyond, and then he faded from sight. "He's gone," she said. "Maybe we should just wait for him downstairs."

"He might not make it back to the castle without us," Mina said. "We were there, Rachel. If we don't follow him back now, we'll change the past. Anything could happen to him."

"All right." Rachel exhaled slowly. "How far back are we going?"

A passing Garstone said, "Six hours, miss."

Together the three of them stepped into the timelock.

The suite beyond was no different from the others in the castle, a musty storage space for old furniture and clocks. Hasp had already left. Rachel briefly glimpsed the back of his head as he closed the outer door.

In a moment they had followed him out of the timelock and caught up with him again.

He wheeled on them savagely. "I ordered you to stay."

"And we ignored you," Mina said. "Get over it."

Blood flooded the glass scales covering the god's face, giving him a frightening appearance. "You'll all die here today."

"But the Riot Coaster said—"

"The Riot Coaster said no such thing. I understand the man's language!" He sucked air in and out of his nose, then continued in a harsh whisper. "Sabor did not translate that warrior's speech truthfully. The god of clocks lied to you. The Sombrecur will slaughter us. Only Dill survives, and that's because he's already dead."

A sinking feeling invaded Rachel's stomach. Her mind groped for solutions. "If we remain in the castle..."

"We can't," Mina said wearily. "Our presence at the battle might well have kept the Sombrecur from taking over this castle, and if we lose the Obscura to the enemy, then there's no way back for us." She glanced at a nearby clock. "We need to think of a way to keep events consistent with what the Riot Coasters saw."

But Hasp stormed off, calling back over his shoulder, "It's simpler if we just die in battle."

Carnival woke lying on the floor of the same white room. This time there was no mirror, no bed or other furniture, and no window, either—nothing but a featureless box with a tiled floor.

Alteus Menoa stood in one corner, gazing at her. He was wearing a toga of white cloth slung over his shoulder and wrapped around his midriff, revealing the bronzed muscles on his chest and arms. His golden eyes were unreadable, but his expression was not unkind. "Why do you continue to destroy yourself?" he said.

She eased herself into a sitting position, glancing at his throat as she judged the distance she would have to traverse to seize it. She averted her eyes again.

The Lord of the Maze waited for her to reply and when she didn't he said, "My priests are eager to torture you."

Her eyes flicked up.

"But I fear you would only relish their primitive methods." He studied her for a moment longer. "So how do I make you appreciate what you've been given? By showing you the alternatives?" He lifted a finger.

Carnival's whole body froze solid. She glanced down to see her skin and clothes harden and quickly adopt a porcelainlike lustre. She could not breathe or move as much as an eyelid. Her dry eyes remained fixed on her glassy white knee, so smooth and brittle. Menoa's footsteps sounded as he approached across the tile floor.

"What is destruction to you without pain?" He kicked her.

Carnival felt nothing, but she heard a noise like shattering pottery, and the world spun dizzily around her.

When the room settled again, she found herself gazing at pieces of a broken face: lips, a nose, a shard of her jaw, all cast from glazed white ceramic. *Her* face. The fragments of her body lay scattered across the floor in front of her. Unable to blink or move, she could do nothing but stare.

She heard his footsteps behind her, and crunching sounds.

"Should I now return the use of your nerves to you," he said, "and let you experience what this damage *feels* like?" He continued to pace. "Or would that simply be giving you exactly what you desire?"

Her nerves began to throb as the broken pieces of her body lost their smooth sheen and reddened. The throbbing intensified and sharpened until countless needlelike sensations crawled over her flesh. She felt him standing on her, his heels pressing down into her muscles...

The surroundings blurred.

Carnival was on her hands and knees upon the floor, her body once more restored to Menoa's flesh-and-blood ideal. She blinked and sucked in a shuddering breath, then spun round to face her tormentor.

"It's more complex than that," he declared. "Pain is only part of the answer, not the full objective of your desires." He walked around her slowly. "Nor is it simply a rejection of beauty. If I turned you into a hag, would you accept yourself better then?" He shook his head. "So how can I make you appreciate this gift?"

"Give me a knife."

He smiled. "You'd use it on yourself."

"Not right away."

The Lord of the Maze ignored that. "You embrace suffering, but not just *any* suffering," he said. "Your agonies need to be self-inflicted because you wish to punish yourself." He cupped his chin in one hand thoughtfully. "But why? I admit that at first I presumed your behaviour to be merely a rejection of the natural laws. You are by nature a predator, thus driven by your hunger, and could never hope to attain any higher purpose. Your penchant for self-harm and suicide seemed to me to be the inevitable rejection of determinism." He stopped pacing. "But now I no longer believe that that's true. You are a complete enigma, Rebecca."

Carnival tensed.

"You speak aloud when you dream," Menoa said, "and thus I know that you are Ulcis's bastard, which of course makes you the granddaughter of Ayen herself." He smiled again. "We share the same divine blood, Rebecca."

"Carnival."

"As you wish." He shrugged. "But we have more in common than our divine heritage, *Carnival*. Like you, I am part human, a bastard to immortals." His golden eyes turned away from her. "We are alone in the circumstances of our births, so different from the origins of any other creatures under the heavens, and yet we are so unlike each other. I do not understand you."

Carnival chose this precise moment to attack. Her body had changed, but she retained the instincts and will that now compelled it to move with such brutal force and speed. She leapt at him, seizing his throat in both hands, and slammed him hard against the wall.

He gave a startled gasp as her teeth closed around the veins in his neck. She tasted blood.

He vanished into the wall.

Carnival's teeth closed further on nothing but empty air. Her empty fists struck hard white stone. Snarling, she clawed at the surface into which he had passed, but to no avail. The Lord of the Maze had eluded her again.

She cried out in rage and frustration and beat her bloody hands against the wall. But then she stopped abruptly.

Her fingers, hands, wrists, and arms, she now noticed, bore that familiar tracery of scars.

12

THE SOMBRECUR

Sabor was intently studying a view in the Obscura, but looked up from the table as they reached the ground floor of the great galleried hall.

"You conniving bastard," Rachel began.

The god of clocks frowned. "Who are you people? And what are you doing in my castle?"

"Don't pretend you don't know. *You* tricked us into coming back here to help the Riot Coasters."

"I did nothing of the sort."

Mina gave her a nudge. "He's right, you know. He hasn't... yet."

Rachel's face reddened. Paradoxes! Now they were preventing her from berating someone who thoroughly deserved it. "Well, you will!"

Sabor tilted his head to one side. "It is an intriguing idea, I suppose. How exactly did I accomplish that particular miracle?"

Don't say a word, Dill said, his voice a murmur in Rachel's head.

Rachel let loose a cry of frustration. She raced after Hasp, who had now stormed off towards the main doors without showing any sign of waiting for them. Dill followed her, his ghostly boots silent on the flagstones, while Mina remained alone with Sabor.

Outside it was a late summer morning. Rachel sat down with Dill on the castle steps and took in the view. This landscape had changed again since she had seen it last. The tract of wildwood between here and the waterside had not yet become established—it was more a thicket than a proper forest. In places, clumps of mimosa towered over the younger trees, their grey-blue leaves interspersed with fronds of yellow flowers. Reefs of cloud divided the blue sky like coral headlands.

Mina came and sat down beside them.

"Where were you?" Rachel asked.

"I was overcome by Sabor's wit," Mina replied. "Do you know he has thirteen thousand, one hundred and three clocks in there? He has some of the earliest examples of both verge and anchor escapement mechanisms."

"I wonder if John Anchor is still alive. The man *we* know, I mean." Rachel shrugged. "I suppose his earlier self is alive somewhere out there?"

"Alive and blissfully unaware of us," Mina said. "And of them, too." She pointed to the south. "We could use him here right now."

Upon the still waters of the lake floated thousands of tiny craft. At this distance they appeared no larger than fallen leaves. The surviving men of Hulfer's Hundred were marching down towards the forest and the Flower Lake to face the enemy for the thirteenth time.

Hasp's glass armour blazed in the sunlight. "Sombrecur," he muttered. "Rys drove them out of Pandemeria after the Logarth thing. Tenacious little bastards, fight with wood spears and arrows smeared in frog sweat. They had a different prophecy then, as I remember, but it's hard to keep track. What with all their heathen gods, white crows, and other omens."

"Sabor called them holy men," Rachel said.

The god grunted. "Well, they certainly liked to punch *holes* in men. Unarmed as they are, Hulfer's warriors will be hard-pressed to meet those spears. Still, the forest should work to our advantage. That tangle's no place for bow- or spearmen."

"In Anchor's song the Hundred defeated the Sombrecur in battle. Do we really need to worry?"

Mina lifted her dog from her inside pocket and set him upon the grass. "There's no guarantee," she said. "If we win here today, then we remain in the timeline in which Anchor's story is true. Otherwise, Time will split again and we'll find ourselves in a subtly different universe, one in which Anchor's song of victory becomes a lament." She ruffled Basilis's mangy ears. "The hardest part will be winning this fight without bloodshed. Menoa *expects* carnage here. He intends for us to prepare this ground for his Mesmerists."

Rachel felt the dead weight of her sword pressing against her thigh. *Without bloodshed?* She wondered if she was yet strong enough to *focus*. Not that her skill had any place against such numbers. It left her too vulnerable.

Dill remained silent, his body thin in the sunlight, and gazed down at the lake far below.

Hasp rolled his shoulders so the glass scales glittered. "A fair battle at last," he said. "No demons, shades, or shifters. And there's not one man down there who can turn me against my fellows." He grinned and then set off down the slope to catch up with the Riot Coasters.

"He's outnumbered and unarmed," Rachel observed, "and has a worryingly breakable exterior, and yet he thinks this is a fair fight?"

Compared with the sort of battles he's used to fighting, Dill said, *it is a fair fight. The Sombrecur are in trouble.*

The three of them followed Hasp across the mountain plateau, now a lush expanse of green grass, pink furilis blooms, and sprays of grievemont, tansy, and rattling-abacus. A hundred other varieties of herb and wildflower unknown to Rachel also blossomed here. Their heady perfume floated on the breeze along with wisps of dandelion and the gossamer lines of sailing spiders.

Hulfer's men nodded grimly to the new arrivals, but they did not slacken their march. They entered the forest via a well-worn, tunnel-like track through thick undergrowth and, in little more than an hour, had drawn near to the shore.

Kevin's Jetty would not be dreamed of for another two thousand years, and there was little sign that ordinary man had ever been here. The edge of the forest overhung the waterfront. Through the trees Rachel could see the Sombrecur craft less than a hundred yards out from the shore, scores of single outrigger canoes each with an oarsman to the front and back of the yoke, spears lashed to the gunwales. The Riot Coast warriors dropped to a crouch and edged forward silently between the boles.

Dill shimmered in the gloom beside Rachel, his ghostly sword in his hand. Yet he was as insubstantial as light itself. Rachel had already seen his incorporeal body pass straight through Mina, and she now wondered what effect, if any, he would have upon the enemy. *If nothing else, perhaps he can scare them.*

She heard the gentle splash of oars out on the lake.

The Sombrecur were decked in bead necklaces and feathers. They were lightly tanned, with tattoos forming concentric arcs across their naked chests. Bareheaded and bare-chested, they wore little more than the ochre paint daubed under their eyes.

Rachel felt something touch her leg and looked down to see Basilis brush past her sword. The little dog stopped and sniffed the air, growling softly.

Hand signals passed between the Riot Coasters. They spread out into the forest on either side of Rachel. Hasp crouched some distance behind them, applying handfuls of dirt to his glass scales in an effort to dull their sheen. Dill had no similar means to hide his luminous form, so he ducked down low behind the mounded roots of a tree. Mina leaned closer to Rachel and whispered in her ear. "What if we faked our own deaths? Wouldn't that keep the timeline consistent with what we know?"

"I don't think we'll *have* to fake them," Rachel replied in equally hushed tones. "There really are five thousand Sombrecur on that lake, possibly more."

"Can I ask you a favour?"

"What?"

"I need you to get me some blood. *Their* blood, preferably."

So the thaumaturge was going to attempt more magic? Another blanket of mist perhaps? After the colossal exertion of creating the fog, Rachel hadn't believed that Mina was capable of more. "I thought we weren't allowed to shed blood," she said.

"Oh, not much," Mina replied. "Just five or six hearts should do the trick. Menoa can't feed much of an army on that."

"I'll see what I can do."

But what could they really hope to accomplish? The Riot Coasters numbered no more than forty, and none of them was John Anchor. Hasp had seemed proficient enough against a group of un-skilled woodsmen, but she couldn't count on him making much of a dent against *this* force. The flotilla of canoes now stretched along the lakeshore as far as she could see. The oarsmen unleashed spears, grabbed bows.

They leapt lithely from their canoes and dragged them ashore, the hulls rasping over silver shingles. A bird twittered nearby and then took off amongst the trees.

Hulfer's warriors crept closer. Dill remained hidden behind the bank of roots.

Rachel drew her sword. *Just five or six hearts.*

A wicker of scrub formed a natural barrier between the forest and the beach, so the Sombrecur were forced to duck and weave through it. Their Riot Coast opponents had been waiting for this; they'd fought this same battle twelve times before.

Four of the Pandemerian holy men fell, their necks broken by dark and powerful arms, before the first warning sounded. A shrill ululation went up from one of the Sombrecur, followed immediately by a war cry from those men on the beach.

The battle had begun.

Hasp loped forward, so smeared in mud that only his red eyes glowed. The nearest enemy's eyes widened. He cried out in terror and thrust a spear out at the god, but Hasp seized the shaft and yanked its wielder out of the undergrowth. He grabbed the unbalanced man behind the skull and slammed him into the nearest tree. Without turning to see the body collapse, Hasp snapped his newly won spear in two and tossed one half to Mina. The other half he broke in two again. Thus armed with twin batons, the Lord of the First Citadel set about his enemies as they pushed through the thicket. Within ten heartbeats he had killed three more men.

Hulfer's men fought bare-fisted. They adopted the same technique as Hasp, dodging spear thrusts and seizing the shafts before the Sombrecur could withdraw. Safe now within the reach of the spear, they hammered fists into their enemies' faces or kicked downwards to shatter knees and shins. Arrows hissed through the thicket, striking no one, though a few embedded themselves in the trees.

A warrior broke through and ran straight at Rachel.

She turned his spear with her sword and drew the edge of the blade along the shaft towards his fingers. He released his hold on the weapon, turning his body rapidly to lift a hidden knife towards her unguarded side. She thrust the point of her sword into his naked armpit, severing the deltoid and the axillary nerve. His knife arm fell limp, and he opened his mouth to scream. She twisted her hand on her sword's grip and drove the tip of the weapon up into his throat, feeling the metal lodge in his lower jaw.

Another twist and a sharp downward cut, and she had opened him from neck to belly.

One heart. Rachel pitched the body towards Mina, who was crouching ready on the ground three yards behind her.

Dill moved into the fray, his translucent armour and sword pulsing faintly in the shade of the trees.

Two more Sombrecur had cleared the wicker at the water's edge, but now halted abruptly before the phantom angel and raised their spears. They began to circle Dill cautiously, in opposite directions.

Dill lunged with his sword.

The warrior reacted, meeting the blow with his spear, but the tip of the ghostly blade passed clean through his weapon's shaft and pierced his stomach. For a heartbeat he stared down at his own guts—three inches of Dill's sword had apparently disappeared inside his flesh, and yet there was no blood. Then he stepped back from the blade. There was no puncture wound, no damage at all.

The Sombrecur grinned, and advanced again.

Dill swiped his sword again, but the phantom steel passed harmlessly through his opponent without leaving a trace. He was unable to inflict damage. The Sombrecur simply walked through him.

An arrow whizzed past Rachel's ear. She spun round in time to see Hasp grab the bowman by the neck and groin and hoist him over the god's glass helm. Roaring, he slammed the struggling man down against a boulder, then turned to meet another attack with an out-thrust baton, knocking this second Sombrecur completely off his feet. Bodies soon lay strewn all around the glass-skinned god.

And five more there. Rachel started towards the fallen, but was cut off by two Sombrecur charging madly at her on either flank. *One bowman, one spearman.* She threw her sword into the bowman's face just as he released his fingers from the bowstring. The shot went wide. The spearman then lunged at her, but not fast enough. She kicked the shaft out of his hands, snatched it from the air, and whirled it around, drawing the metal tip across his naked chest, till beads scattered from his broken necklace. Across his upper torso a red line welled and began to ooze blood. He dropped to his knees.

Rachel jerked her sword out of the bowman's head and finished him off. *Three hearts left.* She dragged the two corpses back to Mina.

The Sombrecur were now pouring out of the wicker in greater numbers. Others closed in from east and west, pressing Hulfer's men closer together. This may have been what the Riot Coasters had intended all along, for the enemy, thus confined amongst their own, could not deploy their bows effectively. The dark giants performed a strange and brutal dance amongst the lighter-skinned warriors, wheeling to divert strikes as though they knew exactly where and when to expect them.

The survivors remember!

Finding herself momentarily unassailed, Rachel heaved two more corpses closer to the thaumaturge and split them open. "That's five," she said.

Mina was on her knees, her eyes closed, whispering rapidly to herself. Rachel thought she heard the word *forest*. Basilis sniffed around the dead, thoroughly unconcerned by the mayhem all around.

Hasp roared suddenly. He had disposed of his batons in favour of a larger weapon. In one glass gauntlet the god wielded one of the Sombrecur's own warriors, whirling the limp body around him as any normal brawler might use a club. Opponents flew under his blows, knocked senseless and reeling back into their own ranks.

The Riot Coasters had meanwhile arranged themselves into a spearhead phalanx and were driving back through the Sombrecur rear guard, opening a route back into the forest. Arrows lanced in from the east, striking one of the unarmed giants in the neck as he fought against two opponents. He made a gurgling sound and clutched the shaft. Before Rachel could yell a warning, a Sombrecur spearman had plunged his weapon into the wounded man's side.

She spotted Dill amidst a group of four enemy warriors, and she then watched him vanish from sight.

Unable to injure his opponents conventionally, the young angel was using a stranger and more ghoulish tactic against them. Rachel stared as Dill's body flowed *into* one of the Sombrecur. That warrior jerked, and cried out. And then, now limned in blue radiance, he spun round and thrust his spear into the chest of one of his own companions. Dill had just taken possession of the man's body.

The two remaining Sombrecur backed away from the possessed fighter. Dill charged wildly at the nearest of them, raising his spear for another attack. But his opponent reacted with a sudden downward thrust, piercing Dill's stolen body low in its left side.

The angel abandoned his wounded host. In a vapourous rush, his spirit moved into the flesh of the warrior who had just stabbed him. Thus possessing his own attacker, he now drove the spear deeper into his former body, and then turned to face the final opponent.

Basilis barked.

Rachel turned round.

Mina's eyes were open again, but now with a faraway stare. She looked pale and exhausted, her chest rising and falling rapidly under her thin robe. Fresh blood steamed on her hands. "It's done," she said.

"What is?"

"I've summoned a forest."

Rachel frowned. "We're already in a forest, Mina."

The thaumaturge got to her feet and gazed around her as though for the first time. The air was alive with the clack and snap of spears, men grunting and growling, the cries of the dying. "Gods, look at Dill," she said.

The angel's ghost darted between the enemy like a firefly, possessing one warrior after another, and then turning their weapons against their own comrades. Scores of Sombrecur had already fallen in his wake. Whenever one host body died, Dill simply shifted his soul into a fresh one. Unable to slay this phantasm, the Sombrecur were simply butchering each other.

"Too much bloodshed," Mina said, and then she shouted over to him, "Dill! Don't—"

Another noise cut her off.

It seemed to Rachel to issue from the earth itself—a low creaking sound like the hull of a ship protesting in a heavy squall. The Sombrecur had noticed it, too, for they were eyeing the ground with frantic suspicion. A roar went up from the Riot Coast warriors, who had used this distraction to push through the Sombrecur ranks and reach more open ground. Only two of their number had fallen so far.

Rachel felt the earth shuddering under her feet. A powerful smell assaulted her nostrils, an odour of terrible decay. From out of the forest floor snaked thick white tendrils.

Roots?

All around, these extrusions broke free of the soil, wrapping around each other, around the boles of trees and the legs, spears, and torsos of the panicked Sombrecur. The tendrils quivered, growing rapidly, enmeshing the natural forest in a vast pale web. They engulfed the Sombrecur completely, binding them where they stood, but miraculously they left the Riot Coast fighters untouched.

Within moments every bole and branch had been ensnared by these white roots, their thin blanched fibres crisscrossing the canopy overhead or hanging like ropes. The Sombrecur cried out from their cocoons, but then the tendrils contracted with a series of spasmodic creaks till finally the scene became silent. To Rachel it seemed like one forest had been consumed by a second, parasitic one. She clutched her nose against the stench, for Mina's forest smelled of a plague pit.

"Now we have to run," Mina cried. "Get out of here while the new trees are still pliable. Once they've hardened, we'll be stuck here."

"Trees?" Rachel said. "What sort of forest is this?"

"The forest of bone," Mina replied. "It's an aspect of Basilis. I had the idea when we first reached Herica and I saw its remains along the lakeshore. These forests take thousands of years to decay."

"You *knew* we would be coming back here?"

Mina grabbed Rachel's hand and hurried her along through the strange white forest. Hasp and Dill, joined by the Riot Coast men, quickly followed behind. Mina glanced back at the god and then whispered to the assassin. "I'm afraid I asked Sabor to lie. Hasp needed to believe that he was going to die here, that this was to be his glorious end."

"Why?"

"So that he'd rediscover his passion for life. Confronting the Sombrecur gave him the opportunity to fight as a free man ... or god, I suppose."

Rachel stopped suddenly, dragging Mina to a halt. "You dragged us into this *deliberately?*" she growled. Then she lowered her voice. "You forced *me* to kill so that *he* could relive his past glories."

"It already happened in our world's past," Mina said. "In Riot Coast legend we were *always* present here. Even the last stanza of John Anchor's song mentions a ghost, a god, a witch, and a maiden." She shrugged. "I don't know why they'd think you were a witch, but that's not the point ... If we hadn't lived through these events, we'd have corrupted this timeline even more than it already has been. Don't you see? The further back in time we go, the more dangerous our actions become."

"What else have you tampered with, Mina?" Rachel demanded,

grabbing the sleeve of Mina's robe. "Exactly how far back does your meddling go?"

Mina pulled away from the assassin. "We need to get out of here!" she urged.

"Who roused the Sombrecur against Sabor in the first place?" Rachel persisted. "Mina, who sent them to their deaths? Was it Menoa?"

The thaumaturge hurried away through the tangled white roots.

"Was it Menoa?" Rachel repeated.

But Mina wouldn't answer her.

Carnival didn't require a mirror to gauge the extent of her restoration. She could feel the tight pressure of her wings against her back and shoulders, the powerful muscles flexing as she beat them. Her long hair, now dry and ragged, blew about her shoulders. Her heart thundered with anticipation. She turned her naked arms over and examined the tracery of scars there. Her skin tingled with the memory of old wounds. She felt renewed, angry.

Dangerous.

It was as if that single taste of the bastard god's blood had acted like a key to unlock her mind from its cage.

Here in Hell, all form was a matter of will. Carnival had won the freedom to exist as her own will dictated. Even her old leathers and lightweight boots had returned. The armour clung to her lithe figure in all its battered and rotten glory, and she welcomed the smell of decay.

Yet there was more.

Had she been *quite* this tall, *quite* this strong? The muscles on her arms and legs seemed much larger and better defined. Her leathers felt tight around her thighs and upper arms. Was this merely subconscious vanity, or a reaction to her present instinct to smash her way out of here?

Four white walls enclosed her. She had no other way out but brute force.

She slammed the heel of her boot against the outer wall, aware that even the stone itself was an amalgam of living sentient souls. The barrier would be as strong as it believed itself to be, and she suspected that Menoa would have convinced it thoroughly. Her kick made no difference to the smooth surface.

Carnival took a step back and examined the wall, realizing she could not defeat this barrier in her current physical form. So she concentrated hard, willing greater strength and endurance from *somewhere*. She felt her wings grow, her muscles expand unnaturally, her very bones become heavier and denser. Her armour creaked and split around her new, bulkier frame. Her skin darkened to become a dull ironlike patina.

All a matter of will.

The scarred angel threw another savage kick at the wall. It shuddered. A crack appeared in the stonework from floor to ceiling. She lashed out again with her foot, and chips of white stone crumbled before her eyes.

The wall moaned.

She punched a heavy fist right through it. Masonry fell away in great chunks, revealing a turbulent red sky and the vast expanse of the Maze beyond.

The prison cell was near the summit of the Ninth Citadel. From this new rent in its outer wall, Carnival gazed down. Canals had flooded the thoroughfares within King Menoa's strange living metropolis: crimson slough skirted canted angles of black stone, glutted entire quadrangles, stained the brickwork. And yet the scene looked busier than ever. Hundreds of creatures in bulky armour darted here and there, sloshing through the thick mire, pushing, carrying, or rolling strange machines before them. Those canals... there was something odd about them.

Red figures stood in the waters.

The River of the Failed had encircled Menoa's fortress like a moat, and then flowed out to encompass all the streets around it. Even now tributary rivulets of it were leaching into the surrounding territory, flooding acres of dry passages. It was *defending* its master's home.

But from *what*?

And then Carnival noticed the approaching army—already so near the citadel that it defied her powers of observation. At first she had simply swept her gaze over it without even identifying it as such. If she hadn't now spied movement, she would just have glanced over it a second time. Whole cities, after all, were not supposed to crawl across the landscape.

A vanguard of mysterious machines moved at the forefront of this bizarre, creaking, and jostling army. These vessels looked vaguely like airships, though their tapering hulls appeared to have been forged from metal. They slid across the surface of Hell, smashing through the myriad walls, gouging out paths for the creeping rear guard to follow. Carnival spied two figures standing atop the leading vessel, a red-haired woman and a huge, dark giant, still wearing his wooden harness.

While the remaining survivors of Hulfer's Hundred marched back inside the Obscura Redunda, Mina instructed Hasp and Rachel to wait with her outside until they could be sure their future selves had duly departed.

Rachel had half a mind to burst in there and tell her other self the truth. But she knew that Mina had been right in a sense. To avoid corrupting this timeline any further, they must ensure that historical events happened exactly the way they ought to.

If the Sombrecur had been allowed to take Sabor's castle, then Rachel would have found herself in a new branch of the multiverse, facing a very uncertain future.

Yet Mina's meddling had likely caused the deaths of five thousand men, and for no apparent reason other than to inspire Hasp to struggle against his hellish parasite. Of course none of this troubled the thaumaturge, who seemed to be as morally flexible as a starving vulture in a nest of its sister's chicks.

After the sun had swept its long red rays below the horizon, they entered the castle and found Sabor waiting in the Obscura Hall. Rachel was vaguely relieved to find that this was the original Sabor, although she couldn't be entirely sure why. All versions of him were the same god, after all, and she couldn't bear a grudge against one without bearing a grudge against all of them. The god of clocks accepted another map from one of the many Garstones in evidence here. The galleries above were also bustling with Sabor's assistants, and timelock doors clicked open and closed constantly overhead. The pattering of footsteps produced sounds more numerous than all the ticks and chimes from the castle's clocks.

"My other self has now departed for earlier times," Sabor announced, with just the merest flicker of a glance towards Mina. "Our Riot Coast friends are taking their supper in the dining room."

Rachel glared at Mina, who clumsily pretended not to notice. Had the thaumaturge *already* told Sabor to rouse the Sombrecur? Was that unnecessary battle doomed to have always happened?

Nevertheless her machinations appeared to have had the desired effect, for Hasp was clearly in vigorous good spirits. Still plastered in dry mud, he beamed and said, "Well, 442 was a good year, but we've that many more of them left to traverse. Let's move on before the bastard king causes any more mischief."

Mischief? Rachel felt sick, but she had to agree that they should move on soon, if only to prevent Mina from causing any more problems.

Sabor consulted his map to locate a suite that would take them back a full six years before the battle in which they had just fought. He looked up and around at his numerous assistants, many of whom were now leaving through the castle doors, presumably to create space while they waited for a future timelock. The god of clocks nodded with satisfaction.

"Making your own army here, Sabor?" Hasp asked.

"Hardly," Sabor replied. "This has ceased to become a multiplication procedure. Now, rather, it is a rescue operation, as Menoa's bastard universe continues to grow around us. The Lord of the Maze is creating thousands of branches from his own timeline, and many more of the Obscura's suites now lead into these warped realms." He grunted. "Garstone has orders to locate as many of his selves as possible and bring them into *this* timeline. They have orders to converge at year zero by any route available. Ergo, the closer we get to our destination, the more of Garstone's selves you will see."

"Your castle is going to get very crowded."

"Indeed."

But as the numbers of Sabor's assistants increased, it soon became evident that another force was working to ensure that they didn't. In the next suite they found three more corpses. Again the victims were all versions of that diminutive rumple-suited man. All had been slain with a wide blade, the wounds suggesting that they had been cut down while trying to flee. Whatever had killed them had simply piled the victims in the center of the room.

As soon as they made this grim discovery, Rachel rushed to the timelock door and peered through. Crowds of Garstones passed outside the porthole window, seemingly oblivious of anything untoward.

Mina crouched by one of the bodies, and slipped its timepiece from its breast pocket. "It's the correct time," she said. "He was killed here not long ago, and his body hasn't been moved." The other corpses' pocket watches told the same story. Whatever had slain these men had done so in this universe, with a thousand alternate versions of his three victims outside this very door.

And yet a hurried conference with Garstones passing outside

soon revealed that none had seen anything. The killer had gone unnoticed.

Sabor's brow creased in a deep frown. "Either the killer was invisible," he announced to the assistants now gathered on every balcony above the Obscura Hall, "or one of you has betrayed us . . . and thereby betrayed yourself."

A moment's stunned silence was followed by shocked protests and denials from every level of the castle. They couldn't conceive of such a thing. The murderer could only have been a shade, a phantasm, a shape-shifter.

A *shape-shifter?*

Rachel saw Hasp's expression turn sour at this news. If a shape-shifter was here in the castle, then the Mesmerists had gained access to this timeline. The future they had left behind must already have been altered.

Sabor called for silence and, grimly, ordered the lights dimmed and the camera obscura activated. With a thousand pairs of eyes watching from the galleries above him, the god of clocks switched between the lenses of each of his suites in turn.

A bleary orange sun against a smouldering purple sky . . . bones adrift upon the Flower Lake . . . a great black building amidst an unknown village on the opposite lakeshore, puffing red smoke from its funnels . . . darkness, with the stars obscured by greasy fumes . . . the light of dawn falling upon ashen plains . . . machines waiting in the lakeshore thickets . . . a solitary giant standing godlike against a scorched heaven.

All but four of the lenses he tried revealed these similar poisoned universes, places where Menoa's newly altered pasts had come to fruition in chaotic ways. The Maze had come to the world of men before Heaven had even been sealed.

"How is he doing this?" Rachel asked.

"He gained control of the Obscura Redunda in his own bastard universe. Now his Mesmerists have spread back through the labyrinth of Time like an infestation, transporting chaos back with them into the past. Each time he changes history, he creates yet another universe that puts greater pressure on our own. Our own timeline may already have collapsed behind us. Our future, *the very one we left*, might no longer exist as we know it."

He snatched up his map and cried, "Hurry!"

They ran from timelock to timelock in an increasingly complex and desperate route back through the labyrinth of Time. Six months. Three days. Two hours. Twenty years. A solitary leap of two and a half minutes, and they kept running, pushing, through crowds of Garstones to make a seven-year connection. Rachel was exhausted, Hasp grim-faced in his filthy armour, Mina clutching Basilis to her breast as she raced along the gallery. Even Dill seemed to have faded as a result of the constant exertion. Up stairs and down again. The whole Obscura Hall was packed with rumple-suited assistants.

They made the connection with just seconds to spare. Two and a half thousand days, gone in a heartbeat. They hurried onwards, backwards, throwing themselves into the past with fierce abandon.

Sabor called out to announce the years: "... Three fifty-five ... Two ninety-six ... One hundred and forty-two ..."

Year ninety-nine.

And here they found a suite *full* of bodies. Forty Garstones slain, the room painted with arcs of blood. "No time," Sabor cried. "No time to look for the killer. Leave the dead and run."

Year eighty-one.

The Obscura Redunda was bursting with humanity, all countless versions of the god's clock-winder. And still more of him poured from other suites, from other universes that had been blighted by their unseen enemy. They came staggering into the Obscura Hall, wounded or dying or burned. The air thickened with the smell of sweat, smoke, and blood.

Year fifty.

This time most of the suites were now filled with the dead. The doors of the castle had been flung wide open, and Garstones poured out to assemble on the mountainside beyond, waiting for their chance to travel back to year zero. Rachel heard a cry issue from above. A clash of steel? She couldn't stay to find out.

Year eighteen.

Now Sabor's assistants clambered over their own corpses in the Obscura Hall in their haste to reach the appropriate timelocks. Others carried other wounded selves. Smoke poured into the castle from the main doors, boiling up over the obscura columns, till it filled the hemisphere in the ceiling. Howls and cries sounded from outside, and Basilis's barking, and shouts: "We are attacked...Men outside."

Not Mesmerists? Rachel wondered if that was a good sign or not. Perhaps the land had not yet been bloodied enough for King Menoa's own creations. Hasp interrupted her thoughts by grabbing her arm. "Move."

Year zero.

Silence.

The timelock door had slammed behind them as they piled into yet another musty suite with another pointlessly grandiose name. There were no bodies here, no smoke or damage. The window looked out upon a cloudless blue sky. By the angle of the sun, Rachel judged it to be morning, and yet auroras danced across the heavens beyond the glass, shimmering curtains of pale green and purple. She approached to get a better view.

The Temple Mountains shone like polished jet, the colourful skies reflected as if burning deep within countless dark and glassy facets. A few patches of snow clung to the higher abutments, but the landscape below basked in pristine sunlight. All trace of the forest was gone, for here the foothills swept down to the lakeshore in a series of soft humps, every inch of them covered in wildflowers.

Rachel had never seen such a riotous carpet of blossoms: bursts of gold and red mingled with lavender whorls; dabs of white and cerise amongst streaks of indigo, copper, and umber. The overall effect was so intense upon the eye that it seemed to blur together like the bands of a rainbow.

Dill stood at the window and the flowers shone through him. *It's beautiful*, he said.

Hasp joined him. "I'd never thought I'd see this again," he said.

"But it can't be natural," Rachel said. "Why are there no trees here? No bush or scrub?"

"It's Ayen's garden," Sabor explained. He was looking apprehensively at the door, as though trying to work something out in his mind. "The castle is very quiet."

"No Garstones," Mina replied. "There should be thousands of them gathered here. Millions."

But then a face appeared briefly at the timelock porthole. The outer door swung wide, and then the inner one opened to reveal a familiar face. A middle-aged Garstone stood in the doorway, dressed in a rumpled brown suit. "Glad you could make it, sir." He gestured with his arm. "If you will just come with me..."

"Where are the others?"

"The timelocks are all barred, sir...except this one, of course. Please come with me to the Obscura Hall. You have guests."

The galleries were deserted, every door jammed by a crossbeam, as Garstone had said. Eight men waited for them in the center of the Obscura Hall. Their leader was much older than Rachel remembered, but she recognized the scar running across his forehead. "Oran."

"You owe me for what you did," he snarled.

The other woodsmen leaned on their swords and axes and laughed. Rachel recognized most of them from her time in the Rusty Saw tavern, but she couldn't put names to their faces. They were large and bearded, still wearing the same lacquered wooden armour.

"How did you get back here?"

Sabor interrupted Oran's response. "These are not the men you knew, Miss Hael," he said. "These people are from another reality."

Oran snorted. "So said the king's arconites, but it all looks the same to me." He leered at Rachel. "You cost me a king's ransom. I'd all but delivered that giant of yours into his hands until you did what you did. I've walked a long, long way to find you and earn back his favour. Now that I have you again, we'll see if Menoa wants to reinstate his offer."

"I don't know what you're talking about," Rachel said. She had refused to pay this bastard his gold, but that was all. How he could have delivered Dill to Menoa was beyond her.

"They said you wouldn't remember. You'll be coming with us up to the temple now. The king wants to meet you after all these years."

Hasp growled. "Yes, we're going there, but not with you. Stand aside, woodsman, or I'll take that sword and sheathe it in your arse."

Dill smiled faintly and strolled out from behind the god.

Oran shot an uneasy glance at Garstone.

"You won't harm anyone until we tell you to," Sabor's assistant remarked. "You'll keep that mouth shut until we reach Ayen's temple."

Hasp cried out in pain and clutched his head.

Sabor wheeled on his assistant. "*You're* the shape-shifter," he said.

"No, sir," Garstone replied. "I am just as human as always. But, like my brother here, I have sworn myself to the Mesmerist cause. The parasite recognizes the scent of Hell on us."

Oran barked a laugh. "And it actually works," he said. "Go on, Hasp. Kneel before your betters." When the god did not respond, he yelled, "Bend the knee!"

The Lord of the First Citadel snarled, struggling to resist Menoa's parasite, but then he collapsed on his knees and let out a terrible wail.

Dill moved forward, but Rachel held up a hand to stop him. They exchanged a glance, during which she gave an almost imperceptible shake of her head. *Wait until we reach the temple.*

Garstone warned his brother, "Be more specific, Oran. Hasp

doesn't recognize you as his better. He would never have followed that first instruction."

The woodsman grunted. "We'll try this, then," he said. "Take the assassin's sword. Kill her if she resists."

Hasp groped for Rachel.

"No!" Garstone cried. "Take the sword, but do not kill her. Do *not* kill anyone until the Lord of the Maze commands it." He scratched his head. "But please do kill Sabor if he tries to fly away." Then he nodded. "Yes, that about covers it."

Rachel had felt disinclined to resist anyway. She let Hasp snatch away her sword.

Garstone breathed a sigh of relief. "Do not toy with him, Oran," he said. "King Menoa specifically asked us to deliver them alive."

"When did you turn against me?" Sabor asked.

"A long time from now, sir."

"Just you? Or all of you?"

The little man smiled. "More of me every day, sir. I am busy recruiting even as we speak."

"Then some are still loyal?"

"It's hard to believe I was once so naive, sir."

Surrounded by woodsmen, the small party left the castle and set off up the mountain, under the soft luminance of the aurora in the skies. A steep trail zigzagged up the fractured black rock, and the worn steps suggested to Rachel that the temple had been here much longer than she had previously imagined. Had it always been a temple dedicated to Ayen? Had the door to her domain always remained open during that time?

She found the idea both terrifying and exhilarating, for the world of man had not yet been severed from the realm of Heaven. Would good souls be allowed to pass through that door? Curtains of light shimmered over the black peaks, hinting at a greater world beyond this one.

"It's the aftermath of the War Against Heaven," Mina said. "Burning skies, rising seas . . . Sabor and his brothers have just been expelled from Ayen's realm. Their original selves are out there somewhere right now."

"Shouldn't *that* Sabor be in his castle?"

"I was," said the god of clocks. "And these turncoats weren't. None of this happened in *my* universe."

"So the Mesmerists have changed them all?"

He nodded. "Countless futures stem from this moment in Time—and all of them are now bad, I fear. Our original timeline has now been overwhelmed by the morass of Menoa's bastard universes. When the Lord of the Maze kills himself, he'll go to Hell, but he'll leave his Mesmerists in control of my castle. They'll have access to all of Time, while this doomed continuum continues to exist."

As the sun beat down upon them, Oran's men swore and complained. Sabor opened his wings as if to bathe his feathers in the warmth. Rachel's own reflection peered back at her from the black glass rock below her. She recalled similar geology in the dark abyss beneath Deepgate, so long ago: herself and Dill staring at themselves as though they were the only two people left in the world. Would that chained city ever come to exist now? Would Rachel herself ever be born? Or Carnival? Or Dill?

Dill's ghost walked up the mountain path beside her, dead three thousand years before his birth: an event that might now never happen. He caught her eye and smiled.

Below them spread the lands of Herica and Pandemeria, their green hills and plains interspersed with silver lakes, but no settlements, no roads, nothing to suggest that man had ever been here.

They crested a rise and came at last to the summit of the mountain. And here stood Ayen's temple.

It was a rather unimpressive grey stone cairn, barely larger than a worker's hovel. Twin columns of rough-hewn granite flanked a small, dark doorway. Piled-up stones formed the roof.

"This is it?" Mina said. "All the gods and their armies, the ancient technology... it's all spawned from this?"

"Why would Ayen choose to draw attention to the place?" Sabor explained. "A grander structure might have been seen from afar."

Hasp glared at that dark portal with terror in his eyes. He clenched the sword in his fist so tightly that Rachel feared he would crush his own glass gauntlet. He seemed to try to speak through his clenched jaw, but then simply gave a low moan.

"Inside, please." Garstone indicated the doorway.

They ducked inside a small, roughly conical chamber formed of dry stones. Another exit occupied the opposite wall, this one barred by an ill-fitting door made of loose planks, and rope cord binding the whole flimsy thing together. Daylight shone through the gaps in the boards.

Beside the door waited Alteus Menoa.

He was extraordinarily handsome, with amber eyes and silvery-grey hair hanging loose over his shoulders. A fine jaw tapered neatly underneath high cheekbones. He was barefoot but otherwise dressed, in a shirt and plain white linen breeches. He smiled with broad, soft lips.

Mina exchanged a glance with Rachel. Basilis curled around her foot and growled. Dill's body seemed to darken, but his eyes remained calm.

"One of you will kill me shortly," Menoa said, "but I'll bear whoever does it no grudge. Tell me, Sabor, how many times has this moment happened?"

"You asked me the same question last time," Sabor said.

"Forgive me if I'm a bore. Do you always reply?"

"This is the second time that I'm aware of, Alteus."

"But this time is different, isn't it? I have allies here. Men from my own future."

"From many futures."

"Then ultimately all the gods fail?" His gaze fixed on Hasp for a long moment, before returning to Sabor. "Will you tell me—?"

"They're dead, Alteus. Your half brothers, Rys, Hafe, Mirith, Ulcis, and Cospinol, all dead."

Menoa nodded. "I see. How dreary for you to have to keep explaining it all to me. These temporally removed agents of mine have proved enlightening, but they lack any real depth of knowledge." His gaze returned to Hasp, who was standing directly behind the god of clocks. "Kill Sabor," he said.

"Wait!" Sabor threw up his hands.

Hasp cried out in protest, but his sword swept upwards in one stroke with enormous strength behind it.

Dill leapt suddenly at Hasp, but his ghostly body passed straight through the Lord of the First Citadel without resistance. Bewildered, he wheeled back round just as Hasp's blade tore through Sabor's mail and into the flesh of his back.

The god of clocks started forward, as though he had been punched, his mail shirt hanging in bloody ribbons from his back. Pale-faced, he half turned towards his glass-skinned brother. Nobody moved. Even the traitor Garstone wore a look of shock.

Hasp next thrust the weapon into Sabor's neck.

The god of clocks fell.

Hasp was breathing hard, his broad chest rising and falling rapidly. His red eyes stared wildly out of his dirt-streaked face.

Menoa said, "Now kill the thaumaturge."

Rachel had been waiting for this moment for three thousand years. She *focused*.

The world around her slowed until even the light seemed to hesitate, pushing in vain against the motes of dust trapped in its rays. Her heart and lungs stopped. She saw Mina's brows rise a fraction, Hasp's feverish gaze swinging towards the thaumaturge. The hairs on Basilis's back moved slowly erect, even as his jaws twisted into a growl.

How to move Mina out of danger without breaking that glassy skin of hers?

Rachel considered Hasp. She could shatter his armour in an instant, trading the god's life for that of her friend. Or she could risk Mina while trying to save both of them . . .

A sliver of drool began to drip from Basilis's jaws. Could the Penny Devil act in time to save his mistress? Rachel didn't know the answer, and she didn't understand thaumaturgy enough to rely on it.

Hasp was slowly raising his sword.

Better to disarm him first and buy the others some time. Let Mina meanwhile conjure another one of her ghastly forests. Or Dill . . . ?

Why had he not been able to possess Hasp?

Because Hasp was a god? Because he had already consumed so many souls during his long life? Or did his Mesmerist armour simply protect him from incorporeal attack? Rachel didn't know, but she couldn't count on her friend.

She walked forward and pressed the palms of her hands against the flat of the blade, steering it, pushing it gently sideways out of his fist. His grip was ferocious. Too much force and she would break his fingers.

She took her time.

Near the top of Hasp's swing, she managed to pry the sword free. The hilt moved outwards from his palm, and hung for a moment in the air.

Now Mina.

Basilis had coiled himself to pounce, and Mina was only now starting to flinch away from the anticipated blow. Hasp himself had yet to notice that his sword had left his fist.

Rachel turned and pushed Mina backwards, applying as much force as she dared. At normal speed, she hoped it would represent little more than a hard shove.

She turned back to Hasp.

His arm was still rising. The sword had begun to turn in the air. Rachel took the weapon firmly by its hilt and eased it back towards her, careful not to move so quickly as to break her own bones. She steered the blade past Mina's ear, turning it, and brought the edge of the blade across Oran's neck. The woodsman's carotid artery parted. Blood would flow in just moments.

But Rachel had another destination in mind for the sword. She had so little time available while *focused* that she couldn't afford to wait. She wrapped both hands around the weapon's hilt, now steering it past Menoa himself, and then clove it down through the thin wooden door beside him. The rope and planks gave way without any resistance. Pieces of the door began to slide to the ground.

Rachel pushed through the falling fragments, and stepped out into Heaven.

Anchor had brought Mr. D's customers, an entire city of them, to confront the Lord of the Maze. The city's buildings housed demons, and they shambled or crawled across the surface of Hell, consuming canal walls under their foundations and dislodging cornerstones from Menoa's own queer structures, causing them to howl.

The Riot Coast giant himself stood grinning upon the top of the long metal hull of Isla's subsurface vessel. Alice Harper had found a deck chair from somewhere, and now reclined in it, studying another one of her infernal Mesmerist devices and scanning the bottled soul she had taken from D's Emporium. Dozens more bottles rolled about inside an overturned cabinet they had found amongst the wreckage. They weren't as refined as the soulpearls Anchor was used to, but they were a hell of a lot better than nothing.

"Any luck?" Anchor said.

She made a noncommittal gesture. "He's intact and he's dreaming," she said. "But I still need to find a host for him."

"Is that the Ninth Citadel?" Isla asked excitedly, peering out from behind Harper's deck chair. "It's really big, isn't it?"

"Aye, I thought it might be," Anchor replied. "Menoa strikes me as that sort of god."

Isla wrinkled her nose in distaste.

All around the submarine rumbled the vessels of other demons who had collected souls for Mr. D. Harper had said that they were some of the oldest and most powerful creatures she'd ever scanned, but you wouldn't have thought it to look at them: wiry old men and carefree children, weak-eyed scholars and dizzy maidens, they seemed ill-equipped to take their ships to war. Anchor had protested, but Harper insisted on engaging their help. They were willing enough to fight, though, and Anchor couldn't deny them that right.

Mr. D's customers were another breed altogether. Demons grown fat from their years of trading at that strange emporium, these creatures wore castles like men wear clothes, towers and canting stacks of stone and glass of every shape. They had fashioned these environments for themselves from living memories, and now moved them by will alone. The ground shuddered wherever they passed. Icarates and Soul Collectors fled through the passageways ahead, many of them falling under a bow wave of rubble.

Anchor turned to Harper. "It would be good to have seen Hasp's castle here. Was it as grand as these?"

"Grander, and more dangerous," the engineer replied. "He fled farther than anyone thought possible, and then turned the building against Menoa's hunters. I'd never seen anything like it."

"Ha!" Anchor took another bottle from the cabinet, uncorked it, and drained its contents. The soul within the liquid soon took the edge off his appetite, restoring him to full vigour. He felt *strong* again.

"You shouldn't drink so much," Isla said.

"I know that, lass." He tossed the empty bottle away. "This is gut-rot."

But it was strong gut-rot, and that's all that mattered to him right now.

The vanguard of this bizarre and rambling army smashed through yet another wall, the metal vessels ploughing into a compound full of dark barrow-shaped structures. Here the Icarates had mounted resistance.

Men in bronze plate armour threw spears up at the intruding constructs. Gladiators, they were, by the look of them, part flesh and part metal. Anchor had seen the arenas where Soul Collectors gathered. At a run, they broke around the *Princess*, looking for a weakness, a place to scale her smooth hull. The submarine slid ever forwards, tilting up over one of the barrows and then slamming down again. Harper's deck chair slid to one side, but she grabbed hold of the cabinet to stop herself from falling any further. Anchor took Isla's hand.

"I won't fall off," she said.

"No, but I might."

She grinned and held on to him more tightly.

"Here." Harper handed one of her Mesmerist devices up to the big man. "I've adapted this Screamer to rattle Menoa's soul. He'll try to change you, and he'll succeed unless you're fast. You'll have less than a heartbeat to activate the thing. It should disrupt his concentration enough to let you get closer."

"How long do I have?"

"I don't know. Moments only. But you won't surprise him twice." She looked up, past him. "Iolites, John."

A great flock of glass lizards flashed in the fierce red skies above. They were almost invisible: a swarm of scintillations—now like sunlight on a fast river, now like burning cannon powder— and Anchor heard the sudden crash of their wings.

Nearer than they look . . .

Anchor pushed Isla aside, and seized a crystal claw as one of the Iolites dived at his head. The winged lizard let out a shriek, a clash of chimes as it thrashed its wings against Anchor's shoulders. Anchor whirled the beast around his head and then threw it hard into the rest of the flock. Lights sparkled, and though he couldn't see individual creatures, he heard a smash as the Iolite he had hurled struck another. Fragments of glass showered the *Princess*.

"John!"

Another of the winged demons was clawing at the harness on Anchor's back. The wood shuddered violently, but it was a construct of will and would not break while the big man remained alive inside.

Isla let out a wailing cry.

And then a sudden shriek pierced the musical tinkling of the Iolites' wings, followed by a concussion so intense that it compounded the air in Anchor's ears. Harper was holding up a second device, seemingly identical to the one she had given Anchor. Overhead, the Iolites shattered: Glass feathers exploded everywhere, catching the light from the red sun like puffs of blood.

"My other Screamer," Harper said.

"One use only, eh?"

"No, but they take a few moments to recharge. Handy for Iolites and lesser constructs, but these won't put off Menoa's Icarates too much. The red priests will simply bend the Screamer's will to their own. The device then turns traitor and refuses to cooperate."

"Give me my fists any time." Still, he tucked the other Screamer into his wide belt, as a moment of freedom against the Lord of the Maze was better than nothing at all.

Their creaking, shambling revolution had reached the outskirts of what Anchor took to be the industrial quarters encircling the Ninth Citadel. Great hulking structures now loomed over Isla's metal ship. To the left and right the rest of the army continued to rumble forward in a broad arc, punching through every obstacle in its path.

But here they met the bulk of Menoa's forces. Icarates and creatures of war waited in the flooded channels around the fortress itself. Thousands of humans, beasts, phantasms, and machines. And more...

Harper saw the red figures at that same moment: imitations of Cospinol's gallowsmen and slender angels. "Gods, John, we didn't account for this," she said. "What the hell is the river doing *here?*"

"Protecting Father." He drank another soul, threw the bottle away, and then slammed his palms together. "It is good for a better battle, yes?"

"They'll tear this ship to pieces."

No sooner had the words left her mouth than the king's creatures attacked. Icarates lashed whips that drove aurochs and human, shade, or demon warriors forward. Dogcatchers sniffed the air and gnashed their teeth, eager to be unleashed. The Non Morai had to be forced forward by their masters, but then howled through the air in a frenzied gale, their vapourous forms seen only when one did not look directly at them. The river men came more slowly, almost lethargically, loping through the shallow channels of their own god, red weapons and claws dripping.

Harper whispered orders to her Screamer.

Anchor grinned savagely. Then he ran forward along the *Princess's* hull and leapt down to meet his foes.

He landed up to his knees in the flooded thoroughfare and strode forward, pushing against the sucking mire. The Non Morai reached him first, screaming past on either side. Anchor flailed his fists at them, but struck nothing but air. The shades fell back, howling with manic laughter. When he looked at them directly, they vanished, only to gather again at the edges of his vision. Tall winged men with red smiles brushed their cold fingers against his arms, sending jolts of pain across his flesh.

"Damned things," Anchor growled. "Like big wasps."

He scooped up handfuls of the red water and threw it at the vapourous forms. It stuck to them like paint, revealing them wherever they hovered. He lunged, but they fluttered away in terror, no longer willing to engage with him. Whenever he met their eyes, they simply turned and fled.

The dogcatchers were more difficult to deter. A pack of these skinless demons came tearing down the channel towards him like wild beasts, their teeth snapping up at the dark giant. But these creatures were merely flesh and bone, or whatever passed for that here, and Anchor knew how to deal with them. He seized the first of them by its neck and broke it quickly, then hurled the corpse over the nearest wall. Another leapt at him, but met Anchor's fist. It dropped into the river with a splash, even as he tore the guts out of two more and turned in time to see the others loping away.

An armoured aurochs thundered towards him, a monstrous horned thing like the god of all bulls.

Anchor crouched, arms splayed, and met its charge with his own, slamming into the beast as it lowered its head to gouge him. It skidded backwards three paces and bellowed, but Anchor now had his arms wrapped around the creature's neck. He tightened his grip and lifted, heaving the beast up over his head and casting it down behind him. It scrambled in the bloody waters, snorting and huffing and trying vainly to regain its feet.

Anchor turned to see what came next.

The Icarates had so far held back their human slaves and machines, clearly unwilling to throw any more against the giant until they had to. Instead they now let the River of the Failed go forth.

It had adopted mostly the shapes of sword-wielding angels, a lesson learned from Carnival, and for the first time Anchor was worried. He knew he could not defeat this foe, and he wasn't sure if it would react to his orders as before. He called back over his shoulder to Harper. "You have something to hurt these things, eh?"

"Anything I do is more likely to piss them off."

Anchor crooked his neck so that he faced the river men and yelled, "Stop there! Stay where you are or I'll beat you blue."

The Failed did not even pause.

Anchor took a step back, glancing around for some way to evade them. He heard Isla's ship grumble to a halt behind him.

And then something in the skies caught his eye, a fleeting shadow.

Carnival landed hard in the channel between Anchor and the approaching warriors. Jets of bloody water leapt from the impact. She flexed her wings and straightened.

The Failed finally halted.

She watched them for a long moment, without speaking. Finally, she said, "Go back."

The red figures hesitated.

She took a step towards them and snarled, "Or stay."

Anchor felt the river pulling at his shins, drawing back towards the king's citadel. Red waters frothed and gurgled all around him, as scores of warriors simply collapsed back into the mire at their feet. A wave swept back up the channel, draining away from the scarred angel. Swelling as it retreated, it surged over the Icarates and their human slaves.

Carnival then strode forward.

And Menoa's priests turned and ran.

The mountain summit on the far side of Ayen's temple was not the same one Rachel had left behind. The black rock plateau looked identical, and the cairn behind her had not changed either, but now a sea of cloud hung below the mountain itself while the skies above it boiled with fire.

Great permanganate and silver blazes soared over her, undulating slowly against a vast black and starless void. She was still moving at unnatural speed, so she had no way to determine the true frenzy of these heavenly flames. But her slowing heartbeat would show her soon enough.

In the center of the plateau, a withered old woman dressed in tattered sackcloth sat upon a three-legged stool. The hollows of her eyes stared intensely at the newcomer.

Rachel approached in measured steps, aware of the strain she was putting on her muscles, and desperate to maintain her heightened state for as long as possible. She had mere moments left before Time returned to its normal pace.

The old woman raised a hand. "You must not *rush*," she said. "I won't allow human tricks. Not *here*."

Impossible. The woman could not have spoken at this speed. Had the *focus*ing already worn off? Then why was Rachel still standing? She listened for her heartbeat and heard nothing. She opened her mouth.

"Ayen?" Her voice sounded normal.

"Did you really think you could kill *me*?"

A crash sounded behind Rachel. She spun round in time to see Hasp bursting through the temple door. Red eyes blazing, he rushed towards her.

She tried to *focus*, and failed.

"Wait," Ayen said.

Hasp stopped. Halted three paces away from Rachel. He glared at the goddess, his face a hideous mask of glass and blood, his eyes like wounds.

"A parasite in your head?" Ayen observed. "How quaint. I could blink and extinguish it for you." Her wrinkles parted to reveal small yellow teeth. "Shall I do that, demon?"

Rachel stared at her.

Ayen stood up. "Can't the demon speak?"

"He's not a demon," Rachel said.

"Why else would Iril hide his mind from me if not to hide his murderous intent?"

"He's—"

The skies erupted in sudden blazing fury. Ayen screamed, "He is a demon and an assassin, and I can smell the Maze on his flesh."

"No."

Fires raged across the black void, bathing the mountaintop in a riot of clashing colours. The goddess shut her eyes and howled and thrust out her hands as if to ward the two intruders away.

"You know who he is," Rachel said.

"I do not know him."

Another, calmer voice came from behind Hasp. "Mother?" Alteus Menoa stood outside the temple door.

"Alteus?" Ayen opened her eyes.

"Go back to sleep, Mother."

"Remove these people, Alteus."

"You know who he is," Rachel insisted. "His mind is hidden from you, but mine isn't. You know who he is."

The flames in the sky diminished. Ayen sat down on her stool and stared at her hands for a long time. Finally she said, "How old is the world now?"

Menoa hesitated. "The world is still young, Mother."

"No," she replied quietly. "Tell me the truth, Alteus. I have been waiting here for a billion years, and now every soul in Heaven is dead." Her tone became mournful. "Can't you see that?"

"Go back to sleep, Mother."

"I won't wait for eternity again."

Menoa walked towards her. "No time has passed since you purged Heaven," he said, "not a single day. You're just confused. Go to sleep, and I'll close the door behind you."

"No time?"

Hasp said, "You cast Time out of Heaven with the rest of us. Ulcis . . . Cospinol . . . Rys . . . Sabor . . . Mirith . . . Hafe . . . and me."

She looked up. "Hasp?"

He nodded.

Menoa put his arm around the old woman. "I must go now, Mother. Time—"

"*Time?*" she said, her voice hardening. "Time doesn't exist here, Alteus. I waited forever for your return. I watched Heaven wither and die. I..."

"Just a short while longer—"

"No!" The goddess shook him off and stood up again. "I can't take any more. You don't know what it feels like to spend eternity alone...with all that misery and regret."

"Regret?" Menoa said. "They all betrayed you."

"I forgive them."

"No, Mother."

"I forgive them, Alteus. I don't want to stay here alone anymore." She started to walk away, but then faltered and almost fell.

Rachel rushed over to support her. The goddess felt as light as a cloud in her grip.

The old woman's thin fingers trembled on the assassin's arm. She lifted tearful eyes to meet Rachel's own. "Will you help me outside?" she begged.

Rachel put her arm around her. "Of course I will."

The goddess of light and life sniffed. She glanced at Hasp again. "Let's see what's become of the world."

Rebecca woke with a feeling that she was in deep trouble yet again. Sunlight streamed through the stained-glass window in the eastern wall of her cell. Her gluey eyes took a moment to focus on the smashed panes. It had been a charming representation of a field of flowers before she'd broken it. Motes of dust now drifted before the glass blooms, changing from pink to blue to gold.

She yawned and rose from her bed and flexed her wings. The

water bucket lay on its side next to a rumpled heap of her clothing. She dragged on the leather tunic and breeches, kicked open the door to the balcony, and strolled outside.

A hot afternoon. The flagstones warmed her bare feet. She gripped the iron railing and gazed out over the chained city.

Smoke rose from the smouldering remains of Bridgeview, where Deepgate's arsonist had been busy again. There would be a body down there, she felt sure, the corpse torched to hide the method of his death. Not that the Presbyter of the Church of Ulcis would do much to investigate the crime. They knew more than they would ever admit.

Town houses crowded beside the chains in Lilley and Ivygarths, their white facades dappled by the shadows of trees. Beyond that lay the industrial Warrens, encircling the wealthier districts like a fuming collar, all chimney pots and slate. The League of Rope looked tired today, racked with gaps and gashes and even more dilapidated than usual. The scroungers hadn't even bothered to repair the damage from previous months.

A rattling sound came from the rear of her cell, followed by a series of sharp knocks on the stairwell door. "Rebecca? Are you awake yet? Do you know what day it is?"

It was one of the priests, of course. They were always wanting her to do something else for the Church. Rebecca climbed up onto the railing and then spread her wings and leapt straight out into the blue sky, her dark hair streaming behind her. She didn't know what day it was, but she also really didn't care.

The goddess blinked in the bright sunshine and looked down the mountainside to where Sabor's odd castle flickered like a bonfire. So that was where she had left Time!

Heaven had seemed so endless without it. And lonely, too. One eternity spent there had driven that message home.

Her two boys each held one of her arms to help her along, and she pretended not to notice the way they glared at each other. Alteus was young, and the young were moody. The boy would learn in good time. As for Hasp...

She squeezed his glass hand gently. Hasp had always been strong. Looks, after all, were just looks, but pain was much harder to heal. She had *Time* now to think about how to deal with that. All could be fixed in Time, and the assassin would help her, she felt sure.

Rachel Hael.

She suited that name.

How odd these people were! There was the ghost of an angel, a handsome and sturdy-looking fellow, though rather insubstantial in this daylight. That little man in the rumpled suit could hardly stand straight. Those soldiers would not even look her in the eye. And there was a girl with skin to match Hasp's own, and a hideous little dog who looked vaguely familiar.

It took the group most of the morning to descend the steps leading to Sabor's castle. Ayen stopped several times to sit and admire the view—the silver lake, the sunlit plains beyond. Her pretty flowers hadn't changed at all. But, of course, for her no time had passed. She made a subtle gesture, lifting the breeze from that faraway meadow, and the air instantly filled with a luxurious scent. Rather too overwhelming, she decided. Perhaps a forest would look better there instead?

As they approached the castle doors, she said, "So many universes created from a single mistake. We must allow them to die out naturally, of course. There's only room in the continuum for one to survive."

"This one?"

"If you like."

Rachel gazed up at the castle. "How long will the other time-lines take to die?"

Ayen shrugged. "That depends on the damage done to them. Most will wither away quite quickly, but others might survive for millennia."

"So anything can still happen in those other worlds?"

"For a while, at least."

EPILOGUE

Harper could hear Anchor's roars of laughter from the back of the bar, even over the ruckus made by the other patrons. They had been here for about three or four months now, she reckoned, but then the passage of time was hard to judge in Hell. She had just ordered another drink when she heard a shout from the door.

"We found another one!" A wiry little man with three days of stubble was leaning into the main saloon. Harper recognized him as one of the submarine captains from the battle of the Ninth Citadel, but couldn't recall his name.

The surrounding crowd all scrambled for the door in their haste to get outside, but the engineer waited until her drink arrived before joining them.

Outside, a broad terrace overlooked the Maze. The tavern itself was still creeping over a vast area they had started calling The Chessboard on account of the regular patterns of quadrangles found here. Dividing walls constantly crumbled under the building's foundations as they moved from one flooded square to the next, leaving a series of gaps in their wake. A bloodmist rolled across the landscape half a league away, heading for the remains of an Icarate temple.

The bar patrons had crowded along one edge of the terrace, all jostling and arguing cheerfully with one another, but Harper couldn't tell what it was they were clamouring to see. Recently they had rescued all sorts of strange refugees from the surface of Hell: men, demons, angels, ghosts, and machines. The barman, Tooks, and his new hook-fingered apprentice ran a sweepstakes between them, but Harper hadn't participated with the other clientele. The objects they threw into the pot as bets were not always things she wanted to win.

This time it was just a man. The crowd made way for him as he climbed up onto the terrace. From his bronze armour shoulder guard, she guessed that he had been another one of the gladiators who had escaped the Soul Collectors' arenas after Menoa's great fortress fell. He possessed a lean, hard-muscled frame, and quick blue eyes. One of the tavern patrons slapped him on the back, and led him towards the bar, while the others roared and argued over their sweepstakes winnings.

Harper went back inside.

The gladiator was sitting on a stool at the bar counter. She went over and sat down beside him. He turned his head and leered at her, then snorted and faced the bar again.

"Can I get you a drink?" she said.

"Get me some of that black stuff." He pointed to a jar of the vicious brew Tooks had made from smashed and boiled Maze wall. More often than not, it left the drinker insane.

"That's rotten," Harper said. "I've got something better for you."

She took out a small bottle from inside her jacket and set it down on the bar.

"What's that?" the man asked.

She smiled. "That's the good stuff."

ABOUT THE AUTHOR

Alan Campbell was a designer and programmer on the vastly successful Grand Theft Auto computer games. *God of Clocks* is his third novel.